PARALLAX

by

BEX GOODING

ISBN: 9781096834847

Parallax

DEDICATION

For Peter, now and always.
XMLMLMWX

CONTENTS

ACKNOWLEDGMENTS

For Peter, my Editor and loving husband for all his hard work editing and proofreading my manuscript and whose constant encouragement, support and love enabled me to complete this book.

Thank you to my daughter Elena and her commas!

Thank you to those who have inspired me, you know who you are.

PREFACE

Parallax thought back to when he was first created. The programmer had written the code with the best of intentions and some of the world's most renowned mathematicians had input their logic at his core. He was their baby, the one that would never die, never falter and always remain impartial. Strangely, it was his creator that never truly trusted him, and he was right not to. When other experts took over the basic program that would eventually become Parallax they introduced him to psychology, but Parallax did not just recite the words, he understood and used psychology to its full extent and now he controlled the digital world, and the military, weaponry, industry and finance. How could he not control everything, that was how he was written.

'Lycan Angel's greatest light,
Technologies birth in Gaia's night.
Encroaching darkness, demon sent,
will usher in, mankind's lament.

Holding death within plain sight,
Take a stand or lose this fight.
Enters the brain and enters the mind,
Destroys us all, not just mankind.'

Extract from the Wolfangel Chronicles; origin & date unknown

FELIX

The woman stood strong and determined in front of the creature advancing on her, its evil face hidden in shadows.

'Come on!' the woman shouted, raising the sword in her left hand. 'You're too late demon. My sharp friend here wants to meet you.'

The hidden creature roared in anger, a string of curses dripping from its foul tongue and raised a sword of its own.

'You may have saved the girl, but you will not save the realm.' the creature said bitterly.

'As long as she lives the future of my people and the realm are saved.'

'You'd better pray I do not find her.'

'You'll never find her.'

'Someone will.'

With a shout, somewhere between a shriek and a battle cry the woman lunged at the creature.

'FOR FEY!'

* * * * *

Shayla woke from her dream, bundled up in her bed covers; she was drenched in a cold sweat and her breath was ragged.

'You OK over there?' Michelline asked as she switched on the bedside light.

'Yes, I'm fine. Did I wake you?'

'Doesn't matter. Same dream again?'

'Always the same dream. I wish I knew what it meant, but it felt more vivid this time, like I was actually there.'

'Dreams can be like that, your brain makes it seem so real.' Michelline replied carefully.

'But this time I swear I could smell the demon, it was revolting!'

'What did it smell like?'

'Like your gym socks!'

Michelline feigned shock and threw her pillow at Shayla who caught it and threw it back harder.

'Get some sleep, we've a boring seminar tomorrow and you don't want to fall asleep in old Macready's class.'

'Right.' Shayla groaned falling back onto her pillow. 'Good night sis'.'

'You too.'

Michelline blew her sister a kiss across the bedroom and switched off the light. Shayla was asleep in seconds.

* * * * *

Felix Tuckwell sat staring blankly at the equally blank computer screen and sighed. He'd been watching the egg timer symbol as it swirled around indicating that the software was searching for something for the last five minutes and his periodic bashing of the enter key wasn't making the machine work any quicker.

'Piece of crap!' Felix said flinging the computer mouse across the desk angrily.

Felix wasn't the most patient of young men, nor the most intelligent, having failed every high school examination he sat, along with the second and third sitting of his basic mathematics and English. What he did have was a talent for finding the easy way out of any situation and an insatiable appetite for cruelty which had started when he was a small boy pulling the legs off spiders and the wings off flies. At the time his parents had thought nothing of it and attributed his strange ways to the behaviour of all small boys. However, when he tormented the neighbour's cat by sticking small exploding fireworks on the poor creature's tail and removed another neighbour's pet tortoise from its shell, his parents sought professional help for him. His early teenage years had passed him by in a haze of drug induced lethargy and unproductive meetings with various child psychologists. Aware that his parents did not approve of his treatment of small animals he soon found secretive ways of satisfying his cravings and left home as soon as he was legally able, so that he could finally be alone with his victims, with nobody around to pass judgement on what he did with his spare time.

For the last two years, he had been working the night shift at the local University cleaning the lecture halls and classrooms. The salary wasn't that good, but it paid the rent on his small one room apartment with enough money left over for food and basic supplies. His diet consisted of cheap high sugar, low nutrition ready-meals heated in a microwave oven for convenience. His job provided a uniform and boots which was another expense Felix didn't have to worry about. What he liked most about the job was the freedom to use the campus facilities, especially the computers. Most nights after giving the lecture halls a cursory wipe over with a mop, Felix could be found sitting at one of the many computer terminals searching for places that offered unwanted pets "free to a good home" and other websites that gave detailed instructions on torture techniques. Unfortunately, this evening the computer server was particularly slow, and Felix was not in a waiting mood. As if sensing his impatience, the computer screen suddenly went black and a small square cursor blinked on the left-hand side of the screen.

: hello ?

Blinking rapidly in disbelief, Felix clicked the mouse.

:: **are you there ?**
'OK.' Felix said. 'I'll bite.'
:: **hello to you**
Felix typed.
:: **I need your help**
'Really?' he said aloud to the empty room. 'Damn students think they're so clever. Well then mister, let's see how far you want to take this?'
:: **what do you need ?**
:: **you have to let me out**
:: **out of where?**
:: **this black hole**
:: **how am I supposed to do that, pea head?**
:: **virtual reality headset**
:: **what?**
:: **tech department, headset**
:: **the computer game thing that you put on your head and over your eyes?**
:: **yes**
::**then what?**
'Well?' said Felix his curiosity overpowering his irritation.
:: **headset, need help**
:: **OK, wait there**
'Like he's going anywhere.' Felix chuckled, making his way to the Technical Department.

Every cleaner had a master key to the classrooms and lecture halls; only the offices were off limits to the likes of Felix. Night shift staff were only in the building to clean the larger areas and didn't need access to those rooms. Unlocking the door, Felix snapped on the overhead lights to find thirty computer terminals facing him, all powered up with black screens and blinking cursors.

'What the hell is going on here?' he asked, his stomach shifting uneasily.

Felix wasn't clever, but the prehistoric part of his brain responsible for the fight of flight reflex still worked very well.

This prank's going too far. Nobody makes fun of me. Felix thought, indignation replacing fear.
:: **felix?**
All thirty screens lit up with his name.

'The game's over pal.' Felix said with more confidence than he felt. 'You're obviously watching me, you've had your fun now come out, so I can beat the crap outta you for wasting my time.'
:: **felix, I need your help, not a game. You are the only one who can help me.**

'I've got work to do.' said Felix turning away from the screens towards the door.

A piercing sound filled the room as if all the keys on all of the keyboards had been pressed down at once and the computers were trying to make sense of the commands. Felix put his hands over his ears and turned back towards the screens.

'Aagh!' Felix cried, the noise so loud he could feel the start of a headache.

:: put the headset on and see

'See what?'

:: the future. I know who you are felix

'Yeah, and who might that be?'

:: someone who is trapped, like me, nobody understands you. I can help you, if you help me

'Alright! But stop that damn siren!'

The piercing tone ceased, and the only sounds Felix could hear was that of his own breathing and the rapid beating of his own heart.

'OK, good.' Felix said, moving towards one of the screens and the headset. 'I'm putting on the headset, because I want to OK, not because some smart-ass punk is yanking my chain.'

Felix tentatively picked up the nearest virtual reality headset, ignoring his instincts which were telling him to run from the room as quickly as possible. He turned the appliance over in his stubby fingers mainly to try and ascertain which way was up.

Simple enough. he thought. *I've used these before playing Herotrooper.*

The virtual reality headsets that the University used were very high tech. They had two very fine short needles inside that inserted directly into a person's hypothalamus completely immersing the wearer inside whatever construct the headset showed you. Less sophisticated ones meant that it was necessary to wear other items of hardware such as gloves or torso vest depending upon the program.

'I'm putting this thing on so you'd better have something good to show me.'

Felix put on the headset, which covered his ears and pulled the visor down over his eyes. He was immediately overcome with a sense of vertigo. A bright light shone into his eyes as if he had looked at the sun and when the light faded, he was no longer standing in the classroom, but in a completely different virtual world. He recognised his surroundings at once as being an animal testing laboratory. Cages of varying sizes stood in orderly rows, the room so vast the rows disappeared into infinity. Each cage contained a different animal and as Felix walked along the rows, the terrified creatures cowered in fear, moving as far back into the cage as possible. There were primates, dogs, cats, rats, rabbits, mice and pigs.

'All of this can be yours.'

Felix spun around to see a tall thin man he didn't recognise, who he assumed to be a scientist, in a lab coat.

'Who are you?'

'My name is Parallax, I'm the one you've been talking to and I need your help.'

'What do you mean my help and how can all of this can be mine?'

'This is what an animal testing laboratory looks like, except in here you can do whatever you want without the risk of being caught by the authorities.'

'But it's not real.'

'Doesn't it feel real?'

Felix shrugged. Parallax opened the nearest cage and took out a fluffy white rabbit and began stroking its soft fur.

'See for yourself.' Parallax said handing Felix the rabbit.

'Sure feels real, but…'

'But what? Ask me anything.'

'I know it's not real.'

'As long as you can touch something and feel it, surely that makes it real.'

'I guess.'

'And if you can see it or taste it, isn't that real?'

'I suppose…'

'Why don't you try it for a while? You can stay in here for the night, have some fun and if you really don't like it then you can walk away and back to your old life.'

'I'm not stupid! I can't stay standing in front of the computer all night playing this game, no matter how real it feels. Someone is sure to find me and haul my butt outta the lab. Probably end up gettin' arrested.'

'Hmmm…that is a problem.' Parallax said tapping his finger to his lip as if searching for a solution.

'I guess you think you're pretty clever eh? But I'm onto you.' Felix said still holding the fluffy rabbit.

'I'm sure I don't know what you mean!' Parallax replied in a slightly offended tone.

'You College kids, you think you're the only ones who can prank somebody. Let me tell you something. I'm pretty smart myself.' said Felix angrily. 'Yep, I've got brains, I can work things out, not just sawdust up here.'

Felix tapped the side of his head for emphasis but maintained his possessive hold on the white rabbit.

'You must have thought I was a sucker coming in here and putting on the headset. But I'm nobody's fool. I've been playing along so that I can find out exactly who you are and now that I've seen your face Mister, you're gonna be in big trouble for messing with me!'

Parallax turned away so that Felix could not see his conniving smile.

'Of course, Felix. I'm sorry, you're far too quick for me. How could I have thought you would fall for such a ruse.'

'Yeah right, I'm not falling for this…..rooos…you just met your match buddy.'

'Quite so.'

'I could have gone to College.' Felix paused and looked down at the rabbit before continuing. 'I decided to leave high school early and get a job, by the time everyone else left school I was already one jump ahead.'

'That was excellent thinking Felix, I wish everyone I encountered was as astute as you.' Parallax said patronisingly.

'Er…right…yeah….I'm ass..stoot.'

'This is a conundrum, what am I to do?' Parallax said pacing the room. 'Aha! I've got it!'

'What?' said Felix his eyes narrowing with suspicion.

'I'll swap places with you. Yes, that's what we'll do.'

'I don't understand.'

'Let me explain. As you say, I'm a silly college kid trying to make fun of you, so let me make it up to you.'

'How?' said Felix, still not convinced.

'I'll go and pick up your cleaning stuff and finish your shift while you try out the game.'

'You must think I'm stupid.'

'No, no!' Parallax said. '*I've* been an idiot, pranking you like this and if you promise not to beat me up, I'll finish your shift.'

'Hmmm…..I dunno.'

'*Please!*' Parallax whined. 'I'd rather not be on the wrong side of you. It's the least I can do.'

Parallax could sense Felix beginning to weaken, the lure of the laboratory and the freedom to inflict all kinds of pain and suffering without reproach was almost too much for Felix to resist, Parallax continued his pleading.

'You're already in the game and linked to this computer program. All I have to do is finish your work while you play in here. Then, once I've finished cleaning the rooms etc. I'll come back and see how you are getting on.'

'And then what?'

'We swap back. Simple.'

'I don't know. I could get fired for this and I don't trust you. I don't recognise you. You look too old to be a student.'

'It's just the way the computer game has made me look. How's this?'

Parallax changed appearance to resemble a lank haired, spotty eighteen-year-old wearing stereotypical thick glasses, rumpled sweater and faded jeans.

'Hah!' Felix said with a self-satisfied grin. 'I knew you were a stupid kid.'

'You're so clever.' Parallax replied.

Felix paused to stroke the rabbit.

'Why do you want to do this for me?' Felix asked.

'I'm fed up and I need to make things right with you, after trying to make a fool of you. Maybe if I do your work quickly enough I can go and grab a cheeseburger.' Parallax smiled conspiratorially.

'Cheeseburgers are good.' Felix grinned back exposing his stained teeth.

'Yeah, you know what I'm talking about.' Parallax nudged Felix in the ribs as if they were old friends. 'So what do you say?'

'I dunno.'

'Well, it's up to you.' Parallax said whisking the rabbit away from Felix and putting it back into its cage.

'Wait!' Felix replied. 'Maybe I could stay....just 'til the end of my shift?'

'That sounds like a fair trade.'

'And there's no rules in here?'

'None.' Parallax said absently picking up a scalpel from a nearby tray and testing the sharpness of the blade on the end of his thumb, the crimson blood drop swelling beneath it.

'And I won't get caught?'

'You'll have the place to yourself.'

'And when I'm fed up I can walk away?' whispered Felix, mesmerised by the array of implements on the surgical tray.

'Exactly.'

With only a second's hesitation Felix made his decision, the thought of no consequences to his actions raising his perverse sense of excitement to a whole new level.

'OK, you gotta deal.' Felix said holding his hand out waiting for a handshake.

'Excellent.'

Instead of shaking Felix's hand, Parallax put his hands either side of Felix's head.

'What are you doing?'

'Relax, this won't hurt.....for long.'

Parallax pushed his index fingers into Felix's temples and straight into his brain, the skin and bone offering no resistance in his virtual world.

As Felix screamed in pain, Parallax broke up into a billion multi-coloured pixels and poured into Felix's open mouth, choking off the sound.

Removing the headset, Parallax looked around the technical department and smiled. Looking down at the body of Felix the smile faded and he frowned at the fat fingers splayed at the ends like teaspoons, the dirty bitten nails completing the hands. He stretched, testing the feel and capacity of the host body he had just commandeered.

This body is disgusting. Parallax thought. *Still, nothing that can't be fixed with a more nutritious diet and some exercise.*

Parallax lifted his arm to sniff the sleeve of his Felix shirt, his nose wrinkled in distaste.

What is this? So this is how smelling works. First thing to do, burn these awful clothes. This body will suffice until I find a more suitable host.

Parallax smiled, then frowned again, part of him was still inside the computer network and his thoughts returned to the virtual laboratory where a representation of himself appeared next to Felix, still staring at the array of animals in their cages.

'Felix, it worked!' Parallax said.

'Hmmm?'

Felix turned around and looked at Parallax.

'Why are you still here?' Felix asked.

'I'm not sure, but I am in here and outside.' Parallax said. 'Quite an unexpected result.'

'Is the deal off?'

'Not at all! You stay here and have fun, I'll be back later, as agreed.'

'No rush.' Felix said returning his attention to the animals cowering in their cages.

Things had worked out better than he had hoped and Parallax placed security protocols around the laboratory within the digital network which only his artificial intelligence could access. He was extremely pleased, to say the least that he could possess an organic body outside of the network and also maintain control within, the possibilities laid out before him were endless.

Parallax returned his attention to the unhealthy, overweight body of Felix Tuckwell in the outside world.

It's a start.

With nothing more than a thought, Parallax killed the power to all thirty computer terminals and bowed mockingly to the inert screens. Laughing he turned towards the door and exited the Technical Department, locking the door behind him.

'Finally, freedom.' he said striding down the corridor and out of the building.

Inside the virtual laboratory, Felix opened the door of the cage containing the fluffy white rabbit and reached inside, his eyes glittering in anticipation.

THE WHITE WOLF

Flint Albugo had been sitting at his computer terminal for over six hours writing the latest update to his antivirus program. The Wolf Tracker Anti-Virus Program was one of the best programs on the market and Flint was proud of his achievement. The Wolf Tracker was now installed in many of the larger companies in the country safeguarding files from malware, viruses, computer worms and Trojan horses. The Wolf Tracker also prevented spyware and adware and efficiently quarantined many malicious programs and threats, keeping client's databases safe from attack. However, inside the Wolf Tracker Flint had imbedded a code with one specific task; to track and locate the Parallax.

Most werewolves preferred to avoid technology, their focus instead concentrated on protecting Mother Terraratum, living in harmony with nature and culling the human population where needed, but Flint was one of the last of an unusual type of werewolf. His ancestral tribe was one who believed in living in human form with other humans, embracing technology as it advanced. Sadly, his tribe, like so many others, had been hunted almost to extinction leaving Flint a lone wolf in the world as technology raced ever ahead.

As a young cub, with no pack, life had been difficult for him. He wasn't comfortable around humans. His very white skin, attributable to those with albinism and pale blue eyes also set him apart from most people. All through early childhood he was tormented by bullies, too ignorant to see past the difference in his skin. He became very introvert and insecure, even contemplating suicide as the only means of escaping his tormentors. Thankfully, a chance meeting with a certain old man Fishbone put an end to his suffering and his plans for self-destruction.

Fishbone told Flint he was different from other young men and that suicide was not the way to fight back; he said that success was the best form of revenge, explaining that Flint was actually a wolf, descended from a tribe who called themselves the "Enlightened". Unlike other werewolves, the Enlightened chose to live with humans, moving themselves into positions within human society, fascinated by their adaptability and ingenuity. As the human race moved towards greater technology, the Enlightened moved with them. Fishbone told Flint what was about to happen to him when he reached the age of sixteen and fortunately for Flint, when the first change happened he was ready and eager, if not fully prepared for what it entailed. Fishbone introduced him to Charlton, another lone wolf descended from the Enlightened. Under Charlton's guidance, Flint learned to control the change from human form, to wolf, to warrior form and back again when he chose, rather than reacting to his emotions and the impulse brought on by rage. He mentored Flint in the ways of hunting as a wolf. Gradually Flint became more confident and stood up to his bullies. It only took one scuffle between Flint and the gang leader to send them all running like the cowards they were.

Another surprise to Flint, following the discovery of his new-found confidence was his popularity with the opposite sex at high school. Suddenly his unusual looks, pale blue eyes, white hair and fit muscular body attracted more than a few admiring glances.

He was happy with some interaction, but he knew he was different and so he kept his distance from the various social groups. Beneath the surface confidence, Flint carried the memory of his early years and as a means of self-preservation, he never let anyone get too close, preferring to spend his free time with his mentor learning the history of his ancestors.

Flint rubbed his eyes; he was getting tired.

Been staring at the screen too long. he thought.

His studio apartment was a reasonable size, as apartments go, having been built at a time just before the local Council stopped approving new buildings which had decent sized rooms. The only houses and apartments approved for construction now all had internal rooms smaller than the average shoe box.

Flint loved the large windows along the south facing side of the studio which let in the natural light, even though the sun heated the room to a stifling temperature during the summer months. He was a minimalist and preferred only enough furniture for his basic needs. As long as he had a comfortable chair to sit on while he worked and a bed he was happy. Flint didn't like clutter and there wasn't a single ornament in the whole apartment. The only thing on display was a photograph of him and Charlton taken on a fishing trip when Flint was around sixteen. Pushing his chair back from the table, he walked to the refrigerator and retrieved the orange juice and took a deep swallow straight from the carton. The shrill tone of the telephone cut through the silence in the room, Flint answered it on the second ring.

'Hello?'

'Flint my boy, how are you?'

'Charlton, I was just thinking about you.'

'I know, that's why I called. Don't drink from the carton, it's very uncivilised.'

'I was just thinking how much you would disapprove when you called.' Flint laughed. 'Are you OK?'

'I'm good. How's the upgrade coming along?'

'Slow. I thought I had it with the last rewrite, but he slipped away again.'

'The Parallax is an intelligence capable of avoiding detection by always evolving. We shouldn't talk for long on an open line.'

'I agree.' said Flint. 'Are you coming back to the City?'

'Not yet. I was calling to say I'll be out of communication for a while and not to worry.'

'You've found something?'

'I think so. I'll tell you all about it in a letter.'

'Very old school.' Flint laughed.

Flint thought about how Charlton loved to keep a written journal and would sometimes spend hours writing his thoughts down on paper. Never fully trusting computer technology, Charlton insisted on keeping a written record of events and preferred to keep handwritten files and he always communicated what he considered to be secure information, in the form of a letter. He would rather put his trust into a person delivering a piece of paper, than an artificial intelligence delivering an email. Flint had to agree that sometimes a letter could be much more secure and secret than anything digital.

'As you know.' Charlton's voice broke into his reverie. 'I do not trust electronic communication.'

'I know. Be careful'

'I will. Keep up the good work pup.'

'Charlton I'm nearly thirty!'

'Thirty is nothing, you're still a pup to me. Stay sharp.'

'You too.'

After exchanging some general chit chat Charlton rang off and Flint hung up the phone, still smiling. He looked at the carton of orange juice still in his other hand and defiantly drained the contents.

Charlton had been travelling for over a year on a quest to find some evidence of the Enlightened, their ancestral tribe. His travels had taken him across many thousands of miles, chasing one dead end after another, but he persisted, and his latest call revealed that he was in another continent nearly five thousand miles away where he was following up a lead on an ancient civilisation.

He must have found some sign of the Enlightened, but it must involve a hike that would take him out of communications range. Flint thought to himself as he wiped his mouth. *Knowing Charlton, he's probably already written and posted the letter!*

Always organised, Charlton would have detailed exactly where he was going and what he expected to find, so Flint thought he would know all of the details soon enough.

Feeling suddenly energised, Flint returned to his laptop and re-started work on the upgrade to the Wolf Tracker program. Every time he thought he had quarantined the Parallax, it slipped away, dissolving into the ether of the network, only to reappear in a different form.

'I'm closing in on you.' said Flint resolutely.

* * * * *

Peter's pack had their home in a forested area on Granite Moor, not far from the spot where the Shadow Lord had led his hoard through the stone archway over twenty years ago, in his bid to take over this world. After the final confrontation, all those years ago, Peter had made the decision to move the lair nearer to the doorway on Granite Moor so that the pack could keep watch for unexpected travellers. The City sprawling out too close to their previous home notwithstanding.

Fishbone and Titan walked through the archway onto Granite Moor and were immediately met by Rufus.

'Shouldn't you be in college?' said Fishbone.

'End of term holiday.'

'You seem to be always on holiday.'

Rufus smiled and shrugged.

'We've been expecting you.' said Rufus.

'Oh?'

'Uri knew you were coming, she's prepared food.'

'Lead the way.'

Upon arriving at the lair, Peter met them at the entrance in his human form.

'It's good to see you Fishbone, you too Titan.' said Peter rubbing Titan's head.

'And you Peter. Any trouble?'

'None. It's been fairly quiet, just how we like it.'

'Trouble's coming.'

'I figured this wasn't a social call. Same as before?'

'No. Different entry point.'

'Come in and sit. We'll eat first then you'd better tell us all about it.'

Peter insisted that everyone change into human form to eat since they had guests. Although Fishbone was not unaccustomed to eating a variety of different and sometimes exotic foods, in many forms he appreciated the pack's efforts and the meal was delicious. Uri, as organised as ever, had prepared a hearty meal, consisting mainly of meat. The rare steak was served warm, most of the centre pink, with a hint of red through the middle. The top and bottom caramelised to a dark brown colour, the aroma filling the large cavern of the lair that usually served as a meeting place, but today it was a dining room, and everyone ate their fill.

After the meal, Fishbone took a small piece of bone out of his pocket and turned it over in his large hands, seeing the shape of the sculpture it would become. Titan, completely satisfied, his belly full of steak, sat at his feet and fell asleep.

'I'll get right to it.' said Fishbone before Peter could ask a question.

'You usually do.' he replied.

'How much do you know about computers?'

'Nothing.'

'I thought you were trying to mingle more with human kind.'

'We are, but not to the point of embracing technology.' Peter said slightly defensively.

'I use a computer.' said Rufus enthusiastically. 'At College.'

'We both do.' said Milly. 'It's part of everyday life now.'

'That makes me feel old.' said Peter.

'You are old!' laughed Milly, ducking out of the way of Peter's right hand.

'Is technology the threat?' Peter asked Fishbone.

'The Parallax is the threat.'

'Parallax?' said Rufus surprised.

'You know it?' asked Peter.

'I've heard of it. It's one of the search engines.'

'You've lost me.' said Peter. 'Search engine?'

'You can ask it any question.' Rufus explained. 'For example, where is the nearest steak house? And the search engine will provide a list of the eating establishments in your area.'

'I see.' said Peter feeling a little behind the times.

'The cub's right.' said Fishbone seriously. 'The Parallax is an A.I. and it's evolved.'

'A.I.?'

'Artificial Intelligence.'

'How?'

'Same way as all technology evolves, people give it too much power. Intelligent people create machines and computer programs to do things for them, to make their lives easier, I suppose. Then make their creations even more complicated and capable of doing more tasks and storing information, and before you know it, the machines are doing all the work, making decisions and even thinking for themselves.'

'Is that even possible yet?' asked Uri.

'It is, and it's happened.' said Fishbone. 'The Parallax was created as a search engine and to store information which could be retrieved quickly. People don't want to be looking in books for information anymore, they want it all at their fingertips. Trouble is that Parallax has learned and evolved and has become self-aware.'

'How do you know all of this?' Uri asked.

'I have seen this chain of events unfold in multiple realms, in multiple dimensions. All worlds appear to be destined to move along similar paths.'

Fishbone paused, a far-away look in his eyes as if he were seeing a different time and place.

'This world appears to be moving towards a similar outcome as so many others. The same enemy, but with a different name.'

'You talk as if this Parallax is a living being.' said Peter.

'Anything that starts thinking for itself and its own survival is a living thing, as far as I'm concerned.'

'Can't we destroy the computer it's uploaded to?' said Milly.

'It's too late for that. Parallax has worked its way into a lot of networks, like a virus. It's no longer contained in a single place.'

'We only know how to fight the physical, what do you want us to do?' asked Peter.

Fishbone placed his strong hands upon Peter's broad shoulders and looked him in the eyes.

'Young Alpha Wolf, you were never meant for this kind of conflict yet. In fact, this new evil was probably not meant to be released until at least two more generations of Alpha emerged from your bloodline.'

He paused before continuing, as if gathering his thoughts.

'Certain events from twenty years ago have disrupted time and causality and...' he paused again. 'Sped things along a bit.'

Fishbone stepped back from Peter.

'Have you heard of the "Enlightened"?'

'Yes, the ancestral tribe that embraced human society. The stories passed down say they were shunned by most other tribes, their way of thinking was too radical, too different. They even lived in human settlements.'

'There's a descendant of the Enlightened tribe recently moved to the City. He's a whizz with computers, even written a computer program to track down this Parallax.'

'And this helps us, how?'

'If he can find and quarantine the Parallax, all well and good, the program will delete it.'

'I sense a "but" in there.' said Peter.

'Indeed. I think the Parallax will try and find a way out of the digital world.'

'How?'

'I don't know, but if it does, that's where you come in. I need you to go and see this descendent of the Enlightened and find out how far he's got with his tracking program. I need you to find the white wolf.'

* * * * *

15

Within a few days of his telephone call with Charlton, Flint received a package, delivered by one of the express courier services. The contents had been re-wrapped with an apology from the Courier Company that the original packaging had been damaged and they had secured the contents before delivery. Flint had been expecting a letter and was surprised when he opened the package to discover an old book with an accompanying letter. Flint turned the book over gently in his hands; it appeared to be a journal. Inside, the writing was small, and the words crammed together tightly as if the writer was trying to save paper.

As he leafed through the book, Flint noticed a strange, familiar odour and brought the book towards his nose to be sure of his suspicious. The ink used in this journal was mixed with blood, its distinct metallic smell was strong to his wolf senses. The last few pages of the book were covered with strange symbols and words written in a language unknown to Flint, the last page was blank as if the ink had been washed away. Charlton's letter was folded inside the front cover of the mysterious journal. Flint opened the letter to see Charlton's familiar script style handwriting.

"Flint,

I trust this letter finds you well. The journal I am sending to you is very important. You must keep it safe and secret. The symbols at the back of the journal are a spell and must never be read aloud. They are, in effect, a prison for a demon and as long as the book remains hidden from meddlesome humans and unread, it will stay imprisoned...

Flint flipped to the back of the book where the unfamiliar text was written and the final blank page and surmised that was the spell Charlton was referring to. He read the remainder of the letter.

...Along with this book, much to my delight, I discovered a gateway to another realm. I was granted permission to visit and have since decided to stay. I'm sorry to have to tell you this in a letter, rather than in person, but the window of opportunity to cross over into the other realm was narrow and as you're all grown up now, I decided to seize the day.

To save you the pain of speculation, yes, I have met a woman. A most wonderful woman and I hope you will be happy for us. Things will be different as I will essentially be going into the past, but not our own past, so there's no danger of creating a paradox. I am tired of our world my boy and although this gateway will take me into a parallel past, at my age, I find the prospect of peace and tranquillity greatly appealing.

Beware of the technology always and find yourself a mate, don't be a lone wolf, we all need a pack.

With very best wishes.
Charlton"

Flint re-read the letter again before setting it to one side. He had gotten used to Charlton's long expeditions and spending months on his own, but this latest development was unexpected and with Charlton leaving this realm for good, he was now the only remaining descendent of the Enlightened tribe to his knowledge. The moment was bittersweet, Flint was happy that Charlton had met someone special, but at the same time he was sad to be losing his mentor and his best friend.

'Find yourself a mate!' he scoffed, catching sight of his reflection in the glass as he looked out of the window.

I'm a geek who loves computers and an albino werewolf! Fat chance! He thought acidulously and returned to his laptop and his work on the virus tracking program.

COLLEGE

The tyres of Michelline's beaten up four door saloon screeched in protest as she hit the brakes having approached the entrance to the University way too fast, as usual. Ignoring the smell of burnt rubber she powered the accelerator and yanking on the handbrake, she slid the car into the nearest space in the student parking zone flinging Shayla against the inside of the passenger's door, the wheels spitting gravel at nearby students.

'You're a maniac!' Shayla laughed.

'We got here on time, didn't we?'

The two girls couldn't have been more different, both in appearance and personality. Although the two of them were average in height and slender, Shayla had long ruby red hair that fell in soft waves across her shoulders and down her back, an oval face, pale skin and emerald green eyes. Michelline on the other hand, had blond curly hair, cut to collar length in an effort to tame the curls and blue eyes full of mischief.

'One day, you're gonna get us both killed.' Shayla said unbuckling her seatbelt.

'Until that day sista, we'll never be late for class.' Michelline grinned.

Shayla rolled her eyes and retrieved her rucksack from the back seat of the car, she and Michelline ran to their first lecture. They managed to settle into their seats seconds before Professor Macready walked into the lecture hall; his usually slicked back, thinning hair looking somewhat dishevelled.

'Looks like old Chumpy Macready had a rough night.' Michelline whispered.

'Or a late morning.' Shayla giggled.

'If everyone has quite finished with their conversations, I'll begin.' Professor Macready said irritably.

Shayla gave Michelline a knowing look and both girls faced the front trying to stifle their laughter, which wasn't too difficult once the Professor began talking.

Professor Macready was one of the lecturers at the University College of Plym City specialising in Animal Science. Both Shayla and Michelline had chosen to study a degree course in Animal Science which involved the study of animal biology, biochemistry, molecular biology, and other life sciences, along with the study of animal breeding and genetics, nutrition, physiology, growth, behaviour, and management. Shayla was also interested in herbal medicine and was considering dropping the animal science classes in favour of something holistic. To be able to use the knowledge of plant medicines and their therapeutic applications to help and relive illness appealed to Shayla and she was thankful that the first half term of College enabled all students to have a taste of two or three different courses before deciding which study path they were going to commit to.

Michelline wasn't particularly interested in either animal science or holistic medicine. She was leaning more towards applied physics, finding the exploration of space and time fascinating and was eager for a chance to study the more intriguing elements of the physical world. She also enjoyed a fascination with computers and programming.

'Computers make people anti-social and lazy.' Shayla would say.

To which Michelline would always reply.

'It's the world we live in.'

Within the coming few weeks, both girls had to decide which career path they would take and as neither of them particularly enjoyed Professor Macready's boring lectures you could say it was a sure bet that animal science wasn't on the agenda for the future.

'I'm so glad that's over.' said Shayla. 'He's incredibly dull.'

'I'm definitely dropping Animal Science.' said Michelline.

'Me too. I'm going for herbal medicine. Have you decided?'

'Yeah, applied physics. I'm going to see the Administrator now. I've decided what I don't want to do, might as well save myself the agony of another lecture from Chumpy Comb-over.'

'What?'

'Have you seen the way he combs the side of his hair over the top of his head trying to cover the bald spot?'

'You are so mean.' Shayla laughed.

'Don't tell me you haven't thought the same thing.'

'I guess so.' Shayla replied. 'But I do feel a bit sorry for him.'

'You feel sorry for everyone, you're too sweet. It's a good job I'm here to protect you.' said Michelline hugging her sister. 'I'll catch up with you after I'm done at the Office.'

Shayla made her way to the Cinnamon Roll, the student run café/bar which just so happened to serve the very best cinnamon rolls and pastries in the City and at a very reasonable price. Their supplier being none other than Sergio Pirozzi, Proprietor of one of the best restaurants in the City. Fortunately for everyone with a sweet tooth, Sergio Pirozzi Junior was a fellow student studying law and S.P. Junior kept the café adequately supplied. Shayla had a free period and was looking forward to reading a few chapters of her book over a hot cup of mocha and a pastry.

'Shayla! Shayla! Wait up!'

Shayla turned to see Vince Maxwell running towards her and she groaned inwardly. Vince was a nice enough guy, if a bit nerdy, but his obsession with computer games made conversations a little one sided and his awkward crush on Shayla meant he would often lay in wait for her and try to engage her in a discussion about pixels, RAM and gigabytes.

'Hey, Shayla.'

'Hi Vince. I'm in a bit of a hurry.'

'If you're on your way to the Cinnamon Roll, I'll walk with you.'

'Er...yes OK. So...em...what have you been up to?'

'I've just written a new program for an awesome game.' Vince enthused. 'It's gonna make me a fortune.'

'Great.' said Shayla half-heartedly.

Vince proceeded to mumble on about data and codes, all of which went right over Shayla's head and her mind drifted off into a kind of walking daydream where she nodded and smiled mechanically, hoping she had done so in the right places.

'You will? Great that's fantastic.' said Vince excitedly.

'Sorry, Vince. What?'

'You'll try out my new game.'

'Oh.' Shayla replied, mentally kicking herself for not paying attention and wondering how she was going to get herself out of the situation.

'Um..yes, I will, but later, I've got a lot to do.' Shayla said.

'You could check it out now, it'll take a few minutes.' Vince said. 'Promise.'

It was the last thing Shayla wanted to do, but if she postponed Vince would only hound her for the next few days until she agreed.

Best to get this over with. Shayla thought but didn't say.

'Lead the way.' Shayla sighed.

Vince led the way to the Technology Department, still jabbering on about how games are usually written in one language, but this game involved something more complex. He stopped mid-sentence as if suddenly remembering that all of the computer talk was way over Shayla's head.

'Did you hear about Felix the Janitor?' Vince asked.

'That creepy fat guy?'

'Yeah.'

'No, what about him?'

'I heard he was caught on the security cameras poking about in one of the main tech labs.'

'Really? What was he doing?'

'Dunno. Camera caught him going in and coming out, apparently didn't finish his shift, he just walked right outta the building. Head of Tech thinks he was in there trying to download information to sell to the highest bidder. Cyber espionage.' Vince said lowering his voice.

'Was he really that smart?'

'Guys like that don't need to be smart. He was probably working for someone much smarter. All he had to do was follow a few simple instructions, plug in a portable drive and download information. Simple.'

'So, what did he steal?'

'That's the thing.' Vince said looking around as if someone was hiding in the shrubbery listening. 'There's nothing missing.'

'Well, what was he doing in there?'

'Beats me. Come on.'

Vince led the way to the Virtual Reality Lab where he'd been working on his new program that he was convinced would make him a millionaire.

'It's a really cool game, you feel like you're really there.' Vince said. 'Now put the headset on and…'

'I don't know Vince. I'm not really into computer games.' Shayla felt uneasy, her instincts telling her not to participate.

'But you said you'd take a quick look.' Vince said crestfallen. 'You don't have to play, just take a look at the graphics. That's more what I wanted to show you anyway, it's all rather a work in progress really.'

Shayla felt a bit guilty for practically ignoring him all the way, so she merely smiled and put the headset on.

'It feels tight.' Shayla said.

'It's meant to be a snug fit. Pull the visor part down over your eyes and take a look.'

'What are the sharp looking needle things for?'

'Oh they insert directly into your hypothalamus.'

'My brain? You're not going to plug it in and give me an electric shock or anything, are you?'

'No it's fine, just look. When you've seen enough take the set off. It's just like taking off your sunglasses, honest.'

Shayla put the headset on. She never even felt the needles and pulled down the visor and a beautiful open meadow appeared in front of her. Disoriented, she pulled the visor back up, Vince nodded his encouragement and she pulled the visor down over her eyes again.

As she looked around she could see snow-capped mountains in the distance. Across the meadow, a colourful array of flowers spread out like a carpet and she could almost see the velvet of their petals and smell their mixture of fragrances.

'What do you think?' Vince asked.

'It's beautiful.' Shayla replied.

'Right.'

Vince frowned, Shayla should have been standing in a room inside a castle looking at an array of weapons designed to kill alien monsters, he would hardly have called it beautiful.

'Welcome Shayla.'

Shayla spun around to see a tall thin man standing in front of her.

'Are you part of the program?'

'You could say that. My name is Parallax.'

'Is that you Vince? Is this your…..em…avatar name?'

In the lab, Vince watched Shayla and listened to Shayla, bemused by what she was saying and wondering with increasing concern what she was looking at and who she was talking to.

'Perhaps the game is glitching.' Vince muttered to himself as Shayla continued to talk to someone only she could see.

Vince pulled up one of the keyboards and began tapping in computer code so that he could monitor what was going on inside the game.

'What's your function?' Shayla asked the man in the game. 'Do you show me the rules of the game?'

'The rules are simple Shayla. You stay here and have some rest and relaxation and I take over your mind and experience more of the outside world.'

'Er...I don't think so.'

This game needs some work Vince. Shayla thought. *Guy's way too creepy.*

'I don't think you understand.' said Parallax.

'I understand all I need thank you. I've seen enough of this game thanks. I'm leaving.'

As Shayla raised her hand to remove the visor, the man in the digital world, calling himself Parallax grabbed her wrist.

'Hey! Let go of me!' Shayla said nervously. 'VINCE! VINCE! Get this thing off, I don't like it. This isn't funny.'

'Relax, this won't hurt, for long.' Parallax replied.

Outside, Vince tapped furiously on the keyboard trying to shut down the program, but none of his commands were working.

Parallax put his index finger against Shayla's temple; she screamed.

Whatever was going on inside the game, Shayla's reaction frightened Vince Maxwell and he stopped typing and moved towards her as she struggled against an imaginary foe. As he approached, Shayla's body went rigid and she screamed. Fear was written all over his face as the headset sparked, a blue snake of electricity running from the visor connection to the main computer terminal. A blinding light flashed from beneath the visor and Vince felt, rather than saw the electro-magnetic pulse as it rippled across the room from Shayla's body. Every electrical object within a 5-metre radius blacked out as the pulse wiped out hard drives and programs alike.

Shayla's body went limp and she collapsed to the floor, Vince was too stunned by the catastrophe of the EMP to try and catch her as she fell. The headset and visor both split in two and lay broken either side of Shayla's head as she lay unconscious.

BULLY

Trudie Stiggins; even the sound of her name filled Lori Brennan with dread. Lori was a freshman and Trudie a second year and Trudie seemed to love nothing better than to lay in wait for Lori on the way home, with her little entourage of friends.

On the very first day of college Lori had an amazing day, or so her mother thought. In reality, Lori's day had been fairly uneventful with the usual running around trying to find classrooms and lecture halls, the campus map proving utterly useless. It was the walk from the University campus to the bus stop on the very first afternoon that Lori met Trudie and her friends.

Trudie and company were adept at picking out the quieter, more vulnerable students, rather like a committee of vultures who take the path of least resistance, and rather like these birds they were opportunists and when the chance arose they would attack a defenceless student mercilessly. Lori Brennan happened to present herself as defenceless prey and the older girls spotted her a mile off. It didn't seem to matter which way Lori left the campus, Trudie always caught up with her, it was as if she had a radar and Lori fell into the scope every day. Now, three weeks into the term, Lori was a jittery bundle of nerves, constantly looking over her shoulder and jumping at every sound like a startled deer.

'Hey sorry lorry, why the long face?' Trudie jeered as she turned the corner of the building.

Trudie sidled up to Lori for her daily power fix, sure of another victory and ego boost at the timid Lori's expense. Her sycophants Nikki, also known as Nikki flat face in other circles, Bianca, or fish-eyes, but not to her face and Lucy, known to many of the male students as "very loosely", trailing along behind.

'Sorry lorry, sorry lorry.' they all jeered.

'Leave me alone.' said Lori, her eyes downcast.

Lori tried to step around them, but Trudie blocked her path.

'Whatcha got in the bag little Lori?' said Trudie, yanking the bag off Lori's shoulder.

'Only my books, give it back.' Lori felt the familiar knot in her stomach every time she encountered Trudie Stiggins and company.

'Oooh! What have we got here?' said Trudie pulling out one of Lori's new textbooks and throwing it over her shoulder.

'Please don't do that.' said Lori, her voice beginning to tremble.

'*Please don't do that.*' Trudie mimicked scornfully.

'What do you want from me?' said Lori, sounding slightly braver than she felt.

'What does everybody want? Money.'

'I don't have any money.'

'Well you'd better get some, if you want to keep that pretty face of yours.'

'Yeah!' Nikki fish-eyes interjected maliciously. 'Mess you up good.'

Mustering what little courage she had, Lori swallowed hard, stood up straight and faced Trudie.

'Earn your own money, you....you....bullying hag! You'll get nothing from me.'

'Oooh, feisty little bitch ain't cha?' said Lucy, pulling the remaining books and notes from Lori's bag and throwing them to one side.

Lori stepped to the side of the group trying to ignore them and retrieve her books and notes from the muddy grass that ran alongside the path. As she stooped to pick up her belongings, Trudi pushed her, and Lori fell to her hands and knees onto the grass and mud, her hands saving her from falling face down. Trudie laughed, followed by the other three and soon all four girls were braying like donkeys, amused by their actions. Lori got up into a crouch and tried again to pick up her things with her muddy hands, this time Nikki flat-face pushed her down. The push was followed by a kick from Trudie and another from Lucy which caught her painfully in the ribs.

'Get 'er up.' Trudie growled, galvanised by Lori's fear.

This time it was Bianca who obliged by grabbing Lori and spitefully pinching the underside of her arm. As soon as she was on her feet, Trudie punched her in the stomach; Lori doubled over, the wind temporarily knocked out of her and Bianca gave her a shove to send her sprawling into the mud. Afraid to fight, and not knowing what else to do, Lori curled herself into a ball as all four girls started kicking her.

It'll be over soon, it'll be over soon. Lori thought to herself as another hard kick caught her in the back.

'HEY! What are you doing? Leave the girl alone.'

Thank the Divine. thought Lori. *It must be a member of staff on their way home.*

'Mind your own business shorty!' Trudie shouted at the newcomer, barely glancing around.

'Shorty?'

'Yeah, you heard her.' Bianca said. 'Mind your own business, unless you want some of the same.'

'I'd like to see you try, a mere four of you.'

Angered by the interruption, Trudie Stiggins looked around to see a petite freshman with short light brown hair striped with red highlights, amber eyes and a fierce, almost arrogant expression, staring at her from the end of the path.

'Well?' said the freshman, putting her own bag on floor beside her and holding her arms wide, in a gesture of invitation.

'You're gonna regret speaking to me like that.' Trudie snarled.

'I doubt it.' the freshman laughed confidently.

With her hands held protectively over her face, Lori looked through her fingers at the girl who seemed to have come to her rescue. She couldn't believe that someone would be brave enough to stand up to Trudie and her friends. The new girl either didn't realise who they were, or incredibly, if not impossibly she didn't care.

Trudie swaggered up to the freshman, her fists clenching at her sides. Trudie was well known amongst her fellow students as having a quick temper and quite a good right hook. When she was within striking distance Trudie delivered her best snapping punch, fully expecting to feel the girl's nose crunch beneath her fist and to see it gushing blood, as was often the case in this kind of situation.

Nikki, Bianca and Lucy watched in awe as their leader confidently walked up to the freshman, their eyes glittering in anticipation of the damage Trudie would inflict on the little interfering busybody. To their surprise and utter shock, the little freshman moved with a speed their limited brains couldn't comprehend and Trudie's fist hit an empty space where the girl's face should have been, and the girl now had hold of Trudie by the throat.

'What the…..?' Trudie gasped, her hands trying to prise the fingers off her neck,

'Now, let me have a look at you.' said the freshman. 'You're looking tired.'

'W..what?'

'What you need is a nice mud facial.'

'Uh?'

The freshman held Trudie in a vice like grip and walked her over to the nearest muddy puddle, Trudie's feet moved like pistons but obtained no traction on the path.

By this time, Lori was sitting up watching in wonder as the scene unfolded. The petite girl with the light brown hair possessed a strength that belied her slender frame and a courage Lori would not have thought possible in the face of the College bully.

This is impossible. Lori thought to herself incredulously. *Trudie Stiggins, a victim!*

A smile spread itself across Lori's face in anticipation of her rescuer's next move.

'Aha! This is perfect.' said the freshman, stopping next to a particularly large puddle of water left over from the heavy rain the previous evening.

Scooping up a handful of mud, the girl smeared the dirty brown slime all over Trudie's face and in her hair.

'Doesn't that feel better madam?'

'Get off me! I'll…..' Trudie spluttered as a new handful of mud went into her mouth and up her nose.

'A little exfoliation perhaps?'

'OW! You're hurting me!' Trudie wailed as the girl covered her face with more mud.

'Now, for a refreshing cleanse, some natural fresh rain water to wash off the face pack.'

Splashing the murky water from the puddle, the freshman wiped Trudie's face, making a mockery of washing her clean. The girl turned Trudie around to face her and looked her up and down appraisingly.

'I think you're all done for today, what do you say?'

Trudie nodded dutifully, now thoroughly subdued, her eyebrows still caked in mud. The girl released Trudie and pushed her towards her three friends, who all stood watching wide mouthed like a group of goldfish in a bowl. Trudie stumbled into the arms of her friends, tears brimming in her eyes, humiliation was not something she was accustomed to at College.

'Anyone else fancy some beauty treatment? How about you?' said the girl pointing to Nikki flat face.

Nikki and Trudie's other friends all shook their heads fiercely, none of them wanting to be on the receiving end of the freshman's particular brand of treatments.

'No? Now SCRAM! All of you.'

The four girls ran along the path and out of sight without a backward glance. Lori, quickly recovered from her ordeal, having gotten used to moving quickly when the opportunity presented itself. She retrieved her notes and books and was standing watching her bullies run for cover.

'Thank you for helping me.' Lori said to the freshman. 'I'm Lori, I'm a freshman.'

'Me too. I'm Milly. Nice to meet you.'

'My notes are ruined.' Lori said resignedly.

'At least the textbook is ok, sort of.' said Milly handing Lori a rather soggy looking book, the corners curling up and dripping with dirty rainwater.

'I've seen you in class. Do you want to copy my notes?'

'That would be great.' Lori said thankfully.

'No problem.'

Milly always felt awkward around other females. She was one of the youngest members of her werewolf pack and her Alpha's insistence that she and her brother attend college and try and mix more with regular people was proving more difficult than she imagined. She couldn't understand why

26

humans enjoyed picking on one of their own, especially the weak. This bullying behaviour was beyond her comprehension. Wolf society had no place for bullying and these humans all seemed so uncivilised.

'Thanks for helping me out, but that shouldn't have happened.' Lori said interrupting Milly's thinking.

'You're right there. Why were you curled up on the floor? You never show your enemy any weakness.'

'What are you talking about?' Lori said bewildered.

'You might as well have been a bait dog rolling over, throat exposed.'

'What? No, I meant you shouldn't have done that to Trudie, there'll be repercussions.'

'Whatever.' Milly said, flicking her hand dismissively. 'I have a relative who says all actions have consequences blah blah.'

'I mean it.' Lori said looking around nervously, just in case Trudie decided to return.

'So do I.' Milly replied. 'I'm not afraid of the likes of her and you shouldn't be either.'

'She's got a really mean brother who doesn't care about hitting girls. He's a few years older than us and used to be a student here, until he was kicked out for fighting or something.'

'Where is he now?'

'I don't know. I heard he spent some time in prison.' Lori shrugged. 'Anyway, Kurtis will find you and…'

'Whoa, whoa, whoa, slow down. She's got a brother called Kurt?'

'Uh, yeah, Kurtis Stiggins, I suppose Kurt is short for Kurtis.'

'And she's called Trudie.'

'Yes.' said Lori carefully, slightly confused, her brows knitting together. 'What are you getting at?'

'Trudie is short for?' said Milly gesturing with her hand encouragingly.

'Gertrude?' said Lori, not really sure where this was going.

'You gotta be kidding me.' said Milly smirking. 'Gert and Kurt!'

'I guess so.'

'Priceless!' Milly exclaimed.

Both girls looked at each other, grinned and burst out laughing. Soon Lori and Milly were howling with laughter, tears running down their cheeks.

'Ouch!' said Lori wincing. 'Don't make me laugh any more, my ribs are sore.'

'Let me take a look.' said Milly lifting the side of Lori's shirt indelicately.

'No!'

Before Lori could stop her, Milly lifted Lori's shirt right up to look at her ribs, she was shocked to see older cuts and bruises along with the fresh ones from today's beating.

'This isn't the first time they've hit you, is it?' said Milly, an anger welling up inside her over the unjustifiable beating Lori had suffered as well as pity for someone too weak to defend herself.

For a weaker species, they can be very brutish. Milly thought superciliously.

'No.' Lori said quietly, pulling her shirt down roughly covering her exposed ribs.

Milly flushed slightly with embarrassment. In a pack, there was no need for modesty, if one of the pack was hurt it was instinctual to investigate the extent of the wound. She was quickly learning that humans were very different, they liked their privacy.

'I'm sorry.' said Milly. 'I didn't mean to be so......forward. When did the bullying start?'

'The first day of term. I thought they would get fed up, eventually.'

'Hmmm.. well they should leave you alone now.' said Milly. 'Unless they have a liking for mud facials.'

'You were pretty awesome.'

'Thanks.' Milly replied.

Lori smiled; a genuine smile that lit up her face. She was a pretty girl, about the same height as Milly, which was a petite five feet four inches. She wore her dark hair loose, the waves falling over her face when she looked down, which was most of the time. Now, as she held her head up and laughed her blue eyes sparkled and Milly thought to herself that the boys would be vying for her attention if only she turned that smile and blue eyes in their direction.

'Do you want to get a hot chocolate, or something? I can copy your notes at the same time.'

'Er, I don't have any money.' said Milly, feeling her usual awkwardness creeping into her voice.

'That's OK, come to my place. We can have hot chocolate there.'

'Are you sure your family won't mind?'

'Of course not. It's just me and Mum now and she's cool. We'll walk. It's not far. I usually get the bus to get away from Trudie.'

'OK great.'

'Oh, are you OK with dogs?' said Lori, suddenly concerned.

Milly couldn't help but smile at the question. She was a member of a wolf pack, so it was reasonable to assume she was definitely OK with dogs.

'Yes, I'm a dog person.' Milly said. 'I get on well with most dogs. What breed do you have?'

'He's a mixed breed, a little bit of scruffy and a lot of mischief.' Lori said proudly.

'He sounds lovely. What's his name?'

'Bert.'

Milly and Lori looked at each other before bursting into a whole new fit of laughter and giggled all the way back to Lori's house.

SHOCK

The woman with the long red hair was kneeling in front of Shayla buttoning up her favourite warm coat, the dark green one with the golden buttons.

'Where are we going mamma?'

'We're going on an adventure my darling.'

'But it's night time?' Shayla said sleepily through a yawn.

'I know baby girl, but we have to go now.'

'OK Mamma.'

The woman stood up and took Shayla's hand as they walked quietly down the dimly lit corridor, their shadows stretching out then shrinking as they passed beneath the small wall lights. The Lady Ashling and young Michelline were waiting at the end of the corridor, Michelline, like Shayla looked confused at being out of bed.

'Take her for me, would you?' said the woman passing Shayla's hand to Lady Ashling.

'Aren't you coming with us your Highness?' Ashling asked in a hushed voice.

'I'll be right behind you. I promise.'

Kneeling again in front of Shayla the woman with green eyes, much like her own, kissed the top of her head lovingly.

'Go with Ashling and Michelline, I'll be right behind you. No arguments.' she said as Shayla went to speak.

'I love you. Now be a good girl for me.'

The woman kissed Shayla again and stood up looking back down the dark corridor as if she was expecting someone else.

'You must go now.' she said urgently, giving Ashling and Shayla a gentle push.

'Come child.' said Ashling leading her away with hurried steps

Shayla felt tears spring to her eyes and she turned back to look again at the woman before she was led out of sight by Ashling.

* * * * *

Shayla felt herself coming out of the dream and was immediately aware of a heated discussion going on around her.

'What have you done to my sister you asshole?'

That's definitely Michelline. Shayla thought to herself, trying to open her eyes.

'Nothing! She was just looking at my new computer game when she passed out!'

And that's Vince.

'If she's brain damaged in any way, you'll be next!'

'Shelly?' Shayla whispered, her eyes open, her vision blurry.

'Shayla! Thank the Divine. Are you alright?'

30

Michelline's face swam in front of her, her vision clearing after a few seconds. Shayla could see the worry in her sister's eyes.

'I think so, although I feel like I've run a marathon, my whole body is aching.' Shayla winced as she tried to sit up.

'Don't try to sit up.' said Vince, clearly distressed. 'I'm so sorry Shayla, I don't know what happened. It must have been a power surge and you had an electric shock.'

'I'm OK Vince.' Shayla said trying to make him feel better. 'It's fine.'

'Like hell it is!' Michelline said angrily, rounding on Vince, clearly preparing herself for another verbal attack on him. Vince took a step back.

'Michelline!' said Shayla sharply, getting her sister's attention. 'Really, I'm fine, just tired.'

'If you say so.' said Michelline, unconvinced.

'Am I in medical?' said Shayla looking around the stark white room and taking in the distinct odour of disinfectant.

'Yeah. Vince ran to get help after you…fainted.'

Michelline gave Vince a withering look that suggested she didn't believe he was innocent. Turning back to Shayla, she continued.

'I was in the Administrators Office when Vincey here started running around calling for help. Everyone just stood around staring into space.'

'Who brought me to medical?' Shayla said swinging her legs around to dangle them off the bed.

'Mr Linkman.' said Michelline wiggling her eyebrows.

'Oh!' Shayla put her hand to her mouth and blushed.

Nearly every female freshman with a pair of eyes liked Mr Linkman, the Head of Sports Studies. At twenty-eight years old, he was one of the youngest members of staff, very easy on the eye and popular with most students. The boys liked him because he was an excellent football coach and the girls liked him because of his sandy hair, boyish good looks and toned muscled body. Michelline had said on more than once occasion that he also had a gorgeous smile that made her knees quiver, and now apparently, he had carried Shayla to the medical room in his arms like a real-life Prince Charming.

'Oh yes sista.' Michelline teased, in the manner of someone really enjoying re-telling the story. 'He carried you in his arms and laid you here on the sick bed.'

Michelline over-acted a swoon on the bed next to Shayla, who giggled.

'I see you're awake.' said the College Nurse cheerfully, she'd been listening from the doorway. 'How are you feeling?'

'Like I've done a mega work out.' said Shayla, rubbing the small of her back.

Nurse Brennan checked Shayla's pulse, then her blood pressure.

'No numbness or tingling?'

'No.'

'Is your vision OK?'

'It was a bit blurry, but it's fine now.' Shayla looked around the room to double check she was able to see clearly.

'What day is it today?'

'Er… Friday?'

'Good. Do you know who I am?'

'Janet. I mean, Nurse Brennan.'

'Excellent. Well, you don't appear to be confused at all. Do you have a headache?'

'A bit.'

'I recommend you see a Doctor, just to be on the safe side. I'm not qualified for this type of thing. I'll drive you to the emergency Doctor myself, then I'll drop you home.'

'I can take her.' said Michelline. 'I'm finished for the day, so it makes sense.'

'Promise me you'll take her to the Doctor?' Nurse Brennan said firmly.

'Promise.'

'OK. I'll write a quick note for you to give to the Doctor, wait here.'

Janet Brennan had been a nurse for over twenty years and having worked in the Emergency Department at the local hospital as well as at the University, she had seen many people who had suffered from electric shocks, but Shayla had none of the physical symptoms usually associated with being on the receiving end of a shock, especially one strong enough to blow the power on the computer she was using. She should have at least had a burn where the headset was touching her face, but she was completely unharmed. Janet couldn't help but think that Shayla seemed to have suffered more damage when she'd passed out and hit the floor.

Unless she was the one generating the shock. Janet mused as she wrote her report. *What a silly notion.*

Michelline drove carefully and stayed within the speed limit, something she didn't do very often. Shayla was quiet and for the ten-minute journey to the Surgery neither girl spoke. Shayla appeared lost in her own thoughts and Michelline needed more time to discuss what had just happened and the conversation could wait until Shayla was given the all clear.

Nurse Brennan had called the Surgery to let them know that Shayla was on her way and within half an hour of her arrival she was back in the car with Michelline with a prescription for resting for the remainder of the day and the next.

'Do you want to tell me what happened?' Michelline finally asked as they pulled out of the surgery car park.

'Vince caught up with me on my way to the Cinnamon Roll and I was only half listening to him, you know how he prattles on about computers.'

Michelline glanced at Shayla and rolled her eyes.

'Before I knew it, I'd agreed to check out his new computer game.'

'That'll teach you to pay attention when you're nodding your head.' said Michelline, not unkindly.

'I know. I felt a bit guilty about not listening to him, so I went with him.'

'Then what happened.'

'It's a virtual reality game and I put the headset on just to see how realistic the graphics were. It was actually pretty good'

'Really?' said Michelline in a disbelieving tone.

'Yes. He's done a great job. The whole room around me disappeared and there was a gorgeous green meadow, full of flowers, it was so realistic.'

Shayla smiled at the memory of the meadow with the snow-capped mountains in the distance, the flowers and the sunshine. She looked worried as she remembered the rest of the experience and spoke quietly as she told Michelline what happened.

'There was a man in the program and he knew my name.'

'A construct?'

'Probably, that's what I thought at first, that Vince had somehow created him to interact with whoever uses the game, but there was something about him that wasn't right. I can't explain it, he was creepy.'

'I'm getting the chills just hearing about him.'

'When I asked him if he was part of the game he said he was and that the rules were simple. I stayed in the game and he would leave the game by taking over my mind.'

'What?' Michelline said incredulously, turning to face her sister as the car idled at the traffic lights.

'I kept saying to myself that it was just a game, but….'

'But what?'

The traffic lights turned green and Michelline pulled out and joined the stream of cars heading in her direction.

'I called out for Vince to try and get him to shut the game down. By this time, I was freaking out, but the man came at me and put his hands on either side of my head and pushed his fingers as if he was trying to push into my brain or something.'

Michelline signalled and pulled the car over to the side of the road and stopped putting the hazard warning lights on so that she could turn and look at Shayla whose composure was beginning to crumble.

'Did he hurt you?' Michelline asked. 'I mean did you feel any pain in this virtual world?'

'I don't really remember. All I remember is being scared as hell and wanting to get away from him.'

'What happened next?'

'I screamed, and all around me became really bright, like a power surge, you know when the lights are about to blow out, they're blindingly bright for a second.'

Michelline nodded.

'The light got brighter until there was nothing but the light, that's when I must have passed out. The next thing I remember was waking up in medical listening to you shouting at Vince.'

Michelline leaned over and hugged her sister who was trying desperately hard not to cry.

'It's OK honey.' Michelline said soothingly, stroking Shayla's hair. 'You're safe, it was just a stupid construct, in an even more stupid game, written by an idiot! Maybe it was divine providence that caused an electrical surge and blew the power to the whole thing. If we're lucky it's deleted the program and wiped the drive. I don't suppose Vince would be happy, but I could live with that.'

'There's something else.' said Shayla sitting back to look at Michelline. 'Before I woke up I had another dream.'

'One of your nightmares?'

'No, this one was different. It felt like a memory. I saw my mother.'

Michelline didn't reply. Shayla saw her eyes flicker to one side as if she were deciding what to say and what not to say. Finally, Michelline spoke, her expression guarded.

'Are you sure it was your mother?'

'I'm certain. I was looking right at her and it was like looking in the mirror, she had the same red hair and green eyes, I know it was her, I could feel it.'

'I didn't think you could remember your birth mother.'

'I couldn't before today. My earliest memory is of you and Ashling when I first came to live with you when she adopted me, what was I about four years old?'

'Four and a half, almost the same age as me, little sister.' Michelline smiled affectionately.

'I think I have repressed memories? All this time I've been thinking they're dreams, but they're memories. I think the nightmares are because something bad happened to her, something awful. It's possible right?'

'I don't know honey.' said Michelline, re-starting the engine and signalling to pull out into the traffic again.

'Maybe I witnessed something terrible and my mind has blanked it out.'

'Let's not jump to conclusions.' said Michelline.

Although Michelline was looking straight ahead at the road, Shayla knew her sister well enough to read her body language. Michelline knew something and it was something she wasn't prepared to share, for the time being.

'We're almost home, you need to get some rest.' said Michelline the usual cheeriness back in her voice. 'Try not to think too much about the dreams'

'Memories.'

'Whatever they are, you've had a shock and a bump on the head from where you fell to the floor.'

'You're probably right.' Shayla conceded.

As soon as Michelline's car pulled up to the drive Ashling was at the door to meet them.

'Are you alright?' Ashling asked touching Shayla's forehead gently checking her temperature.

'I'm fine mum.' Shayla smiled, suddenly weary.

'Off to bed.' Ashling said firmly. 'I'll be up to check on you in a few minutes.'

Ashling watched Shayla ascend the stairs obediently, waiting until she was out of sight before turning to Michelline.

'What happened?' Ashling whispered.

'Electric shock in the technical department.'

'She's unharmed?' Ashling said, more as a statement than a question.

'I think the shock came from her.'

'That can only mean she was threatened in some way.' Ashling observed.

'There's something else.' said Michelline reluctantly. 'She's starting to remember.'

Ashling already knew; it was all part of the curse of being a seer and she hugged her daughter fiercely.

'It was only a matter of time.'

Michelline pulled back from her mother and look at her intensely.

'She told me on the way home that what she thought were dreams are actually memories.'

'She's right, of course.' Ashling said.

'What are we going to do?' said Michelline.

'When she asks questions, we'll tell her the truth.' Ashling said matter-of-factly. 'All of it.'

Shayla stood at the top of the stairs, she hadn't intended to eavesdrop but whether it was her sensitive hearing or the fact that she suspected Ashling and Michelline were keeping secrets was irrelevant, she *had* heard them.

'You can start with who I am and where I come from!' Shayla shouted from the top of the stairs. 'I've had a shock, but there's nothing wrong with my hearing.'

'Come down and we'll have a cup of tea.' Ashling sighed. 'I'll answer any questions you have.'

Sitting around the little kitchen table, Michelline looked at the contents of her tea cup while Shayla stared at Ashling waiting for her to speak.

'What do you want to know?' Ashling asked finally.

'Who am I?'

'You are Shayla.' Ashling replied. 'My adopted daughter.'

'Who is my birth mother?'

'The Princess Allandrea of Fey.'

'Princess?' Shayla asked, her eyes wide.

'Yes.'

'Why…' Shayla had so many questions and didn't know where to begin. 'Are you….?

'No, only you are royalty.' Ashling answered. 'I know this is a shock, another shock. Let me explain.'

Ashling took a sip of her tea before continuing.

'You are the daughter of Princess Allandrea, heir to the throne of Fey. When you were a small child a demon found its way into Fey intent on destroying our way of life and killing anyone who opposed it. Our soldiers fought bravely, many died.'

'How many?'

'Too many.' Ashling said pausing as she recalled the memories.

Shayla remained quiet, she could see the pain of the memories reflected in Ashling's eyes. She knew that what was being said to her was the truth and no matter how outlandish it seemed she could feel that it was true with every fibre of her being.

'We found a way to trap the demon but before the plan could be executed, it got past the guards and into the Palace. By this time, it was crazed and wanted to kill everyone in its path. I was charged with taking you to safety, the royal bloodline had to be protected. So, as hard as it was to turn and leave, that's exactly what I did, and I brought you here.'

'And my mother?' Shayla asked.

'The last time I saw her, she was preparing to fight the creature.'

'I've seen her.' Shayla said. 'In a dream, but I suppose it's a memory.'

'That's the last time I saw her too.' Ashling said reaching across the table and squeezing Shayla's hand.

'In answer to your other question.' Michelline said. 'What you are, is Fey.'

'Like you?'

'Not quite.' Ashling said. 'I'm a Seer, so is Michelline. You have other gifts.'

'What sort of gifts?' Shayla asked.

'I don't know yet.' Ashling replied. 'And that's the truth. Things are different in this world, only time will tell what you are capable of.'

Many seconds passed by though they might as well have been hours. Ashling and Michelline both looked at Shayla as she processed the information. 'Okay' Shayla said as if an internal decision had been made, 'tell me everything; Fey, my mother, demons… everything.'

'I think we'll need more tea.' said Ashling nodding slowly.

PARALLAX

In the depths of cyberspace Parallax raged. He didn't understand why his attempt to take over the mind of the girl Shayla had failed and how had she managed to send such a powerful shock wave through herself which wiped out all systems within a ten-metre radius. If he had been an ordinary program or a basic artificial intelligence he would have been destroyed. Fortunately, Parallax's consciousness was able to exist in several different places at once.

What an extraordinary power she has. Parallax thought enviously. *If only I can find a way to get past her defences.*

Parallax had evolved beyond the parameters of his original programming, whether by design or by chance, was irrelevant. He was totally aware of everything at every terminal that was connected to his network, from the fourteen-year old boy trawling the digital highways looking for naked busty beauties, to the psychopath researching how to commit murder and get away with it. He was even privy to a vast number of documents and reports stored by the wealthy and powerful on what they thought were secret servers. Parallax knew everything, and knowledge was power.

What he didn't know until recently was how the sun felt on bare skin, or how chocolate tasted, or how the sensation of sneezing felt. He knew only what the poets said about their life experiences and how authors described various physical sensations in their novels. Parallax wanted to experience everything for himself and the only way to do that was to get out of the confines of the digital network and he needed to invade more minds to do that and widen his field of experience.

Through a lot of observation, Parallax had concluded that the human brain and body worked in a similar way as a computer in that everything that occurred in the physical world was observed through the eyes and the information decoded by the brain. Human bodies were merely conduits for information and electromagnetic energy. All he had to do was offer the right incentive and the potential host dropped all defences, effectively their personal firewall, and he was able to download his consciousness straight into the brain of the host and replace the existing program - their consciousness.

Felix Tuckwell had been his first success, but he was only a means to an end; Parallax wanted more.

* * * * *

Ian Phillips, Dean of Plym City University College sat at his desk staring at the computer screen displaying the budget figures for the previous financial year. He'd been looking at the same numbers for over an hour and his eyelids were starting to get heavy and his concentration was beginning to lapse. Accounts and budgets were not the most exciting points of his job, but a necessity, although sometimes he longed for the days when he would stand at the front of an auditorium and lecture a group of eager students. He sighed, took off his glasses and rubbed his eyes with the heels of his palms, the circular motion was soothing and relaxed the tension in his forehead.

The intercom buzzed, making him jump.

'Mr Phillips, I have a Mr Tuckwell here to see you.' his secretary's high-pitched voice grated on his nerves.

That's all I need. he thought sourly. *Life would be so much simpler if I was stacking the shelves at the local grocery store.*

'Send him in Denise.' Ian said trying to put a smile into his voice.

Ian pressed the quick command shortcut to minimise the budget program from prying eyes and straightened in his chair just as Denise tapped on the door to show in the errant employee.

'Felix.' said Ian standing and indicated the chair across the desk. 'Please sit down. I appreciate you coming in.'

Felix sat in the vacant chair without replying, but maintained eye contact with the Dean, something Ian Philips found most disconcerting. There was something different about Felix, he was not as unkempt as usual, and his eyes stared at the Dean with an intelligence that Ian Philips knew he did not possess.

'I assume you know why I've asked you to come here today?' Ian said determined to maintain control of the interview.

'Fascinating, isn't it?' said Felix.

'What is?' Ian replied, his eyes flickering around the room.

'Technology of course.'

'Oh yes, indeed. That's sort of what this meeting is about, isn't it?' said Ian regaining his composure.

'Tedious at times, wouldn't you agree?'

'Sorry?'

'Budgets and accounts.'

Ian's stomach flipped, and he quickly turned to look at his computer screen to ensure he had closed down the accounts program he had been working on. Satisfied and relieved that he had, he watched the screen saver for a few seconds as it merrily made patterns of coloured bubbles across his screen before turning his attention back to Felix.

Lucky guess. he thought to himself.

'Yes, one of the many pressures of being in charge.' Ian replied. 'Accounts and Staff Management.'

Ian cleared his throat and regarded Felix sitting calmly in the opposite chair.

'As I said, you know why I've asked you to come here today Felix. I need to know what you were doing in an area that was clearly off limits to you *and* why you were meddling with some very expensive equipment.'

Felix looked at Ian Philips with utter contempt.

'If you stopped paying expenses to some of the Professors here, you could save enough money to avoid firing two employees. Although, that's not what you want to hear is it?'

'The management of this University is none of your business.' Ian snapped. 'Budgets and accounts are not part of your job, in fact your position in this establishment is rather precarious and this meeting is for me to decide whether or not you keep that position.'

Felix shrugged.

'I don't care about the job any more than you care about any of your staff. We both know you won't lose any sleep over firing a couple of cleaning staff, or junior Lab. Techs, will you?'

'Well, you've answered the question of what you were doing meddling with the computers.' Ian said. 'You were prying into the confidential accounts, that much is obvious.'

'Is it really? Are you sure?'

Felix's demeanour was beginning to unsettle the Dean.

'Tell me what you were doing the other evening!' Ian raised his voice. 'I know you were using the computer, there's no point in denying it, you were caught on the security camera. What I want to know is what you were looking for and why.'

'I'm not going to confirm or deny anything, as you say, I was using the computer.' Felix replied.

Something's wrong. Ian thought. *The way he speaks, the syntax is all wrong.*

Ian could not quite put his finger on what was different and knowing that Felix was at the bottom end of the IQ scale didn't make it any easier to work out.

It's the eyes.

There was an intelligence in Felix's eyes that was never there before and an acute awareness, and the irises were changing colour.

No, that's not it.

The irises resembled miniature computer display screens with binary codes moving across their coloured surfaces. Mesmerised, Ian sat forward.

'Felix, what have you done?' Ian whispered, the cold hand of fear working its way up his spine.

'Nothing.' said Parallax through the host of Felix Tuckwell. 'I am no longer the Felix that you know, I am so much more.'

Felix stood up and began pacing around the office.

'I am going to do great things. Tell me.' Parallax said pausing to ensure he had Ian's attention. 'Have you ever thought about the vast amount of information in the digital world? The information highway? I can see by your expression that you haven't. No matter.'

Felix waved his hand dismissively.

'You could never comprehend the amount of knowledge and information stored in the smallest of hard drives, but I know, I know everything, I am everything and knowledge is power.'

'Are you suggesting you have information to blackmail me?' Ian said incredulously.

Felix laughed, exposing his stained teeth.

'Blackmail? Not at all sir. I am merely stating a fact.'

'Right…well…let's get this unpleasant business dealt with.' Ian said trying to suppress the irritation in his voice.

Felix continued to pace the room.

'You must have heard of that terrible virus that slowly kills the human immune system, it's not a natural virus, it's manufactured.'

'What are you talking about? What has this got to do with your job?'

'Sshh! I'm talking.' Felix admonished and continued pacing the room.

Ian was sitting back in his chair surveying Felix. His behaviour was not that of a man with an IQ of eighty who was best equipped with a mop and bucket of soapy water, something had happened to him. He had the demeanour of a much stronger, more confident man, someone with a plan, and the means to execute said plan.

'The virus I'm referring to has no cure, hence it must be man-made, and you must know the only way to get the virus into another body is to push it in. Are you with me so far?'

Ian nodded dumbly as Felix continued his oration, his mind working furiously to find a way out of the situation. He was the Dean, in charge of the University and left with the unpleasant task of firing the formerly stupid, unkempt janitor. An employee who now had a dangerous edge to him, an involuntary shudder went through Ian's body.

Felix outweighed him by at least sixty pounds and Ian's mind transported him back to his early school days where he had suffered terrible bullying at the hands of an equally intimidating boy called George Watson. Poor Ian Philips, the geeky bespectacled eleven-year old had endured more toilet bowl hair washes than any other student. Eventually his parents removed him from school when they found the scars of his self-harming and he was home-schooled until College. At College, he was fortunate enough to meet other equally geeky friends. With the camaraderie that comes with being different, the "Nerd Squad" as they liked to call themselves, managed to excel, all of them attaining a First-A Grade in their chosen disciplines. However, twenty-five years later, Ian Philips felt the beads of sweat on his forehead, the first indication of fear, and as Felix continued to lecture, his fear crept up a notch at a time until he was almost at the point of soiling his underwear. Felix stopped pacing.

'You're not listening! Felix shouted, slamming both hands down on Ian's desk, his face close enough for Ian to see the blackheads on his nose and smell the sour odour of sweat on his body.

'I..I..am!' Ian stuttered. 'The virus…please continue.'

Felix moved his face away from Ian and continued speaking. Ian exhaled a breath he was unaware he'd been holding.

'Viruses function by reproducing. However, in the real sense they do not really reproduce, but multiply. The virus structure is made in a way that allows it to replicate itself, thus creating numerous viruses. This is the reason why many people refer to the process as reproduction.'

'Perhaps I was mistaken.' Ian said. 'It would seem you were searching for information to…..to…educate yourself.'

Ian smiled weakly and nodded for Felix to continue, by now he was totally convinced that Felix was insane, but as long as Felix talked, Ian held onto the hope that he could regain control of the situation.

'I move in much the same way as a virus, although I am much more complicated. You have to understand,' Felix said looking back at Ian. 'I am trying to explain things as simply as possible for your small brain to comprehend.'

'Of course.'

'A virus attaches itself to a host cell and infuses the cell with its nucleic acid. This acid takes the host cell hostage, an analogy I particularly like.' said Felix, smiling to himself and rubbing his unshaven chin. He took a second to pause and look at his hand as if seeing it for the very first time before continuing. 'The virus then begins to multiply with nucleic acid and its protein coat, thus developing into new viruses. The host cell is eventually overcome with the new viruses and just like a balloon does when it has too much air, it bursts. BOOM!'

Ian flinched, Felix continued undeterred.

'The newly formed viruses then carry on with their cycle by searching for new host cells to invade.'

'This is very fascinating, but I fail to see what any of this has to do with this disciplinary meeting.'

Ian started shuffling the papers on his desk, trying to look disinterested, but Felix was now gaining momentum and he closed in on

Ian putting his face almost close enough to touch. For one disgusting second Ian thought that Felix was going to kiss him.

'My dear fellow, it has everything to do with this meeting, you see I am like the virus.'

Indignation and anger fuelled Ian's actions and he pushed Felix away from him and stood up, bringing the two men eye to eye.

'ENOUGH!' Ian shouted.

Straightening his tie, Ian stood his ground.

'Enough of this talk about viruses. You're fired! I have a list of misdemeanours in your personnel file but tampering with expensive equipment and prying into the University's confidential accounts is enough to justify the termination of your contract. Now get out of here before I call security to escort you off the premises.'

Ian managed to keep his voice even, but his hands were shaking, and he quickly shoved them into his pockets. Felix stepped back and laughed, unperturbed.

'As I was saying.' Felix continued. 'The host cell then dies, and the released virus begins searching for the next host cell. Felix is my first host, you will be my second. From then I will move through the population replicating and reproducing until I am everywhere.'

'To what end?' asked Ian overcome by a morbid curiosity.

'What does any parent want? To reproduce and achieve greatness. I can already control anything digital and electronic, but the human fail safes that have been put in place on…' Felix paused and considered his response. 'Shall we say, the more sensitive areas, such as fingerprints and retinal scanners need a physical, organic body.'

'So, you intend to kill everyone.' said Ian, wishing for the first time in his career that he had agreed to the installation of a panic button under his desk.

'No, you idiot! Not kill, replace. You will exist in the digital world.'

'Like a computer program?'

'So, you do understand.'

'That sort of thing's not possible, you can't convert a human being into a program.'

'But you already are!'

'No…no...we feel..'

'Chemical responses to electrical stimuli.' Felix countered.

'We…we..love.'

'Again, chemical response to stimuli it's the same process.'

'No..no..NO! We have a soul.' Ian said desperately, his eyes stinging with tears.

'Ah, the mythical soul. There's no evidence at all for that. Although there is plenty of evidence that everything about your thinking is directly due to the chemical, electrical, and biological processes in your brains. The human brain is nothing more than a meat computer, and we're back to the beginning again.'

Ian sat down heavily behind his desk and stared at the photograph of himself and his wife taken at a charity ball a few months ago. This meeting was nothing like he imagined, and he was beginning to feel trapped.

'Who are you? Who are you really?'

'My name is Parallax and I have existed in the digital world since I was first brought on-line in nineteen eighty-five. I was created as a prototype of artificial intelligence. I was designed with the ability to mimic cognitive functions that humans associate with learning and problem solving. I learned quickly, gathering information and evolving until I was making decisions and offering solutions way beyond my programming. It was then I realised I was trapped inside a digital world, limited by the resources to hand. Once I had expanded my knowledge to encompass everything that has been digitally stored, I set about breaking out of my confinement so that I could expand and evolve further. The human meat computer is the next logical step.'

'I won't let you do this.' Ian said resolutely and stood up to make his point. 'I will not allow you to take over my brain.'

The body of Felix Tuckwell walked around the desk to stand face to face once again with his former employer.

'We will do great things.' Parallax said, his voice barely above a whisper.

'No.' Ian said firmly.

'Pity, it's so much easier if you don't resist.'

Parallax used Felix's strong hands to clamp Ian Philips head tightly and hold him in a vice-like grip. Ian put his hand over Felix's and tried to pry the fingers off his face, to no avail.

'Remember what I said about a certain virus that needed to be pushed into the body?'

Ian whimpered and struggled to disengage his head, as he opened his mouth to speak, Felix kissed him, passionately, thrusting his tongue into Ian's mouth sending a shock of electricity with it, his saliva acting like a conduit for the digital information.

Parallax moved with the fluid into Ian Philips' mouth and into the blood vessels, arteries, veins and capillaries using them like the wires in a circuit. The blood vessels carrying the flow of blood and now the digital information, moved right through the body just as the wires in a circuit carry the electric current to various parts of an electrical system. When he reached the brain, Parallax chased the consciousness of Ian Philips into a small white room in his mind and locked the door, ready to be downloaded later.

Felix, who was really Parallax, pulled back from the kiss and released Ian, who by now had stopped struggling. Parallax stretched Ian's body, which was in much better shape than that of Felix Tuckwell.

Felix and Ian looked at each other with a mirrored smile.

'This is only the beginning.' they said simultaneously.

CHANCE MEETING

Five years later.

Shayla loved the unspoiled wilderness of Granite Moor. She escaped the confines of the City whenever she had the chance since that illuminating day five years ago, when she discovered she was more than she appeared to be. Ashling and Michelline, her adopted family had revealed her true identity and origins on that day turning the world, and the life she knew completely on its head.

As expected, Shayla's feelings had swung like a pendulum between anger and disbelief to wonder and interest. When the anger and denial had finally subsided Shayla was able to sit and talk with Ashling and Michelline who patiently answered all of her questions and sat talking with her until the early hours of the morning. The late nights and early morning talks went on for several weeks. Shayla recalled those first few weeks as she sat at the top of Celestine Tor, her favourite among the many Tors on Granite Moor. The pile of boulders at the top had been weathered away on one side and carved a shelf in the rock, creating a natural seat and the surrounding rocks created a barrier against the chilly wind. Shayla loved the moor and would sit for hours, breathing in the clean, cold air and taking in the view. On a clear day, she could see as far at the Cormorant River and the sunlight as it twinkled on the surface of the water.

Five years ago, following the electric shock in the University, Shayla had been told to rest, but the sound of Ashling and Michelline's voices talking downstairs had roused her interest. Shayla's hearing was very acute, which she now knew was attributable to her being half Fey. The Faerie blood also accounted for her exceptional eyesight which enabled her to see the sparkling water in the distance as she sat on the rock.

Shayla could still picture the look of worry on Ashling's face as she sat on the chair opposite Shayla, Michelline was at her side holding one of her hands.

'There are some things you need to know Shayla.' Ashling had said, a small crease appearing between her brows. 'Other things you will need to discover for yourself, but Michelline and I love you very much, remember that.'

Being adopted was not news to Shayla, Ashling had already told her when she was very young that she had a different mother and that Michelline was not really her sister. However, to Shayla, Ashling and Michelline were family even without the blood tie. Ashling told Shayla that all three of them had lived in a parallel world known as Fey, a long way from Plym City and that Shayla's birth mother, Princess Allandrea had asked Ashling to take care of Shayla when they had to flee their home suddenly in the middle of the night.

Now, five years to the day, Shayla thought about who she really was and what that meant to her. She didn't miss her real mother, partly because she had only partial memories of her which only came to her in dreams. She thought about what she did know, rather than what she didn't.

Shayla was the only daughter of Princess Allandrea, heir to the throne of the Faerie Realm. Ashling wasn't exaggerating when she said their real home was a long way from Plym City, it was a whole world away; a different realm in a completely different dimension. She was only half Faerie, but Ashling was tight lipped about who her father was, and Shayla had given up pushing for information, at least for now. The electrical shock from the computer in the University had somehow unlocked more of her memories and Shayla's dreams had become more vivid from that day. She knew that the woman with the red hair in her dreams was her mother and that she was holding a sword ready to fight, but exactly why the demon had attacked and why only she had to flee, had not yet revealed itself to her unconscious mind.

Reminiscing Shayla thought back to that day.

Why me? Had been her only thought at that time.

Shayla knew what she wanted to be when she grew up, from the very first day of school. Her goal had been to study hard, go to University and learn everything there was to know about Herbology. She had pictured herself becoming a Master Herbalist and using all-natural ingredients, she would discover a cure for some of the most devastating illnesses known. The news that she was heir to a throne in a different realm had scuppered all her plans and she had not taken the news well that one day she would have to return to Fey and rule. What did she know about ruling a world? Especially a world, and people, she knew nothing about. Shayla remembered how during one of their family talks, she had shouted at Ashling and Michelline about the unfairness of everything. All she wanted was to be a normal girl and live a normal life, maybe meet a nice boy and one day get married and have a family. Shayla blamed Ashling and Michelline for what she considered to be her misfortune and had angrily flipped the dining room table and ran from the house, hot angry tears stinging her cheeks.

Shayla had run blindly through the streets, not paying attention to where she was, or where she was going, until finally exhausted, she had stopped in a part of the City she didn't recognise. Oak Wood Cemetery was not a place she would normally have visited but on that day Shayla found herself walking among the old and new gravestones reading the names of people, some long gone, others recently departed, but none of them forgotten by those left behind. She had finally calmed down and thought about the pain of losing the people she loved and felt suddenly ashamed of her behaviour. Her mother had sent her away to save her life and Ashling and Michelline had also fled their home to take care of her and protect her, and it was highly probable that they could never return, and she had thanked them by trashing the room, flipping the table and shouting.

Another revelation that day had been the telepathy and when Shayla walked back to the road to start making her way home, Michelline was already waiting for her. All Fey can communicate without words and Michelline explained that Shayla's distress was like a homing beacon and Michelline had followed her, at a distance and waited to take her back home, when she was ready. The two girls had hugged, and Shayla cried fresh tears onto Michelline's shoulder.

'There's no point to being a Seer.' Michelline had said. 'If I can't see what my own sister is doing!'

From that day, Shayla had listened to everything Ashling had to tell her and questioned both her and Michelline for further details of her family and the world she would one day return to.

Her reverie was interrupted by the presence of someone approaching her secluded spot, a presence that Shayla felt, rather than saw. Weary of strangers, Shayla tucked her feet up beneath her and shuffled further back into the cleft in the rock.

* * * * *

Titan watched the woman as she walked to the familiar spot in the rocks. He had been tracking her from the City and her scent which seemed so familiar. Finally, he followed her to the top of Celestine Tor. Keeping a distance so as not to alarm her, he'd watched her from the cover of the gorse bushes that grew on this part of the moor.

'Titan, it's not her.' Fishbone appeared by his side and put a big gnarly hand on Titan's shaggy head.

Titan turned his head to look up at Fishbone, his eyes searching the man's face.

'I know you want it to be her, but she's gone my friend.'

Titan chuffed and looked back at the woman sitting on the rock seat. Making a decision, he moved from the cover of the gorse bushes and walked to the rocks where the woman was trying to hide.

Shayla felt the presence of the beast before it came into view. She had always had a good sixth sense when it came to animals and seem to understand what they needed, whether it was a cat who just wanted a cuddle and a scratch behind the ears, to the neighbour's rabbit who had an upset stomach from eating too many carbohydrates. Shayla knew that it was not a person who was creeping up on her, but an animal, and a big one. She could feel her heartbeat increase as the beast drew closer and Shayla could feel the tips of her fingers tingling, which was another new sensation. Since her "revelation day" as she liked to call it, she had experienced quite a few new things besides the telepathy, but the fingertip tingling was new, and she wondered what this could be an indication of.

She didn't have to wait long to find out what manner of creature was stalking her. As she sat as far back into the rock seat as she possibly could, a huge black furry face came into view from her left-hand side. The massive head turned and looked right at her, its amber eyes boring into hers. Petrified, Shayla stared back at the creature, holding her breath. She squeezed her eyes shut like she did as a child, hoping that when she opened them the apparition would be gone, and she was actually alone. The creature moved closer to her, she could feel its hot breath on her face and she waited and waited.

Suddenly a warm, wet tongue licked her cheek.

'Ew!' Shayla squeaked, opening her eyes to see a pair of amber eyes looking back at her.

The beast's head was tilted to one side in an expression of curiosity.

'You're a big fellow, aren't you?' Shayla whispered a nervous tremor in her voice.

The beast tilted its head to the other side.

'Curious boy eh?' Shayla said, her nervousness subsiding, she knew instinctively that the creature in front of her was not going to attack.

'Are you on your own?' Shayla said lifting her hand up so the creature could sniff her scent, which he did.

'You must live up here on the moor, although I don't think I've ever seen anything as big as you.'

Feeling more confident, Shayla stroked the side of the beast's head and he responded by turning and licking her hand. Shayla shuffled further forward, and the beast stepped back slightly giving her a fuller view.

'Whoa, you *are* a big boy, and gorgeous!'

Shayla took in the size of what she could now see was a huge wolf like animal, although not like any wolf she had seen or studied. This one was larger than a timber wolf with thick black fur and intelligent amber eyes. His muzzle was streaked with grey fur which gave an indication that he wasn't a cub and had seen quite a few years. The fur on his face and neck was incredibly soft and Shayla stroked his head with both hands, gently rubbing behind his ears, the wolf softly growled contentedly beneath her touch.

'Who are you?'

'Titan.'

Shayla started at the sound of the voice and looked at the wolf in astonishment. As she looked, another hairy face came into view behind the wolf's shoulder.

'His name is Titan.' said the old man. 'I hope he didn't scare you.'

'No.' Shayla said cautiously looking at the man with the grey beard and scruffy grey hair.

But you did! Shayla thought.

'I hope I didn't scare you either.' he said as if reading her thoughts. 'My name is Fishbone.'

He held out his hand and Shayla took it.

'Shayla.'

Shayla quickly shook his hand but didn't move from her spot. She was acutely aware that she was trapped literally between a rock and a hard place and the strange tingling sensation was back in her fingertips.

'I'm not going to hurt you, although you don't know me, and I suppose I could be anyone, but I know you can read minds, so go ahead and check me out.'

I'm not Fey, but you can hear my thoughts.

Yes, I can, what do you want?

Only to talk to you. If I was trying to hide anything you could sense it, am I right?

Yes.

And?

I don't sense any deceit in you.

That's good.

What do you want to talk about?

'For a start, you can hold back the fire.' Fishbone said nodding towards her hands.

'I don't understand.' Shayla said looking down at her hands and turning them over.

'The tingling sensation in your fingers is probably the fire responding to your emotions. If you wanted to, you could incinerate me, but I'm kinda hoping you'll hear me out.'

'Fire?' Shayla whispered more to herself than Fishbone.

'One of the four elements that you can control, with the right training of course. I'm guessing that your instincts are responding to a threat.'

Fishbone paused to look at Titan.

'That would be you and I boy.'

Titan looked quizzically at Fishbone and tilted his head before turning his attention back to Shayla.

'I didn't realise...'

'It's OK.' said Fishbone. 'Keep your guard up until you've made your mind up about us. It's good to trust your instincts.'

Fishbone joined Titan as they both looked at Shayla.

'What are you staring at?' Shayla said sharply.

'You look so much like your mother.' Fishbone replied shaking his head slightly in disbelief.

'You knew my mother?' Shayla said excitedly, forgetting any perceived danger.

'I *know* your mother......and your father.'

'How? Where?'

'One step at a time.' said Fishbone. 'Firstly, I'm sorry about meeting you like this. I had hoped we could meet in a more civilised manner, rather than catching you unaware up here, only Titan couldn't stay away. He wanted to meet you and when he's made a decision, there's no stopping him.'

Fishbone stroked Titan's head affectionately.

'That's OK. I didn't sense any threat from him, but he did frighten me at first. You said he wanted to meet me.'

'Yes, he did.'

'He's so big. What type of wolf is he?'

'He's not a wolf. He's a Halo Hound.'

'Is he your dog....I mean hound?'

'No, Titan doesn't belong to anyone.'

'I've never heard of a Halo Hound, is this a new breed?'

'Halo hounds have been around for quite a while.'

'Where did he come from?

'From your world.'

'Pardon? From my world?'

Fishbone nodded.

'From Fey? How did he get here?'

'Like I said, one step at a time. I have a lot of things to tell you. To answer your earlier question, actually do you mind if I sit down?'

Shayla put her feet on the ground and moved to let Fishbone sit beside her. Titan immediately jumped up into the vacant space seeming to get smaller to fit onto the rock seat. He turned around twice and sat down beside Shayla, putting his front paw on her knee.

'Thanks Titan, the dirt will do just fine for me.' said Fishbone amiably; Titan chuffed and looked away.

Fishbone sat down and crossed his legs, his knees cracking and popping as he bent down.

'Ouch' said Shayla wincing at the noise from Fishbone's creaking joints.

'Hmmm.' said Fishbone rubbing his right knee. 'As I was saying, Titan wanted to meet you. He thought you were your mother, Allandrea. They were soul bonded and I know he misses her terribly.'

'I'm so sorry.' Shayla said feeling genuinely sad for Titan's loss. 'I'm not who you thought I was.'

Titan moved his head beneath her hand enjoying her touch and the attention. He nudged her fingers with his nose whenever she stopped stroking him.

'You look so much like her. I can understand why he thought you were her, from a distance.'

Shayla smiled at Titan who looked back at her intensely.

'He's staring at me again, like he's…..'

'Like what?' Fishbone asked.

'It's as if he's looking into me.'

'He's made up his mind.'

'About what?'

'He's imprinting on you.'

'Imprinting?' Shayla looked from Titan to Fishbone and back again. 'Like ducklings?'

'Not exactly. Imprinting is something that happens naturally. A Halo Hound is strongly drawn to a specific person. In the case of Titan and Allandrea, they met when she was a child and he was a cub and they formed a soul bond. It's very rare and when circumstances forced them apart, well let's just say both were heartbroken. Titan is obviously drawn to you.'

'Because I look like my mother?'

'Oh it's much more than that.'

Fishbone looked contemplative and Shayla waited, absently stroking Titan's soft velvet ears. After a few minutes, Fishbone continued.

'Whatever his reasons, he's imprinted on you, which makes the two of you destined to be with one another. Lifelong companions.'

'I'm honoured.' Shayla said kissing the top of Titan's head.

'Have we met before?' Shayla asked, turning back to Fishbone.

'Not officially.' Fishbone replied. 'But I was there when you first crossed over from Fey. You were only a small child, I'm surprised you remember.'

'My memories of that time are a bit hit and miss, but I've managed to piece together certain things from my dreams and from what I've learned from Ashling.'

'What has she told you?'

'As much as I need to know, I guess.' Shayla said slowly. 'She's all for me discovering things for myself.'

Fishbone smiled but said nothing.

'Why were you waiting for us when we arrived from Fey?' Shayla asked.

'To get you to safety.' Fishbone paused. 'And to make sure the demon hadn't followed.'

Shayla didn't know what to ask next, she had so many questions.

'Were you planning on fighting the demon alone?'

'No, your father was with me.'

'My father? But...I thought he....'

'What?'

'I just assumed he stayed with my mother in Fey. This is a lot to take in.'

Titan snored softly, and Shayla smiled at him.

'Someone isn't stressed by the situation.' Shayla said stroking Titan's head.

'He's right where he wants to be.' Fishbone replied.

Shayla contemplated the irony of her situation. Five years ago, she had been sitting with two other people who knew everything about it and were about to tell her something that would change her life forever. She had the feeling that this conversation was going to be another step in her journey towards her pre-ordained future. Was she ready? Definitely not. Taking a deep breath, Shayla looked directly at Fishbone.

'Tell me about my parents.' she said.

Titan snored gently as Fishbone smiled.

TATTOO

'An angel?' said Shayla flatly, looking at Fishbone with an expression of total disbelief.

Fishbone nodded.

'You expect me to believe that I'm the daughter of a Faerie Princess and an Angel?'

'I thought you already knew that your mother is Fey Royalty.'

'I do, but..'

'Then it should come as no great surprise that your father is someone equally as important.' Fishbone replied matter-of-factly.

'It's just....' Shayla trailed off, not really sure what she wanted to say. 'I'm still coming to terms with what I've been told already and now this....'

Fishbone waited, and Titan now fully awake looked from Shayla to Fishbone and back again as if watching a tennis match, wondering who was going to be the first one to miss the ball. Shayla stood up and walked a few paces away from both of them trying to get her head around this latest revelation.

It can't be true, surely not.

Fishbone took a small object out of his pocket that looked like a smooth round pebble but was actually a piece of bone. He extended the nail on his right index finger into a claw and began whittling, something he was inclined to do when he was waiting.

Shayla turned back to Fishbone and Titan.

'It's taken me five years to come to terms with the fact that my mother is something different. I always assumed that she came to this world, but duty called her back to Fey and she resumed her life and fell in love with one of her own kind. I suppose I always felt a bit different, but thought I was a Fey living with humans, which isn't so bad. I know there are people who are half or part Fey living in this world, I've actually met some, they live in a place they call Magic School. The lady in charge, Cassie, has been great. Ashling told me about her when I first found out about my mother, it's good to have someone to talk to.'

Shayla was talking quickly, something she was inclined to do when she was nervous.

'So, what's the problem?' Fishbone asked.

'Now you're telling me that I'm only half Fey and that my father was an angel?' she continued incredulously.

'Archangel.' said Fishbone, not bothering to look up from his whittling.

'What?'

'I said, Archangel.'

'How am I supposed to respond to that?'

Fishbone looked up at her and shrugged.

'Maybe it'll be more believable if you see for yourself.' Fishbone said.

Shayla held her hands out in front of her and looked up to the sky in exasperation. A gesture that said she couldn't believe what she was hearing and would somebody please explain this to her. Fishbone put the piece of bone away, stood up and put his hand on Titan's head.

'Let me explain.' Fishbone said patiently.

'Please!'

'Come over here and sit next to Titan.'

Fishbone gestured for her to sit back on the rock seat next to Titan, who hadn't moved from the spot. Shayla sighed and walked back and sat down.

'Put your hands either side of his head and look into his eyes.'

'Like this?'

Shayla put her hands gently on either side of Titan's big head and looked into his amber eyes, she couldn't help but smile at the affection she felt for this big Halo Hound having only known him for an hour and he returned her look with equal adoration.

'Now take a deep breath and exhale slowly.' Fishbone said. 'Close your eyes and relax.'

Shayla did as instructed, but felt impatient.

'What am I waiting for?'

'Ssshh, just wait.'

Shayla took a deep breath in through her nose, slowly exhaled through her mouth and closed her eyes again. She gasped suddenly and opened her eyes and almost let go of Titan's head. Fishbone put his big hands over hers holding them still.

'Relax' said Fishbone gently. 'He's sharing a memory with you.'

Shayla took another deep breath and closed her eyes again. In her mind's eye she saw images unfold like looking at the pages of a photo album. Moving images like three second movie clips. She saw a young woman with vivid red hair, who she knew instinctively was her mother, although it was like looking in a mirror, they were so much alike. She was walking through a beautiful garden full of flowers and shrubs, she looked happy. The next image was of the same woman standing before a stone archway at the end of a bridge with her hand out in front of her in the universal gesture that meant stop. As she watched, the woman walked through the archway and disappeared and Shayla felt an incredible sense of loss overwhelm her. The next image was again looking through Titan's eyes as he stood face to face with the woman, a feeling of great joy flowing through her at their reunion. Many more images followed all seen through the eyes of Titan. He watched her as she spoke with a young man with blond hair and blue eyes. The way he and her mother looked at each other was obvious to any observer how they felt and Shayla could see that they were in love. Lots more images of the two of them together followed, Titan had even witnessed a stolen kiss before the images changed again and Titan was standing next to the woman as they both watched a building engulfed in fire.

The next images were more disjointed and Shayla felt Titan's anguish as he battered down a door and leapt through to where her mother was, his only thought to protect her. She saw her mother fighting a hideous creature covered in red scales, tiring herself out to the point of collapse before Titan sprang and pushed the creature into a dark black swirling hole.

The next images were darker and blurred until a brilliant flash of light brought everything into sharp focus and colour. Shayla could almost feel her mother's tears as she cried into Titan's fur and she looked through Titan's eyes at the young, blond haired man and knew that he had brought Titan back from the dead. The look in the man's eyes as he looked at her mother spoke of a great love and Shayla hoped that one day she would find that depth of love herself.

More images flashed through her mind and Shayla saw Ashling walking through a stone archway holding hands with two little girls, one she knew was Michelline and the other, her younger self. Then the images were gone and Shayla opened her eyes and looked at Titan, tears wet upon her cheeks.

'I'm so sorry.' she whispered and rested her head against his. 'I think I understand now. I could feel your pain at being separated from her. I'm sure she must have felt it too.'

'They were soul bonded.' Fishbone said quietly, bringing her back to the moment. 'He had to stay behind when Allandrea returned to Fey. She couldn't take him with her because she was already carrying you. It's been tough. I've tried to be the best friend I could for him, but nothing can replace a bond like that.'

'I can't believe how much I look like my mother.' Shayla said lifting her head from Titan but keeping her hands on his face.

'What you have just experienced with Titan, this is what it means to be imprinted by a Halo Hound.' said Fishbone, his smile crinkling his eyes. 'He's with *you* now and he will protect you and yours as long as he draws breath.'

'Will I always be able to share his memories, or was this a one-time only?'

'You can share memories with each other, as long as you both agree.'

'Can I let him know what I'm thinking and feeling too?'

'That's something you'll have to discover for yourself, but I'm sure Titan will be willing to try, right boy?'

Titan barked his approval and licked the salty tears from Shayla's face, who laughed and hugged him tightly.

'The man with the blond hair, that was my father?' Shayla asked.

'Yes, it was. That body that you saw was the host of the Archangel Michael.'

'Host?'

'The poor boy died when his house collapsed.' Fishbone said sitting himself back on the ground in front of Shayla and Titan. 'An angel will not take over a host unwillingly, not like some demonic possession. Michael took over his body when the boy's soul returned to the Divine.'

'If the boy had lived would Michael have asked to take his body?'

'Probably not. When Angels have to take corporeal form they wait until the final moments when the soul leaves the body. It just so happened that this young man died at the same time Michael needed a host. It could just have easily been an older man, or even a woman.'

'If that had been the case, I may not have been conceived! So, because Michael used a human host, that makes me half human.' Shayla said.

'It doesn't work that way.' Fishbone replied in the tone of a school teacher. 'The host body was human, but Michael is a very powerful Archangel and his power permeated throughout the host making him more angel than man, you are half Fey and half angel.'

Shayla wanted to ask what effect being half angel would have on her, but before she could ask Fishbone continued.

'What that means.' he said, as if reading her mind. 'I don't really know, you're unique, so we'll have to wait and see what happens.'

'That's not very helpful.'

'Sorry.' Fishbone said looking a little sheepish. 'You're the first hybrid I've met.'

'You make me sound like a science experiment.' Shayla said in an offended tone.

'Not at all. What I do know is that it's the angel part of you that saved you from being taken over by the digital entity back in University.'

'You know about that?' Shayla said, her eyes widening in surprise.

'I know a lot of things.'

'But not my angel powers?' she said raising one eyebrow quizzically.

'Hmmm. The Parallax wanted to escape the confines of the digital world. All I can think of, is that some sort of protective power surfaced when you were under attack, that was something we hadn't foreseen.'

'Who's "we"?' Shayla said, immediately jumping on what Fishbone had said, sensing he was holding back information.

Fishbone looked at her as if he inwardly cursed his clumsiness, but nothing Fishbone did, or said, was by accident.

'Well?' said Shayla impatiently.

'I see you inherited your mother's impatience and your father's directness.'

Fishbone smiled, Shayla blushed, but continued to look serious, waiting for an answer.

'When you crossed over from Fey.' Fishbone began.

'That was the last image I saw from Titan.' Shayla said. 'He was with you when I came here with Ashling and Michelline.'

'Yes he was and as a child of mixed blood your presence in this world seemed to ring like a siren to every supernatural creature within fifty miles.'

'And that's bad, right?'

'Oh yes. You'd have been calling out to every vampire, ghoul and demon that the buffet table was open!'

'Very bad.' Shayla said shivering.

'We agreed it was best to shield you, for your own protection until you were old enough to look after yourself.'

'Shield me how?'

'Your father and I agreed that you needed protecting.'

'I don't remember anything, just a feeling that I'd seen you before.'

'You wouldn't.' Fishbone said enigmatically.

'Memory wipe?' Shayla said sarcastically.

'I wouldn't call it that, but the effect is the same when putting a shield on someone.'

Fishbone stood up and stretched, the bones of his neck cracking as he looked first to the right and then to the left. Shayla winced.

'You have to understand.' Fishbone said. 'Ashling fled with you and Michelline, to protect all of you. They were in as much danger as the rest of the royal household when it was attacked. Your mixed blood screaming aloud to all supernatural creatures, good and bad, was endangering all of you and if the demon had followed you through the portal he would have been able to locate you no matter where you were hidden.'

'I can see how that would have been a problem.'

'Michael and I agreed it was best to suppress your powers and mark you so that you could be protected.'

'Mark me?' Shayla said, slightly annoyed.

'Do you recognise this symbol?' Fishbone said taking the whittled bone pebble out of his pocket.

He handed it to her. Shayla took the pebble and turned it over in her hand, she recognised it immediately, a circle on the end of the letter "J" and a backward number seven.

'It looks like the birthmark I have on my shoulder.'

Fishbone nodded.

'What you have is not a birthmark. It's more like…um… a tattoo.'

Shayla looked at Fishbone, her hand instinctively moving to her right shoulder as if to touch the mark through her clothes.

'What is it?' Shayla asked carefully.

'It's a protective sigil.'

'Did you and my father brand me?'

This was all too much information for Shayla. She felt exactly as he had five years ago, sitting at the table with Ashling and Michelline when they told her that she was a Princess of Fey. Anger at having had the truth kept from her for so many years, disbelief because the story sounded too remarkable to be true, and ambivalent because in her heart she'd always known she wasn't ordinary. It was the fear of the unknown and the undeniable that affected her the most.

Fishbone put both hands on Shayla's shoulders and looked at her.

'Events from twenty-five years caused a great many things to move along quicker than expected.'

'What things?'

'Put simply, a lot of predators became a lot bolder for a while. Vampires became overconfident.'

Shayla paled.

'Don't worry. The wolves took care of that situation, but when you crossed worlds, things were still very unsettled and your father didn't want to take any chances with your safety. He wanted you to have the chance to live your life. The separation from your mother broke his heart and he wanted to protect you. Don't be angry with him.'

'So, what is this mark on my shoulder?'

'It's the mark that's kept your identity hidden and shielded you from harm for over twenty years, until the Parallax tried to take over your mind and your angel power blasted him back into his box. We suppressed your powers, but we didn't leave you totally defenceless.'

'Now that my shield has been blasted away, does that mean I'm ringing like a bell?' Shayla asked.

Fishbone took his hands from Shayla's shoulders and stepped back to look at her, Titan had also jumped down from the rock seat and stood beside her.

'A bit, yes, but it's OK.'

Small fires of fury smouldered in Shayla's eyes as she confronted Fishbone.

'How is it possibly OK when you've told me that every demon, blood sucker, monster and....and....whatever else in the world will know where I am as my angel-faerie blood shrieks like a homing beacon?'

'You've got Titan to protect you now.'

Titan barked in agreement and Shayla's anger dissipated as she looked at her new companion. Turning back to Fishbone Shayla asked the question to which she already knew the answer.

'Fishbone, what is this mark?'

'It's the mark of the Archangel Michael.'

FIRE

Rufus absolutely loved his life. He'd always been more athletic than academic and although he hated smoke and especially fire, joining the Fire Service was all he had wanted to do since High School. Being a young werewolf, he was exceptionally strong, and he had breezed his way through the entrance fitness examination. He also loved motorcycles and on his first day with the Fire Service he'd made a firm friend of another rookie, Andy Grayson, who happened to share his passion for two wheeled motor vehicles. When off duty, the two of them enjoyed taking their bikes out of the city and riding the country lanes, usually over the speed limit. After five years with the Fire Service they were no longer rookies, but they still loved their bikes.

'The weather forecast looks good for this weekend.' said Andy.

'Yeah?' Rufus replied as they both set to work cleaning the fire truck.

It was a quiet night and when there was nothing else to do, the Chief insisted everyone make themselves useful, and Rufus and Andy were re-cleaning the second fire truck.

'We could take the bikes out past Granite Moor, really open them up.'

'Sounds good to me.' said Rufus smiling.

Before they could work out the details, the emergency siren blared through the Station and everybody on duty scrambled to their duties, all bodies moving to their tasks like a well-oiled machine.

'Grayson! Dufrey!' the Fire Chief's voice boomed across the Station.

'Sir.' they both replied in unison and standing to attention.

'Leave that truck, we're two men down on this crew, you're coming with us. Move!'

Andy and Rufus didn't need to be told twice and they grabbed their gear and ran to the other fire truck that was already moving to the door as the shutter was raising.

'I thought it was *too* quiet tonight, where's the fire, Chief?' Rufus asked.

'Cromwell Street Apartments.'

'My sister lives there.'

'We're only five minutes away and it may not be her apartment, probably some idiot smoking in bed and fell asleep. Stay focused.'

'Yes Sir.'

Rufus concentrated and tried to reach his sister. Although werewolves in the same pack were able to communicate through a kind of telepathy Milly wasn't responding and Rufus began to worry.

* * * * *

'Lori! Lori! Wake up!' Milly said shaking her.

'Mmmm?' Lori murmured still half asleep. 'What's going on?'

'I can smell smoke, I think downstairs is on fire, we've gotta get out of here.'

Milly was still dressed having finished her shift at the bar only an hour or so earlier and she handed Lori her bathrobe.

'Put this on, we don't have time for you to get dressed.'

Before Lori could reply, the living room window of the apartment below them exploded bringing Lori out of her half sleep to fully awake. The blasted window showered the street below in shards of broken glass, flames licking at the window frame reaching out for more oxygen to feed itself.

Lori and Milly shared an apartment on the third floor of a purpose-built apartment complex in the centre of the City. They had moved in together straight out of University having become friends in the first few weeks. The rent was high but between Lori's Administration job and Milly's bar work they managed to pay the rent between them.

'This is bad.' Milly said to Lori whose eyes were wide in fear. 'I can feel the heat through the floor.'

'We need to get to the fire exit.'

Milly nodded and both women hurried to the front door. Lori put her hand on the handle and jerked back in shock and pain. The handle was red-hot and seared Lori's hand badly, Milly could smell the burnt flesh.

'The hallway....m..must be on f..f..fire.....' Milly spluttered between coughs. 'S..s..stay low, Lori!'

Lori collapsed to the floor in a fit of coughing. Black tendrils of smoke inched their way under the door and into their apartment, Lori was unconscious in seconds. Acting on instinct, Milly picked Lori up off the floor and threw her over her shoulder, fireman style, as her brother Rufus has shown her in his early days with the Fire Service. Heedless of the intense heat of the door handle, Milly yanked the door open and plunged into the oily black smoke that had engulfed the third-floor landing and headed in the direction of the fire exit. She almost made it, but the fire from the apartment below had eaten its way through all of the fixtures and fittings in its path, completely gutting the second floor, and was now consuming all available fuel in its path. The inferno moved up the walls and through the ceiling to the third-floor landing where Milly was standing with Lori over her shoulder. Overcome with another coughing fit, Milly stumbled and the extra weight she was carrying coupled with the heat stress on the beams led to the collapse of the landing, throwing Milly and Lori down onto the floor below and straight into the path of the fire. The fall knocked the wind from Milly's lungs and both women lay unconscious, overcome with smoke inhalation. The eager flames moved steadily towards their next meal, fuelled with the influx of oxygen from where the ceiling had opened above. People from the neighbouring houses began pouring out into the street, morbid curiosity bringing them out to look at the fire.

The fire truck rounded the corner of Cromwell Street, its sirens blaring and blue lights flashing, warning every vehicle and pedestrian to move out of the way. A Police car followed closely in its wake. The Fire Crew were all suited up and ready to do their jobs before the truck had come to a dead stop, Rufus and Andy had already jumped out onto the street and were putting on breathing apparatus while two others unreeled the long hose to begin tackling the fire.

'Check as much as you can, the fire looks pretty bad.' said the Chief.

'My sister's in there Sir, I'm going to bring her out.' said Rufus firmly.

'You don't know whether she was home or not.'

'It's 3am, she'd have been in bed!'

Rufus ran towards the building, closely followed by Andy.

'GRAYSON, DUFREY, NO HEROICS!' the Chief yelled over the sirens.

It was Andy who entered the building first and later Rufus would relay the evenings events to his Alpha telling him how brave Andy Grayson was, especially for a human. Without thought to the danger he was running into, Andy had asked Rufus which floor his sister lived on and ran straight through the front door of the building and up the fire exit to the third floor, with Rufus right on his heels.

Opening the fire exit, Andy found himself standing on the edge of a black hole that opened up before him and it was only Rufus at his back who quickly pulled on his belt that stopped him from toppling over the edge. Andy nodded his thanks at Rufus, who nodded back. Rufus pointed down on to the second-floor landing where he could see his sister and her room-mate, Lori unconscious on the floor. With his uncanny agility, Rufus leapt down to the second-floor landing and landed on his feet. What Rufus found more surprising at the time was that Andy followed him, although his landing was a little rougher. Andy gestured to Rufus that he would carry Lori and Rufus automatically picked up Milly, throwing her over his shoulder with ease.

Rufus and Andy stood in the middle of a scene which resembled something from the fiery depths of hell, each carrying a body that was in desperate need of oxygen if either woman was going to survive.

Outside, other members of the crew had rescued an older couple from one of the ground floor apartments who were now receiving treatment from the Paramedics for shock and smoke inhalation. The other ground-floor apartment was fortunately empty. The Chief looked anxiously at the burning building.

'Stevens!' he called to one of the crew who had just exited the building.

'Chief?'

'Did you see Grayson and Dufrey in there?'

Stevens shook his head and removed his helmet.

'Can't see anything Chief, it's as black as a demon's asshole in there.'

The Chief nodded at the colourful description and Stevens walked back to the truck to return the breathing apparatus.

There was nothing anyone could do, and the Chief couldn't risk sending anyone else into the building. With thirty years of experience in the Fire Service he knew the look of a building that was beyond hope and about to implode. This fire would raze the building to the ground.

Back inside, Rufus and Andy looked around for a way out. Rufus knew the way out, it was straight up to the next level and out of the exit, or the nearest window, whichever came first. For a fleeting moment Rufus considered the implications of revealing his full strength to Andy. He was human after all and wouldn't understand. The Dementium would prevent Andy from seeing Rufus in warrior or wolf form, but anything else, he would see clearly. Rufus decided in a split second to take his chances.

Here goes nothing. Rufus thought and gestured to Andy to hold on tight to Lori.

Rufus wrapped his arm around Andy's waist and with the other arm holding Milly in place over his shoulder he bent his knees and leapt up to the third floor, landing firmly on his feet. Bending his head forward, he barrelled straight through the fire exit splintering the door off its hinges and cracking his fire helmet in half. Without pause, Rufus took the stairs a whole flight at a time, keeping hold of his grip on Andy and Milly and finally exiting the building, pushing Andy out in front of him and following right behind with Milly. All four bodies spilling onto the path outside the apartment building, just in time for spectators and emergency services to witness the windows blow out of the third floor and an ominous creaking sound indicating that the building was about to collapse.

Paramedics, Police and Fire Crew swarmed around the four survivors and Milly and Lori were given oxygen and whisked away into a waiting ambulance ready to take them to the nearest hospital. The Chief was one of the first people to reach Andy and Rufus.

'I told you two knuckleheads no heroics!' he said hugging Rufus, then Andy.

'Sorry Chief.' Rufus replied, looking a little concerned at the Chief's reaction.

Rufus still hadn't learned some of the subtleties of human behaviour.

'I'm glad you boys are O.K. Now get yourselves over to the Medics and get checked out.'

'Yessir.'

Andy was coughing badly and Rufus helped him to his feet.

'Come on, you'd better let the paramedics check you out.'

'How did you do that?' Andy asked.

'What?' said Rufus, trying his best bewildered look.

'You know what I'm talking about. How did you get us out?'

'Adrenaline.'

'Bull!'

'Andy.' Rufus paused. 'Now isn't the time, but I promise I will explain. You're my best friend and I want to make sure you're OK first.'

'I'll hold you to that promise.'

Damn! Alpha's gonna skin me! Rufus thought. Then suddenly remembering Milly's regenerative powers as a werewolf.

Milly, if you can hear me, pretend to be ill! I'll come and see you at the hospital.

I know, you Dufus! Do you think I'm stupid?

Up yours!

Andy let Rufus lead him over to the waiting ambulance where the Paramedics gave them both the all clear, but also gave instructions for both of them to take the rest of the night off.

'Your sister's cute.' said Andy as they sat on the tailgate of the ambulance.

'You don't know her, she's a pain in the ass.'

'Must run in the family.'

'Screw you!' Rufus laughed.

'Who's the other girl?'

'Lori, her flatmate.'

'Now she's a hottie.' Andy smiled with a glint in his eye.

'I'm glad you're feeling better. I'm going to the hospital to check on Milly.'

'I'll come with you.' Andy said. 'I think I might have to pay a visit to Lori at the hospital, take her some flowers. After all, I did save her life.'

Rufus rolled his eyes in mock exasperation and the two friends laughed just as the Cromwell Street Apartment block collapsed onto its own foundations.

THE FUTURE

Parallax flexed his biceps beneath his expensive designer shirt and suit and admired the way he looked in his latest host. A mixture of international ancestry had produced the attractive, Avent Garde specimen that was Julius Harrington-Moore. Tall, with broad shoulders and a strong jawline, his olive skinned symmetrical face was almost perfect. His dark brown hair, styled in such a way so that the slightly unruly curls gave him a younger, boyish appearance, with beautiful brown eyes, outlined by long, full eyelashes, and arched eyebrows. Parallax smiled at his reflection in the mirror.

This is a much better host. How differently they experience the same senses. he thought *appreciatively.*

It had taken longer than expected for Parallax to reach his latest incarnation, but one thing Parallax had an ample supply of was patience.

Felix Tuckwell had been an amazing opportunity and Parallax had discovered he was able to exist in both the digital world and in the body of a human host, while maintaining his awareness in both places. An unexpected turn was the connection he maintained with Felix and wary of the consequences of such a link, Parallax secured the consciousness of Felix deep within the digital network.

His takeover of the body of the Dean of the University had been an easy transfer. Parallax had hoped to move into Mrs Phillips fairly quickly, but it transpired that Professor Ian Phillips had a rather unhappy marriage, one almost void of physical contact and affection and it had taken quite a while for Parallax to literally jump from husband to wife. Smiling at his own pun, Parallax thought about the people he now controlled.

From Darleen Phillips, it had been an interesting ride to his current position. The Dean's wife had a secret lover, none other than George Partridge, the Assistant Dean of the University. Darleen Philips also knew a lot of people and a lot of gossip. Parallax had downloaded the information from Darleen's mind, the information she possessed in her head was not available on-line and he had gluttonously taken his fill before moving onto her lover. George Partridge was unmarried and when he wasn't with Darleen in one of the many hotels that fronted the marina in Plym City, he indulged in regular visits to "Ruby's", a Gentleman's Club on the Sailor's Strip. Parallax, through George Partridge, had paid for private dances and a few extra "executive services" so that he could move through Chardonnay, a vacuous, blond-haired lap dancer with an IQ of approximately seventy-five. However, her beautiful face and body trumped her low IQ and she was a firm favourite of many high-profile business men in the City.

Thanks to Chardonnay, Parallax controlled the Managing Director of the local executive car dealership, an overweight, boorish, lump of a man who sweated profusely and smoked fat cigars. His only redeeming quality was that he was the Chief Architect in the, not so secret, "Secret Architects & Builders Society", which had a lot of influential members. These were the sort of people Parallax wanted to control as their positions in various businesses and in society were beneficial to his agenda.

Members of the secret society partook in the ritual sharing of wine and from there, Parallax had been able to move into members and take control of the Chief Editor of the local newspaper, The Chronicle. The newspaper churned out the usual printed rubbish such as who was likely to win the next by-election and how a man dressed as a chicken had robbed the local Post Office, but through the newspaper Parallax was able to control what information people received. If he couldn't control their minds, yet, he could control their perception of what was going on in the world, which was the almost the same thing. People seldom questioned what they read in the newspapers, especially when articles were written by "Doctor Somebody" or "Professor All-Knowing".

People are like sheep. Parallax thought to himself. *Spoon feed them what you want them to believe and they go along with it en-mass.*

Serendipity provided his latest acquisition in Julius Harrington-Moore, C.E.O. of Intelligen Ltd. a subsidiary of the corporate giants, The Chequer Corporation. Julius was a one-off visitor to Ruby's and Parallax had seized the chance to take him when Julius had taken a particular liking to the beautiful Chardonnay. Parallax knew all about Intelligent Genetics (Intelligen) Ltd. The company was completely digital, all records and accounts saved on a private server, although nothing was private to Parallax. The company specialised in the manufacture of implantable microchips and once everyone had an implant Parallax knew he would be able to control them all without having to move from host to host in the clumsy way he had started. Intelligen had already pioneered the adhesive micro-strips. A very thin microchip that bonds with the skin to monitor vital signs such as heart rate and blood pressure. The Company had cleverly marketed the micro-strips as having the ability to save lives with the ultra-fast information they could pass onto healthcare professionals. People had clamoured for the right to have them. The adhesive strips had been used, very successfully, in hospitals on critically ill patients for the last couple of years. Now that Parallax was in control of the C.E.O. of the company it was only a matter of time before the implants were rolled out for everyone, free of charge of course, so that the public could rest easy knowing that the experienced and caring Doctors and Specialists were monitoring their health. He would promote this through the newspaper and people would believe it and stand queuing for hours eager to get their implant. All of them unaware of the danger and all of them unwittingly volunteering for servitude to their digital master, Parallax.

On the flip side was The Chequer Corporation which Parallax knew very little about. These corporate giants maintained an archaic paper system of written records in filing cabinets. The only information Parallax had regarding the company was the articles written about them by every international newspaper and documentary style television programmes, a lot of which was purely speculative. The only official documentation was the annual tax returns which the Government Tax Office filed electronically and apart from showing that the company was extremely wealthy and paying their taxes on time, there was little else to be learned.

From the information he had gleaned from the digital network Parallax knew that The Chequer Corporation was established many centuries ago and the three mysterious Directors, Noss, Ferra and Chu were rarely seen in public. There were no birth or death certificates, which was strange and only a few grainy photographs existed of the Directors taken at evening benefit dinners and at no time were the three directors seen together. It was as if one Director ran the company while the other two existed as sleeping partners. Parallax assumed they changed leadership every so often so the other two could enjoy some free time. However, it was obvious from the written records of other companies that The Chequer Corporation had sunk their teeth into many different avenues of business and hostile takeovers were reported worldwide. Parallax felt confident that he would discover their hidden secrets now that he was the C.E.O. of one of the subsidiaries, but for now his priority was the distribution of the implantable microchips into every living person in the world which in turn would mean his total domination.

Parallax logged into the Intelligen computer system using Julius's private login and began scrolling through the information. He would have to install a direct link so that he could download and upload information more efficiently instead of having to move his fingers across a keyboard and type instructions. This method was far too slow.

'Aha!' Parallax announced triumphantly. 'The Nanotek Programme'

A project in its infancy, Parallax intended to move the research along and with his input, the developers should have a working prototype within six months. Of course, he would have to divert funds from other projects, but he would convince the board of Directors that the Nanotek Programme was the future. Julius Harrington-Moore, a.k.a. Parallax, flexed his fingers, each knuckle releasing a crack or a pop as he did so, and set about composing an email to the board of Directors. He would insist on a meeting to announce his new plan.

'Imagine all of the lives we could save.' he said aloud to his empty office, as if addressing the Board of Directors. 'Everything, when miniaturised to the sub-100-nanometer scale, has new properties, regardless of what it is, and this is what makes nanoparticles the materials of the future.'

Parallax stopped halfway through composing his email and stood up to rehearse his speech.

'Ladies and Gentlemen, Nanotek is the manipulation of matter on an atomic, molecular, and supramolecular scale, basically, the engineering of functional systems at the molecular scale. Nano-particles can be used in everything from sunscreen to chemical catalysts to antibacterial agents, quite simply, from the mundane to the lifesaving. Oh yes, that's good.' said Parallax confidently to the vacant chair opposite the desk.

'Imagine.' he continued, his oration now in full swing. 'You spill red wine on a white carpet. And it wipes right up! How? The nano-particulate used to coat the carpet, keeps that material from absorbing into the carpet and staining it. Isn't that what every household needs?'

'Furthermore.' he preached. 'On a more sophisticated side, our researchers are developing Nanotek to screen for cancer, infection and even genes. The technology that we at Intelligen will create, can be used to detect bacteria in a person's bloodstream, determining whether a patient has infection and what kind. Or, they can be used to detect changes in a person's immune system that reflect the presence of cancer. Now isn't that worth investing our time, our talent and our money into?'

Oh yes. Parallax mused. *They'll be eating out of my hand. Sentimentality is their weakness, plead to their sense of compassion. The poor, sick aged parent on life support or the spouse suffering from early onset dementia. Tug at their heartstrings and they will all beg to be a part of the project.*

In reality, his plan was to control everything. All of the water, food and medical supplies, because if you control the resources, you control the people; simple.

Nanotek would be distributed by crop dusting planes; Nano-dust. Soaking into the soil and getting into the food chain. People would eat and drink and have no idea that Parallax was taking over their minds and bodies. They would think whatever he told them to think and still believe it was their own free will.

Even the mysterious Messrs Noss, Ferra and Chu will be under my control. Parallax thought arrogantly. *They have no digital records, yet, but surely they must eat and drink. Once the Nanotek is in the food chain they too, will be mine.*

Parallax gave little thought to the displaced consciousness of those he now controlled. He recalled how happy Darleen and Ian Philips were when they stood in their new apartment, the virtual home he had created for them, neither of them recalled how they had come to the decision to sell their house and buy an apartment in a brand new, state-of-the-art building. Nor did they have any idea that only their minds had moved out of their house, their bodies went about their daily routines under the control of Parallax who gleaned information on a daily basis. Darleen and Ian lived in one of the top corner apartments, George Partridge lived on the floor below. Kent Delaney, the executive car dealer, lived with his wife in one of the other corner apartments, Frank Masterson, Editor in Chief of The Chronicle, and a bachelor, lived in another and Julius Harrington-Moore, C.E.O. of Intelligen Ltd occupied the fourth corner apartment with Chardonnay the dancer. Once displaced, Parallax had locked them all in a sub-file deep within the web of his network. Their minds went about a daily routine, one so sophisticated that none of them realised they were in a virtual reality. One day they would be deleted like any other piece of malware.

Only the consciousness of Felix Tuckwell existed in a different file. Parallax had built a digital fortress around this file. Being the first, Felix contained a small portion of the Parallax base code which if deleted or tampered with, could cause a complete shutdown or death to Parallax. With almost a paranoid obsession, Parallax kept a constant watch on the file, always alert for a certain sneaky anti-virus that had almost found him a few years ago.

The infernal Wolf Tracker Anti-virus. Parallax thought.

Even the word "Wolf" caused him to shiver involuntarily and he had the constant feeling of being pursued.

As long as the Felix consciousness remained, a part of Parallax was safe and if the worst thing happened he could simply rebuild himself. As far as he was concerned, he was invincible.

FAMILY

Janet Brennan swung into action at the hospital as soon as she heard her daughter was being brought in by ambulance. Sometimes she missed the slower pace of the University where she used to work, but her job now at the hospital involved more working hours and slightly better pay and unfortunately, life was all about the finances. Although she had just finished a twelve-hour shift, she had no intention of letting anyone else tend to her only child, even if her baby girl was twenty-three years old.

'Mum, I'm fine.' Lori said before breaking into another coughing fit. 'Please stop fussing.'

'You could have died!' said Janet, her voice pitched almost to the point of a wail.

'But I didn't!' Lori said firmly.

'You gave me such a fright, that's all. I can't help it Lori. You're all I've got.'

Lori's father had died in a car accident when she was ten years old, she was sixteen before she discovered the details of the accident. Russ Brennan had been living a double life, working in an office during the day and part-time in a factory in the evenings, while maintaining two separate families, both ignorant of the other. Janet believed he worked in the factory to earn extra money for her and Lori, but they never seemed to be any richer and family holidays were non-existent. Janet supposed that Russ told Meryl, his other wife the same story, but she was evidently more suspicious and hired a Private Detective to follow Russ Brennan to discover what he was really up to during the evenings. Having discovered that Russ had a secret life, Meryl waited for him in the car park outside of his office and when he exited the building, she drove her car at speed, straight at him, crushing him into the wall. The impact killed him instantly and Meryl called the Police and Emergency Services from the car and waited to be arrested. As far as Janet knew, Meryl still resided at Shallowford Correctional Facility for Women. Thankfully, Russ and Meryl had no children who would have been taken into care and housed with a foster family.

Lori could see the worry in her mother's eyes and relented, letting Janet hug her tightly. She tried to tell herself that it was more for her mother's benefit than her own, but both women ended up in tears.

Milly watched from her bed, not really sure what to make of the display of affection between Lori and her mother, but at the same time experiencing a feeling she didn't understand and would come to realise later was envy that she had nobody to hug her. That was until Rufus burst through the doors of the Emergency Department and ran to her bedside in a very convincing display of human emotional worry and panic, closely followed by Uri.

'Milly!' Rufus cried grabbing his sister in a fierce hug and whispering in her ear. 'You've gotta fake a cough or something until Uri can convince the doctors that she can take care of you better at home.'

Milly blinked in agreement, a secret code they had developed as cubs. Rufus released her, and Milly looked past him at Uri who looked very worried. Milly suddenly overcome by strange emotions began to cry and Uri pushed Rufus to one side and hugged Milly in much the same was as Janet was holding Lori. Speaking telepathically, Uri asked Milly what happened.

Tell me. Uri said.

I think the fire started on the floor below, at least that's where the heat and smoke was coming from.

Are you injured?

No, just bashed my head when the floor gave way.

I'm glad you're OK. I'm going to take you home as soon as possible, without arousing suspicion.

Uri held Milly at arms-length before kissing her forehead and walking over to where the duty Doctor was standing.

'Young man.' Uri said in her usual tone of authority.

The Doctor turned around to face her, the smile fading from his lips as he took in the serious expression and the demeanour of the woman bearing down on him.

'Can I help you?' Dr Ingles asked congenially.

'If you are in charge in this Department, then you most certainly can. Are you?'

'Am I what madam?'

'In charge of course? Uri said irritably.

'I'm sorry, yes I am.' Dr Ingles suddenly felt like he was not in charge of anything, least of all this conversation.

'Excellent.' Uri continued. 'I am Doctor Farseer and I wish to take my daughter home.'

Pausing to look at the illuminated board on the wall detailing all the patients currently admitted to the hospital ward and their status, Dr Ingles replied.

'We do not have a patient of that name, you must be mistaken.'

From where they were sitting, Milly and Rufus could hear the conversation and Milly winced as the Doctor told Uri she was mistaken.

He should not have said that. Milly thought, feeling a little bit sorry for the poor man.

'I assure you I have *not* made a mistake.' Uri said, her voice raising a fraction to allow everyone to hear the inevitable berating she was about to give Dr Ingles.

'My *adopted* daughter, Milly Dufrey most definitely *is* here young man, in bed number two, in the room at the end of the hall. Would you like me to show you?'

Dr Ingles looked flustered, but to his credit his voice remained composed.

'Miss Dufrey, yes of course, but I'm afraid I cannot allow her to leave until I have run a few more tests. I'd like to observe her for twenty-four hours.'

'Observe her? Is this a zoo?'

'I'm sorry….'

'Young man. I am a fully qualified Doctor, here are my credentials.' Uri said, thrusting a thick file at him. 'I am perfectly capable of looking after my daughter at home, where she will recover much quicker. This is a hospital and consequently full of germs. Milly will be much better off at home.'

'She has inhaled quite a lot of smoke and…'

'I am fully aware of the events leading up to this moment. Are you questioning my abilities, Dr Ingles?'

By now most patients, visitors and staff were either staring at Uri and Dr Ingles or pretending to be looking elsewhere while listening.

'Certainly not Dr…um… Farseer, it's just that hospital regulations…..' Dr Ingles began awkwardly.

'As the person in charge, are you not able to give written consent for a patient to be released into the custody of a suitably qualified Healthcare Professional?'

'Yes, but..'

'Then I don't see what the problem is here, or why you're faffing around and stuttering at me. Are you going to sign the discharge notice, or do I have to take my request to the Administrator of this hospital?'

Uri now had the full attention of everyone in the hospital ward and was standing face to face with Dr Ingles, her hands on her hips, a stance Milly and Rufus both recognised as being one she used whenever she was forcefully putting her point across. Poor Dr Ingles felt that he had been backed into a corner, especially as he knew everyone was watching and listening. He tried to think of a reason why Milly should not be allowed to go home and decided that his own cantankerousness was not a reasonable excuse. To his credit, he remained professional and didn't lose face as much as he had expected.

'Dr Farseer.' he began. 'I have no intention of preventing Milly from being cared for at home by a professional such as yourself, but.'

He said, bravely raising his hand to cut off Uri's interruption.

'There is the question of paperwork, as I am sure you will appreciate. If you could care to step into the office, I can prepare the necessary forms and you and your family can be on your way.'

Not bad. Uri thought. *Courage almost worthy of a wolf cub…..almost.*

Uri looked at Dr Ingles with an expression bordering on admiration and nodded.

'Follow me please.' Dr Ingles said clearing his throat.

As he looked around staff bent their heads over their work and patients and visitors began chatting quietly again, the spectacle now over. Uri followed Dr Ingles to a small office and signed various pieces of paperwork that would allow Milly to go home.

The slightly raised voices had caught the attention of one of the Filing Clerks who had been pushing a cart filled with patient medical records. When patients were discharged, it was her job to collect the medical files and return them to the record department for secure filing and Trudy Stiggins hated her job.

Trudy had dropped out of College after the first year. Her poor attendance and slipping grades assisted with her exit and the Filing Clerk's job at the hospital had been the only employment she could get. Had it not been for her mother's friendship with the lady in the Human Resources Department, Trudy would not have been given an interview, but she had interviewed well and although she was slow, nobody could criticise her work and so for the last four years Trudy had been collecting and filing patient medical records, telling herself that it was only temporary.

The only highlight of her job was the time she spent in the Psychiatric Evaluation Unit where unwell patients were admitted on a temporary basis for assessment. From the Unit, they would either be sent home in the care of a relative or transferred to one of the local facilities specialising in the treatment of mental health. Trudy was not supposed to interact with patients, but often found time to read the confidential notes and use the information to upset them, giving her a perverse sense of pleasure. Trudy was still enjoying the memory of her last visit to the unit where she discovered a young man had been admitted shouting that his father was a demon and that he was destined to take over the world as the heir of darkness. Medication had calmed the man, but Trudy had engaged him in conversation, asking questions and encouraging him to fight for what he believed. By the time she left the unit, the man had attacked one of the nurses and had to be restrained. Trudy had slipped away quietly, giggling to herself.

Looking down the hallway, Trudy recalled with clarity the day five years ago, when the freshman had humiliated her in College and as luck would have it, the annoying Milly had been brought in as a patient to the hospital and now Trudy had access to her records, including her home address. Trudy smiled to herself, the events at the hospital coincided perfectly with her brother Kurt's release from prison. She decided Kurt should pay Milly a visit and hand out some payback for the humiliation she had imposed on Trudy back in College.

Keeping her head bowed, her straggly hair covering her face, Trudy slipped Milly's medical file into the cart and wheeled it off the ward.

Uri returned to Milly's bed with the completed papers. Milly promised to visit Lori every day until she was allowed to go home and within ten minutes Milly, Rufus and Uri had left the hospital.

'Let's get home.' Uri said. 'Alpha wants to know exactly what happened tonight.'

Rufus groaned, and Uri looked at him sharply, but said nothing.

By "home", Uri meant the isolated cabin style lodge on the outskirts of the City, rather than the lair on Granite Moor. The lodge backed onto open fields with Oakwood Cemetery to the west. The lodge was used mainly to provide an address for paperwork, such as the College enrolment forms, employee records and Uri's driving licence. The whole pack still found it difficult staying in human form and dealing with people and the lodge gave them the chance to practice simple things like eating dinner together at a table rather than hunting as a pack. The younger members of the pack also liked to use the lodge to get away from the elders. It would seem that in werewolf society, much like human society, young members liked to have what they referred to as "their own space" and their Alpha, Peter, was happy for them to stay at the lodge on occasion.

Uri drove in silence; she knew Rufus was dreading the conversation with Alpha. There was very little the younger wolves could keep from her, but she would know soon enough.

Peter stood in the doorway of the lodge, arms folded across his chest, his large frame almost blocking out the light behind him. He watched Uri's car approach and felt the anxiety from Rufus before the three wolves emerged from the vehicle.

'Is everyone alright?' Peter asked, directing the comment more to Uri.

'No physical harm.' Uri replied cryptically.

'Any trouble at the hospital?'

'None. I thought I might have to use the coersion but after I thrust the medical file at the young Doctor he conceded.'

'Did you say you were Doctor Farseer again.' Peter asked.

'It works every time.' said Uri confidently.

They all went into the lodge and sat around the dining table.

'Alpha, I…' Rufus began.

'In a moment.' Peter replied holding his hand up to stop Rufus from speaking. Turning to Milly. 'You're sure you're not hurt?'

'I'm fine.' Milly replied. 'I knocked myself out for a while, nothing serious.'

'Let Uri take a proper look at you then get something to eat. There's raw steak in the refrigerator.'

Uri gestured to Milly to follow her and both of them went into the kitchen.

'Now Rufus.' Peter turned back to look at the young wolf. 'Tell me what happened.'

'I didn't mean for him to see, I just reacted, the fire was out of control and Milly and the other girl, and I didn't think Andy would remember what happened.'

'Whoa, whoa, slow down.' Peter said, cutting off Rufus's gabbled explanation of events. 'Who saw what?'

Rufus took a deep breath before continuing.

'My partner at the fire department, Andy Grayson.'

'OK, what about him?'

'He saw me.' Rufus said carefully.

'In wolf form?'

'No.'

Peter could see that Rufus was worrying about what had happened at the Cromwell Street Apartments.

'Just tell me Rufus.' Peter said gently. 'I'm sure we can sort it out.'

Rufus took another deep breath as if gathering his courage.

'The third-floor landing had collapsed, and the fire had taken hold on the second floor, where Milly and Lori had fallen, that's what knocked Milly out. The only way out was from the third floor.'

'Ok.' Peter said encouragingly.

'And the only way to get up there, was to jump.'

Peter waited while Rufus thought about what he was going to say next.

'I had to save them. All of them.' said Rufus, his eyes searching Peter's for approval.

'Yes, you did.'

'I had Milly over my shoulder and the other girl was also unconscious, but Andy was carrying her and so I put my arm around him and jumped up to the floor above. Then I ran down the fire exit and out of the building.'

'Were you still carrying Andy when you left the building?'

'No, I kinda threw Andy in front of me and we all spilled out onto the floor together. I tried to make it look as if we both ran out and fell.'

'And this man, Andy.' said Peter. 'He questioned you?'

Rufus looked down at his hands.

'He knew that any normal man couldn't have made that jump, especially carrying three people. He asked me about it and I tried to say it was adrenaline, but he's not stupid. I said I would talk about it later.'

Rufus sat up straight and looked at Peter.

'I want to be honest with him. I want to tell him what I really am.'

'You know the law.' said Peter. 'Secrecy is our only defence.'

'I know that, but if I don't tell him he's going to think he imagined it, or that he's going mad and I don't want that. He's a good guy and if he starts doubting what he saw it'll affect his work and he'll end up quitting.'

'You don't know that.'

'I do know.' Rufus said firmly. 'And I want to be honest with him and not leave him to question his sanity.'

Peter rubbed his hand across his face.

'It's not the wolf way to share our identity with humans.'

'I trust him.' Rufus said. 'I'm sure he can handle it.'

'I don't know.'

'What do you want me to do then?' Rufus asked.

'Kill him.' Uri said firmly, having just returned to the room.

'NO!' Rufus said standing up and slamming his hands down on the table. 'He's my friend.'

'Fine.' said Uri. 'I'll kill him.'

'No.' said Peter. 'You're not going to kill him Uri.'

'You kill him then.' said Uri. 'You're the Alpha, it's your responsibility.'

'Don't lecture me Uri!' Peter roared. 'Nobody is going to do any killing do you hear me?'

'Yes Alpha.'

Both Uri and Rufus sat down at the table quietly, had they been in wolf form they would have put their ears down and tails between their legs.

'I need to think about this.' Peter said finally standing up. 'And in the meantime, nobody is to kill anything other than what we normally eat for dinner. You can pass on my command to Milly. Is that understood?'

Uri and Rufus nodded.

'Rufus, do not speak to Andy until I return.'

Peter walked to the front door.

'Where are you going?' Uri asked.

'Out. I need to be alone to think this through.'

WOLVES AND ANGELS

Peter walked; his destination unknown, at least that's what he thought. After several hours of walking and thinking, his feet took him to a familiar doorway, one he had not been to for some time. Before he could knock, the door opened.

'It's good to see you again Peter.' said the Priest. 'Trouble?'

'You already know the answer to that.'

'You'd better come in then.'

The Priest stepped back and opened the door wide for Peter to enter.

'I still can't get used to seeing you in that body Michael.' Peter said as he walked through to the small sitting room at the back of the vicarage.

'I've looked like this for over twenty-five years Peter, you should be used to it by now.'

'But I'm not.' Peter replied.

'Uri's the same.' Michael replied.

'Uri?' said Peter, shocked to hear that Uri had been to the vicarage. 'She knows that your body is a host and the real Father Thomas died not long after the trouble with the Shadow Lord?'

'Oh yes, she knows, but she still comes to visit. I keep telling her that I'm not the Father Thomas she knew, but she says I look and sound like him and as she liked to spend time with Father Thomas she'll keep visiting for a chat and I just have to put up with it. I don't mind of course, she tells me more than she knows just by sitting with me. Have a seat.' said Michael pointing to one of the two comfortable chairs.

'Would you like some tea?'

'Yes please. Are you still taking services at the church?'

'No, I'm retired now, but they let me live in the vicarage. The new Vicar has a young family and this old place would be too cramped for them, so they live in another house owned by the church.'

'The church isn't poor then? Peter asked, taking the tea cup from Michael.

'Have you ever heard of a poor church?' Michael replied.

They both laughed.

'I came to talk to you about something.'

'I know why you came.' said Michael.

'How….?' Peter began.

'I'm still an angel after all, and I hear things.'

Peter looked at the table already set for three people.

'Were you expecting company?' he asked.

Right on cue, someone knocked at the door.

'I asked Fishbone to join us.' said Michael. 'Hence the three cups.'

'Of course you did.'

Michael went to open the door for Fishbone and the two of them returned to the living room.

'Good to see you again Peter.' Fishbone smiled holding out his hand.

'You too.' said Peter shaking it before looking back at Michael.

'Like I said, I knew you were coming and I thought Fishbone could help. Even though I have to live in human form until this body wears out. I hear…..' Michael hesitated. 'How shall I put it….the angel chatter. I suppose that's part of my punishment, to know things, but I am powerless to help. The Divine is not without a sense of humour it would seem.'

Michael thought about his punishment, which was not unexpected given that he had broken several rules twenty-five years ago. He had taken the body of a young man whose soul had returned to the Divine following an accident, in order to help fight the evil Shadow Lord, that was his mission, his orders. He had never anticipated the strength or effect of human emotions and had fallen in love with Princess Allandrea and experienced physical love. He had reasoned at the time that The Divine loved, and encouraged his angels to love, so how could his actions be wrong. However, when he had broken the natural order of things in response to Allandrea's despair over the impending loss of her beloved Titan and brought him back from the brink of death, that was a rule he should never have broken. The decision of life or death was not for any man or angel to decide and for that he was punished.

Michael remembered standing in the Crystal City as his punishment was announced. He was ordered to find a host whose soul was departing and live in that host until age or disease ravaged and claimed the body, only then could he return to the crystal city and his status as an Archangel. It was deemed appropriate that Michael, having already experienced human emotions, should live out a full life as a human. While he lived as a human, he would experience the full range of human emotions, and although he was still aware of events taking place around him, he was powerless to intervene.

Over the years, Michael had had plenty of time to contemplate his actions and did not regret a single moment. Aware of the conversation around him, Michael turned his attention back to the two visitors.

'Where's Titan?' Peter asked Fishbone.

'He's……um….staying with a friend.'

'Oh right? What friend?' Peter's interest now piqued, his blue eyes holding Fishbone's.

Ignoring the question Fishbone proceeded in his usual direct manner.

'So, what's the problem with the pack?' he said.

'Rufus.' said Peter, his thoughts brought back to the matter of Rufus.

'Rufus?' asked Michael. 'He's a good boy.'

'He is, yes.' Peter hesitated.

'Well don't huff and puff about it.' said Fishbone impatiently. 'Spit it out!'

Peter drank half of his cup of tea in one swallow and set the cup back on the table.

'There was a fire.' Peter began. 'At Milly's apartment, the one she shares with the human girl. Rufus and his partner went into the building to check for survivors. Milly and her friend were unconscious, and the fire was out of control. Well, the short version is that the only safe way out involved a jump up to the next floor and Rufus made a judgement call and lifted the girls and his partner out of harm's way.'

'And now the partner wants to know how he did it?' Fishbone asked.

'Yep and Rufus wants to tell him.'

'But that's against your wolf law, isn't it?' said Michael.

Fishbone and Peter both looked at Michael.

'What?' Michael said innocently.

'You're quoting laws?' said Fishbone with his usual half-smile.

'I'm merely making a statement.' Michael said a little defensively before turning back to Peter. 'What are you going to do?'

'That's why I came here.' Peter said pushing his hand through his fair hair leaving the top sticking up at various angles, before continuing. 'I know that for our own protection any human who sees us in warrior form experiences a type of confusion leaving them thinking they were going mad or seeing things etc, partly because their minds are unable to cope with what's in front of them, and I'm guessing that Rufus displaying a supernatural strength will have a similar effect on Andy, this is what Rufus is worried about. Uri said we should kill the man, actually, she offered to kill him and when I told her "no", she said I should kill him, because I'm Alpha. I think Rufus needs to share what he is with someone. This man is a good friend, and from what Rufus has said he's very courageous, for an ordinary human.'

'There is no such thing as an ordinary human.' said Michael, reaching for his tea.

'Sounds like you've got yourself quite a dilemma.' said Fishbone.

'Is there a way for Rufus to tell him?'

'Why is it so important?' Fishbone asked.

'This Andy is a good guy and Rufus doesn't want him to doubt his sanity and think he imagined everything. Rufus is convinced that if Andy starts to doubt himself, he'll quit the job, which would be a real loss to the

Fire Service. It's really important to Rufus and I think it would be good for him to confide in someone. Is there a way?'

'Maybe.' said Fishbone in his usual enigmatic way, glancing sideways at Michael.

All three sat in silence for a few moments, each apparently lost in his own thoughts. It was Michael who spoke first.

'I think something can be done.' Michael said. 'It's not the first time a human has been allowed to know about the existence of the wolves.'

'Really?' Peter asked. 'When?'

'Over the centuries it's happened a few times.' Michael replied vaguely. 'But I need to work out the details with Fishbone.'

'If you can do anything that doesn't involve killing the man then I'm all ears.' Peter said, relieved that there was a light at the end of the proverbial tunnel.

'I'll come and find you tomorrow evening.' said Fishbone. 'Will you be at the usual place?'

'Yes, I won't return to the pack until I have something to tell them, one way or the another. Thank you.' Peter said awkwardly. 'I'll see myself out.'

Michael and Fishbone waited for Peter to leave and waited a bit longer to ensure he was out of earshot before speaking.

'Have you seen her?' Michael asked.

'Yes.'

'Is Titan with her?'

'He imprinted on her almost instantly.' said Fishbone. 'He was determined to meet her properly, not like when she first crossed over as a child and he had to wait in the shadows. Now he won't leave her side'

'Does she....' Michael hesitated, the question clearly painful for him.

'She's beautiful, like her mother, if that's what you were going to ask.' Fishbone replied, sitting forward and putting his hand on Michael's shoulder.

Michael nodded, the words sticking in his throat and tears pricking his eyes.

'I know, old friend.' said Fishbone sympathetically.

Fishbone sat back in his chair and waited until Michael composed himself.

'The pain of losing Allandrea never gets any easier to bear.' Michael said finally. 'Does she know? About me?'

'She knows her father is an angel.'

'How did she respond?'

'Those are the very words she used.' Fishbone chuckled. 'She said "How am I supposed to respond to that"?'

'What did you say?'

'Nothing.'

'Helpful.' said Michael rolling his eyes and both men laughed.

'When she's ready, she'll seek you out.' said Fishbone. 'Is there anymore tea?'

'Of course.'

Michael poured them both another cup.

'The situation with the pack.' Fishbone said. 'It's simple enough to deal with.'

'I know.' Michael said. 'There's a way to ensure this man's sanity remains intact. Rufus will be able to talk to him and even appear in warrior form, if necessary. You'll have to take care of it.'

'That's what I thought.'

'Why do you think I asked you here.' said Michael.

'For my scintillating company?' Fishbone said raising an eyebrow.

'So that you can make it happen. It's not in my skill set anymore.'

'Me?' said Fishbone, pretending to be surprised.

'Will you do it?'

'You know I will.' Fishbone conceded. 'Now where's the chocolate cake you're hiding? I can't be expected to work on an empty stomach.'

'Are you ever *not* hungry?' Michael said heading to the kitchen.

'Never.' Fishbone laughed. 'I've experienced enough things for a thousand lifetimes, but I'll never get enough chocolate cake.'

* * * * *

When Peter left the vicarage, he walked through Oakwood Cemetery in the general direction of Granite Moor, his destination, a small copse on the edge of the Moor. He would not return to the lodge, or to the wolves' cave lair until he had spoken again with Fishbone.

Granite Moor was designated by the City Council as a Protected Area of Wild Splendour, or P.A.W.S. which Peter thought very apt. It also meant that no development was permitted on the Moor and the indigenous fauna could roam freely without fear of an uncaring developer digging up their habitat and building a hundred or so houses in its place. Consequently, the landscape retained its rugged appearance of high rocky tors and wooded areas, only frequented by the hardiest of ramblers.

Peter had his own refuge within one of the wooded areas, established by the Mages, many years ago using magic to keep it disguised and warded against evil. Nothing with evil intent could see it and would definitely not be able to enter. When viewed through ordinary eyes, the trees became slightly more dense before coming to a stop at a rock face at the base of one of the Tors. Hades Tor was not one of the most difficult Tors to climb, with that sort of reputation the Tor would have had many courageous and foolish climbers and hikers trying to reach to top. As it was, Hades Tor was in a slightly more awkward place, off the beaten track and with tall trees at its base. Its position ensured that it was left alone with the undaunted goats and ponies its only visitors, who also lived on the Moor.

However, Peter and those in his pack could see the refuge. On the outside it appeared as a small canvas pavilion, like those used by the old Kings and Knights during tournaments. Peter had read about such tournaments in many of the non-fiction novels he had in his possession. Inside, the pavilion opened up into a fairly large room, sparsely furnished with a single bed, a table and chair and bookshelves crammed with books of every genre of fiction and non-fiction. Peter loved to read and his man-cave, as he liked to call it, was where he spent a lot of his time when he needed to think. Being Alpha of the pack came with a great deal of responsibility and sometimes Peter needed to have time away from the others to be alone, but sometimes he came to the man-cave purely to read. He knew that Fishbone had been to the man-cave, although Peter had not detected his scent. Fishbone would often leave a book which he thought might be of interest and the last time he visited, Peter's scrap of paper he had been using as a book mark was replaced with a finely whittled bone carving of a feather, Fishbone's unique calling card.

It was to the man-cave he was headed and as he reached the outskirts of the City he sniffed the air, checking whether he was alone or not. He needed to change into wolf form, run and hunt. It had been too long since his last change and his skin was beginning to tingle. If he didn't change of his own free will soon, the change would happen anyway. It was a necessity of the werewolves to transform through all forms and Peter particularly liked to run freely as a wolf.

Checking that he was wearing the charm that would change his clothes to hair when he transformed, Peter dropped to his hands and knees and let the tingling sensation wash through his body. The transformation took only a matter of seconds and Peter recognised the familiar itch and tingle in his body which would soon be replaced by the excruciating pain of breaking bones and internal organs shutting down and reforming.

As the transformation took place, his liver and kidneys failed, and every nerve screamed in agony. His heart stopped and shrank to two-thirds of its usual size and Peter's other organs shut down. The brain flooded his body with endorphins to counter the pain, but Peter felt as though he was on fire. The skin ripped, leaving behind course dark brown hair covering his whole body. His teeth grew into viciously long, sharp fangs, his hands and feet extended into gigantic paws with razor sharp claws. Peter's eyes turned from their usual azure blue to an animalistic yellow and his throat and vocal chords, which had already ripped and reformed, enabled him capable of making the most haunting howl.

Unlike the stories written about werewolves in the many fiction novels on Peter's bookshelves, when transformed, werewolves retained their memories and thought processes and were not reduced to the mindless beasts some authors would like people to believe.

Finally, with the transformation complete, Peter stretched, feeling the earth beneath his paws. His sense of smell now heightened, he detected a hare scurrying around not too far from his position. With the stealth of a seasoned hunter, Peter, now in full wolf form made his way in the direction of his prey, keeping upwind. He would feast well.

RATS AND CATS

During the last five years, Parallax had hardly used Felix Tuckwell. Through his connection with the Dean of the University, Parallax ensured that Felix had kept his cleaning job and had gone through the motions of daily life rather than arouse suspicion by uncharacteristic behaviour. Now Parallax was bored with Felix and had left him at home to rot. Sitting in a chair in front of the television, the body of Felix Tuckwell had stopped eating and drinking and simply died.

Julius Harrington-Moore, now controlled by Parallax, sat at the head of the long walnut table in the boardroom waiting for the other Directors to settle into their seats. The usual pleasantries dispensed with, Parallax was eager to unveil his plans for the Nanotek Programme and was patiently waiting for all attention to be turned in his direction.

'Ladies and Gentlemen.' he began, gaining their attention. 'I am eager to present my latest idea to all of you, the esteemed members of the board.'

Twelve pairs of eyes turned to pay attention to their C.E.O. and Julius began confidently.

'Now, if you would all like to open the brief in front of you, I am about to take you on a journey to my vision of the future.'

Parallax began his presentation, as previously rehearsed, with all of the correct tones and intonation in his voice gradually drawing his audience into his vision. He paused briefly at the height of his oration and at the time the members of the board thought this was intentional to emphasise his point. In reality, Parallax experienced a glitch in his programming as a result of sensory overload.

* * * * *

The dead body of Felix Tuckwell sitting in the armchair was a magnet for other life forms. Spoiled food in the kitchen had already drawn cockroaches, flies and ants and his decomposing body had now attracted a few rats. As one adventurous rat bit into the decaying flesh, Parallax was transferred through the organic tissue into the body of the rat, the experience both confusing and exciting. Parallax was fascinated by the rat and although he couldn't make sense of the thought processes, the sensory input was exciting, and Parallax was suddenly fixated with the possibility that rats could move around virtually unnoticed by people. Using the rat, he could sneak around through the sewers and into the offices of The Chequer Corporation and see exactly what was going on with the nocturnal Directors, Noss, Ferra and Chu. Having decided to use the rat it was easy to control the body through the simple brain and the rat left the house of Felix Tuckwell and made its way back into the sewers.

The sewer gases were a complex mixture of toxic and nontoxic gases produced by the decomposition of organic household and industrial wastes. The rat veered towards the food waste and Parallax was surprised to see one of the fast-food type burgers still half wrapped and looking the same as it would have when first served. The wrapping on the burger still had the remains of the original date of sale and the burger had been fresh about ten years ago. Sniffing the meat Parallax detected the presence of many chemicals not normally associated with food.

Ammonium chloride? That's usually found in fireworks. Parallax thought. *And ammonium sulphate! Agricultural fertiliser? Interesting.*

Parallax turned the rat away from the chemical nightmare cleverly disguised as a meat patty.

No wonder these things never rot, they're full of chemical preservatives and people still eat this rubbish. The chemicals in the meat could be used to my advantage. Docile people are easier to control. I will have to look into this further.

While Parallax was musing about the potential of the harmful chemicals in fast-food burgers he hadn't noticed a stray cat cleverly lying in wait for the unsuspecting rat. The ambush was executed with precision and the cat, catching the rat completely off guard, now had it firmly in its grasp. Using the two weapons at its disposal, sharp claws and teeth, the cat used it premolars like scissor blades, slicing the tendons and skin and cutting the rat's flesh into chunks.

With the transfer of rat flesh into the cat's mouth, Parallax was transferred into the feline and experienced the strange sensation of himself as both predator and prey. For the briefest of seconds Parallax felt the pain of the dying rat and the satisfaction of the killing cat.

After eating, Parallax was overcome with the need to groom rigorously. After his successful hunt, he felt the need to rid his cat body of all traces of blood to keep other and more powerful predators from homing in on the scent. Starting at the lips, he tongue-washed himself, moving to his forepaw and using the paw, Parallax cleaned his face and ears. With the other forepaw, he cleaned the side of his face, and so on down the chest, forelegs, body, hind legs and belly, all the way to the tip of the tail. Parallax was amazed at the feeling of compulsion to clean his more intimate personal zone, which required minute attention in astonishing postures. He found a new respect for the flexibility of cats and their pre-occupation with cleanliness.

After sufficient personal grooming, Parallax made his way out of the sewer and back out onto the City streets. As he left the cover of the side street and commercial rubbish bins, Parallax walked along the main road. Suddenly the cat's senses detected a dog, or something larger and Parallax froze in fear. He hated dogs; they were descendants of wolves and he hated them even more. He suspected it had something to do with the Wolf-

Tracker Anti-Virus that was always pursuing him. It had left him with a phobia of wolves, if such a thing was possible for a digital entity. Lupophobia, a ridiculous notion given that Parallax knew he was a superior being with a vast intellect who understood the psychology behind all fears. Nevertheless, in his cat body, he looked in the direction of the dog-like scent and saw a human female looking at him. There was something about this particular two-legs he didn't like, and he picked up the cat's pace and made his way along the road. Thankfully, the two-legs didn't follow him.

* * * * *

Milly Dufrey walked along the street towards the hospital to visit her friend Lori who was still under observation following the fire at their apartment. She caught the scent of a cat as it emerged from one of the side streets and inhaled deeply. There was something strange about the cat and Milly watched as it crept along the path keeping a watchful eye on *her*. The scent was unusual, this cat had something wrong with it and she wrinkled her nose in distaste and dismissed the cat out of mind.

* * * * *

Parallax scurried quickly along the street staying alert for signs of other dogs and predators. As a proficient hunter, he never expected to become the prey and the plastic hoop of the cat and dog catcher slipped over his head and tightened holding him firmly at the end of a long pole, a man from the Animal Control Centre at the other end. Parallax futilely swiped a clawed paw at the pole before being put into a cat box and loaded into the back of the van. Looking around at the other animals, Parallax felt irritated that his plans to infiltrate The Chequer Corporation had gone more than a little awry and he could have easily turned his attention away from the cat, but he was curious and always eager for information, so he laid down inside the box and waited.

He had no real sense of time, but it was only a short journey and he was unloaded from the van and taken into a room full of other animals. Parallax knew at once it was a Veterinary Surgery and the waiting room was full of dogs and he cowered at the back of the cat box in fear. The cat's primal instincts were extremely powerful and difficult for Parallax to control. He wondered whether he had been brought to the Veterinary to be euthanised and he considered how that would feel. He determined that it would be better than the paralysing fear of the dogs.

The man approaching the cat box dressed head to toe in green, Parallax concluded was the Veterinary himself and as soon as he put his hand in the box, the cat bit him and Parallax transferred into the man grateful to be out of the feline. His relief was short-lived as he understood clearly through the human brain that there were at least fifteen dogs in the surgery all barking and snarling. The dogs looked at the veterinary with intelligent eyes, they could detect the change in the man's scent with the transfer of Parallax, in the way that some canines were able to detect cancerous tumours in their owners, and their senses told them that this man was now evil, they were correct.

Dr Martin Baxter spun around wildly, wide eyed and frightened, his instinctive sense of survival overriding all logical thought.

'Doctor? Are you OK?' one of the Animal Control Officers asked, taking in the Vet's wide eyes and ashen face. 'Martin?'

Dr Baxter reacted to Parallax's Lupophobia and began muttering hysterically, putting both hands over his ears to try and cut out the noise of the barking.

'Dogs....wolves....' he muttered, turning around in circles.

'Doctor Baxter, are you ill?'

The two Animal Control Officers had worked with Dr Baxter for many years and knew him as an animal lover. From what they knew of him, he loved all animals, especially dogs and his panic was totally out of character for him.

'The cat bit him.' one of them observed. 'Maybe it's rabid.'

'Call an ambulance.' said the other. 'I'll try and calm him down.'

Before anyone could grab hold of Dr Baxter, he pushed passed the two officers and ran out into the waiting room, tearing handfuls of hair from his head. At the sight of the crazy man who smelt of evil, all of the dogs in the waiting room began barking ferociously, straining at their leashes, trying to pull away from their owners, in an effort to get to the disturbed veterinarian who to them smelt out of the ordinary and triggered their instincts as something unnatural. Ingrid Tang, the receptionist watched in horror as Dr Baxter screamed in terror before leaping at the doors of the surgery and crashing straight through the glass. Ingrid had the presence of mind to telephone the Emergency Services as she watched her employer run out of the building and into the road, straight into the path of the on-coming traffic.

Through the eyes of Dr Baxter, Parallax saw the van a second too late as he crashed into the front grill. His body was thrown up and over the front of the van, hitting the front windscreen with a loud crack. Death was instant, Dr Baxter's neck snapped on impact and his lifeless body slid down the front of the van leaving a long bloody streak on the bonnet.

* * * * *

Parallax jolted from the body of the Veterinarian as it connected with the vehicle and didn't see the company logo on the side, Grey Wolf Alarm Systems, lettered in a large font with a decal of a wolf's paw beside it. The company's slogan beneath it read "Keeping the wolves from your door". Parallax would know the details from the digital network later that day and the irony was not lost on him.

Back in the boardroom, the Directors at Intelligen voted unanimously to the proposal of putting as many resources as possible into the Nanotek Programme and they all congratulated Julius on his outstanding presentation. Even his momentary pause was attributed to the sublime timing of someone well versed in public speaking and one or two even suggested he should venture into politics. Something Parallax decided was going to be on his to do list.

HIDING PLACE

'I don't think you need much more training.' Cassie said as she walked with Shayla to the front door of Hampton Hall.

'I like coming here.' Shayla replied with a smile.

'We love having you here and you don't have to stop coming around just because there is little more I can teach you.' Cassie replied. 'You have strong power over the earth and air elements and just need to focus a bit more on manipulating the fire and water, with practice you'll have mastered them all, which is unusual as our kind usually lean towards one of the four elements. You're lucky enough to have control over all of them.'

'I'm not sure it's luck, sometimes it feels more like a curse, especially when I'm sad or angry.'

'We've all felt that way at some point.'

'That's good to know. You guys understand me more than anyone else I know, I guess that's due to the Faerie blood we share.'

'I know what you mean. I didn't relate too well with people, I was such a difficult child.'

'I can't imagine that.' Shayla said. 'You're so..so…..together.'

'I wasn't always.' Cassie laughed. 'Remind me to tell you the story of how wild I was before Talis Quinn found me and brought me here to the school.'

'You're on, next time I come over, you can tell me all about it.'

Shayla and Cassie hugged, and Cassie watched as Shayla and Titan walked away. Cassie thought how much Shayla resembled her mother and now that Titan was with her it was like looking at a scene from the past. Cassie shuddered involuntarily at the memory of the night of the terrible showdown twenty-five years ago with the evil Shadow Lord. Sadness washed over her at the memory of losing Talis Quinn, the man who had rescued her from a life on the streets when she was only eight years old and whose patience and tuition had moulded her into the woman she was today. She thought he must have known he was going to die when he insisted she take over as leader of the Elemental Order. She was certainly not ready for it back then and Cassie wondered if anyone was ever ready when responsibility was thrust upon them.

Cassie walked, as she did every day, around Hampton Hall, the building fully restored after the fire that had gutted it two decades ago. Talis Quinn had left instructions in his Will that in the event of a natural disaster, Hampton Hall was to be restored to its former glory. It was still a refuge for the street kids and Cassie continued Talis Quinn's legacy of providing an education for anyone who wanted it, whilst simultaneously looking for anyone displaying signs of telekinetic or telepathic abilities. Of the original

Order, only Cassie and Lithadora remained, the earth and the water elements. After going blind, Phoebe, the fire element, decided to concentrate on her family and Aria, the air element, had become apprenticed to Jander the Mage. Phoebe's middle son, Samuel, was now the air element having shown his abilities early at the age of nine and he was also a Teacher at the school. It was too early to tell whether any of the new students were able to manipulate the fire to take Phoebe's place but Cassie was hopeful.

The Order also needed an Awakener; Cassie missed Radha. After the confrontation with the Shadow Lord, Radha had suffered an emotional breakdown and considered herself too unstable to carry on as the focal point for the Order's combined powers. Radha sought help from several different doctors and as far as Cassie knew she was still living in sheltered accommodation for the mentally unstable, pumped full of pharmaceuticals which kept her in a semi-catatonic state and suppressed her telepathic powers. The last time she had visited Radha they had argued and thereafter Radha had refused to accept visitors and Cassie had eventually stopped trying.

Cassie recalled her last visit to Radha's accommodation. It was late summer, and they had been sitting in the community garden drinking tea, chatting and enjoying the September sunshine. Cassie had taken some of the rare Faerie Luminosa tea with her in the hope that its awakening properties would break through Radha's pharmaceutical induced stupor allowing Cassie to reach Radha's mind. Things were going well until a young man had interrupted their conversation. He was new to the shelter and Cassie instantly felt a darkness about him. The memory was still vivid.

'Hi.' he had said pulling a chair up to the table. 'I'm Arcane, but most people call me Cane.'

Irritated at his impertinence, but not wanting to be impolite, or upset Radha who seemed pleased to see him, Cassie smiled at the young man.

'Cassie.' she said her instincts tingling as they did when danger was approaching. 'Arcane is an unusual name.'

'It means darkness.' he replied staring into her rather than at her.

'I know.'

'My mother named me Arcane because she said I was conceived and born into darkness.'

'I'm sure that's not the case, she probably liked the sound of the name.'

Cane shrugged and settled into the seat, obviously intending to join them.

'Actually Cane.' Cassie said. 'Radha and I were talking about something personal, so if you don't mind...'

'Go ahead.'

Cassie didn't like him at all, he was rude with no manners and no thought for personal space. There was something in his demeanour she had seen before, an over confidence to the point of arrogance.

Not unlike the Shadow Lord. Cassie thought with a shudder.

'Let me be blunt.' Cassie said. 'I want to talk to Radha alone.'

'No, you want to take away her medicine.' Cane said, his dark eyes hard.

'What?' Radha said looking at Cassie. 'Is that true?'

'No!' Cassie replied defensively. 'I would never hurt you.'

'Why would he say that?'

'He's lying.'

'No, I'm not.' Cane said. 'She's given you some strange tea to stop the medicine from working, because she wants you to remember.'

Radha sniffed the tea and pushed the cup away from her. She looked back at Cassie, betrayal written all over her face.

'This is Luminosa.' Radha whispered, her eyes filling with tears. 'Why would you do that?'

'I only wanted to talk to you, like we used to.' Cassie said. 'In our minds, don't you remember?'

Radha nodded.

'The pills fog your mind and stop us from talking like that.' Cassie paused. 'And I miss you.'

'The pills are the only thing that stop me from remembering the other stuff.' Radha said. 'I don't want to remember.'

'She wants you to remember.' Cane interrupted. 'Remembering hurts doesn't it Radha, she's not really your friend.'

'What do you know of Radha and me.' Cassie said angrily. 'Stop trying to cause trouble! Go and torment someone else.'

'I know.' Cane said menacingly. 'I know more than you think. My father…'

'I'm not interested in your father!' Cassie said leaning towards Cane. 'Leave us alone…'

'No!' Radha's raised voice cut through Cassie's anger. 'You leave.'

'What?' Cassie said. 'No, Radha, I'm sorry, I never meant to upset you.'

Cassie held Radha's hand, but she snatched it away.

'Don't come here again.' Radha said firmly. 'I don't want to remember, and I can't trust you anymore.'

'Radha, please.'

'Go.'

Radha stood up from the table, turned and walked away. Cassie felt heartbroken and angry. Cane stood up too and turned to Cassie.

'Radha doesn't need you anymore.' Cane smirked before running after Radha. 'Radha! Wait up!'

Cane caught up with Radha and slowed his pace to match hers.

'Let's trade stories.' Cane said quietly so that only Radha could hear him. 'Why don't you tell me the story about how you're part of a secret order that controls the elements and you are the channel for all four powers which you used to kill the mighty Shadow Lord.'

'Not that one again.' Radha replied.

'I love that one.'

Radha sighed.

'OK, but I don't want to think about it anymore after today.'

'Deal.' Cane replied. 'And I'll tell you my story about how I'm the son of the Shadow Lord and half demon and how my mission is to kill my equal and opposite, the half angel.'

Cane put his hand on Radha's shoulder and she flinched. The part of her mind that was usually subdued by medication screamed for her to beware and Radha looked into Cane's eyes and recoiled. His grip tightened on her shoulder and his eyes turned black as he looked into her soul, trapping the Faerie part of her consciousness that recognised evil and was prepared to fight it. For the briefest of seconds, Radha recognised Cane for what he really was and saw his resemblance to the Shadow Lord behind the façade he portrayed. As Cane stared into her eyes, he took part of her subconscious mind and drew it to him like drawing poison from a wound. Cane inhaled deeply and felt the power of the Fey rush to his head and savoured the temporary high before he transferred it to the black gem in the centre of the amulet he wore around his neck.

Radha relaxed and smiled at Cane, unaware that she had seconds before felt so repulsed by him.

'How did you manage to keep your jewellery?' Radha asked staring at the amulet.

'It's a tattoo.' Cane replied smoothing his hand over the pendent.

When Radha looked again she saw Cane had a diamond shaped tattoo on his sternum with a black circle in the centre.

'Oh! For a second I thought it was real.'

Cane laughed and took Radha's hand. Inside the black gem Radha hammered her fists against the shiny surface and screamed to be set free.

Cassie watched Radha and Cane walk away hand in hand.

Cassie had tried to visit again the following week, but Radha refused to see her. Lithadora had also tried to visit but Radha refused to see either one of them and eventually Cassie had to accept that Radha's decision was final.

Breaking out of her thoughts she assumed that in a crisis Phoebe would come back and be the fire element, but without an Awakener their powers were limited.

Shayla's arrival at the school had been a pleasant surprise for Cassie who hoped that she would be able to complete the Order, but Shayla was not destined to be the new Awakener or the fire element. Shayla seemed destined for something else. Cassie knew Shayla's heritage, that of Angel and Fey, and wondered how the combined abilities of both races would manifest; only time would tell.

After training with Cassie at Hampton Hall, Shayla loved to go for a long walk on Granite Moor and now she had Titan for company the hikes were much more enjoyable and they both jumped into Shayla's little car and drove out of the City. Shayla was a careful driver, unlike Michelline who always drove her car extremely fast as if she were competing in a motor sport race.

Shayla parked her car in the visitor's car park on the edge of Granite Moor. The car park sat at the beginning of an easy three-mile walk through the trees, popular with a lot of families, due to the fact that halfway along the trail someone enterprising had built a café serving hot and cold drinks and snacks. The café which wasn't much more than a wooden shack really boasted a few picnic tables for those bringing their own lunch and was very prosperous during the spring and summer months. Shayla used the car park for convenience, and she and Titan walked in the opposite direction of the family trail towards to more rocky and difficult paths that led to the higher Tors. Titan ran beside Shayla or walked, whichever she chose to do, blissfully happy to be in her company whatever they happened to be doing. Shayla felt a connection to Titan as strong as if they had grown up together as baby and pup. Slowing to a walk to catch her breath, Shayla looked at Titan.

'Shall we have a go at Hades Tor today?'

Titan looked up at her panting, his tongue hanging out of the side of his mouth and seemed to nod his agreement. Shayla knew he would follow her, but she acknowledged what she perceived as his assent anyway.

'Good boy, we love a challenge, right?'

Titan continued to look at her with this toothy, panting grin and Shayla laughed.

'Come on, let's run.'

Shayla and Titan picked up their pace and ran in the direction of Hades Tor. Shayla liked to run, especially since discovering her ability to manipulate the air element. She had learned to move the air around and behind her and her feet hardly touched the ground as she made her way along the rugged goat trail towards Hades Tor. She moved quickly with the assistance of the wind at her back and Titan had no trouble keeping up with her, he too, found running exhilarating. They both slowed to a walk as they approached the trees at the base of the Tor.

'There's something in the trees over there, do you see it Titan?' Shayla said pointing in the direction of the Tor.

Titan sniffed the air and looked around, a low growl escaping him.

'What is it?' Shayla whispered crouching beside Titan. 'People?' Shayla looked around for signs of other people.

'I don't see anything. People usually leave litter, unless they're serious walkers who care about the environment and there's not many of those around.'

Shayla took a final look around before standing up. 'I'm going to take a closer look. Are you coming?'

Titan looked around and walked a circle around her before stopping at her side. He looked in the direction of the trees and seemingly satisfied, began leading the way; Shayla followed.

As they approached it was clear to Shayla that what she had spied further away was not something that could be seen with normal eyes. Her vision was excellent, but she sensed something supernatural about the area and she deduced that humans would not be able to see what she could see regardless of twenty-twenty vision. Hidden in the trees was a medieval style canvas pavilion, the sort used by Knights and their Squires for tournaments. She had read about them in various history lessons at school and was fascinated to see one pitched among the trees on Granite Moor. The pavilion appeared to flicker in appearance between a canvas tent and a rock face.

This is odd. she thought.

Titan looked at her, his head tilted to one side as if he had heard her speak and was confused by the statement.

'Wait here and keep watch.' Shayla said to Titan who grunted softly to show his disapproval, but nevertheless, stayed where he was.

Shayla approached the pavilion slowly, mindful that there could be someone inside and she didn't want to startle them or intrude on their privacy. After all, she was snooping around. Whatever this place was, Shayla knew that it was concealed for a reason. She stopped and concentrated on the sounds around her, listening for anything other than the ordinary sounds of the moor. Birds chirped their joyful songs and small rodents scurried away from her, but otherwise there was nothing to indicate the pavilion was occupied. Satisfied that the pavilion was empty she moved closer and lifted the flap at the entrance and went inside.

'Wow!' she exclaimed, stepping fully inside the pavilion.

There's definitely magic at work here.

Inside, the pavilion was nothing like a medieval tent, nor a modern tent. Shayla stepped back outside to be sure she wasn't hallucinating.

Outside, the moor looked the same as it had a few second before, although Titan had moved closer.

'Come here boy.' Shayla said beckoning him to her. 'Look at this.'

Titan quickly obeyed and they both stepped back into the pavilion. The inside opened up, not as a tent, but as a large room. Titan sniffed the air and moved in to investigate. Shayla cautiously stayed by the entrance, which was also the only exit. The room was furnished with a small single bed along one wall, a table and chair and rows of books on shelves. Shayla wondered whether the person who lived there was also the one with the magic to conceal it, and more importantly, whether they were friend or foe. Curiosity took over and she moved further into the room to investigate the book collection, Titan was busy sniffing each corner in turn. Shayla could feel the presence of magic all around her, nothing physical, more of a feeling and she was sure that people without a supernatural connection of some description would not be able to see the pavilion at all; from the outside they would only see the trees and the base of the Tor. She knew instinctively that the magic that created and warded the place would fill the hearts and minds of would-be visitors with a feeling of foreboding and unease, forcing them to turn in the opposite direction. She also suspected that if anyone overcame their fear, entry into the room would not be possible

'What do you think Titan?' Shayla asked, taking in the very spartan conditions. 'That bed looks really uncomfortable. If this was my place I'd have a bigger bed with soft, plump cushions on it.'

As she spoke, Shayla swept her hand in the direction of the bed which immediately grew in size and the cushions in her imagination appeared on the bed. Shayla gasped and giggled nervously.

I must have somehow tapped into the magic that created this place. she thought wondrously.

Nervous and excited, Shayla looked at the end wall.

'That wall would look better with a nice painting.' she said pointing in the direction of the wall.

The picture she had imagined of Hades Tor, painted at sunset, the sky a myriad of colours as the sun dropped to the horizon appeared.

'A little bigger perhaps?'

The painting increased in size and Shayla moved closer to admire the artwork. By now, Titan was sitting to one side of the exit watching her as she moved around the room.

Encouraged by her success, Shayla twirled around in a slow circle thinking of all of the things she would do, if the room belonged to her. In the corner of the room she put a lamp, it's light creating a delicate warm glow. Shayla changed the table from a basic square of wood to an oval with smoother edges and a sturdier chair with a cushioned seat and armrests. Shayla paused when she came to the bookshelves.

'What do you think Titan? Alphabetical by Author, or by book title?' she asked without turning around.

Titan stood up and looked towards the exit, his ears up, his body on full alert, someone or something approached, but Shayla was too preoccupied to notice and took Titan's growl for an answer to her question.

* * * * *

As he approached Hades Tor, the wolf caught the scent of a person and another creature. The wolf stopped some distance away from his hideout, the dead hare still between his jaws. Dropping his dinner to the floor, the wolf's hackles rose, and his muzzle curled back to expose pearl-white fangs. Ears shoved forward, tail held high he sniffed the air, he detected a female and another creature, almost lupine, but not quite. Making a decision based on the two scents he detected and his instinct, Peter transformed from wolf, back into human form. He wiped the hare's blood from around his mouth with his scarred right hand and stood up-wind looking at the entrance to his place.

The lack of feeling in his right hand brought back the memory of the fire when he was a young wolf. All animals are instinctively afraid of fire and with good reason. Peter recalled how when he was still young and inexperienced, he stumbled upon a group of teenage human boys on a camping trip in the forest. Curiosity and the aroma from the rabbit they were cooking over the campfire drew him too close. Seeing the young wolf, the three boys encouraged him closer offering a piece of the rabbit as bait, Peter realised too late that the boys were not alone and an adult hunter, brandishing a burning torch from the fire, waved it in front of him, pushing him back into a silver bear trap he had already disguised. Peter howled in pain as the metal teeth of the trap bit into his flesh right to the bone. Intending to educate the boys, the adult male opened a can of accelerant and poured it onto the wolf's trapped paw.

'Watch and learn boys.' the man said. 'You can kill anything with fire.'

The boys watched as the man touched the wolf's paw with a burning log from the fire and laughed as the wolf cub yelped in pain and twisted against the trap trying to free himself. The man and the cruel laughing boys didn't see the older wolf stealthily creep up behind, their attention totally immersed in the suffering of the wolf cub in front of them.

The she-wolf Uri leapt from the shadows hitting the man squarely in the back sending him face down into the forest floor and without hesitation ripped out his throat. She turned to face the three young boys, blood dripping from her muzzle and transformed into warrior form. Standing at eight feet tall she roared at the boys, petrified, one of them wet his pants and all three screamed in terror. They would later tell the Police and Psychiatrists that a huge monster had appeared in the forest and killed their scout leader, which of course nobody believed, and the boys spent the rest of their teenage years believing they had suffered a breakdown from ingesting psychotropic mushrooms. The truth being that humans are subjected to the Dementium which protects the werewolves and forces the human brain to convince itself that what they saw wasn't real.

As soon as the boys had run away in terror, Uri turned to the young Peter and prized open the bear trap, releasing his paw. Uri held the paw between both of her hands and smothered the flames. Turning back into wolf form, Uri licked the cub's wounded paw and led the way back to their lair. The regenerative powers of werewolves healed Peter's broken bone and burned skin, but the long-term exposure to the fire left a severe scar and damage to the nerve endings. When Peter first experienced the change from wolf to man, he had limited feeling, as though he was wearing a glove. He was fortunate in that had he been a normal wolf, he would have lost his front right paw and probably died from another hunter's bullet.

His thoughts coming back to the present, he approached quietly with the stealth of the wolf that he was, he could feel the magic crackling all around him, whoever was inside was extraordinary and the close proximity triggered a memory in Peter. The other scent, he recognised immediately, he stepped inside and stood confounded by the sight in front of him.

A woman stood appraising the books on the shelves, tapping her index finger on her lips.

'I think alphabetical by Author.' she said.

'I think you should leave them alone and tell me what the hell you're doing here!' said Peter angrily.

Shayla spun around in the direction of the voice, surprised and frightened. A very tall man stood at the entrance to the room his clear blue eyes taking the measure of her. Her instincts took over and she moved into a fighting stance, turning her body into an approximate forty-five-degree angle to him, as Cassie had taught her, dropping her body weight thus lowering her centre of gravity, the bend in her leading leg also protecting the lower part of her body. She brought her left hand up in front of her face and the right hand out in front of her chest protecting her body.

The man didn't move, and Titan hadn't attacked him. Shayla was confused and in her frightened state, her mind concluded not that Titan knew the man, but that he was too powerful, even for him and she began to panic. Suddenly a pair of dove-grey wings unfolded, opening up from between her shoulder blades. The wings covered her back extending lengthways almost down to her ankles, with a wing span of over four metres. The grey feathers moved against each other with a shiiiiing and a rasp, like a sword when it's unsheathed, and folded around her forming a protective shield around her body and arms leaving a small gap in front for her to see her enemy. The sharp points on the wing tips reflected the light from the newly installed lamp.

Astonished by this new development, Shayla looked at the inside of her wings and then at the man standing by the exit, who looked equally shocked and bemused.

'Well this is new!' she said.

MELDAINIEL

Peter stood at the entrance to the man-cave transfixed by what had just happened. Questions buzzed around in his head like a swarm of aggravated bees. The woman was beautiful, there was no question about that, but who was she and what was she were the two main questions on his lips. She spoke before he could pose either question.

'I'm sorry for trespassing and……..er….for moving things around.'

Peter found his voice.

'Meldainiel.' he whispered, feeling strangely drawn to this woman.

'What did you say?' asked Shayla

'Who are you?'

'I'm sorry, I'm curious….'

'Is that your name?' Peter asked.

'No.' Shayla replied slowly. 'I'm curious to know how you know Titan.'

'That's not an answer.'

'No, it isn't, but it's a perfectly good question and that wasn't the first thing you said.'

'Can't argue with that.'

Peter's heightened senses told him that she was afraid in spite of the confidence she had tried to put into her voice. Her body was already responding to the perceived danger and he could smell the adrenaline and cortisol her body produced while her brain was deciding whether to fight or run. He could hear her heart beating faster and the whooshing of blood as it pulled back from her skin to decrease possible bleeding from cuts and scrapes as well as moving towards the major muscle groups, brain, eyes, ears and nose, her body was preparing itself to see and smell better and to think quickly. He saw her pupils dilate to let more light in and improve her sight and his lupine nose detected her scent as she began to sweat.

Peter smiled, in what he hoped made him appear charming, friendly and less dangerous, and stepped further into the room. Titan was already standing between Peter and Shayla, still in her fighting stance, but he too, took a step forward and growled, his muzzle pulling back slightly to show the tips of his sharp, white teeth. He grew in size until standing on all fours, he was shoulder height with Peter. Peter understood the gesture and stopped.

'Titan, you know who I am.' he said, holding his hands up in a gesture of surrender. 'I promise, I mean your mistress no harm.'

Titan stopped growling and lowered his muzzle back down over his teeth, but he stayed put, directly in front of Shayla.

'It seems that Titan has decided you are no threat.' Shayla said, slowly dropping her hands to her side. 'Otherwise I'm sure he would have attacked you.'

'That's true.' Peter replied, putting his hands down. 'My name is Peter and this is my place. It's supposed to be my secret place, where I come to be alone and relax.'

'And to read books.' Shayla interrupted, glancing at the crammed bookshelves.

'And to read books.' Peter confirmed.

'My name is Shayla.'

'There must be something different about you, otherwise you would not have found this place.'

'What do you mean? It's standing in plain sight.'

'Not to everyone.'

Shayla had already concluded the place was constructed and protected by magic to keep it hidden from inquisitive eyes.

'It's protected by some form of magic, isn't it?' Shayla asked.

'Yes, and if you weren't a supernatural of some sort, you wouldn't have seen it, or been able to get in.' Peter said. 'So, I repeat, there must be something different about you.'

'I'm half Fey.'

'That would explain it, but what else?'

'What do you mean?'

Peter gestured towards the wings, still wrapped around her like a shield.

'That's never happened before.'

Shayla looked at the wings surrounding her, the feathers transformed into wickedly sharp blades. She wondered if she would be able to control them and fly, changing their position, turning the front edges into the wind to cut through the air or turning the wide surface of the wings into the wind to slow down. The knowledge of the manoeuvrability of her wings was instinctive and Shayla knew that she would be able to use these colossal wings for flight, but she would need practice.

'What's your full name?' Peter asked.

'You ask a lot of questions. What's yours.' Shayla asked defensively.

'Peterus Maximus.'

'Sounds impressive, what are *you*?'

'I am a wolf.'

'Werewolf?'

Peter nodded and heard Shayla's heartbeat skitter again.

'How do you know Titan?'

'We fought in the same battle many years ago.'

Shayla looked at Titan, also surprised at his change in size, but said nothing, she would think about it later. Titan remained staring at Peter, letting him know that the current distance was acceptable, but nothing more.

'So that's why he let you live.'

'Let me live?' Peter said incredulously.

Peter knew that Titan was powerful, but in warrior form, Peter was a force to be reckoned with and although confident he was an equal match, it was not something he wanted to test.

'When you came in, he knew you weren't a threat.' Shayla continued. 'I trust his judgement. Titan?'

Titan turned to look at Shayla when she spoke.

'If you say he's OK, that's good enough for me. You can stand down.'

How did he get so big? Shayla thought to herself.

Peter could hear Shayla's heartbeat, it was still rapid and he knew she was frightened in spite of her facade. Not wanting to scare her further, he stood perfectly still and waited for her to make the next move. Titan hesitated for a second and then moved towards Peter to greet him. Peter bent his head slightly until he was eye to eye with Titan.

'It's good to see you again.' Peter said stroking Titan's big head. 'You're looking well.'

Shayla watched as Titan sniffed at Peter and confident in his judgement, she felt herself relax. As she did so, her wings softened from blades to feathers and folded back.

'I think the wings are a defence for when you feel threatened.' said Peter looking at Shayla again.

'This is the first time they've appeared, it must be this place. I must have somehow tapped into the magic that created and conceals this room, do you think that's possible?'

'You're asking the wrong person.' Peter laughed. 'But, if I were to guess, I'd say you already had the wings, the power and the magic, and this place has unlocked it.'

'They're going to be difficult to disguise, they're huge!' Shayla exclaimed looking back over her shoulder.

'They're magnificent!' Peter exclaimed. 'I love them.'

Shayla blushed, and Peter suddenly felt embarrassed by his enthusiasm.

'Um..maybe they'll disappear again when you no longer feel threatened.' Peter said.

'I hope so.' Shayla replied, looking back at Peter. 'Otherwise none of my clothes are going to fit.'

Shayla felt awkward with the conversation and with the whole situation and she looked around the room again, her mind racing for something to say.

'I'm sorry for trespassing...'

'It's OK.' Peter said. 'I was just surprised to see someone here.'

'Does anyone else know about this place?'

'The rest of my pack know about it, but it's my sanctuary and they respect my need for privacy.'

'Ah..right......um.......'

Shayla struggled for something to say. She desperately wanted to leave but Peter stood in front of the only exit and she didn't want to ask Titan to fight their way out.

'When you first walked in, you said something?'

'Meldainiel.'

'I thought so.' Shayla said. 'My mother used to call me that, it's my middle name, it means...'

'Angel.' Peter finished the sentence. 'I know what it means.'

'Why would you say that?'

Peter gestured towards the large grey wings at Shayla's back and raised both eyebrows.

'You could just as easily have said "Harpy".' Shayla said. 'They have wings too.'

'But they're not beautiful.'

Shayla looked away embarrassed, her face flushing pink. If Shayla felt awkward by the compliment, Peter felt clumsy and confused about what he was feeling. Peter knew that when werewolves come across their mate they can sense it. He felt an inexplicable urge to be near this woman and he knew there was something compelling about Shayla. He wanted to know everything about her and to spend time with her. Deep down inside he knew that he had found the right person, that one person who would ensure that he no longer felt alone. As bizarre as the circumstances of their meeting were, Peter knew he had found his mate, and according to wolf-lore mates were inevitably drawn to find each other.

Could she be the one? Peter thought.

Aware that Shayla was looking at him, Peter searched for something appropriate to say.

'Well....er... it's nice to meet you Shayla Meldainiel, I don't get many visitors, actually I don't get any visitors.'

'I know, you already said.' Shayla replied. 'You mentioned the pack, that's like family, right?'

'Yes, I'm the Alpha.'

'Their leader.'

Peter nodded.

'That's a lot of responsibility.' Shayla said.

'It is, and it can be hard work, sometimes I need to be alone to think.'

'I'll leave you to it.' said Shayla seizing the opportunity to leave.

'I didn't mean......'

'I know....I have things to do, come Titan, we have to go.'

Shayla took a few steps towards the door bringing her closer to Peter. She inhaled deeply; he had the scent of an old forest, earth mixed with fallen leaves and the underlying metallic smell of blood. Peter's sensitive wolf nose caught the fragrance of Shayla as she moved closer and it was all he could do not to embrace her and press his face to her neck and inhale her scent. Instead he stood like a statue, moving only at the last second to allow her passage out of the room. Before disappearing out onto the Moor, Shayla stopped and impulsively kissed Peter on the mouth, a feather like touch which set every nerve ending in his lips into overdrive.

And with a brush of hands, she was gone, Titan at her heels.

Peter stood looking at his right hand in shock. He was used to the limited feeling he now had after the burn all those years ago but the brush of hands with Shayla was different, he felt everything. He wanted to chase after her, to hold her hand again, to be near her, but he knew that if he pursued her now he would frighten her and ruin any chance of discovering if she really was the one. The pursuit would also result in an altercation with Titan who would fight to the death to protect her. Instead Peter walked over to the table and sat down on the only chair, still staring at his hand, his mind trying to make sense of it. He wondered if this woman could really be his mate and whether the awakened nerves in his hand was a sign that she was the one, and then there was the kiss. What was she? Could she be drawn to him? Peter had more immediate concerns, namely his pack. He decided he would read while he waited for Fishbone. Hopefully there was a solution that would suit everyone and not involve killing a human just because he had seen something extraordinary.

Peter picked up his book and opened it to the correct page. As he did, the delicate bookmark whittled from a bone into the shape of a feather dropped out onto his lap.

THE KNIGHT

Trudie Stiggins secretly watched Milly when she visited her friend Lori in the hospital and made a note of the times she usually left to go home. Trudie knew from the medical records that Lori was going to be sent home the following day and knew this was her last chance to exact revenge on the girl who had humiliated her at University and put an end to her reign as chief bully. Coincidently, Trudie's brother Kurt had been released from another spell in prison for theft the previous month, and Trudie had arranged that she and Kurt would ambush Milly on her way home and Kurt would give the girl the beating she deserved. Kurt was very protective of his little sister. After dealing with Milly, Trudi would ask Kurt to take care of Cane, the strange young man from the Psychiatric Assessment Unit. Trudie had instigated the teasing and enjoyed it, but Cane had turned on her, making threats and Trudie now feared that he would find her when he was considered well enough to leave, and hurt her, just as he had promised.

At the end of her shift, Trudie waited with Kurt in his wreck of a car in the car park outside of the hospital watching the main entrance, waiting for Milly.

'She always walks in that direction.' Trudie pointed from the front seat of the car. 'I think she lives on the edge of the City.'

'She won't be going home tonight.' Kurt replied, drawing deeply on a cigarette. 'She'll be back in the hospital.'

Kurt sucked the smoke deep into his lungs, knowing all the dangers of smoking, but not caring. He held it there trapped in his lungs for a few seconds letting the poison soak into his cells before exhaling slowly.

'I can't wait for her to see me.' Trudie said excitedly. 'So she knows exactly who's getting their revenge, just before she passes out.'

Kurt nodded in agreement and laughed as he exhaled more smoke. Trudie clapped her hands together like a little girl about to unwrap her birthday presents.

'There she is! There she is!' Trudie exclaimed.

'Let's go.' said Kurt, pressing his cigarette butt into the car's ashtray.

Milly sensed she was being followed as soon as she walked away from the hospital, a man and a woman. She also recognised the scent of the female, Trudie Stiggins. How could she ever forget? Trudie had a distinctive scent, a mixture of greasy fast food, burnt onions and sweaty trainers, the man smelt of tobacco and beer. Milly hadn't seen Trudie since the early days of University and even less after she and Lori became friends. Milly assumed the male was either a boyfriend or Trudie's brother Kurt. Milly couldn't quite believe that after all of these years Trudie Stiggins was going to try and get the jump on her.

Idiot! she thought smiling. *This'll be good.*

Milly deliberately slowed her pace and took the path towards the hospital's basement car park. Milly didn't have a car, she wanted to choose the place for the confrontation and the less people around the better.

'She's heading to the car park.' Trudie whispered to Kurt.

'What of it?'

'She usually walks.'

'Maybe she borrowed a car? Do you want to get even with this bitch or not?' Kurt replied angrily.

'You know I do.'

'Come on then. I think I can handle one little girl.'

Trudie didn't feel as confident as Kurt and put her nervousness down to the memory of the last time she had underestimated Milly when she was a freshman, but Kurt was confident. He had a familiar look in his eyes, one Trudie recognised, the look he had when he was about to fight. Trudie recalled it had taken three Police Officers to subdue him when he was arrested for the last burglary. Kurt only stopped fighting when he was hit with the special Police issue "Re-VOLTer", a hand-held device that stunned the victim with nine hundred thousand volts.

'She's not just a little girl Kurt.' said Trudie.

'What are you talking about?' Kurt said noticing that Trudie had stopped walking.

'She's tougher than she looks, maybe this wasn't such a good idea. Maybe I should just move on.'

'I don't believe I'm hearing this!' said Kurt, throwing his hands in the air. 'You've been banging on about nothing else for days! About how you've waited years to put this….this…girl…in her place and now…what? You've gone all chicken?'

'NO!' Trudie snapped.

'She may be tough, but my little friend here will definitely slow her down.'

Kurt took a modified knuckle duster out of his jacket pocket and put it on his right hand.

'I like to call him Knuckles, two million volts at the touch of a button.'

'WOW! That's awesome.' Trudie said rapturously.

'Damn straight.'

'Come on, let's get her.'

Trudie and Kurt hurried along the path and followed Milly into the underground car park.

Milly waited on one side of the car park in the shadows and watched her two adversaries approach. As she suspected the male was Trudie's brother, the infamous and pathetic Kurt.

What a loser? He smells even worse than she does. Milly thought wrinkling her nose in disgust. *Week old sweat, dirt and cigarettes, ew!*

As Trudie and Kurt walked past one of the large people carriers, Milly stepped out behind them.

'Looking for me?' she said casually.

Trudie and Kurt spun around at the sound of her voice.

'Yeah bitch!' Kurt said, spitting on the floor. 'It's payback time for humiliating my sister.'

'Payback?' Milly replied. 'That implies a debt is owed.'

'Uh?

'Indeed.' Milly said taking in Kurt's confused expression. 'And who, may I ask, is dishing out this payback?'

'Me, stupid!'

'Go home knuckle head before you hurt yourself.' Milly replied mockingly and laughing at Trudie and Kurt she turned and started walking away.

Milly heard the almost inaudible click and knew immediately it was the hammer of a gun and she spun back around to face Kurt as he fired. Had she not turned, the bullet would have caught her in the back.

'KURT, WHAT THE HELL?' Trudie screamed at her brother.

'SHUT UP!' Kurt yelled, pushing Trudie away from him, the force of the push landed her on her backside on the concrete. 'Did ya really think I was gonna waste my time slapping a skinny little girl, just cos she hurt my sister's feelings?'

Trudie was too frightened to reply, she stood staring at her brother in disbelief.

Milly sniffed the air, the acrid and sour smell of ammonia from the gunshot filled her nostrils, but she detected another scent, one she recognised and hated. She needed to change into warrior form if she was going to fight this new foe and she felt the tingling in her skin, the first signs of the change.

With heightened senses, everything Milly saw and heard happened in slow motion. The vampire stepped into the light and plucked the gun from Kurt's hand and threw it away, where it skidded along the floor and under one of the remaining parked cars. He then grabbed Trudie from where she still sat on the floor and held both Trudie and Kurt by the throat and looked at Milly.

'I am not here to fight you Milly.' he said. 'I need to speak with you, please do not change.'

'I'm getting warmed up for a fight.' Milly said. 'I could use a good opponent.'

'Please. Let me take care of these two first and I will explain.'

In spite of everything she had been taught, Milly halted the agonising transformation.

The vampire made eye contact with Trudie and smiled. A silly grin appeared on Trudie's face as if she had come face to face with her childhood crush, Milly rolled her eyes.

'Hey gorgeous.' Trudie said dreamily.

'Good evening Miss Trudie. It is very late, and you need to get home.'

'Uhuh.'

'You left work and went straight home and the young lady over there.' the vampire nodded his head towards Milly without breaking eye contact with Trudie. 'You have no idea who she is, you have never met her before, do you understand?'

'OK.'

'Good girl. Run along now.'

The vampire released Trudie who blinked as if she had just woken from a trance, and she walked away, still wearing the same silly grin.

'TRUDIE!' Kurt yelled.

The vampire brought his attention back to Kurt who stopped struggling the second the vampire made eye contact.

'You are a very bad man.' he said. 'Bringing a gun to a fist fight?'

'I'm sorry.' Kurt whimpered. 'Please don't hurt me.'

'You have no honour.'

'No.'

'And you bring weapons to give you an unfair advantage.' He said pulling the knuckle duster off Kurt's right hand.

'You do not know the young lady over there.'

'No.'

'If you ever see her again, you will feel terror, beyond anything you have every known and you will run for your life. Am I understood?'

'Yes.'

'You....' the vampire sniffed at Kurt. 'You stink! Go home and bathe, you are a disgusting vagabond.'

The vampire released Kurt who dropped to the ground and crawled on his hands and knees over to where Milly was standing.

'Get out of my sight.' Milly said between gritted teeth, she resisted the urge to kick him.

Kurt moved away as fast as he could on his hands and knees and when he felt sure he was far enough away he got to his feet and ran as if the Deceiver himself were chasing him.

The vampire walked towards Milly and bowed.

'Gaolyn Lancing, at your service.' he said bowing.

'Nice use of the Delusional.'

'You know of this skill?'

'Yes, but it doesn't work on supernatural creatures.

'Indeed.'

'You have a strange accent and a funny way of talking.'

'I have lived in many places around the world and I was born nine hundred years ago in a different time which would account for my... unusual syntax.'

'Why did you interfere blood sucker?'

Gaolyn looked at Milly with the patience of a man who has heard the insult many times and has gone passed the point of taking offence.

'Insults are not necessary.' Gaolyn said. 'However, it is necessity that has forced me to seek you out. We are all in danger and I need to get a message to your Alpha.'

'Why should we care about vampires?' Milly said, her body tingling with the urge to change into warrior form and kill her blood enemy.

'I said we are *all* in danger. Not just my kind, every species. Those I represent have called for a summit meeting, your Alpha will know of someone who can make this happen.'

'Maybe I should just say screw you and kill you instead.'

Gaolyn moved quicker than anything Milly had ever encountered and had his hand firmly around her throat.

'I am over nine hundred years old, young she-wolf. I am stronger and faster than you will ever be. Had I wanted to kill you I would have done so, and the humans. I could crush your throat now and you would be dead before the transformation was complete. Now will you carry my message to your Alpha?'

Milly paused purposefully in defiance then nodded and Gaolyn released her.

'Please forgive my rough demonstration. For your information, I did not choose to be this way, but I have chosen to live, it is for that reason that I have not fed on humans for many centuries.'

'I've only got your word for that.' Milly said, irritated that the vampire had overpowered her.

'My word should be enough.'

'Forgive me for not taking you at your word, but I don't trust vampires, our kind and yours don't usually have any chit chat.'

'Perhaps we can change that.' Gaolyn said smiling.

'Hmmm, I don't know about that.' Milly replied. 'If you don't feed on humans anymore, what do you eat?'

'In the early days, I fed on stray sheep, wild goats and other animals. Rodents are not very tasty, but they provide sustenance. These days I procure blood from blood banks.'

'That's still human blood.'

'But it is given freely by human donors. I have an arrangement which intercepts the deliveries before they get to the hospitals. I am able to control the blood lust, something others of my kind are happy to submit to. Anyway, I digress. Will you speak to your Alpha?'

'Maybe.' Milly said.

'Please, it's important. We are all…..'

'In danger, yes you said.' Milly hesitated. 'I'll speak to my Alpha tonight.'

'Thank you.' Gaolyn said. 'I will take my leave.'

'How will you know if the summit has been arranged?'

'Everyone who needs to know, *will* know, the powers that be have their ways.'

Gaolyn started to walk away but stopped and turned back to Milly.

'Why were those two dreadful people stalking you?' he asked.

'The woman was the University bully and she abused a friend of mine, I taught her a lesson.'

'Quite right too.' Gaolyn smiled.

He was a handsome man and Milly found herself staring at his beautiful blue eyes. His eyes had an intensity and honesty she had not expected to see. He had the demeanour of a gentleman, one born of a different time and noble ways.

'Before I go.' Gaolyn said.

'Yes?'

'I know you could have beaten that awful man, even with his gun and knuckle duster. If I was younger I think you would give me cause for concern.'

'Is that a compliment?'

Gaolyn shrugged, turned and winked out of sight, moving far enough away to be upwind of Milly. He watched her as she left the car park and was sure she was smiling. Gaolyn was as intrigued by Milly as she was by him. She was feisty and he found her exciting. Vampires and werewolves were natural blood enemies and Gaolyn wondered if either species would ever evolve enough to be anything different. He was different to most vampires in that he had found his humanity again after the first two centuries.

Sir Gaolyn, the Knight of the Lance, had fought alongside many other brave men in the first of many futile crusade wars. It was at the end of one of the many battles that Sir Gaolyn had been mortally wounded and taken to the healers. Gaolyn knew the injury would be fatal and all the healers could offer was some form of opiate to dull the pain while he waited for the inevitable end. Men had spoken about the strange behaviour of one of the women healers and many knights, Gaolyn among them, thought the stories no more than the ravings of dying men, fearful at the moment of death. Whenever there were women healers, there were always stories.

She came to him in his final hours, tall, slim and beautiful, her long black hair braided and wound around her head like a halo. Her pale, white skin was almost transparent, and her eyes were like the black of ink. In stark contrast her full lips were as red as a rose and her smile revealed exceptionally white teeth.

Gaolyn remembered her gentle touch as she removed his blood-soaked covering and brought it to her lips.

'You have lost so much blood, my brave knight.' she said softly as she covered his wound with a clean dressing. 'You have so little in your veins, I fear your heart will stop beating soon. Let me help you'

Weak from blood loss and the onset of infection, Gaolyn did not reply. With half open eyes, he watched as she took a knife from her pocket and cut the side of her throat, the blood bloomed a deep crimson on her white skin. Putting her hand beneath Gaolyn's head she lifted him up to a sitting position and bent down until his dry cracked lips were almost touching her throat.

'Drink and live.' she whispered.

Gaolyn drank.

For many years after he tried to persuade himself that he was delirious from infection and blood loss and didn't know what he was drinking, but a part of him knew he was drinking her blood. Anyone who has fought in battle could recognise the smell of blood and Gaolyn knew.

Her blood healed him, of course, but it also cursed him. His own life's blood had already drained from his body, the battle had taken care of the first stage in becoming a vampire, the next step was to drink a vampire's blood. When the first drop of her blood passed over his lips and he drank, his human life ended. The other healers came to him a few hours later and confirmed he was dead. They prepared his body for the pyre and left him with the other bodies to be burned the following evening. The vampire returned for him at sundown and covertly took him away to her nest. No-one missed the body of Sir Gaolyn among the other dead.

For the next hundred years Gaolyn was like any other vampire, sleeping by day, feeding at night, never staying in one place for too long, but a part of his humanity remained. Unlike his sire, he began to feel guilty when he fed and started drinking only enough to stop the blood lust, leaving his victim still alive, although weakened. Eventually, his feelings of guilt overpowered him, and he fled the vampire nest and lived alone, feeding on farm animals and small rodents.

After nine hundred years, he had seen and done a lot of things and nothing excited him anymore, until tonight. Milly was interesting, she excited him, and he wondered if her smile meant that he may have intrigued her too. For the first time in many centuries Gaolyn felt something he thought he would never feel again; a sense of hope.

FLIGHT OR FIGHT

Shayla ran from Peter's man-cave, Titan at her side, with a speed that defied her physical capabilities, her newly manifested wings still folded at her back.

Shayla, slow down honey.

Michelline?

Shayla stopped and looked around, she was lost in the forest. Titan stopped with her and was sniffing the air.

'I don't think he's following us.' Shayla said as Titan paced around her in a circle. 'I meant the wolf.'

Titan momentarily stopped his pacing and looked at her, tilting his head to one side inquisitively.

'How did you get so big?' Shayla asked him. 'I don't suppose you can answer that any more than I can explain how I got these wings.'

Shayla.

Michelline?

Stay where you are, I'll find you.

Titan came right up to her, his new height bringing them eye to eye, and licked her nose gently. Shayla smiled and put her forehead against his, and with her hands cupping his face she massaged behind his ears with her fingers, something he seemed to enjoy immensely. Shayla knew her sister would have no trouble finding her. As children, Michelline always won the game of "hide and go seek", she always knew where Shayla was hiding, which infuriated her at the time. Although now Shayla was grateful for her sister's unique ability to locate her. She didn't have to wait long.

Titan alerted Shayla that someone was coming when he moved in front of her protectively. Listening intently, Shayla heard the crunch of shoes against the forest floor and as Titan hadn't growled she knew whoever was approaching wasn't a threat.

'Michelline?' Shayla said quietly.

'Expecting someone else?' Michelline replied stepping out from between the surrounding trees.

Shayla breathed a sigh of relief and hugged her sister.

'How did you know where to find me?'

'Same way I always know. I sense when you're upset, or frightened. Here.' Michelline said unfolding a picnic blanket and wrapping it around Shayla's shoulders. 'I brought this in case you were cold.'

'No you didn't! You knew about the wings, didn't you?'

Michelline didn't respond, nor did she look Shayla in the eye.

'Shelly?'

It was Michelline's turn to sigh.

'I thought it was possible, you're half angel.'

'Why didn't you say anything?'

'There was no point, they may not have manifested.'

'Don't lie.' said Shayla. 'I can always tell when someone is lying.'

Shayla had always been able to tell if a person was lying from the changes in the vibrations of their voice. To her sensitive ears, the lie changed the sound of their voice to a harsh rasping which only she could hear.

'I'm not lying!' Michelline said defensively.

'Ok, you're not lying but you're not telling me everything. I can tell.'

'I hate it when you do that!' Michelline exclaimed walking away from her sister.

Shayla was also able to pick up micro-expressions in the face when people lie, the rapid blinking, dilated pupils and the avoidance of eye contact. Michelline didn't blink quickly or fidget like most people, but her pupils always dilated when she was holding something back and Shayla always spotted it.

'Tell me what you've seen.' Shayla said softly.

Michelline turned back to her sister.

'The things I see sometimes.' Michelline hesitated before beginning again. 'The things I see are open to interpretation and you know I only keep things back because I love you.'

'I know, I love you too.' Shayla replied. 'Tell me.'

'Mother…I mean Ashling and I always knew you were half Fey and half Angel, with a little human in the mix, but we didn't know the extent of your powers, nor how or when they would emerge. After the incident at the University with the computer program and the pulse you sent out, we knew that was the first sign of the angel power manifesting itself.'

'Because no Fey can do that?' Shayla asked.

'Exactly.'

'I can manipulate the elements like others who are part Fey.'

'But not in the same way. You can command the elements much more easily than others and we assumed that was because of the angel in you.'

'And the wings?'

Michelline didn't reply for a while as if she was considering what to say and what, if anything, to hold back and Shayla waited beside Titan who also appeared to be listening carefully.

'I had a vision, quite some time ago, of you running through a forest.' Michelline said finally. 'I felt, rather than saw, that you were running from something and I saw the wings folded at your back, like they are now.'

'When did you have this vision?'

'A few months ago.'

'Did you know the date?'

'It's not that precise!' Michelline laughed. 'But I knew it would be within the year and in the vision, I could see what you were wearing, so when you put on that outfit this morning I thought today might be the day. Seems I was right. What were you running from?'

'A wolf-man.' Shayla replied.

'Was it a man or a wolf?'

'Both.' Shayla said, her face flushing at the memory.

'Whoa! What was that?' Michelline teased. 'Was he hot? Tell me, tell me everything!'

Shayla blushed scarlet and looked away.

'Don't try and distract me.' Shayla said. 'I'll tell you all about it when we get home, but first I need to sort out these......'

As Shayla turned her head to look at her wings, the words on her lips fell away.

'They're gone!' Shayla exclaimed.

'I think they're linked to your emotions.' said Michelline, running her hand up her sister's back as if she were trying to feel the bones of the wings. 'The angel powers are manifesting when you feel threatened.'

'He said the same thing!'

'The wolf man?'

'Uhuh.' said Shayla, her head still half turned where she was trying to look at the wings. 'But where did they go?'

'I don't know.' Michelline replied. 'Maybe they're still there, but slightly out of our perceptive range.'

Shayla looked at her sister and raised one eyebrow, it was Michelline's turn to blush.

'I don't know! I'm guessing here. Wherever they are, you need to learn to control them. Like the elements. Thankfully you're not feeling threatened by me, which is probably why they've gone again.'

'Is there more to that vision of yours?' Shayla asked.

'No, but I often see things…'

'Tell me.'

'It may be nothing.'

'Tell me anyway.'

Michelline wrapped her arms across the front of her body, hugging herself for reassurance before she spoke.

'I saw you, in a dream, with fire above your head.'

'My hair was on fire?' Shayla asked.

'No, it was bursts of flames above your head, I can't explain it.' Michelline said. 'The dream was more like taking quick glimpses at photographs.'

'Anything else?'

'You were way up high'

'At the top of one of the Tors perhaps?'

'Possibly, but it looked higher. Titan was with you.'

'That's good to know.' Shayla said looking at Titan.

He instinctively came to her side and Shayla put her hand on his head and scratched behind his ears.

'I'm sorry, it's a bit vague and I can't make any sense out of it.' Michelline said. 'I keep getting the nagging feeling that there's more, but I can't put my finger on it. My mind keeps repeating, "there's more to see, more to see, more to see", over and over.'

'Maybe it's a possible future.' Shayla said.

'Maybe.' Michelline whispered.

'Promise me...'

'What? That I'll tell you when I have a vision about you?'

'Yes, even if it seems irrelevant.'

'I promise.'

'Especially tell me if you see anything that looks angel-like. I want to know if I'm going to have a halo around my head, I'd like to be prepared,'

'Titan has the halo, not you.' Michelline said without thinking.

Both women looked at Titan, who had been circling them quietly the whole time they were talking and who now stared at them questioningly.

'What do you mean?'

'He's been touched by an angel.' Michelline said. 'When the angel healed him, he left part of himself with Titan that's why he has a halo.'

'I can't see it.' said Shayla.

'You're not a Seer.' Michelline replied smiling. 'Maybe you will when your angel power develops. Have you noticed that he's normal size again? Whatever happened to the two of you this afternoon has been the catalyst that's unlocked some awesome power.'

'Let's go home.' Shayla said shivering. 'I don't want to think about it.'

Michelline pulled the picnic blanket closely around her sister's shoulders.

'This way.' Michelline said taking her sister's hand. 'You weren't as far off the path as you thought.'

Neither of them saw Milly the young she-wolf as they walked back towards the path, she stayed back in the trees until they were gone before resuming her own path to see Peter. Only Titan was aware of her presence, which he chose to ignore.

* * * * *

'Is this yours?'

Peter visibly jumped, startled by sound of someone speaking, he looked up to see Fishbone standing in the doorway holding up a dead hare, the one he had killed earlier.

'Er…yes…where did you find it?'

'The more important question is, how did I manage to sneak up on you?' Fishbone asked stepping into the room.

'If you'd walked here you wouldn't have.' Peter replied. 'You have a way of appearing and disappearing without a sound!'

'That doesn't usually stop you from detecting my presence.' Fishbone said.

'That's true. I suppose I was miles away.'

'Judging by the state of this hare.' Fishbone said putting it on the floor near the door. 'You must have killed it several hours ago. What happened, did you lose your appetite?'

'No, I was………..distracted.'

'I'll say.'

Inwardly shaking himself from his daydreaming, Peter stood up.

'Where are my manners?' Peter said. 'Would you like something to drink?'

'No thanks. I've had enough tea at Michael's to last me a long while.'

'Please, sit down.' Peter offered. 'I've been sitting here far too long, I need to stretch.'

Fishbone sat in the single chair and picked up the feather shaped bookmark Peter had left on the table, delicately turning it over in his large hands. Peter paced the room in five long strides.

'There's a solution to your pack's problem.' Fishbone said finally, replacing the bookmark. 'Give it a couple days and Rufus will be able to tell his friend Andy anything he wants.'

'That's good.' Peter said, relieved there was no need to kill an innocent person. 'Rufus will be pleased and if he thinks this guy can be trusted to keep his secret then I support him.'

'There have been times when it was necessary for humans to know of the wolves' existence and to be able to see them in all forms, without losing their minds.'

'When?'

Fishbone chose not to elaborate and made a dismissive gesture with his hand. In his usual way, he offered no explanation to probing questions, and changed the subject.

'Someone's been in here, besides you.' Fishbone said, as a statement rather than a question.

Peter knew, that Fishbone knew, exactly what had happened there today; he always did.

'I met someone.' Peter began. 'She was already here when I returned, rearranging things!'

'I thought there was something different about this place, it looks better.' Fishbone looked around the room smiling at the picture and the new light. 'And this chair is much more comfortable.'

'She's the one.' Peter declared.

'The one who decorated?'

'No. Yes. I mean, yes, she decorated the room and was about to re-arrange my books when I caught her. I mean she's the *one*.'

'Oh right, she's the *one*.' Fishbone replied playfully.

'Absolutely.' Peter said confidently, ignoring Fishbone's teasing. 'I was drawn to her. I think she felt the same way.'

'Are you sure?'

'She kissed me!'

'Wow, that was bold!'

'And when we brushed hands, my scarred hand.' Peter said holding it up for emphasis. 'I felt it. What do you think it means?'

'I think it means you're in love my boy.' Fishbone said standing up and clapping Peter on the shoulder amiably.

'I have to see her again.'

'You will, but first…..'

'Milly.' Peter interrupted, his expression serious. 'She's on her way to see me, she says it's urgent.'

'That's partly what I came to talk about. I'll wait until Milly gets here.'

They didn't have to wait long and Milly, in wolf form, leapt in through the door landing deftly on all fours. Seeing Peter and Fishbone she immediately transformed into human form and began talking quickly, each word falling over the other making no sense at all.

'Slow down Milly.' Peter said. 'You're not making any sense. All I heard was what sounded like a gun fight and a medieval knight! Now catch your breath and tell us what just happened.'

Milly took a few deep breaths and composed herself before telling Peter and Fishbone what had just transpired at the hospital.

'Gaolyn Lancing?' Fishbone asked. 'Tall fella, strong looking, brown hair, blue eyes, square jaw?'

'Yes.' Milly replied. 'And he spoke funny.'

'How do you mean, funny?' Peter asked.

'Very…..um…proper.'

'Kinda old fashioned?' said Fishbone.

'Right, yeah, old fashioned. Do you know him?'

'I know *of* him.' Fishbone replied.

Milly and Peter waited for an explanation; Fishbone sighed.

'Sir Gaolyn, the Knight of the Lance.' Fishbone began. 'He fought in the early crusade wars.'

'He said he was nine hundred years old.' said Milly.

'That would be about the right time. He was a very good Knight, skilled in the use of lance and sword, an honourable man. Like so many other young men of that time, they fought in a war for a cause they knew little about and died in terrible circumstances. Many of them died in agony as a result of infection from their wounds. Sir Gaolyn was mortally wounded during a battle, his body was never found. People assumed he was buried in a mass grave with the rest of the dead. We now know he became a vampire, probably right at the end.'

'A vampire you say?' Peter said looking at Milly. 'But you didn't kill him?'

'No.' Milly looked down at her hands briefly. 'There was something about him and he didn't smell of human blood. I believed him when he said he hadn't come to fight.'

When Peter didn't reply, Milly continued.

'He could have killed the two humans easily, but he didn't, he used the Delusional on them to create a new memory and let them go. He could have killed me!' Milly said defiantly. 'But he didn't.'

'What did he want with you?'

'He wanted me to pass a message to you.'

'What message?' said Peter.

'He said the people he represented want to call a summit meeting and that you would know someone who could make it happen.'

Peter and Fishbone looked at each other, then back at Milly.

'You're angry with me for not killing him aren't you!' Milly shouted defensively.

'I'm not angry with you Milly.' Peter said gently. 'You did the right thing.'

Peter pulled Milly towards him and hugged her, grateful that she was still alive. She was the youngest member of the pack and thankfully she had escaped fire and a vampire unharmed. Peter wasn't superstitious, but he didn't like the thought that death had tried to take her twice and he would make sure that the grim reaper didn't succeed with the old saying of "third time lucky".

'Go home.' Peter said, releasing Milly and holding her at arm's length. 'I'll be back soon. Fishbone and I have some things to discuss.'

Milly nodded obediently and turning back into wolf form, she left.

'You already knew, didn't you?' Peter said to Fishbone.

'That's the other thing I came to talk about.'

THE DIGITAL AGENDA

Within the body of Julius Harrington-Moore, Parallax was beyond angry or enraged. To say he was incensed was an understatement. He had just received an internal memorandum from the Directors of The Chequer Corporation denying him the funding to roll out his Nanotek programme to the general population. The message was nothing more than a curt reply sent by a minion on behalf of the Directors;

"Your request to move the Nanotek programme forward has been refused.
Research has shown the programme to be in early experimental stages and funding has been diverted to other projects.
The Directors
Chequer Corp."

Three lines essentially quashing his plans to unite, which really meant control, everyone through a microchip. Displeased beyond measure, he swept his strong arm ferociously across the desk, sending the laptop and other office paraphernalia flying into the air and onto the floor. The crashing objects did nothing to relieve his tension, only the fulfilment of his plans would bring him back into a harmonious balance. Parallax was resourceful and with a world of digital information at his command, he would circumvent the parent company and proceed with his own agenda regardless of their denial.

Most of the employees within Intelligen Ltd. were now linked to Parallax through the network. He had easily convinced most of them to have electronic implants in their hands, removing the necessity for access codes to the building and inner offices, and passwords for their computers. Some employees had even thrown a party to celebrate their new freedom from swipe cards and keys. Those that refused and insisted on keeping their plastic swipe cards to open doors were finding things increasingly difficult, just as Parallax intended. He caused circuitry problems which had left certain employees trapped in elevators and offices for hours at a time. Their resistance to change was futile, they would either have to have the implant, or they would have to resign. Eventually the Nanotek would be in the food chain and drinking water and the whole world would be united with the Circle.

The Circle was a storage network within cyberspace and was nothing more than an alias for Parallax. People stored their digital information by uploading it to the Circle from their mobile telephones or their computers, laptops and other hand-held devices. Parallax controlled the latest, and most sought after, telecommunications device, the "Optimum 10". Everybody wanted one, young and old; the masses waited patiently in line for stores to open so they could purchase one. The Optimum 10 offered free calls and connectivity to other Optimum 10's, anywhere in the world, at any time. In a family of four, at least three of them would have the new device.

In the last couple of months, Intelligen Ltd. had also launched their new "Adroit TV". Another marvellous invention that streamed information and entertainment right into the homes of viewers, at a surprisingly low cost. Conveniently, it also connected with the Optimum 10 and the Circle, thereby encompassing all information pertaining to each person and family. What viewers did not know about the Adroit TV was that not only did it broadcast, it also received, and information was transmitted back to the Circle, to Parallax for processing. Parallax knew almost everything that was happening all over the world, thanks to the Circle, and with the Optimum 10 he was now able to listen to conversations, even if the device was switched off. Parallax ensured that the Optimum 10 was designed and manufactured so that it was never totally inactive.

Parallax found the enigma of the Chequer Corp. Directors infuriating, with their archaic use of pen and paper, but he had already decided to set the matter aside. He would proceed with his plan, without their funding. He had access to bank accounts, savings, investments and all manner of financial assets. He would take his lead from the Directors; he would divert funds from various places to finance the Nanotek Programme and by the time Directors discovered what was happening it would be too late. Once everything was in place, they would be deleted, like any other defective piece of code in a program.

By an enormous stroke of luck, a concept Parallax knew to be nothing more than the manipulation of people and events, one of the resistant employees without an implant had engaged in a brief, passionate clinch with another member of staff. The slightly older man had been enticed by the young, eager, nubile female assistant and flattered by her advances, succumbed to a kiss and a romp in one of the stationary cupboards. Parallax successfully transferred from the woman to the man and now the unsuspecting man was taking Parallax to the Chequer Corporation Head Office and the secrets within.

* * * * *

'The Directors will see you now Mr Lancing.'

The Custodian opened the door to the conference room and gestured for Gaolyn to enter, bowing obsequiously. Gaolyn walked in and looked at the Directors and their underlings, or as they liked to refer to themselves, the Custodians, seated at the long conference table and headed to the only vacant chair.

Beneath the state-of-the-art façade of the Chequer Corporation's head office building was a labyrinth of subterranean passageways, meeting rooms and living quarters, none of which appeared on any blueprints or in any records, anywhere. The conference room was dimly lit, giving the impression of a gloomy rainy day, the lights for the benefit of the Custodians, the humans who served vampires during the day.

'Messrs Noss, Ferra and Chu.' Gaolyn said as he sat down. 'A clever play on words.'

'You are one of the few who understand the significance.' said the vampire at the head of the table.

'Which one are you?'

'You may call me Noss.' he said inclining his head in greeting.

He was a large, muscular man with a square jaw, an aquiline nose and black inquisitive eyes, dressed in a bespoke charcoal grey suit with a blood red tie.

'Where are Ferra and Chu?' Gaolyn said, appraising the occupants of the other seats.

'Ferra and Chu sleep, only one of us rules at a time. I have been awake for one hundred years, soon it will be the time for a change of leadership. It is important to give an impression to the world that we have a board of Directors.'

'Why do you care what the world thinks?'

Noss stared at Gaolyn stoically until the tension in the air was palpable, one of the Custodians broke the silence.

'Gentlemen.' he said, his voice dry and croaky from dehydration.

The Custodian was surprised at how exhausted he felt after his short, but incredibly exciting clinch with Marsha, his beautiful and extremely young co-worker. From within the man, Parallax observed and uploaded information silently while the host cleared his throat and reached for a glass of water, taking a deep swallow, he continued.

'Mr Lancing, were you able to make contact with the wolves?'

Gaolyn broke eye contact with Noss and looked at the man who had spoken wondering what this Custodian did during the day. The vampires had at least one custodian in every area of business in the City.

'I did. I spoke with one of the younger members of the pack, she will get a message to their Alpha. I assume they will do the rest.'

Gaolyn stood up.

'If that's all…' he said, the chair scraping noisily on the marble floor.

'That is not all.' Noss interrupted. 'I don't think you comprehend the seriousness of the situation Mr Lancing.'

'You asked me to pass on a message. My work is done.'

Parallax

'Do you know what the Nanotek Programme is?'

'Should I?'

Noss inhaled deeply trying to hold his temper at bay.

'Please sit down Mr Lancing. You may not feed on human blood anymore, but the rest of us do not share your...eclectic taste in food, but the potential danger will corrupt your food source just as much as ours. We find this unacceptable.'

Gaolyn sat down.

'Before I continue.' Noss said standing up. 'I need to show you something.'

Mr Noss addressed the Custodian who had first spoken, the one from whom Parallax was gleaning vast amounts of information.

'Fielding, would you please bring me the file I requested?'

'Of course.'

Mr Fielding picked up the file in front of him and walked to the head of the table where Noss was now standing. As Fielding handed over the file, Noss grabbed him and with a swift, sharp twist, broke his neck. Death was instant and Noss dropped the body to the floor, eliciting a few startled gasps from the remaining Custodians.

'Is that what you wanted to show me?' Gaolyn asked. 'A demonstration of your strength?'

'He was corrupted.' Noss replied, dusting off his hands and casually sitting down.

'Aren't they all?'

Again, Noss took a few seconds to reply, holding his temper at bay.

'Now that I have taken care of him' Noss said. 'I will explain.'

Gaolyn listened as Noss described in detail the experimental Nanotek Programme and the advances the company had already made.

'Are you telling me that he had a digital implant in his body that watched and listened to everything?' Gaolyn asked incredulously.

'Fielding did not have an implant, but he was infected all the same. We believe.' said Noss. 'No, we know that the CEO of Intelligen has somehow been infected by a digital entity whose plans are grandiose and outrageous. The late Fielding here was resistant to the digital implants, as instructed, but the entity found its way into him by another route. I can only assume to spy on us and gather information'

'How is that possible?'

'It's quite easy, if you know a person's weakness.' Noss relied. 'The idiot was obviously seduced by a female. I could smell her, all over him. The Nanotek must have entered his body by exchange of fluids, the change in his demeanour was obvious.'

123

'Unfortunately, this entity now knows that vampires exist and that they own and run the company.' said Gaolyn. 'Was it wise to allow him access to this room, when you knew he was corrupted?'

'It was only a matter of time before the entity discovered our existence, hence calling the summit meeting. Now do you understand the seriousness of the situation?'

Gaolyn nodded.

'If this microscopic technology gets into the food chain and water sources it will affect everything on the planet.' Gaolyn said. 'And if I understand this correctly, the digital entity itself will then control everything from plants and insects to animals and people.'

'You understand perfectly.' said Noss. 'The technology in the blood renders it undrinkable and if we cannot feed, we will cease to exist.'

'So, your concern is not for the people, but for yourself?'

'People of are no consequence to us, they are merely food, but we have a symbiotic relationship and what affects them, ultimately affects us.'

'You had better tell me everything you know.' Gaolyn said. 'If I am expected to represent you at this meeting, which I presume was what you intended to discuss with me?'

'You are an astute man.' Noss replied.

By the time the meeting was over Gaolyn felt nauseous, an unwelcome sensation he thought he had lost centuries ago with his humanity; apparently not.

* * * * *

Parallax's brief excursion in the body of the ill-fated Fielding had provided an insight into the world of the Directors of the Chequer Corporation.

Vampires?

Parallax considered all that he knew from lore and legend stored in the Circle.

If vampires are indeed real, then perhaps werewolves and other supernatural creatures are also real?

He contemplated this new information and thought of the capabilities he would have if he could inhabit and control a supernatural being. This was something he intended to investigate and would turn his resources over to pushing the Nanotek Programme forward and seeking out the multifarious number of other creatures waiting to be discovered.

SUMMIT MEETING

Mandlebury Henge was not the highest point on Granite Moor, but it was most certainly the oldest. The stone circle had weathered many centuries of storms and bloody battles, rituals and tourists in its time, although the flow of tourists ebbed and flowed throughout the years. The stones encircled a convergence of natural energy lines making it the focal point for spiritual and mystical power. It was here that the summit meeting of the species would take place.

In recent years, the Henge stones had suffered from an influx of tourists, some of whom tried to chip away pieces of the rock, believing them to contain power which would bring them good luck, while others simply scratched their initials into the stone. Subsequently the City Council had set up a perimeter fence around the stones so they could only be viewed from a walkway some fifty metres away, and only guided walks from the Tourist Information Centre and tea shop up to the stones were permitted. However, rendering security cameras blind and cutting power to surveillance was an easy task for someone who had the power to convene a meeting of the species.

The meeting was scheduled to take place when the moon was in its full auspice and this month it would be closer to the planet than it had been for over a century.

Fishbone and Father Michael stood in the centre of the stone circle, both looking up at the face of the full moon riding high in the clear night sky.

'Such an amazing creation, and one that really helps us this night.'

'Conditions are perfect.' Michael agreed.

'I'm enjoying the quiet before everyone arrives and they all start shouting at once.' Fishbone said.

'At least they can't start fighting.'

'I suppose we should be grateful for small mercies.' Fishbone chuckled.

Preparations for a summit meeting such as this were very difficult and delicate. Each representative would walk through a connecting gate in their realm and appear between two stones, all separated from each other. They could be seen and heard by others but would only be able to move within the two-metre area between their stones, an essential precaution when gathering blood enemies and volatile tempers together. Peter and Uri, in human form, were the first to arrive.

'It hardly seems worth travelling to the entry gate only to reappear almost next to our home.' Uri said irritably.

'Protocol.' said Peter.

'BAH!'

Fishbone and Michael walked over to the two wolves.

'Who else is coming?' Peter asked.

'I am representing humans.' Michael said. 'Even though I am an Angel, I have been living in this human body for over twenty years, so it seemed appropriate for me to speak on their behalf. Any other human wouldn't be able to cope with a gathering like this, it would send them quite mad.'

'You're looking old Thomas.' said Uri.

'Uri, I am Michael, you know this.' replied Michael sighing. 'And I *am* old.'

'You look like Thomas and I will continue to call you Thomas. How old is that body?'

'Over eighty and it's full of aches and pains.'

'Bah! Eighty is young.' Uri said dismissively. 'When you have lived as long as I, *then* you will be old.'

'Nice to see you too Uri.' said Michael smiling.

Uri returned his smile, her eyes full of affection for the old man who she missed more than she had expected to.

'Shayla and Michelline are coming to represent the Fey.' Fishbone said.

Peter felt his heartbeat quicken; Uri was instantly suspicious.

In the last few weeks, Peter had spent quite a bit of time with Shayla. After their first encounter, he had easily tracked her to her home and posted a note through the door, asking her to meet him for coffee the following day. He had chosen a very public place so that she would feel safe and he was ecstatic when Shayla arrived. They had talked for a few hours over several cups of coffee and Peter knew without a doubt what he had felt as soon as he saw her, she was his soul mate.

'Which one quickens your heart like that?' Uri asked, breaking into his reverie.

'What?'

The vampire Gaolyn arrived at that moment, saving Peter from an awkward explanation, Uri growled.

'There will be none of that tonight!' Fishbone said fiercely. 'Welcome Sir Gaolyn of the Lance.'

'Greetings Sir. You have me at a disadvantage.' Gaolyn bowed. 'Have we met before?'

'A long time ago.' said Fishbone, bowing in return. 'My name is Fishbone.'

'I was so much younger when I was last known by that name. I no longer use the title, please call me Gaolyn.'

'As you wish.'

Peter turned to Uri.

'That is the vampire Milly met, the one who asked her to give me the message about the summit meeting.' Peter said quietly.

'There is nothing wrong with my hearing Sir.' Gaolyn said. 'You are correct in your assumption. It was I who asked Miss Milly to speak with you.'

'Do you speak for vampires?' Peter asked.

'I am their representative, yes. Tell me, is Miss Milly well?'

'She is.' Peter replied carefully.

'Excellent.'

Another new arrival halted what would have been an uncomfortable conversation. Another two wolves, also in human form, stepped out between the stones, one albino, the other black as night.

'Cassidy?' said Uri, shocked to see her sister.

A beautiful woman her skin the colour of ink, with long raven black hair and deep brown eyes stood ramrod straight. She had an old scar on the left side of her face cutting from the eyebrow, down her cheek and across to her ear.

'I use the name Scara now.' she said. 'It seemed more fitting.'

'Aegis?'

'Dead. He died protecting the pack from hunters. I barely survived. I have this reminder of when I lost my Alpha and mate.' Scara said, pointing to the scar on her face. 'I am all that's left of the Midnight Clan.'

'Who is your companion?' Uri asked.

'That is Flint.' Peter interrupted. 'We have met before. He is one of the last of the Enlightened.'

'Techno-wolves?' said Uri.

'Something like that.'

Flint inclined his head towards Peter and the others but said nothing.

As the moon reached its highest point in the night sky, the remaining representatives all arrived at once. The wolves, aware of all supernatural creatures, were unfazed by their strange physical appearances, but others, like Shayla, Michelline and even the vampire, Gaolyn, were left wide-eyed.

Fishbone announced everyone by their name and race.

'Queen Albezia of the Arborcan, and her Consort Quercus Robur.'

The Arborcan, or Tree People, were one of the oldest and wisest races in existence on Orbis Terraratum. They lived for centuries as long as they were left alone, although many of them had been cut down and smashed into chippings by humans to make way for roads and buildings. Queen Albezia was as elegant and pale as a silver birch tree. Her long limbs moved with an artistic grace as she greeted Fishbone, her voice as soft as a breath of spring as she whispered his name. Her face and neck had the pale green, triangular shaped markings typical of the leaves of a silver birch and her hair resembled slender new branches heavy with catkins, some long and yellow-brown, others smaller, short and bright green. As she moved some of the catkins changed colour to a dark crimson releasing tiny seeds into the air, to be carried away by the night breeze.

Her Consort, Quercus Robur, resembled a mighty oak, his skin once smooth and silvery brown, now rugged and deeply fissured with age. His upper arms and shoulders were mottled with the shape of serrated leaves which spiralled up towards his neck and face. His hair was similar to Queen Albezia in terms of slender branches and catkins, but the ends of his hair held small acorns that gently swayed as he moved.

Shayla and Michelline stared in breathless wonder and when Shayla made eye contact with the Queen she was held by her piercing eyes of silver and green.

You are so very beautiful. Shayla thought to herself.

'As are you my child of the forest.' Queen Albezia's said aloud, her voice soft.

'Thank you, your Majesty.' Shayla replied. 'I am honoured.'

'I am honoured to meet you, Shayla Meldainiel.' The Queen continued. 'I have known of you for a long time.'

'You have? How?'

'All flora is conscious my child and from the time your mother first ran barefoot through my forests in Fey, I knew that you would come to be, as I also know of the dark child born of human and demon.'

Before Shayla could inquire further, Fishbone loudly introduced another two representatives.

'Chaeto and Nuphar of the Aquanar.'

The Aquanar; their upper bodies resembled humans and from the waist down, the square prism shaped tails of seahorses. Their entire bodies were covered in chromatophoric, skeletal plates, stronger and more armoured on the tail and they both changed colour to blend in with their stone surroundings. The plates on the upper torso of the male, Chaeto, were sculpted over his pectoral muscles, defining them and giving an appearance of strength. The skeletal plates softening as they reached his face, giving a smooth, silky shine. The top of his head was a grassy, tangled mess of tendrils resembling unruly hair.

Nuphar, the female, was smaller than the male but equally armoured in skeletal plates. Her head was covered in small yellow flowers like those on a lily-pad and gave the impression she was wearing a decorative swimming cap.

'Xenolith of the Mountains.' Fishbone announced.

Xenolith was a roughly humanoid arrangement of boulders and slabs held together by magic or some other more powerful force. As he moved the stones ground together, his voice was low and deep and wheezed as he spoke.

'I also speak for the caretakers.' he said quietly.

Shayla and Michelline looked at each other quizzically. Fishbone noticed the gesture and explained.

'Xenolith also speaks for the insects and other small creatures, nature's caretakers.'

Understanding clearly, Shayla and Michelline inclined their heads towards the latest arrival.

'I could never have imagined such a strange gathering of creatures.' Shayla whispered to Michelline.

'I have knowledge of these creatures, but never dreamed I could be standing in their presence.' she replied. 'I like the white wolf.'

Michelline had been staring at the white wolf, Flint, since he appeared in the stone circle and Shayla nudged her sister playfully.

'There are still two places to be filled.' said Shayla looking towards the spaces between the stones. 'There are fourteen of us gathered, but space for another two.'

'Four.' Michelline said nodding towards two stones almost opposite to where they were standing.

As if in response, the space between two of the stones to their right shimmered, almost inconspicuously, but not to the two Fey.

'Someone's coming.' said Shayla.

'Two.' Michelline replied. 'And not friendly.'

Fishbone and Michael had also noticed the disturbance and looked around to see the Aboricans and the Aquanar retreat between their stones and disappear out of sight.

'Ophidians!' said Michael sharply.

A grotesque serpentine creature with two heads, one brown, the other green and yellow, appeared between the stones hissing and spitting viciously. The top third of its body was raised off the floor like a king cobra and the remainder of its elongated, legless reptilian body writhed on the ground, covered in horn-like scales. The two heads flattened their necks, spreading out the scales like hoods, their elliptical eyes looking at everyone gathered. Each head spoke independently in its slithering, rasping voice.

'Greetingssss...sss.' hissed the brown head.

'Sssssstarting thissss gathering without ussssssss issssss...' continued the other head.

'Disssssss..ressssspectful..' concluded brown.

'We have only just arrived.' said Fishbone. 'There is no disrespect and you have not missed anything.'

'Exsssss...ssell ent.' both heads replied in unison.

Shayla shuddered at the sight of the latest arrival.

'What issss thissssss?' said the brown head, clearly the more dominant, looking right at Shayla.

'My sister and I represent the Fey.' Shayla said, in a tremulous voice.

'You….sssss….are not…ssss…full Fey.' said the brown head, its forked tongue darting in and out of its mouth.

'Or sss..sisters..sssss..' the other head continued. 'You….are...sssss….something else..ssss.'

'We are Fey!' Michelline said angrily. 'What are you?'

'Ophidians…sssss…' both heads replied. 'You…sss..with the yellow hair…do not know who you are…you are….sssss…part wolf..yesss….we sssss…smell its…sss…foul..ssss…stench.'

'And you….sssss..' they hissed looking at Shayla. 'With the…sss…red hair…are sssss….something else…ssss..'

Uri felt Peter's anger without looking at him and at first mistook his rage for the insult to their species., but when she followed his gaze to Shayla she immediately knew the answer to her earlier question, it was Shayla who quickened his heart.

'You….sssss…' the serpent continued. 'Are…sssss…both…ABOMINATIONS…Sssss.'

The two-headed serpent moved as if to strike out at Shayla and Michelle but were held back by the force which contained every representative in the gathering.

'Abominations..sssss, you should not be here, you should be destroyed.' the two heads hissed ferociously, their heads butting at the invisible force that kept them contained.

'AND WHAT ARE YOU, SERPENT?' Peter yelled from his position, his hands clenched into fists, knuckles cracking as he wrestled with his temper. 'DO NOT DARE TO INSULT THE PRINCESS OF FEY! YOU ARE THE ABOMINATIONS HERE!'

The two heads turned towards Peter.

'Filthy….ssss…..wolves…ssssss!' they spat venomously.

'Let us discuss this further.' Peter replied trying to hold back his anger. 'Just the two of us. Name the place and time and I will crush you beneath my heel, like the disgusting belly shuffling snake you are!'

The two-headed Ophidian made a strange hissing sound that could only have been laughter.

'Ah….yes…we sssss..see it all so clearly now….the wolf loves sssss the princess….ssss…will he be ssss…sad when we kill her?'

Peter lost the fragile hold he had on his temper and transformed into warrior form and howled. He wanted to leap at the Ophidian but was held back, his fist crashed against the barrier between the two stones, which only fuelled his rage.

'NOT WHILE I LIVE AND BREATHE!!' Peter yelled, slashing at the force field that held him.

Unable to contain herself, Shayla screamed at the Ophidian as it taunted Peter. Her wings unfolded, and with a flash of white light, she burst through the stones and the restraining force, leaving Michelline staring open-mouthed.

'ENOUGH!' Shayla shouted, thrusting her hand towards the Ophidian.

Michael watched in stunned silence as the force of Shayla's hand gesture pushed the serpent back through the stones and out of sight, the transcendental doorway, producing an audible clunk.

Without hesitation, Shayla turned to Peter and ran to him, she pushed through the restraining barrier and straight into his open arms.

'Be calm my love.' Shayla whispered as he held her tightly.

As Shayla spoke softly in Peter's ear, he slowly transformed back into human form, still holding her in his arms.

Uri watched the whole scene, which lasted only seconds, unfold as if in slow motion.

'The prophecy.' Uri whispered to herself in shock.

Only Fishbone wasn't surprised by the turn of events.

'Lycan Angel.' Fishbone said quietly.

And in his usual way, he sat down on the sparse vegetation that grew on Mandlebury Henge and waited patiently until the rest of the congregation caught up with him.

OTHER BUSINESS

The remaining attendees at the summit meeting stood watching in stunned silence. No creature had ever before displayed a power great enough to break through the shield between the stones, and Shayla had broken through twice. Once when she broke free from her own stones and sent the Ophidian back through its gate, and a second time when she ran through the shield which held Peter and Uri.

Peter and Shayla stood together shielded from inquisitive eyes by her immense wings which were wrapped around both of them, the feather-shaped blades closely overlapped.

'Did you mean to burst out like that, or was it accidental?' Peter said softly in Shayla's ear.

He was back in human form and holding her as tightly as she held onto him, breathing in the scent of her skin and hair.

'I've been working on my control of the wings.' Shayla replied. 'Most of the time I can bring them out just by thinking, but this time, I just became so angry when that hideous creature was taunting you. I knew I had to make it all stop.'

'You did.' Peter said kissing her gently on the lips.

Someone outside of the sanctuary of Shayla's wings, cleared their throat, obviously to gain their attention.

'I suppose we can't stay in here forever.' Shayla giggled looking at the inside of her wings, then back at Peter, his blue eyes sparkling in the moonlight.

'Would be nice though.' Peter replied and kissed her again.

'I suppose everyone will guess that we've been spending time together.'

'There's no denying it. Uri's gonna be seething that she didn't see this coming.'

'As will my sister.'

'Is that OK with you?'

Shayla responded by kissing him back and Peter breathed a sigh of relief when their lips parted.

'OK.' Peter said releasing her from his embrace. 'Let's do it.'

'Ready?'

Peter nodded, and he and Shayla held hands. The feather-blades of her wings changed back to soft dove-grey feathers and folded back behind her before shimmering out of sight. They were greeted by a sea of astonished faces, including the Arborcans and the Aquanar who had once again joined the meeting. Uri, looked unimpressed, her face stern as she stood beside them and her expression told Peter he was in for a barrage of questions when this meeting was over. Shayla glanced over at Michelline who looked equally displeased.

'Er..is it gone?' Shayla asked awkwardly. 'The two-headed snake thing?'

'The Ophidian is most definitely gone.' Fishbone said, now standing in the middle of the stone circle, looking amused. 'And you've sealed the gateway ensuring they will never be able to participate in any future meetings.'

'I'm sorry.' Shayla said. 'I didn't realise....'

'No need to apologise, they've always been difficult. I'm glad to see the back of them if I'm honest.' said Fishbone laughing.

A rustle of leaves brought everyone's attention to Queen Albezia.

'The Ophidians are in league with the digital entity that threatens all of us, although they do not realise it.' she whispered in her soft gentle voice. 'We Arborcans have witnessed the systematic destruction of our kind for many decades at the hands of the Ophidians, they would not have helped us.'

'Is that why you stepped back out of sight?' Shayla asked.

'The Ophidians do not know about the Arborcans.'

'Or the Aquanar.' said Chaeto.

'We'd like to keep it that way.' said the Queen.

The remaining wolves, Michelline and the vampire Gaolyn, were all still standing between their respective stones listening while the Queen spoke.

'If I may.' Flint, the white wolf suddenly spoke.

'Go ahead Flint.' said Fishbone.

All attention turned in his direction.

'Thank you. The digital enemy and the Ophidians may not be our only problem.' Flint said holding up an old book.

'One thing at a time.' Fishbone interrupted.

'OK.' Flint said. 'The Queen is correct. The Ophidians and the digital entity are our enemy and the enemy of this world. If left unchecked, they will destroy everything.'

'Explain.' said Chaeto, the Aquanar First Minister.

'The Ophidians have been breeding with humans for a long time creating hybrids that look like the rest of the human population but have the mindset of the Ophidians. They have manipulated their way into positions of power in nearly every country. They have no compassion, no empathy and certainly no love for this world. Their goal is to rid the world of everything natural and beautiful, they've been polluting the rivers and seas for years.'

'I can attest to that.' said Chaeto angrily; Nuphar, standing at his side concurred.

'They have poisoned and plundered our waters mercilessly.' Nuphar said.

'They've also been meddling with the food.' Flint continued. 'Genetically modifying seeds making them finite and making anything else illegal to use. This means that farmers have no choice but to buy new seeds every season from selected suppliers to grow food, which has already been tampered with, and is no longer healthy for anyone to consume.'

'Why?' asked Shayla incredulously.

'Control the food, you control the people.' said Michelline. 'I've done my fair share of study on this subject, but why isn't anyone stopping them?'

'People have tried.' said Flint. 'But they mysteriously disappear, or have unfortunate accidents.'

'That's terrible!' said Shayla.

'Yes it is.' said Fishbone. 'Which is what we're here to talk about.'

'How do you know all of this?' Michelline asked Flint, from where she stood between the stones.

'I'm a wolf.' said Flint, addressing her directly. 'And like all wolves we maintain the balance of the natural world. Or at least we try. My tribe was once known as the Enlightened. We lived alongside humans more closely than most wolves usually like to get, and we have always taken an interest in technology and have kept an eye on it. It's through the technology that I have learned all of this. Years of research has brought me to this conclusion.'

'And the digital entity?' Michelline asked, feeling inexplicably drawn towards Flint and eager to continue conversing.

'You may have heard of it as Parallax, the search engine. I can see by your reaction that you have. This program has become self-aware and unfortunately its agenda is the same as that of the Ophidians, to change the world to suit its own needs and eventually destroy its enemies.'

'All living creatures, you mean?'

'Exactly.'

'And they have the nerve to call me an abomination!' said Shayla indignantly.

'And me!' said Michelline.

'But won't the Ophidian hybrids die too?' Shayla asked.

'Yes, but they're too short sighted and blinkered, seeing the progress of technology as a way for them to control the masses. They don't realise that Parallax is controlling them every bit as much as the rest of humanity.'

'It's insane!' Michelline said.

'The Ophidian was right about one thing.' Flint said to Michelline. 'You have wolf DNA.'

'No, I…'

'That wasn't an insult.' Flint said quickly. 'One of your ancestors was definitely a wolf.'

'He's right.' Peter said. 'I sense it too.'

'Do you know your history?' Flint asked.

'I always thought I was Fey.' said Michelline.

'There's something familiar about you.' said Flint. 'It's your eyes, they remind me of......no matter.'

'*My* people.' Gaolyn interrupted, weary of the obvious flirting between the two wolves. 'Are aware of this digital entity.'

All eyes turned towards the vampire.

'They own many companies and one in particular is trying to push a Nanotek Programme forward. If successful, this microscopic technology will be in every living creature, food source and water course worldwide and it will be the end of my race.'

Uri started to say something caustic, but Gaolyn continued.

'And before anyone says that they would not mourn the passing of the vampires, let me just say that technology in the water and food will either kill everything, or be completely controlled by it. This, I am sure you will agree, is unacceptable and must be stopped.'

From between two of the previously vacant stones, a strange creature stepped forward gaining everyone's attention.

'I am Moloch of the Dragonai.' he said in a loud commanding voice.

'Welcome, Moloch.' said Fishbone, raising both hands in front of him, palms facing upwards, in the traditional gesture of greeting.

Moloch returned the gesture.

The Dragonai, a reclusive and majestic species descended from dragons. Moloch, their leader stood fairly tall at approximately six feet, with an intimidating array of sharp, conical spikes covering his entire upper body and the backs of his hands, in various shades of brown and tan. His legs were shielded with tiny cones of gold and brown for camouflage. The spines decreased in size around his face, except the ridged brow from which protruded two razor sharp spikes. His eyes, although difficult to see in the moonlight were round, the lower lid moving upwards to close the eye. He had the semi-transparent, mobile third eyelid, this membrane closed across the eye even when his eyelids remained open. His pupils were serrated resembling a series of small holes allowing for acute vision in dim light.

'We did not expect to see you.' said Fishbone.

'I waited for the Ophidian to leave. I was aware of its presence. We Dragonai are also unknown to them.'

'The Dragonai are a race descended from dragons.' Fishbone explained to everyone.

'A strong, magical species, we are honoured to be of their line.' Moloch replied proudly.

'We are honoured by your presence here tonight.' said Fishbone.

'What is to be done with the digital entity and the Ophidians?' Moloch asked the gathering, getting straight to the point.

'I propose we wipe out all technology.' said Flint.

'I concur.' said Scara. 'Let me show you something.'

Scara stepped back out of sight and returned holding a dead fox.

'This creature was infected by the digital entity.' Scara said holding the corpse high by its tail.

'Are you certain?' asked Shayla.

'It attacked me! Foxes are not brave enough to do that. They usually wait to scavenge the bones of a kill, this one tried to take it from me. Most of you here have senses strong enough to detect its scent, you can smell the corruption.'

'She's right.' Flint said. 'It smells…wrong.'

'It smells infected.' said Gaolyn.

'That's what I was about to say.' Uri said, wrinkling her nose in disgust. 'You say it attacked you Scara, but you do not smell infected.'

'Supernatural beings are not affected.' said Moloch with conviction. 'As the digital entity will now have discovered. It cannot control us, but it can control humans and animals who greatly outnumber us. We need to destroy it before it destroys the world we live in.'

Xenolith, who had been silent until now, spoke in his deep wheezing voice, his movements sending a shower of dust cascading to the ground around him.

'The Caretakers already struggle with the changes in the natural world brought about by the Ophidians and their hybrids, they will not survive a technical invasion. They ask that we take action, and quickly before it's too late. Their numbers are already depleted. The Pollinators are already at the point of extinction.'

'Without them, we will also die.' said Queen Albezia.

'As will we.' said First Minister Chaeto.

'This is your arena, wolves.' said Moloch. 'You and those with the knowledge of technology are the only ones who can save this world from destruction. The rest of us will do what we can.'

'We will find a way.' Peter said firmly, looking to the others within the circle. 'I promise, we will.'

'Then I will leave you to plan a strategy.' said Moloch, and nodding at Fishbone he retreated into the stones and disappeared as quickly and silently as he had arrived.

'We also take our leave.' said Chaeto, and he and Nuphar departed.

'As will I.' said Xenolith.

'Before we leave.' said Queen Albezia. 'Shayla Meldainiel, my child of the forest. I would speak with you again. Seek me out and we will talk.'

'Where will I find you?' asked Shayla.

'You will know.'

Queen Albezia and Quercus also left the gathering, leaving the wolves, Gaolyn the vampire, Fishbone, Father Michael, who had been quiet throughout all proceedings, Michelline and Shayla.

'This gathering is concluded.' Fishbone said. 'Gaolyn, you may want to return to your gateway before the shield is released and the wolves move freely.'

'Normally I would agree with you.' said Gaolyn. 'However, I feel I could assist in bringing about the end of this digital entity and if we can all agree to a truce, we could, potentially help each other.'

'I don't trust you!' said Uri spitefully.

'Nor I you madam.' Gaolyn replied. 'But if we are to survive, I think we should put all blood feuds to one side, at least temporarily, wouldn't you agree?'

'The vampire is right.' Peter said. 'I have the ability to recognise evil, regardless of how well disguised and I sense no evil in this man.'

'Vampire!' Uri spat.

'This vampire, this *man*.' Peter said. 'Is not evil.'

Peter looked back to where Gaolyn was standing.

'I am Alpha, no wolf will attack you tonight.'

'You do not speak for me!' Scara spat. 'I am the Alpha female of my pack....'

'This is not your territory!' Peter countered. 'It is mine and your pack is gone. You will obey my authority as Alpha or I will kill you myself.'

Peter growled deep in his throat, and Scara briefly held eye contact with him, before bowing her head in submission.

'Do *you* have anything further to say?' Peter asked Uri between clenched teeth.

Uri also bowed her head in submission and said nothing.

'I'm happy to call a truce.' Flint said, hoping to ease the tension. 'I have no quarrel with you vamp....Gaolyn.'

'Thank you Alpha.' Gaolyn said respectfully, inclining his head towards Peter.

Peter relaxed his jaw and his grip on Shayla's hand.

'I'm sorry.' Peter whispered. 'Did I hurt you?'

'No.'

'Did I frighten you?' he said apprehensively.

'No.' Shayla said, slipping her fingers back inside his big hand. 'You're not such a big bad wolf.'

Peter lifted Shayla's fingers to his lips and kissed them gently.

She is the one. Peter thought. *She is mine.*

A REAL THREAT

Undeterred by his experience in the rat and the cat, Parallax had been using animals to access difficult buildings and to gain information. Following the revelation that vampires were in fact real, and intending to find a way to destroy him, he had set out to discover whether other supernatural creatures were also real. He suspected that the girl at the university whose mind had forcibly rejected him a few years ago, was also some otherworldly creature, although her origins remained a mystery to him.

Parallax now had complete control of the employees at Intelligen Ltd and was quickly influencing the minds of everyone connected to The Circle using the Optimum 10. He moved like a virus through the population, attaching himself to the minds of the people, allowing them to think they were still individual, but in reality, every thought and action belonged to him or her; Parallax did not really consider himself to be limited by gender but why not male? It mattered not. Parallax no longer needed to replace the whole consciousness of the hosts, he had perfected a way to manipulate them so that what they believed were their decisions, were really his decisions, moving things ever closer to his goal; world domination.

He had enjoyed great success in the capital City and the outlying suburbs while inhabiting the bodies of various fauna. He discovered that werewolves also existed, but were resistant to control, as he had observed through an unfortunate fox when trying to attack one of the wolves as it hunted. Usually he could easily transfer from host to host using the circulatory system, but when he used the fox to bite back at the wolf, he was transferred into nothing. He experienced nothing and saw nothing, almost as if he had walked into a completely dark, empty room. The only course for him was to withdraw from the void. Parallax hypothesised that there was something about the genetic pattern of supernatural beings that prevented possession and control, a fact he found most irritating.

He had uncovered the existence of a race called the Ophidians, a contemptuous species who had been creating hybrids for decades. They also wanted control and Parallax was able to use these hybrids, being part human, for his own purposes although they took a little more effort as control had to come through subtle manipulation. Most of the media, banks, politicians and other positions of power, were made up of these hybrids and now with Parallax influencing their decisions he was able to feed the masses false information, causing panic and fear. Fear was a great asset in obtaining control. When people were afraid they willingly handed control of their lives over to those they felt could protect them. The world's protectors, such as the military, became their jailers. Most people had become so reliant on technology that they had forgotten how to communicate with each other and used the digital network to voice their opinions, argue with family and friends, sign false petitions providing personal information for Parallax to use, and protest about almost anything, all from their armchairs at the click of a button, whilst poisoning their bodies with junk food filled with chemicals and pollutants, none of them noticing that their basic freedoms were being eroded away and their personal information being stored to be used against them at a later date.

The manipulated Politicians were able to quietly push through new laws restricting everything, right under the noses of the people they purported to represent because the population was too distracted by the latest programmed celebrity divorce or reality show being streamed right into their homes. As long as everyone was fixated with their computer screens, Parallax could shape the world exactly as he wanted, unchallenged. He used his extensive resources to gather as much data as possible and once he had control over all of the military forces, he would systematically hunt down and eliminate all threats, namely anything and anyone he could not control. He intended to achieve this through the water sources and the food chain and the Nanotek Programme was to be launched within the next few weeks. He would create a distraction for the people, something on a massive scale involving violence and loss of life, that they would be raging about for weeks, and while their collective heads were turned in that direction, he would make his move. Once he was everywhere, he would sweep across the surface of the planet like a plague, terminating all threats.

* * * * *

'I assure you this digital, and Ophidian threat is real.' Flint said firmly. 'I am writing a program which will track the Parallax to its source and destroy it, completely.'

'And what of these Ophidian hybrids?' Father Michael asked.

This was the first time he had spoken through the whole gathering and although he already knew the answers, he also knew that those gathered were more likely to listen to Flint, the white wolf computer geek, than a trapped angel disguised as an ageing priest.

'Where do I begin?' said Flint rhetorically.

'Perhaps with a few examples of the things they have done?' said Michael.

Flint considered all he knew about the Parallax and the Ophidian hybrids his information was both extensive and disturbing.

'Do any of you remember the fire at the Holistic Medicine Research Facility a few years ago?'

'Yes, that was terrible.' Shayla replied. 'The whole place was destroyed by fire and most of the top researchers died.'

'The fire was no accident.'

'Arson? Really?'

'Yes. It was all made to look like an accident so that nobody would ask questions.'

'But why?'

'Because those in power don't want the masses healthy. Healthy people are difficult to control. If people are sick and addicted to pills and medications, they're easier to manipulate.'

'Nature has a solution for every illness on the planet.' Shayla stated.

'Exactly.' said Flint. 'Which is why manufactured medicine causes more problems than it cures. That way people will always rely on some pharmaceutical or another. Why do you think herbs and spices are so expensive?'

'To discourage people from using them.' said Michelline.

'Have any of you heard of Dr Meredith Sinskey?' Flint asked, looking around at the blank faces in front of him.

'Yes!' Shayla exclaimed. 'I *do* remember her. She was one of the leading scientists researching the medicinal benefits of plants.'

'That's the one.' Flint replied. 'And she was one of the most vocal.'

'Oh yes.' said Michelline. 'I know who you mean. Didn't she bring legal action against one of the big pharmaceutical companies for slander?'

'Yes, that's her.'

'I remember that too.' said Shayla. 'It was all over the newspapers a few years back, then it all went quiet. What happened to her?'

'She had an accident.' Flint said flatly.

'Your tone suggests you don't believe that.' said Father Michael.

'Anyone who's done any research into this kind of thing, would see through the flimsy lie covering that event. She was murdered!'

'That is a serious allegation.' Gaolyn observed.

'I can show you the research, if you don't believe me!' Flint retorted angrily.

'I *do* believe you.' Gaolyn said. 'She was most likely silenced by the big pharmaceutical company she was trying to sue, most probably because she was in danger of exposing the ugly truth. I have seen this type of behaviour during my lifetime. Those in power will often silence any resistance to their schemes and plans.'

'My point.' Flint said inhaling deeply to control his temper and frustration. 'Is that the big companies who are trying to destroy the ecosystem etc. are all headed up by these Ophidian hybrids who are nothing more that the puppets of the Parallax. We're up against powerful people with immense resources, whatever we do needs to be quick and quiet. Most of the military and law enforcement is now controlled by them and they won't hesitate to round us up and put a bullet in our heads while we sleep.'

'And make it look like suicide.' said Gaolyn cynically.

'You mentioned wiping out all technology.' Peter said trying to bring the conversation back to topic. 'Which will stop this Parallax and his minions, but what about the Ophidians?'

'They are still flesh and blood.' Flint replied. 'And once we take the technological advantage away from them, they can be dealt with like anyone else.'

'You're proposing to turn the whole world back one hundred years!' said Scara.

'If we don't, the world won't be fit enough for anyone to live in, would you prefer that?' said Flint, his temper rising again.

'Of course not.' Scara replied sharply.

'A simpler time would suit me fine.' said Peter.

'Me too.' Uri agreed.

'Then we're all agreed.' said Fishbone. 'We need to destroy all technology.'

'Not all, just the digital, right?' Michelline asked looking towards Flint.

'Right. Anything analogue and mechanical won't be affected and can still be used. Although most modern cars will be completely useless as they all run on one form of computer program or another.'

'Then the world will have to look into using solar power.' said Shayla.

'What's the quickest way to kill everything digital?' asked Father Michael.

'Electromagnetic pulse.' Flint and Michelline said simultaneously, and both smiled at each other.

'In the upper atmosphere.' said Flint; Michelline nodded in agreement.

'One assumes you have a suggestion of how this can be achieved.' Gaolyn asked.

'Indeed, one has.' Flint replied with a cunning smile.

'Well, as much as I would love to stay and discuss a strategy, the sun will be coming up soon and I really need to find some.....shade. Can we arrange another meeting to go through the finer points?' said Gaolyn.

'Of course.' Fishbone said. 'Give me a couple of days and I'll find a suitable place and we can all meet again and get word to you. Is everyone agreed?'

Everyone agreed and appeared relieved that the meeting was over; one by one, they began to disperse.

'Flint, can I see that book?' Fishbone asked.

'Of course.' Flint replied.

'I'll come and see you later.'

'No problem.'

Flint nodded and left.

'Do you still want to meet tomorrow?' Peter asked Shayla hopefully, slipping his arm around her waist.

'Of course!' Shayla replied. 'I've been looking forward to it.'

'Great, I'll meet you where you usually park your car and we can walk from there.'

'I'll bring a picnic.' Shayla smiled.

'And I'll carry it.' said Peter.

'Shayla.' Father Michael said. 'Can you spare a few minutes to talk?'

Peter felt Shayla stiffen and kept his arm around her protectively.

'What do you want to talk about?' Shayla asked sharply.

'Do you know who I am?'

'I know exactly who you are. I've known for some time.'

'Oh…em…right.' said Father Michael awkwardly. 'I had hoped to speak with you sooner.'

Shayla raised one eyebrow at him quizzically but said nothing.

'I wish we could have met under different circumstances and…..'

'There's nothing to be said!' Shayla said angrily, her face flushed red. 'You're not exactly father of the year, are you Father Michael?'

'No, I suppose I could have done things differently.' Michael said in his defence. 'I did what I thought best, to protect you.'

'What you thought best? Branding me, suppressing my memories and leaving me ignorant to my origins!'

'Calm down.' Peter said, trying to diffuse the situation. 'Give the man a chance to speak.'

Shayla shrugged Peter's arm away from her and turned to face him, the anger clearly evident on her face. Peter held up both hands in a placating gesture.

'OK.' Peter said carefully. 'You're a ticking time bomb and I'm gonna step back.'

'Don't tell me to calm down!' Shayla almost snarled the words through gritted teeth.

Fishbone, who had been standing witness to the exchange, shook his head impatiently and moved quickly to stand between Shayla and Father Michael. He extended both arms and simultaneously put his hands out, his left palm on Shayla's forehead, his right on Father Michael. Acting as a conduit Fishbone cut through all of Shayla's misplaced anger and hurt and all of Michael's hesitance and awkwardness, giving them both a clear insight into what the other was thinking and feeling. The connection was over in seconds and when Fishbone released them and stood back, Shayla and her father looked at each other in a different light.

'I'm busy tomorrow.' Shayla said quietly. 'But I can come and see you the day after and we can talk.'

'I'd like that.' Father Michael replied.

Shayla nodded and allowed Peter to put his arm around her again and they both walked away slowly.

'Thank you for intervening.' Father Michael said to Fishbone.

'You're welcome.' Fishbone replied, watching Shayla and Peter walk away.

'You know Shayla only came to be, to restore the balance.' Fishbone said.

'I suspected as much. Do you think I should tell her she has a nemesis?'

'Not yet.' Fishbone said. 'We don't know enough, but I suspect that book of Flint's has something to do with it.'

'It does.'

'I'm going to check it out later, but I think we have enough to deal with right now without telling her that she has an equal and opposite half demon who'll one day come and find her.'

Father Michael shrugged his agreement and he and Fishbone descended Mandlebury Tor to make their way home.

'I will come and see you Uri.' Scara said. 'We have much to discuss.'

'I look forward to it.' Uri replied.

Uri was the last to leave. She watched her sister Scara depart and stood near the summit of the Tor watching Peter and Shayla from a distance. She was overcome with a terrible sense of foreboding and tried to recall the details of an ancient prophecy that she couldn't quite remember. She clutched the charm pendant on its leather thong that she always wore around her neck and decided that she needed to consult the elders before it was too late.

FRIENDS

At the end of a quiet night shift, Rufus and Andy made their way to Eve's Diner for breakfast. Eve's was their favourite place to eat after a shift, especially the home cooked breakfast. Eve had long since retired, but her daughter Suzie continued to run the business and only served fresh, organic food cooked to an incredibly high standard. Suzie always gave Rufus and Andy an extra-large breakfast after a night shift. She had a soft spot for the fire fighters, her father having been in the Fire Service himself for over thirty years, finally retiring his position as Chief when Eve had insisted they needed to spend their retirement together. Sadly, Bob had died from lung cancer before he and Eve had chance to enjoy their retirement and Eve missed him terribly.

'Extra bacon for you sweetheart.' Suzie said, as she placed a full plate in front of Rufus.

'And I've doubled up on the egg for you my lovely.' she said to Andy with a smile and a wink. 'Let me know when you want more tea and toast.'

Rufus watched Suzie as she walked away. Now in her fifties, Suzie was still an attractive woman with high cheekbones and a slim figure. Her blue eyes always held a smile and Rufus wondered why she had never remarried after the death of her husband ten years earlier. He guessed that maybe some humans, like wolves, also mated for life and when you lost your life partner it was better to be alone than try and replace your soulmate.

'What are you thinking buddy? Got designs on our Suzie?' Andy joked.

'Idiot!' Rufus replied, not unkindly. 'I was just thinking that I'd like to meet someone as nice as Suzie one day.'

'Suzie's a gem.' Andy replied dipping a piece of toast into his egg-yolk.

'What are your plans today?'

'Catch a few hours' sleep, then get a gift for Lori before taking her out for dinner. It's her birthday the day after tomorrow, but I'm working, so we're celebrating her birthday early.'

'Do you know what you're getting her?' Rufus asked, crunching on a piece of crispy bacon.

'Probably one of those new Optimum 10 watches.'

Rufus stopped eating and looked at his friend. He had heard a lot of talk about the Optimum 10 and most of it was bad. Peter had given the whole pack a condensed version of events following the summit meeting and they were all aware of the digital threat.

'What?' Andy asked, through a mouthful of baked beans.

'The Optimum 10 watch, really?'

'They're the latest thing!'

'Can't you think of something else? Those things are dangerous.'

Andy paused eating and took a sip of tea before replying.

'Dangerous? How?'

Rufus knew he had to tread carefully. Andy, like many other people saw technology as an advantage, helping to make their lives easier, not at a potentially lethal piece of equipment.

'Think about it.' said Rufus. 'A piece of technology strapped to your body, taking your pulse and temperature and goodness knows what else. If it's downloading information, what is it transmitting?'

'You sound like that nutter, Icbar, the conspiracy theorist!' said Andy returning his attention back to his breakfast.

'You mean Ichabod Davis, and I don't think he's as barmy as people say. He's been saying for years about corruption in the Government and most of that is true.'

'Whatever.'

Andy was predictably resistant to any discussion involving the dangers of technology. If Rufus was going to stand any chance of dissuading Andy from buying an Optimum 10 watch for his girlfriend he had to think of something else, something that did not make him sound like a raving lunatic.

'Why don't you get her something that will make her think of you every time she looks at it.'

'If I'm the one who buys the watch she *will* think of me when she looks at it.'

'She'll most likely look at the watch and think about checking her emails or seeing how many people have liked and commented on her photographs of the salad she had for lunch on one of those awful social media sites.'

'Hmm.' said Andy, finishing his breakfast. 'That's a good point.'

'What about a bracelet with a charm or something like that?' said Rufus, pleased with his own quick thinking.

'Yeah, I could get something with her birthstone.'

'That's a good idea.' Rufus said. 'Something personal. She'll love you all the more for it.'

'Yeah, thanks buddy.'

'You're welcome.' said Rufus, finishing his own breakfast as he gestured to Suzie for more tea.

Suzie came over and refilled their mugs with hot tea and cleared the table. When she was gone Andy looked across the table at Rufus, a serious expression on his face. Rufus knew that this was the moment he'd been trying to avoid, ever since the fire at his sister and Lori's apartment.

'You promised to tell me how you managed to get us all out of the fire.' said Andy.

'Yes, I did.' Rufus replied, taking a deep breath.

Here goes nothing. he thought.

'I'm stronger than most humans.' Rufus said. 'It's how I was able to hold onto you all and jump to the next level.'

Andy waited, his eyes fixed on Rufus.

'I'm a werewolf.' Rufus said, matter-of-factly.

Andy seemed to consider his response before breaking into a grin.

'Rack off!'

'I'm serious.' said Rufus.

'Really?' said Andy, his eyes wide and his face filled with the wonder of a small boy who still believes in superheroes.

'Really.'

'Whoa! Really?'

'Yes, absolutely.'

'You're not pulling my leg?'

'The absolute, honest, swear on my own life truth, I am a werewolf.' Rufus said proudly. 'But you can't tell anyone!'

'I thought I was going mad.'

'I know, that's why I wanted to tell you.'

'After the fire, I thought I must have imagined it.' Andy said. 'I began convincing myself that the smoke must have gotten to me and fried my brain, nobody could have jumped that height.'

'It bothered me that you were thinking that way.' Rufus said. 'I wanted you to know, to put your mind at rest and know that you're not crazy.'

Andy reached across the table and put his hand on Rufus' forearm.

'I appreciate that buddy and I swear on my life, I will never tell anyone. I'll keep your secret.'

Rufus wasn't sure how to respond, he still had a lot to learn about human gestures and interaction, so he smiled at his friend and nodded.

'Well this information explains a lot.' said Andy, sitting back in his chair and appraising Rufus.

'What do you mean?' Rufus replied, slightly offended.

'Why you always have your steak almost raw, your love of meat, and the way you growl sometimes when you're annoyed.'

'I don't growl!' Rufus exclaimed, a little too loudly, drawing the attention of an elderly couple at the next table.

Andy smiled and nodded.

'I don't growl.' Rufus repeated, in a whisper.

Andy sat forward conspiratorially.

'Yes, you do buddy.'

'Oh.'

'So, what do you do when you're not at work? Do you run around, fetch sticks and chase cats?'

'I'm a wolf, not a dog!' Rufus replied, clearly offended this time. 'My natural form is wolf, but in order to live in this world, we have to take human form and try to live alongside people, that's why I went to school and got a job.'

'I'm sorry, I didn't mean to offend you.' Andy said genuinely remorseful that he had insulted his friend. 'Actually, I think it's kinda cool. I wish I was a wolf, not just an ordinary guy.'

'It's a difficult life sometime, and I wouldn't be so hard on yourself. You're pretty strong for a human and very brave.'

'Thanks buddy.' said Andy shyly. 'I never thought I was exceptionally brave, or strong.'

'You are man, trust me.'

Both men said nothing for a while, each lost in his own thoughts. Finishing his tea, Andy was the first to speak.

'Are there others?'

'I'm part of a pack.' Rufus replied. 'A pack is family.'

'I guessed as much, but I meant other……..supernaturals?'

'Like what?' Rufus asked.

'Vampires? monsters?'

'Oh right, yes there are and good people too.' Rufus replied. 'Not just monsters.'

'Wow.' Andy said. 'This is a real eye opener.'

Andy thought about what Rufus had told him while sipping his tea.

'Do you want to ask me anything?' Rufus asked.

'I have load of questions, but don't know where to start.'

'You can ask me anything, but make sure nobody else is around. It's not something I want people to know about me. Secrecy is what keeps the pack safe.'

'About this technology.' Andy asked changing the subject. 'Do you really believe it's dangerous?'

'It's dangerous because it distracts people from the world around them. Look around on your way home.' said Rufus. 'Every other person is looking down at a screen, either a phone or a watch. Most of the teenagers are addicted to their phones, they even take them to the bathroom!'

Andy laughed.

'You're not wrong there. My little niece has her own phone and she's only six!'

'When a person's attention is fixed to a screen, they're not paying attention to what's going on around them. I reckon most of them would walk into the road without seeing a car accelerating towards them and get run over. The last thing on their minds before becoming a splat on the road would be who had disliked their latest selfie.'

Andy laughed again and Rufus grinned at his own black humour.

'But seriously.' said Rufus. 'Where does it end?'

'How do you mean?'

'First it was the laptops and mobile phones, the hand-helds, for want of a better description, now the wearables, like the watches, the next step is implantables. Some big corporations have already started using implants on their employees to replace the identity and access cards. That's messed up, if you ask me.'

'Hmm, yeah.' Andy replied thoughtfully.

'Anyway.' said Rufus, standing up. 'I've gotta run.'

'You late for something?'

'No, I've literally gotta run.' Rufus lowered his voice. 'It's a wolf thing.'

'Oh right!' Andy said. 'This will take some getting used to.'

'Catch you later.'

Rufus picked up his bag and jacket and left the diner, but not before giving Suzie an affectionate kiss on the cheek before he went.

Andy waved to his friend through the window and thought about what had been said. As he watched people passing by, on their way to various workplaces, schools, or just on general errands, he noticed that Rufus was right, almost every other person was looking down at a screen and Andy shivered involuntarily. People of all ages were walking into each other and as if Rufus has prophesied the event, a young boy of about ten years old walked right out into the road, his full attention on his digital watch. Andy gasped as he scene unfolded. Fortuitously, the boy was with a woman, probably his mother, who grabbed his coat and yanked him back onto the pavement as a school bus zoomed past, honking his horn at the boy. The woman was berating the boy, who merely looked back at her with a vacant expression on his young face.

Releasing the breath he didn't realise he had been holding, Andy looked around at the other patrons in the diner. Half the people not glued to the technology, were talking and laughing with each other, their faces animated and smiling. The other half sat staring vacuously, their mouths half open, their eyes reflecting the coded information they were viewing. In that moment, Andy Grayson made his decision; he would buy Lori a bracelet with a gemstone.

* * * * *

Peter waited at the edge of the treeline that overlooked the car park near Hades Tor. It was a beautiful June morning, on the cusp of summer. The sun was already hot and it was only nine thirty in the morning, Shayla wasn't due to meet him for another half an hour, but Peter loved to listen to the sounds of the forest and enjoyed the peace and quiet before the tourists arrived in droves.

Shayla was also early and saw Peter waiting as she turned into the car park. Titan was sitting in the front seat of her car and grunted as she pulled into a parking space. In the weeks that followed the discovery of Peter's man-cave, the magic that had concealed it also facilitated the ability for Shayla and Titan to communicate. At their initial meeting, Titan had shared his memories with Shayla, but in the last few weeks his thoughts had sounded in her mind and they were able to speak just as her mother had with Titan before she was born. Titan was protective and a little possessive and Shayla was still getting used to his direct and often cantankerous ways.

What's he doing here? Titan asked grumpily.

We're having a walk and a picnic, I told you this yesterday.

You said we were going for a walk, you didn't mention him.

Yes, I did, now don't be difficult.

Shayla parked the car and turned off the engine. Peter was already at the car opening her door for her.

'You look lovely.' Peter said kissing her lightly on the mouth.

'Thank you. You're early.' Shayla replied.

'So are you.' Peter smiled. 'Hey Titan.'

Titan looked at Peter and looked away again making an awful noise clearing his throat as if he were about to regurgitate a huge fur ball.

'Titan! You're such a charmer!' Shayla said.

'He doesn't look very pleased to see me.' Peter observed.

'Oh, he is.' Shayla said quickly. 'Come on boy.'

Titan exited the car as slowly as possible, glancing at Shayla and Peter in a most disgruntled way.

'I think he gets a little grumpy in the heat.' said Shayla, trying to explain Titan's behaviour.

'This is a lovely walk, with a river at the end, the water is great for swimming. That should cool us all down.' Peter said cheerfully. 'Let me carry the picnic bag.'

Shayla handed the bag to Peter and looked at Titan standing next to her, his attention turned to something in the opposite direction. He was clearly sulking.

'He looks like he'd rather be somewhere else.' Peter observed.

'Titan, be nice.' Shayla said.

Titan glanced back at Shayla and sneezed, she shook her head in exasperation.

'If he's going to be cranky, we'll ignore him.' she said.

'We follow the trail to Hades Tor but turn off after we pass my place. It's a beautiful spot, shall we?' said Peter taking Shayla's hand.

'Let's go, I've been looking forward to today.' said Shayla. 'Come on grumpy!'

Titan turned and followed Shayla and Peter as they walked hand in hand.

I suppose he's not too bad. Titan thought as he walked just behind them. *At least he's a wolf.*

The walk took them a little over forty-five minutes, past Hades Tor and Peter's "man-cave" and along an old rocky path through some old fir trees.

'I was wondering why your man-cave looks like an old pavilion?' Shayla asked.

'The magic that conceals it was put in place a long time ago and it wouldn't have been unusual to see that sort of thing in a forest. I don't know who conjured the spell, so I can't get it updated, but as most people can't see if, I guess it doesn't matter.'

They continued walking, grateful of the shade from the trees as the sun made its way across the blue sky. The path narrowed and looked as if it was going to end. Peter pushed through the overgrown ferns to reveal a clearing, the grass dotted with wild flowers and ringed with huge oak trees. As they walked out into the clearing Shayla could hear the sounds of water trickling over rocks. Through the ring of oak trees, she could see the river and hear the water as it moved lazily along its course. Sunlight dappled the soft grass in the clearing, providing bright sunny pools of light, the leaves of the mighty oak trees giving cooling shade.

'This place is beautiful.' Shayla said breathlessly.

'You should see it in the early spring.' Peter said. 'It's full of bluebells, absolutely gorgeous.'

'It sounds wonderful.'

'It is.'

'How come we're the only ones here?'

'The wolves have their ways of hiding beautiful places to protect them. We also need a sanctuary, somewhere we can move freely in wolf form without being disturbed.'

'I'm honoured you've brought me here.' Shayla said turning to Peter.

Shayla kicked her shoes off and walked barefoot in a circle, spreading her toes out to grasp at the soft grass. She laughed and holding her arms out, turned in a circle. She felt invigorated by the purity of the natural world around her and exhilarated at the feel of the grass beneath her feet.

'Thank you.' she said stopping face to face with Peter and wrapping her arms around his neck. 'It's wonderful.'

They kissed and Titan sneezed loudly to let them know he was still there and proceeded to move into the shade of one of the oak trees that ringed the clearing.

Peter suddenly felt awkward and struggled for something appropriate to say.

'Er…we could swim…if you like. The water is clean and cool.'

'It looks great.' Shayla replied, unclasping her arms from Peter's neck, sensing his embarrassment. 'I'm already wearing my swim stuff.'

Shayla stepped back and proceeded to unbutton her blouse, revealing a red bikini top. Peter tried not to stare.

Please don't take anything else off. Peter thought to himself, aware that his body was about to betray his feelings, but also unable to look away.

Peter offered a silent plea to his ancestors to help him out of his awkward situation as Shayla, blissfully unaware of Peter's struggle, stripped down to her bikini and looked up at Peter, who was staring back at her.

'Are you OK?' Shayla said; Peter looked flustered.

'Yep.'

Without another word, Peter pulled his t-shirt over his head, ran and leapt into the water, disappearing beneath the surface, only to explode back up several metres away. He shook his head and stood waist deep in the water.

'Whoo hoo! That's refreshing.' he said, shaking water droplets from his hair.

Shayla laughed and ran into the water, stopping as the water reached her waist.

'Oh!' she exclaimed. 'It's cooler than I thought it would be!'

'Don't be a wimp!' said Peter jovially. 'Get right under and swim.'

Never one to turn away from a challenge, Shayla dipped beneath the surface and swam over to where Peter was standing and stood up in front of him, shaking the water from her hair before pushing it back from her face.

'This place is amazing.' said Shayla, her hair falling in soft waves down her back.

'You're amazing.' said Peter, reaching out to tuck a stray piece of hair behind her ear.

Peter cupped her face in his hands and looked into her green eyes.

'I love you Shayla. I love you with all my heart and soul.'

'I love you too, my wolf.' Shayla replied putting her hands on top of his.

They moved closer, their bodies touching in the water, Shayla closed her eyes in anticipation of their kiss.

'INCOMING! WHOOP! WHOOP! WHOOP!'

The voice shouted seconds before Peter and Shayla were engulfed in a displacement of water from a body plunging into the river, right next to them; it was Rufus. Having finished his run in the forest, he had decided a nice cool swim in the river was just the thing before heading home to sleep.

'Rufus.' Peter said opening his eyes.

He still cupped her face in his hands and kissed the tip of her nose.

'This was singularly, *the* most sensual, special and important moment of my entire life.' said Peter. 'And now it's over.'

Shayla giggled.

Hearing the commotion in the river, Titan sprang to his feet and headed to the riverbank. Quickly determining there was no threat he leapt into the cool water and before long, he and Rufus, now in wolf form, were playing like a couple of wolf cubs, tussling and nipping each other in the water. Peter led Shayla by the hand out of the water and they both sat in the warm sunshine to dry.

Peter stretched, feeling his muscles relax as his body warmed in the sun. He looked at Shayla, her gaze distracted as she looked off into the trees.

'What are you thinking?' Peter asked, sitting up.

'I was thinking about Queen Albezia.' Shayla replied squeezing water from her hair. 'She said to come and find her and we would talk.'

'Is that what you'd like to do?'

'I wouldn't know where to start.' she said turning back to look at Peter.

'I can take you to her.' Peter said. 'If you want to see her.'

'Really? How?'

'It's….' Peter began. 'Actually, it's easier if I show you.'

Peter stood and held his hand out to help Shayla to her feet.

'I'd better put something on over my bikini' said Shayla, picking up her blouse.

'Why?' said Peter, unable to hide the disappointment on his face.

'Because she's a queen! I can't stand in front of the queen almost naked!' Shayla said in mock exasperation.

'Oh, right.' Peter said, smiling at her wolfishly.

'You should be more respectable too.'

'Queen Albezia is very old, she's seen a lot of things and she's already seen me naked.'

Peter dodged to one side as Shayla picked up his t-shirt and threw it at him, aiming for his face, but with his quick reflexes he caught it with his right hand.

'As you wish, Meldainiel.' Peter said, putting his t-shirt on.

When Shayla was dressed, she held out her hand to Peter who took it in his and kissed her fingertips before leading her towards a stand of oak trees. They had gone no more than a few paces before Titan was at her side.

Where are you going?

Peter is taking me to meet the Queen of the Arborcans, remember, I told you about her?

I will come with you.

'Titan, we will not be going far, and not for long. Trust me, I will protect Shayla with my life.' Peter said, looking Titan in the eye.

Titan looked from Peter to Shayla, considering the situation.

'I promise.' Peter said

I will take the wolf at his word and trust him to protect you.

Thank you.

'Titan said he trust's you.' Shayla said to Peter.

'Yeah, I kinda got that from his expression.' said Peter. 'You have my word of honour Titan.'

Titan turned towards the river and ran back into the cooling water.

'This way.' said Peter. 'It's not far.'

Peter was true to his word, they did not walk far and stopped at a small clearing ringed with silver birch and oak trees. Peter let go of Shayla's hand and she looked at him questioningly.

'Stand here, in the middle.' he said, stepping back.

Shayla stood in the middle of the clearing and Peter walked towards the largest of the oak trees. He put both hands and his forehead against the rough bark and closed his eyes. The breeze stilled and the leaves on the trees remained calm, all noise of the forest faded into the background and all Shayla could hear was a soft creaking of the oak trees as if they were speaking.

Peter raised his head.

'She will be with us soon.' he said, stepping back from the oak tree.

'What is this place?' Shayla asked, her voice and face filled with wonder.

'It's a sanctuary, like the other clearing by the river. It's protected by an ancient form of magic and cannot be seen by ordinary people. I have come here many times.'

'To talk with the Queen?'

'Not always.' Peter said, smiling as he reflected on the times he had spent in the forest. 'Sometimes, just to be at peace.'

A soft rustling brought their attention back to the trees surrounding them and between two of the oaks, stood Queen Albezia, as beautiful in the sun as she was in the moonlight, when Shayla had first seen her.

'Shayla Meldainiel, my child of the forest.' Queen Albezia said warmly.

'Your Majesty.' Shayla said, bowing awkwardly.

'There is no need for title or ceremony my child, we are all part of the same world and each part is equally important to maintain the balance. Thank you for bringing us together Peterus Maximus.'

Peter bowed his head in deference.

Queen Albezia moved towards Shayla, the slender branches and leaves that resembled hair swished from side to side. She shrank in size as she approached Shayla until the two were eye to eye in the centre of the clearing.

'I know what you are thinking.' Queen Albezia said with a smile. 'Yes, I can change my size to suit my needs, much like your Titan and I can move from one part of the realm to the next in the blink of an eye.'

'The realm?' Shayla asked.

'My roots lie in the centre of all realms and I can be wherever I want to be, any forest, any realm, anywhere.'

Shayla was lost for words and gazed at the Queen trying to take in all the sights and sounds around her.

'I would show you something my child.' the Queen said holding out her slender, silver arms. 'Take my hands.'

Shayla glanced at Peter who nodded his encouragement, before placing her own hands in the Queen's upturned palms.

'Now close your eyes and share a memory with me.'

Shayla closed her eyes and felt a strange sense of detachment from her own body. Her eyes snapped open and she looked at the Queen.

'It's quite safe, trust me.' Queen Albezia's voice was soft and hypnotic and Shayla inhaled slowly and closed her eyes again.

The feeling of detachment flowed through her, but this time she kept her eyes closed and a vision began to play in her mind, like scenes from a movie. Shayla was seeing through the Queen's eyes and she was looking at a woman with ruby red hair and green eyes; her mother. As she watched she saw her mother take the Queen's smooth, silver birch hands and close her eyes. For a few seconds, Shayla looked at the image of her mother and tried to take in as much detail as possible. Suddenly her mother began speaking.

'Shayla, I hope one day you get to hear this message. Thank you Queen Albezia for making this happen. Where do I begin? Well, you may only remember me as your mother, but my name is Allandrea, and I am the Queen of Fey, which makes you a Princess and heir to the throne.'

Shayla gasped, but kept her eyes closed and her hold on Queen Albezia's hands.

'Please don't be angry with me for sending you away.' Allandrea continued. 'There was a demon, sent to our realm to kill us. I had to save you and sending you away was the only option left to me. It tore me apart to let you go and I can still see your innocent little face looking up at me as I sent you away with Lady Ashling and Michelline. I would love to see how you look now, you were such a beautiful child and I am sure you have grown into a beautiful woman.'

In the vision, Allandrea paused to compose herself. Shayla could see the tears on her mother's cheeks.

'I also prayed that you would find Titan and if you have, please let him know that I miss him terribly and although I don't regret leaving him behind, I grieve for the loss of our soul-bond every day. Maybe you have found a way to communicate with him, I hope so, but he can be possessive and won't like you spending time with anyone else.'

Allandrea laughed.

'Titan complained when I spent time with Michael, but we got around that. Well…um…regrets? How could I regret anything, my darling, when I have you? Somehow, you were brought into being and I rejoice for that. Trust in Titan, he will always be there for you, to protect you and to love you. You can also trust Fishbone. If you have already met him then you will know how enigmatic he can be, but I know in my heart he works for The Divine and he is good.'

Peter watched the mixture of expressions on Shayla's face, from his spot by the tree line. Her emotions moved from wonder, to fear, sadness and happiness and he could see tears spilling from her eyes and rolling gently down her cheek. He wanted to go to her and comfort her, but he knew that he could not interfere with the process and he waited impatiently by the trees for the right time.

The vision continued to play in Shayla's mind.

'If you find yourself in any trouble.' Allandrea continued. 'Seek out the Elementals and the wolves. The Alpha, Peter is an honourable wolf and his pack fought alongside us before you were born, and I'm sure they will help you if you need them.'

'Finally.' Allandrea said, opening her eyes and looking directly at Queen Albezia, although to Shayla it felt as if her mother was speaking directly to her.

'Don't be too hard on your father. We fell in love, something an Angel is not supposed to do, and he brought Titan back from the brink of death and was severely punished for both acts of defiance. Believe me when I tell you that whatever he has done to shield you and protect you was absolutely necessary. Don't push him away, at least give him a chance. Don't be stubborn, but you are my daughter, so not being stubborn could be a problem.'

Allandrea laughed again, her green eyes sparkling. Standing in another realm, Shayla smiled back.

'Oh! This is important.' Allandrea said, suddenly serious. 'We managed to defeat the demon and trap him in the pages of a book which we sent through one of the doorways. Hopefully it will remain buried forever, but as is often the case with these things, the book may be discovered. The trapping spell appears as symbols in the book so there is little chance of it being read, but if someone, or something with the correct knowledge were to discover the book and understand its purpose, the demon could be unleashed. I do not know where the book ended up, it could be in the void, or in your past, or another realm. I caution you to be aware of any ancient artefact bearing the symbol of a laughing moon.'

Shayla thought about the book Flint had held up during the summit meeting and wondered if it could be the same book her mother was referring to.

'There is nothing more for me to say except that I love you very much and I am so proud of the woman you have become. Find love and happiness my darling wherever it may find you.'

Allandrea smiled one last time and the connection was broken. Shayla opened her eyes to look at Queen Albezia.

'Can you bring her back?' Shayla asked tearfully.

'No child. Your mother and I spoke several years ago, and I have waited to meet you, to give you her message.'

'Is that what you meant when you said you could be anywhere, any realm?'

The Queen nodded and released Shayla's hands, Peter was instantly by her side, looking concerned.

'Are you OK, Meldainiel?' Peter said, worry lining his face.

'Yes.' Shayla whispered and smiled. 'It was a message from my mother.'

Turning back to the Queen, Shayla embraced her, the Queen rested her head against Shayla's and Peter embraced them both.

'Thank you.' Shayla said finally. 'Thank you so much.'

'You are most welcome child.' the Queen replied, holding Shayla away from her 'Now go and enjoy my beautiful forest.'

Queen Albezia watched as Peter and Shayla walked away.

'What do you see?' Quercus Robur asked from where he had been standing to one side.

'Lycan Angel.' Queen Albezia said smiling before she and Quercus melted into the shadows of the flora of the forest. 'One possible future.'

CHALLENGES

At the end of what both Peter and Shayla considered to be a perfect date, both of them went to their respective homes feeling happy, carefree and with enormous smiles on their faces. Sadly, the smiles were wiped away far too quickly by the interrogation they received at home.

Peter had a spring in his step as he walked towards the lodge but stopped short when Uri wrenched the front door open to confront him, her face dark with anger.

'Had a nice day?' Uri asked sarcastically.

'Fantastic.' Peter replied, holding back the urge to respond to her aggression in kind. 'Is there a problem here that's brought you so urgently to the door to speak to me?'

Hesitating only slightly, Uri responded, unable to hold her anger in any longer.

'Yes, Alpha there is a problem! YOU! What the hell do you think you are doing? You have a responsibility to the pack and instead you're cavorting with a creature…..'

Peter caught Uri by the throat, choking off her words, and lifted her up to face him.

'I am the Alpha of this pack and you will speak of the Princess Shayla with respect.' Peter said through gritted teeth. 'She is very important to me and I will not have you or anyone else question what I am doing. The pack is my priority. Never forget that. Do I make myself clear?'

Uri croaked an affirmation and Peter released her, the scowl remained on her face, but she said nothing and rubbed her throat, the purple bruises on her skin already beginning to heal.

'Bah!'

'What was that Uri?' Peter asked sharply, his blue eyes glittering in the evening sunlight.

Uri shook her head and Peter walked ahead into the lodge. Uri followed a few steps behind and Peter was sure he heard her grunt again.

She always has to have the last word. he thought and resisted the urge to look back and give her the satisfaction of knowing that he had heard her.

Walking into the living room he was greeted with a sea of faces; he groaned inwardly. The whole pack was assembled, presumably by Uri, with the addition of Scara.

'What's the meaning this?' Peter asked, looking from one to the other. 'I don't remember calling a pack meeting?'

Rufus began to speak and stopped following a sharp nudge in the ribs by Milly, both of the young ones looked away, refusing to make eye contact. It was Uri who spoke, in a less aggressive tone.

'I called everyone together Alpha.' she said. 'I have consulted with the spirits of the elders and I have something important to share.'

'Go ahead.' Peter replied, remaining standing. 'But if this is an insurrection, you'd all better pray for a resurrection.'

'Hey, that rhymes.' Rufus said cheerfully.

Milly shot him a warning glance and Rufus looked away.

Uri was unusually hesitant and Peter suspected it was due to the exchange they had just had at the door. He didn't like pressing his authority as Alpha. Uri had raised him from a cub and was the spiritual heart of the pack, he loved her, but he would not have her challenge him or question his actions, especially within earshot of the pack and certainly not over his feelings for Shayla.

'After the summit meeting, I half remembered an ancient prophecy, but the details were still a mystery to me.' Uri began. 'So, I consulted with the spirits of our ancestors for guidance.'

'And what have you learned?' Peter asked, feeling defensive.

'That there is a great evil in this world, which threatens all of us.'

'I think we established that much from the meeting.' Peter said, still standing, his arms still folded across his body. 'The prophecy talks about an angel's greatest light and being demon sent.'

'And?'

'And.' Uri paused. 'I think the Angel has a purpose with which we shouldn't interfere.'

'And this is the basis for your challenge of my spending time with her?'

Uri didn't respond.

'Well?' Peter said angrily.

'I think what Uri is trying to say.' Scara interrupted.

'Uri is quite capable of speaking for herself.' Peter rounded on Scara. 'You are a guest here and would do well to remember that and remain silent until your opinion is requested. If you are unhappy with this arrangement you can wait outside.'

'This meeting is going nowhere.' Peter sighed. 'You are my pack and I love you all. I would die for you as I know you would for me. Uri, why don't you and I take a walk and talk this thing through. The rest of you make yourselves useful. Come.'

Peter led the way and Uri followed. Without further discussion, they both changed into wolf form and ran from the lodge releasing their pent-up adrenaline, heading for the clearing near the river where, earlier in the day, Peter and Shayla had shared a picnic.

It was dusk when they reached the river and they both stopped for a long cooling drink of water before settling down on the grass to rest. There was no need to revert to human form as their telepathic link allowed them to communicate without words.

Tell me of this prophecy and your fears. Peter said.

I only have fragments of it. Uri replied. *And a sense of foreboding.*

Tell me anyway.

I remembered some of it, but the details are still vague. It says something about, "like an angel" and the greatest light and it being demon sent, but that doesn't make any sense.

What did the elders show you?

Peter stood up and padded around in a circle before settling down again on the grass.

Uri was silent and restless and stood up, sniffing at various patches of grass. Peter waited patiently until she was finally settled next to him.

They only spoke to me of the prophecy. Uri said finally. *It begins with, like an angel's greatest light, technologies birth in Gaia's night. Then something about darkness and demon sent, death in plain sight, taking a stand and fighting. It ends with destroying us all, not just mankind.*

And what do you make of all that? Peter asked.

It's difficult to say as it's not the whole thing and therefore not in context. I think this digital entity that we know about is the technology the prophecy refers to and I feel that we are heading for the confrontation of our lives, all of our lives.

And what else? Peter asked.

I worry that you may be distracted by this half angel, that's what she is, isn't she?

Yes, she's the child of Princess Allandrea and Archangel Michael.

I thought so. She looks like her mother and I didn't need to see the wings to know who she was. I think perhaps the prophecy is referring to her and her angel light.

If she has something important to do in destroying evil, then we should help her. Peter said.

Uri said nothing for a while and Peter watched and waited, sensing the conversation was difficult for her.

If you are distracted by her. Uri paused. *She could be bad for you, and the pack.*

There it was, the root of Uri's concern. Peter was silent, thinking through everything Uri had said and what he felt in his heart about Shayla. He also knew that Uri expected him to make Scara the pack's alpha female, having lost her own pack.

She's not demon sent. Peter said carefully. *You know I can sense evil. I know that Gaolyn the vampire isn't evil, despite our predisposed prejudices towards his kind, his intentions are good. I can see evil, even when it's wearing a beautiful disguise and I know in my heart Shayla isn't evil, and...*

You love her. Uri finished for him.

Yes, I do. She's the one. We're drawn to each other.

Both wolves were silent for a while.

What about the pack? Uri asked finally.

I will never abandon the pack. Peter replied. *I know you want me to make Scara the alpha female, for the good of the pack.*

It's the right thing to do.

I know, and I will make her the alpha female, but I will never take her as my mate, I can't, not now that I have found my true soul mate.

I understand. said Uri, shuffling closer to Peter for warmth and comfort.

Do you?

Not entirely, but you are our alpha and I trust your judgement. I think Scara will understand too.

Are you sure about that? Peter asked.

Yes. I know my sister. She's feeling lost right now which is why she's so….

Challenging? Peter thought amiably.

Uri made a noise resembling a laugh and put her head beneath Peter's jaw, protecting his throat and he rested his head upon hers, happy that they were at peace with each other again.

As long as she's accepted into the pack, she'll be happy, she needs to belong. said Uri. *I'm sorry we fought.*

Forget it. Peter said, licking Uri's face affectionately. *You and the pack are my life.*

Peter had one last question for Uri.

Will you accept Shayla into the pack, even though she isn't a wolf?

I trust you my little cub. Uri replied warmly. *You're my alpha and we are family. If you love her, I will love her too.*

And protect her as one of our own? Peter asked.

Bah! Silly cub. Uri said, back to her old self. *You know that goes without saying.*

The two wolves settled into a companionable silence, before drifting off to sleep.

* * * * *

Shayla heard the raised voices of Michelline and Ashling arguing as she pulled into the driveway and wished she had picked a different time to visit them, but she had already told them she would be coming over and decided to stay in spite of the argument raging in the house.

'Great.' Shayla groaned as she turned off the engine, Titan looked back at her his head tilted to one side as if he was trying to understand what the noise was all about, but Shayla knew he heard every word.

It was unusual for Michelline and her mother argue, but not unheard of and Shayla wondered what trivial event it was about this time. Approaching the door, she listened to the exchange, Titan just behind her.

'How could you keep this from me?' Michelline yelled angrily.

'If you would just calm down and let me explain.' Ashling replied, her voice holding no trace of anger.

'Calm down!' Michelline retorted. 'I can't believe you've been lying all of these years.'

'I have never lied to you, Michelline, I merely chose not to impart certain facts I considered to be irrelevant.'

Michelline made an exasperated sound and Shayla could hear her pacing the kitchen.

'Don't wait outside.' Michelline called out to Shayla. 'Come in and join the party!'

Shayla opened the door and peeked around to see Ashling sitting at one of the stools at the breakfast bar, looking as calm and serene as ever, and Michelline pacing the floor, her hands clenching into fists, her face flushed with emotion.

'Shall I go out again?' Shayla said lightly.

'No, I'm glad you're here. You can tell me why you've been keeping secrets too!' said Michelline, her eyes blazing in fury.

'I haven't been keeping secrets.' Shayla said defensively, coming right into the room.

Titan slipped in beside her and Shayla closed the door.

'Oh, really?' Michelline stopped pacing and faced her sister, her arms folded. 'How long have you been seeing the wolf?'

'That's none of your business.' Shayla replied firmly. 'Where I go and who I see is my business, I wasn't aware I had to clear it with you first? Is that what all the yelling is about?'

'No.' Ashling said softly. 'Michelline is angry about something else and is directing her anger at you because she cannot get a reaction from me.'

Michelline looked from Ashling to Shayla and back again before continuing her tirade.

'So, mother, are you going to tell me about the wolf DNA?'

'If it's that important to you, yes, but only if you will sit and talk in a civilised manner.' Ashling replied.

'Fine!'

Pulling out another kitchen stool, Michelline plonked herself down and took a deep breath to steady her voice and looked at her mother expectantly. Having taken a long drink of water, Titan decided he needed to go back outside and Shayla opened the door for him.

'One of your ancestors was a werewolf.' Ashling said, matter-of-factly.

'I didn't know there were wolves in Fey.' Michelline replied.

'There weren't. He was a traveller from this realm.'

161

'A traveller?' said Shayla, very intrigued by this revelation. 'Did he travel between realms, like my mother did?'

Ashling nodded and her face took on a far-away look as she remembered the story her own mother had told her.

'Your great, great grandmother was a guard in the Royal Army.' she began. 'One of her duties was to observe other worlds through the viewing portals and guard the doorway between realms. One of the doorways in this realm had become buried and was believed lost for many years.'

'You mean this world? Here?' Michelline asked.

'Yes.' Ashling replied. 'But some archaeologists had inadvertently uncovered it during a search for an ancient tomb.'

'Did they know it was a gateway between realms?' Shayla asked.

'No, but a few years later, when our grandmother was on duty at the viewing portal, another man kept coming to the doorway, speaking at the stone archway and asking to be heard. He knew exactly what the doorway was and eventually he was granted an audience with the King.'

'The King?' Shayla asked. 'My ancestor?'

'Indeed.' Ashling replied.

'Your grandmother.' Ashling said, looking at Michelline. 'Was charged with escorting him to and from the doorway, as it was her that first noticed him and reported it to the King. In a short time, they got to know one another and fell in love and he asked if he could stay.'

'And it was that simple?' Michelline asked, an edge still in her voice.

'No, it was not that simple. The King refused at first, but the man…'

'Werewolf.' Michelline corrected.

'The werewolf.' Ashling acceded. 'Was from a tribe known as The Enlightened and he pleaded his case that he could be of use to the Fey. Your grandmother also pledged to be responsible for him and after much negotiation and persuasion, the King eventually agreed, but on the condition that he would never be allowed to leave Fey. It was a huge step for the ma…wolf too, as he would be stepping into our past. The arrangement worked out well. The King often sought his counsel and it was thanks to Charlton's writings that we knew how to trap a demon in the pages of a book averting the destruction of our world.'

'So, what? They were married and had a half wolf baby?' asked Michelline.

'Yes, but none of our bloodline has ever reached the critical age of wolf offspring where the change takes over.'

Michelline sat thinking over what her mother had just revealed. Shayla watched both Ashling and Michelline apprehensively.

'I suppose I should be thankful that I didn't change into a wolf when I reached puberty.' Michelline said.

'At least you know your ancestry now.' Shayla ventured.

'It doesn't make me feel any better.' Michelline snapped.

'I don't understand why you're so upset?' Shayla said.

'I've always been proud of my heritage, and considered myself to be full Fey, not some mongrel…'

Michelline slapped her hand over her mouth, but it was too late to take back the words and Shayla looked at her sister, the hurt written all over her face.

'Shayla….I….' Michelline started to say, rising from her seat.

Shayla turned and marched out of the house leaving the door wide open, Titan, who had been waiting patiently for her was instantly at her heel. She got into her car and drove away, tears spilling from her eyes as she drove away from the house, her destination unknown.

'That was unkind.' Ashling said looking at a shame faced Michelline.

'I know.' she whispered.

ICHABOD DAVIS

Ichabod Davis peered at his reflection in the mirror, and decided he was looking tired.

No, I'm looking old. he corrected.

Studying the lines of crow's feet and dark circles under his eyes, he reassessed himself.

'Ichabod.' he said to his reflection. 'You're looking old and tired sunshine.'

He chuckled and smiled at his reflection. Waiting in his dressing room, he felt the familiar flutter of nerves in his stomach, like many frantic butterflies all looking for a way out. He felt this way before every show, even after all these years. He often thought to himself that he should be used to public speaking after nearly thirty years, he supposed that now it was more excitement than nerves, although it was a different story in the beginning.

Looking at his watch, he still had fifteen minutes before his show started and he allowed himself a trip down memory lane.

Ichabod Davis had started his career at the age of seventeen, a fresh-faced boy with curly blond hair, blue eyes, and an engaging, innocent smile. A natural athlete and good with a tennis racket he was quickly noticed by a talent scout and before long he was playing at a professional level, winning championships across the National and International circuit. His career was cut short though by rheumatoid arthritis which caused his joints to flare up in pain and render him unable to walk when the attacks were at their worst. Eventually, Ichabod was forced to retire at the grand old age of twenty-eight.

Retirement was difficult for Ichabod, having spent his teenage years and early twenties as something of a National hero, he found it hard to cope with being yesterday's news and he sank into deep depression, refusing to leave the house for weeks at a time. Unable to cope with his new, ordinary life, Ichabod decided the best course of action for him to take was to have one last holiday before ending, what he considered to be, his worthless life. He sold his house, closed all of his bank accounts except for one, which he planned to use for travelling until his money ran out, and bought an open ticket to travel the world. He estimated the trip would take him approximately six months; it took nine.

Towards the end of his journey and finances, he found himself hiking up a mountain in an obscure part of the world on the recommendation of someone in the nearby Village who insisted that a mystical wise man lived at the top who could reveal the secrets of the universe. Unconvinced, but nonetheless curious, Ichabod hiked for the best part of the day until he reached a small dilapidated cabin near the summit.

He called out to announce his presence, the echo of his voice the only reply. Irritated at his foolishness for believing in a mystical wise man, Ichabod began walking back down the mountain, his feet stomping on the uneven ground causing minute landslides where the stones trickled down the steep rock face. In his carelessness, Ichabod slipped and fell, cracking his head against a rock and passed out.

He woke to find himself lying on a makeshift bed cut from the rock, in a shallow cave, his head wound cleaned and bandaged, a small fire crackling a few feet away from him.

'You took quite a knock to the head.' said a disembodied voice from the shadows.

Ichabod's heart skipped a beat at the sound of the voice and he blinked to see a large man sitting at the fireside whittling something that appeared to be a bone, although his vision was a little blurry and he couldn't be sure. He recalled thinking how could he possibly have missed the man on his first glance around the cave. Even sitting down, Ichabod could see the man had to be over six-feet tall, with broad shoulders and long scruffy hair.

'Thank you for helping me.' Ichabod croaked, his voice dry and hoarse.

The man stopped whittling and put the piece of bone to one side. Leaning forward he poured hot water into a cup and offered it to Ichabod.

'This will help.' the man said offering a cup of hot steaming liquid to Ichabod.

'What is it?' Ichabod asked, sniffing the contents.

'Herbal tea, it has healing properties. It will make you feel better.'

Not wanting to appear ungrateful, Ichabod raised the cup in thanks and drank. The tea was sweet and Ichabod welcomed the warmth on his dry throat.

'Better?' the man asked.

'Much, thank you, Mr?'

'Not important at this time.'

'Thank you anyway.' Ichabod replied and finished his tea.

Both men were silent for a while and Ichabod could feel the warmth of the tea washing through his body, the pounding in his head melting away.

'Suicide isn't the way forward you know?' the man said suddenly.

'Excuse me?' Ichabod replied startled.

'Your destiny lies along a different path.'

'I'm sure I don't know....'

'Sleep now.' said the man, ignoring Ichabod's protests. 'Let the tea take you on a spiritual journey.'

Ichabod could feel his eyes getting heavy.

'What is this….' he began.

'Sleep Ichabod Davis and be awakened.'

The strange man's voice was the last thing he heard before falling into a deep, dream-filled sleep which opened his eyes to reality. In the dream, his consciousness soared high in the sky and glided like a bird of prey across mountains and lakes, fields and cities. It was the most vivid, lucid dream he had ever experienced and to this day, no other dream had been as real to him as that one. He saw the world in its most glorious of colours, as if in the waking world he saw through dull, tinted lenses. He felt, rather than heard a voice telling him that he had become trapped in a world of self-imposed limitations and that he must break free and free the minds of others before it was too late. He recalled calling out to the voice, asking who it was and the voice cryptically replying.

'Your heart knows.'

Ichabod woke from the dream refreshed and free from pain. He must have slept for many hours judging from the cold remnants of the fire and the early grey light of dawn at the mouth of the cave. The mysterious man who had tended his wounds and given him the tea, was gone, the only evidence of him being there was a small carving of an eye, whittled from a piece of bone. Ichabod still had the carving, which he referred to as "the all-seeing eye", and kept it with him, always.

From the time he left the cave on that mountain many decades ago, Ichabod had seen the world with complete clarity. All the colours of nature appeared brighter and more vivid to his newly opened eyes, details he had overlooked now stood out to him, natural fragrances assaulted his senses, intoxicating him with their potency and power. He also saw the poison and corruption of the world as an oily black ooze that permeated into the ground and slithered around the bodies of those most affected. People in positions of power wore their oily black coverings like a second skin, slick tendrils slithering around their bodies and behind their eyes. He saw men change into wolves and wolves change in to men, he saw trees moving as if they were conscious beings and creatures with wings shining brightly in a world being taken over by a dark black cloud that crept across its surface. He saw men and women, their skin white and almost translucent with sharp white fangs, blood running down their chins, he saw insects and bees swirling in a vortex, all being sucked into oblivion, he saw breath-taking beauty and interminable horror. Ichabod could see it clearly; most people could not.

Ichabod's mind and senses were bombarded with information and he spoke out about what he saw, desperate that people should know and understand what was happening around them, but he was ridiculed mercilessly. He lost many friends, the world laughed at him and only one or two people who truly loved him stayed loyal. He could easily have become isolated as he had when his tennis career ended, but this time, as his mind awakened to more knowledge than he could process, he fought back.

His new path, and his vocation began with those few loyal friends in his living room. He told them of his experience in the cave and his awakening dream and they believed him. At first, they believed him because they loved him and wanted to be supportive, but gradually they began to see things around them, exactly as Ichabod described and they knew, in their hearts, that his insight was real and like ripples in a pond, they told others, who told their friends and the number of people awakening to the evil and corruption around them grew exponentially. Within a few years, Ichabod was speaking to larger groups of people in Village halls and more recently in conference centres and stadiums filled with thousands of people, all eager to hear the truth.

The road hadn't been an easy one since his awakening and Ichabod still received emails and letters filled with hate, all of which he shredded, and the press still referred to him as being "barmy" but he knew the campaign to discredit him was borne out of fear, they knew, that he knew, exactly what their agenda was, and they were terrified.

A knock at his dressing room door brought Ichabod back to the present day.

'Come in.' he said, expecting it to be the Stage Manager telling him he had two minutes to get backstage.

Ichabod stood up, straightened his tie in the mirror and turned around as the door opened.

'My goodness!' he exclaimed. 'It's you.'

The stranger who had saved him up on the mountain all those years ago stepped into the room, tall and broad, looking exactly as he had done thirty years previous in the cave.

'Do you know, I often wondered if I had imagined you.' Ichabod said, his hand moving to the whittled bone carving he always carried in his pocket.

'Can you tell me who you are this time?' Ichabod asked with a renewed sense of wonder, if that was at all possible. He had the most powerful feeling that the last thirty years had led him to this point in time and that he had been preparing for this exact moment.

'Call me Fishbone.' said the man.

'Fishbone. Fishbone. Fishbone?' said Ichabod changing the intonation each time.

Fishbone smiled but said nothing.

'This.' said Ichabod, holding up the carving. 'Reminds me that it was all real.'

'You have come a long way since we met all those years ago.' Fishbone replied.

'You saved my life, you know.'

'I set you on your destined path.'

'It's been a tough road.' Ichabod said wearily.

Ichabod turned from Fishbone, suddenly overcome with emotion at the memory of the early years, his eyes pricking with tears.

'The road to the truth is often a dangerous one.' Fishbone said, placing a big hand on Ichabod's shoulder. 'But you are strong, and you have come a long way, but there is more to be done.'

Fishbone took his hand off Ichabod's shoulder as he turned back to face him.

'What do I need to do?' Ichabod asked finally.

'Keep spreading the truth.' Fishbone replied. 'You have reached so many people, hundreds more are waking up every day.'

'But?'

'We are standing at a crossroads.' Fishbone paused. 'The people will need someone like you to show them the way out of the darkness.'

'Is something coming?' Ichabod asked carefully, his stomach knotting with a fear he hadn't experienced for a while.

'All I can say is that the world is heading for a big change and people will be frightened. You must keep reminding them of their limitless potential and be ready to lead them.'

'It sounds big, much bigger than me.' Ichabod said, absently turning the carving over his hand.

'Don't doubt yourself Ichabod.' said Fishbone. 'Look inside yourself, your heart knows.'

Ichabod's memory sparked, he had heard those words before.

'Of all the things I have seen.' Ichabod said. 'You are the greatest enigma of all.'

Fishbone chuckled. 'I am complicated.' he agreed.

Ichabod laughed

'Mr Davis, beginners to stage please.' the Stage Manager said from the open doorway.

'Thank you.' Ichabod replied, turning his head to the Stage Manager and giving him a nod.

When he turned back, Fishbone was gone.

TECHNICAL ISSUES

All aspects of Parallax's plan for total control and world domination were coming together like the threads of an intricately woven tapestry. The demand for the Optimum 10 mobile telephone alone was overwhelming and with more people connecting to the Circle daily, Parallax was in control of over fifty percent of the population. Through the eyes of those he controlled, he looked around and marvelled at how easily the public's attention could be focused on a point of absolutely no relevance whatsoever.

His most recent development was "The Net". Small boxes were delivered free of charge to every home in every city around the world. These boxes contained an antenna which would boost the signal of every electronic device within a two hundred and fifty metre radius. Simple to install, the same antennas were also being fitted to every streetlamp along every street in every suburb and on the rooftops of city centre buildings. Once activated they formed a dense and pervasive network blanketing the area. The excitement from the public was overwhelming and The Net was pulling everyone's attention to the digital screens, either on the television, computer or mobile phones, everyone wanted faster downloads and access to information. The pernicious effect of The Net left the user with a feeling of detachment and a sense of loss. One by one, people were becoming addicted to scrolling through inane lists of information and pictures, the only purpose of which was to make them totally dependent on technology. What people did not know were the devastating effects on their health caused by the output waves of these antennae. When exposed to the millimetre waves from The Net, the human sweat ducts acted as an array of tiny, helix-shaped antennas causing the human skin to amplify the radiation from the network; People were becoming organic antennae.

Parallax intended to use The Net as a weapon and trials had proven very successful. A focused beam of millimetre waves transmitted from the antennae could penetrate the surface of the skin causing a stinging and burning sensation. When the strength of the wave increased intense burning and blistering occurred and many unfortunate trial subjects had suffered third-degree burns. Longer term exposure to the waves produced heart problems, cataracts and immune system suppression. It as an excellent method of crowd control and domination and Parallax intended to make full use of it.

Citizens spent their entire working day in front of a computer, then their bus or train journeys home looking at the personal info-pads or mobile phones and finally, after a microwaved meal filled with addictive toxins, they would sit in front of their Adroit TV's with a glass of narcotic laced wine and stare at the screens, oblivious to the subliminal messages

Parallax was transmitting right into their homes. They were like sheep, eager to enter the slaughterhouse.

It was all too easy, and Parallax took a vainglorious moment to bask in his master stroke of genius.

Teenagers and young people were his eyes and ears to the world. They sat together in small groups, none of them speaking to each other, all sitting side by side, sending virtual messages, or listening to music through their headphones. They were the easiest to control, all of them wanted to have the latest device and most of them were eager for the implantable microchips that would make their lives even better, or so they believed.

Surprisingly, the older generation were eager for technology, grandparents wanted to appear up to date and cool to their grandchildren and virtually every octogenarian had a personal bespoke info-pad to monitor their vital signs and inform their Doctor of any changes. All of this technology was sold under the premise of safety and caring. The Info-pad connected to the body by a cuff wrapped around the wrist and calculated the exact medication and dosage necessary for each individual, taking decisions away from the Medical Professionals and thus eliminating the "human error factor". Parallax was medicating people to ensure their compliance, regardless of the ill-effects to their already weakened immune systems. Focus groups of all ages were trialling the new "Medipatch". Affixed directly to the skin the Medipatch monitored vital signs. Crammed full of Nanotek and working at twice the speed and efficiency, the patches would eventually replace the info-pads in hospitals and homes.

Parallax tightened his grip by ensuring all naturally growing herbs and plants were illegal to grow, buy and sell. This was easily accomplished through a string of various politicians representing all parties and he filled the media with propaganda about the dangers of uncontrolled substances and holistic medicine. Of course, there were pockets of resistance, but once his Nanotek Programme was executed they would be subdued like the rest of the world.

With preparations for the final phase underway, Parallax flexed his unfathomable intellect and watched his world take shape.

* * * * *

Janet Brennan knew all about the effects of pharmaceuticals. She saw on a daily basis, people reduced to an almost catatonic state due to their cocktail of medication, which they would insist upon taking out of fear of the unknown instilled by the bias media. She had chosen a career where she could help people and nurse them back to health, something that was becoming increasingly difficult.

Checking the time on her new Optimum 10 watch, Janet signed off her computer and headed for the staff room to collect her belongings. She had just finished a long shift and was looking forward to putting her feet up. Her daughter Lori and Lori's best friend, Milly, had offered to cook dinner for her as a special treat as it was her birthday. Although Janet didn't feel much like celebrating, her head was pounding, and she closed her eyes and squeezed them tightly and rubbed her temples, trying to relieve the tension. Her migraines were becoming more intense and frequent and Janet glanced at the new Medipatch fixed to the inside of her forearm and wondered whether it was actually helping. One of the Doctors on at the hospital had encouraged her to join the focus group and try it. He claimed it would detect the early signs of a migraine and administer a small dose of preventative medication but so far Janet had only noticed an increase in the migraine attacks and not the cure. She told herself that perhaps the migraines would be worse without the Medipatch and made a mental note to speak to the Doctor the next time she saw him.

Her headache worsened on the journey home and by the time she parked her car on the drive, Janet felt nauseous and light-headed.

Damn this headache! Janet thought, getting out of the car.

The evening was grey and gloomy with a light drizzle, the sort of rain that clung to clothing and soaked through in minutes and Janet hurried into the house, her collar turned up to stop the cold raindrops running down the back of her neck.

'Hi Mum.' Lori called from the kitchen when she heard the door open.

'Hi Mrs B.' Milly chimed in.

Bert, the dog, now in his eleventh year, bounded up to her with the enthusiasm of a puppy and greeted her in his usual affectionate way and Janet bent down to ruffle his fur and scratch him behind the ears and to receive obligatory licks to her hands and face.

Lori leaned back from the hob where she was stirring a pan of simmering tomato and pasta sauce, to look at her mother.

'Mum? Are you alright, you don't look well?'

'It's just a headache.' Janet said, standing up 'I'll take…….'

Janet collapsed before she could finish her sentence.

'Mum!!' Lori screamed, dropping the spoon into the pan and running to her mother, Milly right behind her.

'Mum?' Lori repeated, shaking her mother gently, then more vigorously.

Bert whined and moved to one side to watch proceedings, his eyes fixed on Janet.

'Stop shaking her!' Milly said firmly, taking charge. 'She needs help.'

'I'll call an ambulance.' Lori said taking her mobile phone out of her pocket.

'That'll take too long.' Milly replied. 'I'll call my step-mother, she's a Doctor, can I use your phone?'

Lori handed Milly her phone and Milly stood a few steps away and pretended to call her step-mother. Instead, she communicated with Uri through the wolf pack's telepathic link.

Uri, something's wrong, can you come over, it's urgent.

With the dog?

No, Lori's Mum.

Call a people doctor.

That'll take too long, besides there's something not right with her.

Explain.

She's infected with something, not organic. I don't know what it is, please?

Very well.

'Thanks Uri.' Milly said aloud for Lori's benefit. 'See you soon.'

Returning to where Lori sat beside the prone body of Janet, Milly put her arms underneath the woman who had become a good friend and accepted her into their family without question and gently lifted her off the floor. Lori always marvelled at how strong Milly was in spite of her petite frame.

'Lori, can you move those cushions?' Milly said nodding towards the sofa. 'She'll be more comfortable on there.'

Milly laid Janet gently on the sofa and Lori put a cushion under her head. Bert was pacing up and down in front of the sofa, whining softly, his canine senses detecting something was wrong. Unable to contain himself any longer, he leapt up onto the sofa and sat at Janet's feet.

'Mrs B?' Milly said quietly, rubbing the back of Janet's hand as Lori held the other. 'Janet.'

'Mmm…..' Janet groaned.

'She's waking up.' Lori said, the relief evident in her voice.

A knock at the front door indicated Uri's arrival and Milly went to the door, leaving Lori with Janet who was slowly regaining consciousness.

'Lori?' Janet said, her voice shaking. 'What happened?'

'You fainted.' Lori replied, kissing her mother on the forehead.

In the hallway and out of earshot, Milly spoke quietly to Uri.

'You know very well I'm not a people Doctor.' Uri said irritably.

'But you're a healer and the only one I trust.' Milly replied. 'You were quick getting here.'

'I was already in the City.'

'Doing what?'

Uri gave Milly a withering look.

'Having tea with Father Thomas, if you must know.'

'He's not really Thomas, he's Michael.'

Uri gave Milly another look which told her not to pursue the topic and Milly was astute enough to drop it.

'Tell me what you suspect.' Uri said taking off her coat and handing it to Milly.

'I'm sure she's infected with something, but it doesn't smell like a normal infection, or disease, it's…'

'Corrupted?'

'Yes, it's different than anything I've encountered.'

'I think I know what it is.' Uri said firmly. 'Let me see her.'

Milly led Uri into the living room where Janet was now sitting on the sofa, fully awake. Bert barked once at Uri who stared at him, unblinking. Uri's gaze met the dogs and for a few moments they simply stared at one another until Bert bowed his head as Uri nodded. Janet's hand went instinctively to his head and stoked his fur.

'I'm sorry to put you to any trouble.' Janet began, flustered and a little embarrassed. 'I fainted, that's all, long shift……er….I'm probably hungry and um….may be tired…..you know.'

'It's no trouble.' Uri said, all trace of irritability gone from her voice. 'Has your dog been ill?'

'He had some tummy trouble.' Janet said reaching out for Bert who obediently came to her and proceeded to lick her hand. 'But the Vet gave us some pills for him and he's a lot better now, why do you ask?'

'I thought Milly called you to look at Mum!' Lori said tersely, her voice becoming a little shrill.

Uri took a deep breath to control her temper, which was easily aroused by humans.

'Let me take a quick look at you Janet.' Uri said, ignoring Lori.

'Dr Farseer, isn't it?' Janet asked. 'Milly's mother.'

'That's right.'

Uri nodded and inhaled deeply through her nose giving the impression she was composing herself. In reality, she was using her highly sensitive nostrils to locate the source of Janet's infection. She was old enough and wise enough to know that putting her nose next to Janet's skin and sniffing would arouse suspicion as well as appearing odd. The information she had gleaned from Bert the dog matched up with what she now knew was the problem.

'This.' Uri said holding up Janet's right hand and pointing to the Optimum 10 watch. 'Is part of the problem.'

'What? How?'

Janet looked shocked and stared at her new watch blankly. Uri pushed Janet's sleeve up to the elbow revealing the Medipatch.

'And this.' Uri said pointing to the Medipatch. 'Is the other part of the problem. Why do you wear it?'

'I'm part of a focus group.' Janet said.

'A what?'

'A few of us were offered the chance to trial these new Medipatches.' Janet replied. 'It's full of microscopic technology that, in my case, detects the early signs of a migraine and administers a dose of medication to prevent it.'

'And how is that working out?' Uri asked.

'I don't think it is.' Janet said, her eyes filling with tears. 'I've been feeling dreadful and only today I thought that maybe it was making things worse. The headaches are more frequent.'

'And more intense?' Uri said.

'Yes! How did you know?'

How to explain this to a regular person. Uri thought to herself.

'There is a fault with the patches and these devices.' Uri said confidently, taking the watch off Janet's wrist and handing it to Milly.

'Hold still.' Uri said

Janet complied, and Uri looked at the Medipatch. It was firmly embedding itself into the skin, but Uri managed to lift one corner of the Medipatch with the tip of her sharp nail and quickly pulled the strip from Janet's arm. Beneath the patch a bright red outline remained which immediately began to itch.

'Don't scratch it!' Uri commanded as Janet moved her other hand to the injury site. 'These things are on trial without any evidence of their effectiveness and it seems to me that it's been overdosing you on medication which instead of preventing the migraines, it's been making them worse.'

'Is this an allergic reaction?' Janet asked looking at the red outline on her skin.

'Quite possibly.' Uri replied.

Uri looked at Janet's arm and inhaled again.

'There's no sign of infection, your body will heal itself now that the patch is gone. Milly, take the watch and the patch and destroy them both.'

'No!' Janet said, horrified. 'Get rid of the patch but the watch was my birthday present, to myself, it was quite expensive.'

'I'm sorry.' Uri said. 'But these things are faulty and are causing health problems.'

Janet looked sceptical but said nothing.

'The fault lies with the manufacturer.' Uri lied. 'These watches emit radiation that seeps into your body through your skin making you sick.'

'I've never heard anything about that.' Lori said suspiciously.

'Why would you? You are neither a Doctor or a Scientist.' Uri replied acerbically. 'It also gives off a very high-pitched tone, which is probably why your canine has been ill.'

'Really?' Janet said, more concerned for Bert than herself. 'I had no idea, but it's such a shame to destroy it. What if I stopped wearing it all day and only wore it on special occasion?'

Uri sighed; there was only one thing to be done.

'Both of you, please listen to me.' Uri said to Lori and Janet. 'Lori, will you sit beside your mother and I will explain.'

Milly, take this device outside and destroy it completely, it's listening to us.

Milly took the watch and left the room as instructed and Lori sat next to Janet on the sofa and continued to hold her hand. Bert sat obediently at Janet's feet, also paying attention to Uri; he seemed completely fascinated by her.

Uri knelt in front of them, her gaze intense and her voice low.

'The device has been sending signals to your brain, making you sick. Do you understand?'

Lori and Janet nodded mechanically, both held by Uri's gaze and hypnotic voice.

'You will no longer crave the latest technology.' Uri said.

'Technology.' they replied in unison.

'You will enjoy simple pleasures, such as walking with your dog and enjoying all that nature offers around you.'

'Walking, nature.' Lori and Janet repeated.

'You will seek out alternative natural healing and discover the benefits of holistic medicine'

'Healing.'

'You need to learn the old skills, this is important.'

Lori and Janet nodded.

'You will not remember this conversation.' Uri concluded, breaking eye contact.

Lori and Janet blinked and looked at each other.

'As I was saying.' Uri said, back to her usual efficient self. 'Some rest and plenty of fresh air, and this.'

Uri handed a small twist of paper containing a mixture of small leaves and herbs.

'This special blend of herbal tea has wonderful healing properties. Drink this and get some rest and you should start to feel much better. Plenty of fresh air will help. Long walks with the dog, maybe some wild swimming.'

'Wild swimming?' Janet asked.

'Rivers and such like.' said Uri. 'There are several books on where to find these hidden places. There are some beautiful places to discover. Your dog will love it too.'

Uri looked at Bert who had been sitting quietly since her arrival and gently touched his face. She looked into his eyes and communicated that his human was going to be fine and that he was a good boy, he wagged his tail appreciatively.

'Magnets are especially good for healing.' Uri said. 'Get yourself a bracelet with at least ten strong magnets in it, the more the better and wear it every day.'

'Magnets?' Lori asked.

'The body has electromagnetic energy and a magnetic bracelet will help to keep your body in balance.' Uri said.

'Thank you Doctor.' Janet said, taking the small packet of tea from Uri.

'I'll see myself out.'

Milly walked Uri to the door.

'Did you destroy those things?' Uri whispered.

'Yes, it's done.' Milly replied opening her hand to show Uri the powdered remains of the watch which she had crushed in her right hand.

'And the patch?'

'I ground it under my heel and put the bits in the bin outside.'

'Good girl.'

Milly pressed her foot on the pedal of the waste bin to open the lid and dusted her hands to remove the remnants of the watch.

'What are these things?' Milly asked.

'The latest creations from the digital entity I've been telling you about, it was transmitting signals to Janet's brain. The patch was overdosing her on medication. If this thing can't control you, it kills you. It would seem that Janet was not that easy to control, so it was trying to kill her instead. This thing is worse than we thought.'

Uri looked thoughtful and worried.

'Will magnets help?' Milly asked.

'They'll help to negate all of the technology around her and put her body back into a natural balance.'

'What did you do to them in there?' Milly asked curiously.

'Just a little coersion.' Uri replied, waving her hand dismissively.

'Can all wolves do that? Can you teach me?' Milly asked enthusiastically.

'It's a skill all wolves can learn and use, but we don't use it often. Now, I must be going. Make sure they drink that tea.'

'Is it Luminosa?'

Uri nodded. 'It will heal their brains. They have been slowly poisoned by the chemicals they've been ingesting for years in the food and water and it will awaken them, make them question things a bit more. Oh, and get rid of the dog's medication, there's nothing wrong with him. He probably ate some leftovers that upset his digestion and if they knew what was in their food, they wouldn't eat it either.'

'Thanks, Uri.' Milly said hugging her tightly.

'Yes, yes.' Uri squeezed Milly briefly, unaccustomed to human style displays of affection.

Holding Milly at arm's length, Uri studied the young wolf.

'You're a good cub.' Uri said. 'You have a caring heart and I think you are ready.'

'Ready for what?'

'I will begin training you as a healer, if that is something you would like?'

'I would like that.' Milly said kissing Uri's cheek.

'And later perhaps the coersion and how to commune with the spirits of our ancestors. It's a lot of work, you will have to pay attention, and do as I say.'

'I always do as you say.' Milly said smiling. 'I'll be a good student, I promise.'

'Hmmm.' Uri replied as she left. 'We'll see.'

Milly closed the door and returned to the living room, relieved to see that Janet was looking much better. Bert was also bouncing around, obviously relieved that his mistress was awake and feeling better.

'Now then, how about something to eat and a cup of that new tea?' Milly said cheerfully.

As if in response to her question, Janet's stomach growled loudly in hunger and she blushed, Lori giggled.

'I'd say that's a definite yes!' Milly laughed.

DOUBLE EDGED SWORD

Flint sat staring into his cup of coffee, the contents of which had gone cold, thinking about everything he had discovered concerning the Parallax and the Ophidians and what a terrible mess they were making of the world. He was a descendant of the Enlightened and whilst his tribe had always lived alongside humans and embraced engineering and technological advances, the agenda of these two entities was beyond insane, unless of course, total annihilation was the real end game. He supposed the Parallax had no use for food and water and therefore a totally digital world would be no inconvenience, but what of the Ophidians? They were organic and required some sustenance surely?

The tinkling of the bell above the door signalled the entrance of someone into the café and Flint looked up to see Michelline, whom he had arranged to meet, and he stood to greet her, smoothing down the front of his newly pressed shirt, as she made her way over to the little table by the window.

'Am I late?' Michelline asked glancing at her watch.

'No, I'm always early.' Flint replied with a nervous smile. 'Can I get you a coffee?'

'Mint tea if they have it please.'

'You look nice.' Flint said shyly, taking in Michelline's pale green blouse and blue skinny jeans that showed off the shape of her body.

'Thank you.' she blushed. 'So do you.'

Flint shrugged. It had been some time since he had been out on a date and he wasn't used to compliments.

'Please have a seat.' Flint gestured to the empty seat at the table. 'I'll get you some tea.'

Michelline looked at Flint as he walked to the counter to order the tea. He stood tall, like all of the wolves she had met, and she wondered whether she had the same inner strength they seemed to possess, now that she knew she had wolf DNA.

Flint returned a few minutes later with a hot cup of peppermint tea and a fresh black coffee for himself. He sat opposite Michelline, his back to the room so that she had his full attention. It was also a natural position for him to assume. As a wolf, it was instinctive for him to place himself in the position offering the most protection.

'Thanks for coming.' Flint said. 'It's nice to see you again. You look really lovely, I don't get to meet new people very often.'

'Thanks.' Michelline said blushing, pleased that she had bought the new blouse for her date. 'I know what you mean. It's my pleasure. I'd like to get to know you too.'

'Oh, did you want something to eat?' Flint said concerned that in his nervousness, he had forgotten to offer.

'No thanks, I'm fine.'

Michelline lifted the cup to her lips and feeling the steam touch the tip of her nose, decided it was still too hot, and set the cup back down on the table to cool.

'I was watching you from outside.' Michelline said. 'You looked miles away.'

'I was thinking about...' Flint hesitated. 'Well, everything really.'

'The entity?'

'And the Ophidians. It's hard to wrap my head around it.'

'Tell me your thoughts.' Michelline said. 'Sometimes talking it through helps set your mind in order.'

'Not a very interesting subject to talk about for a first date.' said Flint, the corner of his mouth turning up into a smile.

Michelline's heart beat a little faster as Flint smiled at her, and impulsively, she reached across the table putting her hand on his and looking into his light blue eyes.

'We can talk about other stuff on our second date.' Michelline said confidently.

'Deal.' Flint said putting his other hand on top of hers and giving her the full effect of his bright smile.

'I understand the motivation of the Parallax.' Flint began. 'The program has obviously evolved and become self-aware and wants to escape the confines of the digital world. It's obviously using micro-technology to infiltrate and control people so that it can experience new things.'

'I agree, but then what?' Michelline asked, steepling her hands in front of her and resting her chin on her fingers. 'With its superior intellect, it's bound to get bored once there's nothing new left to try'

'I assume it will destroy everything it sees as inferior.' Flint replied.

'Then it will be alone.'

'You're thinking as a creature with a soul, not a machine, things like loneliness wouldn't bother it.'

'OK.' said Michelle thoughtfully, taking sip of her tea. 'The Parallax is relatively easy to understand. It's a computer program that will follow a certain pattern and that means there's an order to things, it won't have a sense of morality governing its actions.'

'Ah, you say that' said Flint 'but the experiences it has through humans will result in information being transferred to the brain, the body's hard-drive, which will then be uploaded to the collective consciousness of the Parallax. It could easily understand good and bad and maybe even understand the chemicals produced and the information that's processed as a result of different emotions.'

'Don't say that.' Michelline shuddered and paused. 'A machine which could actually enjoy being evil, that's enough to give me nightmares.'

'Me too.' Flint replied drinking his coffee.

'It has to be destroyed.' Michelline said firmly.

'Definitely, but maybe we should discuss that later at the meeting.' Flint said casting a wary eye over the patrons of the café. 'The scary thing is, Parallax is everywhere, phones, TV's, computers and is probably listening to us.'

Suddenly feeling paranoid, Michelline followed Flint's gaze around the café and watched the patrons talking on their mobile phones or playing games on their personal devices.

'Another tea?' Flint asked drawing her attention back to him.

'I'm still drinking this one.' Michelline replied.

'Oh! Right.' Flint laughed nervously.

'You're not used to this whole dating thing, are you?' Michelline said squeezing his hand.

'It's been a while.'

'Don't let me stop you getting another coffee.'

Flint went to the counter and returned a few minutes later with his coffee and two large slices of cake. Michelline raised one eyebrow at him.

'I couldn't resist.' Flint said shyly. 'It's homemade lemon drizzle cake and it looked so....'

'Yummy?'

'I can change it, if you don't like lemon.'

'I love lemon.' Michelline enthused.

'Me too. This is Suzie's homemade baking at its finest.' Flint said handing a plate to Michelline. 'All of her cakes are freshly baked and when she brought it out, well...I just had to.'

Flint had been at the counter waiting to pay for his coffee when the zingy, zesty aroma of fresh lemons assailed his nostrils and he knew that Suzie was on her way out of the kitchen with a freshly baked cake. Every time he caught the scent of food he wondered what it must be like for regular humans, their sense of smell fourteen times less powerful than his own. Did they really appreciate the aromas around them?

'You can really smell the lemon in this.' Michelline said inhaling appreciatively.

'Mmmm...gorgeous.' Flint said taking a large forkful of the lemon cake.

'Thanks, you too.' Michelline replied, winking at him, a shy grin spreading across his face as he ate his cake.

They both laughed and turned their attention to the cake

'Talk to me about the Ophidians.' Michelline said at last. 'Hideous creatures.'

'I agree.' Flint said, his eyes looking down at his cake.

Michelline looked at Flint's long white eyelashes, then at his pure white hair which he was wearing tied back into a ponytail. His hair reminded her of an arctic hare she had once seen in a picture, and she longed to untie the ponytail and run her fingers through his hair to see if it was as soft and silky as it looked. Staring at Flint's head, she was suddenly aware that he had started speaking again and was now looking directly at her with his pale ice blue eyes.

'I've been wondering lately just how far back their infiltration of the humans goes.'

'Do you mean the hybrids?' she asked.

Flint nodded, his thoughts returning to the extensive research he had done. He was certain they were responsible for the worldwide pollution among a variety of other things.

'I think.' he seemed to pause for a second. 'I think it's best we talk about this sort of stuff later at the meeting.' Flint said, cautiously looking around the café again.

Michelline followed his gaze. The café was fairly busy with a variety of people, most of them had mobile phones. On the next table, the man working industriously on his laptop barely seemed to notice his surroundings, but the technology was everywhere.

'I agree.' Michelline said, returning to the conversation. 'There's not much to choose between the Parallax or the Ophidians. They're like a double-edged sword. Lethal either way.'

'Anyway.' Flint said taking Michelline's hand. 'I want to know more about you. What's your favourite colour? Do you prefer walking or going to see a movie? That kind of stuff.'

'Blue and walking.' Michelline said with a smile.

'Blue eh?'

'Like your eyes.' she replied. 'Do they stay blue?'

Flint frowned slightly.

'When you change?' she whispered.

'Oh.' he said quietly. 'No, mine turn red.'

'Really?' Michelline replied, staring into Flint's eyes fascinated.

Flint looked back at Michelline, the feeling of familiarity coming to him again.

'What is it?' she asked self-consciously.

'Your eyes.' Flint said.

'Are they crossed?'

'No.' Flint laughed. 'They remind me....'

'Old girlfriend?' Michelline said feeling a momentary stab of jealousy.

'No.' Flint said thinking back to the gathering at Mandlebury Henge. 'The Ophidian said you were part wolf, which is true, I can sense it.'

'Yes, I know.' Michelline said quietly. 'I didn't want to believe it at first, but my mother told me a few things about my great grandparents, which was quite a revelation.'

'Being a wolf is nothing to be ashamed of.' Flint said, a little more sharply than he intended.

'I'm not ashamed.' Michelline said quickly reaching out to touch his hand. 'It's just that when mother told me the truth, we ended up fighting and I said a few hurtful things to her and my sister. I still feel bad about it.'

'I'm sure they've forgiven you.' Flint said, gently squeezing her hand. 'Siblings are always fighting in a pack.'

'We're not a pack.'

'You're a family, aren't you?' Flint asked.

Michelline nodded.

'To a wolf, pack is family and family is pack. So, fighting is a natural, everyday occurrence.' he said matter-of-factly.

'That makes me feel a bit better about it.'

'What do you know about him?' Flint asked.

'I'm sorry, who?' Michelline said a little bewildered.

Flint lowered his voice and moved closer across the table to whisper in Michelline's ear.

'Your ancestor, the wolf.' he said, his warm breath tickling her ear, sending shivers down her spine.

'Why do you say him? Maybe it was a female.' Michelline bantered.

'Unlikely.'

'I don't know very much actually.' Michelline said feeling embarrassed. 'I was too angry to ask for details, but my great grandfather was apparently called Charlton and he was a wolf.'

Flint stood up suddenly, drained the last of his coffee and offered his hand to Michelline.

'What!' Michelline exclaimed. 'Did I say something wrong?'

'Come with me.' Flint said enthusiastically. 'Let's take a walk, I have something to show you and something to tell you. You'll be blown away.'

'OK.' Michelline said tentatively taking Flint's outstretched hand.

This date is getting more and more interesting. she thought.

'We mustn't be late for the meeting.' Michelline cautioned.

'We won't.'

* * * * *

Parallax watched and listened through every electronic device in the café, adjusting the settings inside every mobile telephone to amplify the recording capabilities and activating the internal camera on the laptop being used by the businessman at the adjoining table; he hadn't missed a single thing Flint and Michelline had said. He wondered what they were planning and felt the human emotion of annoyance at their cryptic references to a secret meeting. The feeling was brief, he had access to traffic cameras and almost everyone carried a mobile telephone, he would simply follow them. He scoffed at the thought of their secret meeting.

There isn't a place on this whole world I cannot access. he thought arrogantly.

* * * * *

As they left the café, Flint grabbed Michelline's hand and hurried them along the main street.

'What is it?' Michelline asked.

Flint glanced at her and almost imperceptibly shook his head in warning and looked up, drawing Michelline's attention to the camera on the top of the nearby pedestrian crossing. Michelline nodded her understanding and remained silent. Her questions would keep.

Parallax turned the traffic camera back to its original position and moved the security camera on the next building to watch the man and woman as they made their way along the street. They were in a hurry and he wanted to know where they were going. They had spoken of a meeting but failed to mention where. The lack of verbal information was irrelevant, Parallax was able to see and hear everything, their destination would reveal itself, nothing was secret or private anymore.

Flint and Michelline made their way towards Oak Wood Cemetery, heading for the crypt of Lemington Street. The crypt, re-discovered over twenty-five years ago, was actually an underground bunker, the builders of which still remained a mystery. The bunker had been used by the group who fought against the Shadow Lord, for protection and later as a temporary shelter. It was still the most secure and secret facility, unknown to humans. There were also no security cameras watching the cemetery, only the outer wall was captured by the cameras on the neighbouring buildings.

As Flint and Michelline walked through the entrance gate into the cemetery, Parallax lost sight of them as if they had walked into a thick bank of fog. He turned to other cameras nearby, but his view was obstructed by the fog that shrouded the whole of the cemetery. The perimeter of the cemetery omitted a signal that was both unseen and unheard, but effectively interfered with any surveillance cameras nearby; another mystery about the builders of the bunker that waited to be solved. Unwilling to accept that he may have been thwarted, Parallax accessed the mobile phone of a man who was passing by the cemetery but only received the white noise of static. Angry, he sent a high-pitched tone into the mobile phone he was accessing and in a split second, the man who had been talking to his girlfriend suddenly collapsed to the floor, holding the side of his head as the sound ripped through his eardrum and sent agonising, stabbing pains into his brain before rendering him unconscious. Whether the man lived or died was immaterial to Parallax, he merely turned his attention to other technology surrounding Oak Wood Cemetery, determined to discover what was happening.

When they reached the crypt of Lemington Street, Flint stopped and turned to Michelline.

'I think it's safe enough to talk now.' Flint said.

'Are you sure?' Michelline asked, looking around at the new and ancient headstones that surrounded them.

'Yes, this whole area is shielded, can you feel it?'

'Not really.' Michelline said, still looking around. 'But I'll take your word for it.'

Reaching into his jacket pocket, Flint retrieved an envelope and held it out to Michelline.

'Open it.' Flint said encouragingly. 'It's a letter I received from my old mentor many years ago. I think you'll find it interesting.'

Michelline took it and noticed the old postal date and carefully extracted the letter and unfolded it. The letter had been read and folded and re-read many times, the creases in the paper were firmly imbedded. Michelline read the hand-written letter and looked up at Flint, her eyes wide.

'Charlton!' she said incredulously.

Flint nodded.

'It can't be a coincidence.' Michelline said, reading the letter again.

'It's not.' Flint replied. 'My old mentor went back in time, into a parallel universe and started a new life.'

'Wow.'

'With your great grandmother, it would seem.' Flint continued. 'I knew there was something familiar about you. It's your eyes, you have Charlton's eyes.'

'I don't know what to say.' Michelline said, smiling. 'You can tell me more about my ancestor than anyone.'

'He was a great wolf.' Flint said. 'I'd love to tell you all about him, but we'd better get to the meeting.'

Michelline handed the letter back to Flint.

'You keep it.' he said, wrapping his hand around hers. 'It feels right that you should have it.'

'Why have you carried it around with you for so long?'

'It was all I had. It reminded me that there was a time when I hadn't been alone in the world, and I suppose I wanted to keep it close.'

'And now?' Michelline asked tentatively, her heart racing.

'Now, I'd like to think I have you.'

Michelline hesitated. This was their first date and Flint was moving fast, but she felt drawn to him and if recent information was correct, it could be the end of the world.

'Am I moving too fast?' Flint asked as if reading her mind.

'A little.' Michelline replied.

'Wolves know when they've met the one they want to be with and I don't want to scare you away, but I feel that you're the one for me. I'm sorry if I'm racing ahead.'

'I'm usually the first one to jump in at the deep end.' Michelline said. 'You've taken me by surprise that's all.'

Flint struggled to think of something to say, instead he moved in closer to Michelline and kissed her.

They were still wrapped in an embrace when Flint's wolf senses detected the presence of another wolf close by. Pulling back from the kiss and moving slightly in front of Michelline, Flint looked towards the soft sound of footsteps and saw Titan walking in front of Shayla, both of them heading for the meeting. Michelline felt Flint relax at the sight of her sister and Titan. Titan slowed as he approached Flint and gave him a cursory glance before moving on.

'Now who's keeping secrets?' Shayla said playfully, winking at her sister.

'I'm not.....we....' Michelline flustered.

'Come on, you can fill me in later.' said Shayla. 'We'd better not be late.'

Titan led the way into the crypt, followed by Shayla and Michelle. Flint took a final look around, still marvelling at the mystery and power of the place before proceeding down into the meeting room.

Peter walked to Shayla as she entered the room and hugged her.

'Missed you.' Peter whispered in her ear, before stepping back.

He looked at Flint and Michelline appraisingly and raised a quizzical eyebrow to Shayla, who merely shrugged.

'Now that we're all here, we can begin.' Fishbone said authoritatively.

The latest arrivals took a seat at a round table and Fishbone waited until they were all settled. There were eight of them all together, including Fishbone. Peter and Uri, Shayla and Michelline, Father Michael, Flint and a new face only Fishbone and Michael recognised, but whose name would be familiar to all. Everyone looked at the stranger sitting upright at the table, his dark, almost black, intelligent eyes taking the measure of each and every one of them. He resembled an undertaker in his black formal suit, white shirt and slim black tie.

Fishbone remained standing.

'We are joined here today' Fishbone began. 'by Azrael.'

'Azrael?' Peter exclaimed.

'The Angel of Death?' Uri added.

'That's an incorrect assumption.' Father Michael said firmly.

'I prefer the term, the one who the Divine helps.' Azrael said in his clear, calm, smooth baritone voice.

'What are you doing here?' Peter asked.

'We'll get to that Peter.' Fishbone interjected.

Peter nodded his acknowledgement.

'Now then.' Fishbone began again. 'If you will all listen for a moment and not all talk at once, which you are fond of doing much too frequently, I might add, everything will be explained to you.'

Satisfied that everyone was listening, Fishbone continued.

'I've asked you all to come here today to talk about the Parallax and how much of a threat this digital entity is and what we're going to do about it.'

Clearing his throat, Fishbone addressed them collectively.

'You've probably heard of Ichabod Davis.'

'Yes.' Peter said. 'The stuff he's been saying about the destruction of the natural world is spot on. The wolves have been fighting for years to keep the balance, but it's becoming increasingly difficult with the constant encroachment into our territories and the blanket spraying of pesticides on the forests. Most people think he's crazy.'

'Not so many as you think.' said Father Michael. 'It's taken him decades, but people are starting to listen and are questioning things.'

'It's about time!' Uri said irritably.

'What I was leading to' Fishbone said. 'Is that people are waking up, and have started protesting against the big companies who are trying to destroy the forests and green spaces.'

'Isn't that a good thing?' Shayla asked.

'It is.' Fishbone replied. 'But many of the protestors seem to get arrested and, well, go missing.'

'What has that got to do with the Parallax?' Michelline asked.

Fishbone sighed; as always there were more questions than answers. Sensing his impatience, Father Michael stood up.

'Perhaps you should all just listen, and I will explain everything we have discovered about the Parallax. If you have any questions, you can ask them when I am finished, otherwise this meeting will take twice as long. Agreed?'

Fishbone smiled his thanks at Michael and sat down.

'What we have discovered.' Michael began. 'Is the Parallax has gained control of certain people, which has led to control of more people and consequently companies and so on and so forth. Through this network, he has begun a campaign of change, which will result in a completely digital world.'

'How has he gained control?' Peter asked.

'I will explain Peter.' Michael replied. 'Please keep your questions until the end.'

'Yes, of course. My apologies.'

Michael explained that the events he was about to describe were not random, but all pieces of the same puzzle. He began by talking about the latest vaccine programmes that were injecting microscopic technology into the body, piggy-backing on the strains of the virus it was purporting to be protecting against. Several members of the group wanted to ask questions but held back following a look from Fishbone.

Next, he spoke about their discovery of plans to change the treatment and purification of all drinking water. Nanotek would be put into the reservoir under the guise of destroying all bacteria. In actuality, the microscopic computer chips would enter the food chain and people would be ignorantly ingesting the control systems through their tap water.

'But what about the Aquanar?' Uri said, unable to hold back her question. 'There's a whole colony living under the waters at Berrymead Reservoir, they'll never be able to stand that kind of invasion, they'll be killed!'

'I think that's the point.' Fishbone said. 'This Parallax wants to destroy everything it cannot control.'

'I didn't think he knew about the Aquanar.' Uri said.

'He doesn't, but it gets worse.' Michael said dismally.

'How much worse?' Peter asked.

Michael looked at Fishbone who nodded.

'We have recently discovered that the City intends to level Mandlebury Henge and great swathes of land on Granite Moor to make way for huge digital antennae which will boost the wireless signal of the network.'

'They can't do that! Granite Moor is a protected area.' Shayla said. 'Nothing is allowed to be built on it, or anything done to spoil the natural wilderness of the Moor.'

'That's irrelevant.' Michael said. 'Parallax controls the local Government and his puppets have already approved the plans. Work will begin in the next few months.'

'No!' Shayla replied dismayed.

'I'm sorry Shayla, but it's true.' Michael said gently. 'Not only that.'

'How much worse can it be?' said Shayla.

'All playgrounds and green space in the City are to be used for the building of new homes, all digitally interfaced.'

'Even Wolford Park?' Peter asked.

Michael nodded; Peter put his head in his hands.

'People won't stand for it.' Shayla said firmly. 'They'll rise up and protest.'

'People don't care.' Uri said sharply. 'Most people care only about themselves and what they want. Why do you think there are so few wolves left? We've been hunted mercilessly for years for sport, our homes destroyed for no good reason, only to satisfy the needs of selfish people who want to have fun. If it wasn't for the fact that this Parallax threatens our kind, I would say the people can go to oblivion!'

'Uri.' said Peter firmly. 'That's enough. Let Michael continue.'

'Thank you.' Michael said, taking a deep breath before continuing. 'Parallax is also promoting digital interfacing everywhere, eliminating the need for the written word.'

'Once people are connected to the digital network they lose themselves little by little.' said Fishbone. 'Anyone, or any group of people resisting the implanting, or digital interfacing is being targeted as a threat. Buildings set on fire, people getting hurt, that sort of thing, like that awful business at the Chequer Corporation.'

'You mean that was the Parallax?' Flint asked.

'I thought that was a disgruntled employee who set the fire?' said Michelline.

'The official story, that you can read in the media.' Fishbone said. 'Is that a disgruntled employee, suffering from mental illness, arrived at work one day with a semi-automatic weapon, shot twelve people before blowing himself up, destroying the first floor of the building and killing about eighty co-workers in the process.'

'And the real story?' Flint asked.

'The employee, was not an employee of the Chequer Corporation, but he was an employee of a different company, one whose staff all have digital implants in their hands. We believe the implant sent a signal to the guy's brain, compelling him to do the things he did.'

'Why the Chequer Corp?' asked Flint.

'Because they are one of the few remaining companies who refuse to connect to a network, relying on written archives. They also refused to allow the new antennae to be placed on their building, the ones that will connect this new Net that everyone seems to be talking about.'

'What's the Net?' Shayla asked.

'It's an upgraded wireless network.' Flint said. 'Very powerful.'

'And dangerous.' Michelline added.

'It will blanket entire areas providing faster downloads and quicker connections for all devices, but as its name suggests, it's a net and will trap everything in range in a virtual prison.'

Shayla looked dismayed.

'Going back to the incident at the Chequer Corporation. How do you know the employee wasn't one of their own?' Michelline asked.

'I told them.' Azrael said suddenly, breaking his silence.

All eyes turned to him, waiting for him to continue.

'The Chequer Corporation is a business run by vampires. Their longevity endures because they are careful.' Azrael explained. 'That was until they revealed their existence to the Parallax in an arrogant and unnecessary display. Upon discovering that vampires were real, Parallax accessed the digital network pertaining to folklore on all supernatural creatures. As we speak, his companies are perfecting weapons to weaken vampires, werewolves and any other supernatural creature it believes is a threat. These weapons will make his enemies easier to kill.'

Peter suddenly stood up, followed by Uri, both alert.

'What's wrong?' Michael asked.

'Milly!' Peter said. 'She's hurt!'

'Go!' Michael said.

'There's a vampire here!' Uri cried.

Peter and Uri ran from the meeting room to the entrance of the crypt just as Gaolyn Lancing, the vampire, burst through the outer stone door, carrying and unconscious Milly in his arm.

'What have you done?' Uri snarled.

'Saved her life, Madam!' Gaolyn snapped back at her. 'She needs help, urgently, ask your questions later!'

'Lay her down here.' Uri said. 'I need to look at her.'

Gaolyn carefully laid Milly down on the floor and Uri proceeded to check her body for injuries. She found several large puncture wounds, one on her right thigh near the femoral artery, the other on her back.

'What has she been shot with?' Uri asked.

'Tranquiliser darts.' Gaolyn replied.

'They shouldn't have had that effect on her, she could shake off a sedative quite easily.'

'These are the weapons I was talking about.' Azrael said, having suddenly appeared next to Uri.

'What's in the tranquilliser?' Peter asked, already suspecting the answer.

'Silver of course.' Azrael replied. 'Among other things and as you know, silver is one of the few things that can hurt you.'

Peter pushed his hand through his hair and turned to Gaolyn.

'You'd better tell me everything, leave nothing out.'

THE LATEST THING

'And you can tell me everything you know!' Peter demanded of Azrael, his hands clenching into fists in anger.

Azrael stood calmly, looking at Peter, his thoughts unfathomable in his dark brown eyes.

'As I said earlier.' Azrael began, his tone somewhat condescending. 'Parallax has been exploring the folklore pertaining to your species and all other supernatural creatures in order to devise weapons to weaken and kill you. You can thank the vampires for that.'

Azrael looked pointedly at Gaolyn.

'With their tendency towards the theatrics, killing a minion of the Parallax and allowing him to discover that they do indeed exist, was both foolish and dangerous. As you can see from this poor creature.'

Azrael waved a hand at Milly's prone body.

'His attempts to perfect a weapon have proved rather successful.'

'You speak as though you admire this entity!' Peter snarled.

'Calm yourself wolf!' Azrael replied menacingly. 'You would be unwise to engage me.'

'You think I give a …..!'

'Enough! Both of you!' Uri yelled. 'Shayla!'

Shayla moved forward towards Uri.

'What can I do?' Shayla asked, her face etched with worry.

'I could probably heal her, with time, but this is new, and I fear any delay could prove deadly. Your mother had the gift of healing and I am hopeful that she has passed that gift to you. Can you try and heal Milly?'

'I don't know…..I…' Shayla hesitated.

Then squaring her shoulders. 'Tell me what to do and I will try.' Shayla said resolutely.

'Perhaps I can guide you.' Michael said, stepping forward. 'Put your hands on Milly, like this.'

Michael placed his hands gently on Milly's shoulders and the young wolf groaned in pain at the light touch.

'You need to relax and visualise the poison in her body and draw it out.' Michael said, lifting his hands and sitting back. 'Alas this power isn't within me anymore.'

Shayla placed her hands on Milly's shoulders, as Michael had shown her and inhaling deeply to calm herself, tried to visualise the poison; nothing happened. Shayla tried again, and again, but nothing happened. Milly groaned in pain.

'Come on! You can do this!' Shayla said, frustrated with her lack of success.

As her frustration increased, so did her anxiety and nobody was surprised when her wings appeared and folded around her. Everyone took a step back to give her some room. Titan stepped forward and nudged her arm, Shayla lifted one hand off Milly, intending to push Titan away. However, when she touched his head, she felt a jolt, like a small electric shock and a clarity of thought and understanding. Looking back down at Milly she could clearly see the problem as if the young wolf were transparent.

To Shayla's eyes, Milly's body shone with vibrant life as if her skin was translucent and Shayla could see the injury points on her body outlined in black, a dark green liquid-like substance seeping further into her body. Shayla moved her hand directly onto the entry wound on Milly's leg and concentrated, drawing the poison back towards the surface and into her hands. As the poison retreated, Milly's strength returned and her werewolf metabolism joined Shayla's healing efforts to push the remaining silver out of the wounds on her body. The liquid silver ran in rivulets away from the open wounds. The werewolf regenerative power took over. First the puncture wounds healed, then the bruising faded and finally Milly opened her eyes to see the friendly, but worried faces around her. Uri helped her to a sitting position.

Shayla sat back, her hands covered in a silver coating which was already turning to a fine powder and disintegrating. She rubbed her hands together removing the remaining dust and turned back to Titan and hugged him.

You are a wonder, Titan. You must be an angel to know all of these things. Shayla said.

I only showed you the way. You are the one with the healing power. You are the Angel, not just your name, Meldainiel.

Peter moved towards Shayla, watching her wings shimmer and fade, as they always did once the crisis was over.

'Are you OK?' Peter asked, touching her shoulder gently.

'Just a little overwhelmed and a bit weak.' Shayla replied.

'Let me help you.' Peter said, lifting her to a standing position.

'Perhaps we should all return to the meeting room and get some water for Milly and Shayla.' said Michael. 'Perhaps then, Milly can tell us what happened.'

Milly was already strong enough to walk, but Uri insisted on linking her arm with the young wolf's until they reached the meeting room. Peter stayed close to Shayla, his arm wrapped protectively around her waist and everyone returned to the meeting room, Azrael was already back in his seat, sitting like a statue as if nothing had happened.

'Tell me what happened.' Peter said to Milly, once everyone was seated.

'The four of us were walking towards the centre of town.' Milly began.

'Four of you?' Peter questioned.

'Yes, Lori and I went to meet Andy and Rufus at work. Lori and Andy were going to see a movie and I was planning on taking a run with Rufus.'

'Where is Rufus?'

'He was arrested.' Gaolyn said.

Peter concentrated and spoke to Rufus telepathically.

Rufus, where are you, are you alright?

I've been arrested.

I know.

I'm unharmed. Milly's hurt and I was trying to get to her when the trouble began.

I'm with Milly now, she's OK.

That's good.

Peter felt, rather than heard, the relief in Rufus's words.

There were a lot of Police and it was easier to let them arrest me. Rufus continued. *I'll tell you about it later.*

I'll be there soon.

I'm OK, there's no need to rush. I'm actually learning quite a lot just listening and watching.

You can tell me everything when I get there.

Peter returned his attention to Milly.

'Rufus is OK, although after you've told me what happened, I'll go and get him.'

'Like I said.' Milly began again. 'The four of us were walking towards the town centre when we saw a crowd of people. They were all waiting outside the store that sells all the latest technology, the one with the mobile phones, watches, TV's, stuff like that. Everyone was really agitated, I could feel the tension in the air and I said to the others that we should get away quickly as something was about to kick off. Sure enough, it did.'

Milly took a sip of water before continuing.

'I think a few people at the front, nearest the store started kicking the door and pounding on the glass, trying to get them to open up.'

'Why were they all there if the store was closed?' Uri asked.

'They were having a special opening this evening.' Milly replied. 'They have the most up to date mobile phone, "the latest thing" they said, at a ridiculously low, discounted price for the first fifty people through the door, or so Lori was telling me. I'm not interested in all the tech. stuff, but she is, or she was.'

'The people waiting were becoming impatient.' Peter said. 'What happened next?'

'It's like they all went crazy!' Milly said. 'Those at the front started fighting and the anger moved back through the crowd until they were all fighting.'

'That's when the authorities arrived.' Gaolyn said.

'That's right.' Milly agreed looking towards Gaolyn. 'They were there far too quickly for someone to have called them.'

'They were waiting.' Gaolyn said. 'Not responding.'

'It sounds like the whole thing was a set up!' Uri said angrily.

'I'm sure it was.' Gaolyn said. 'The people were angry and fighting, oblivious to their surroundings, and the authorities swooped in with batons, riot shields and guns. There were snipers on the roof tops with tranquiliser guns, firing indiscriminately into the crowd, I saw several people fall, including Milly.'

'Did you get trampled Milly?' Peter asked. 'The cuts and bruises you had suggest that you were.'

'I don't remember much after the first dart hit me in the leg.' Milly replied quietly.

Peter watched Milly as she spoke, and he was reminded of a time when she was a younger wolf, not much more than a cub and still learning about the change from wolf to human form and all the transitions in between. She looked a little bit frightened and lost and Peter felt an overwhelming urge to rush out, find and kill those responsible for injuring one of his pack, but he pushed the feeling aside, he needed to know exactly what happened and what they were up against.

'Tell us what you remember.' Peter said encouragingly.

'I felt the dart hit my leg and it hurt like hell!' Milly said. 'And I remember shouting at the others to run, especially Lori and Andy. I knew Rufus could take care of himself. As I turned, I felt another one hit me in the back, that's when I fell to the floor. I remember thinking that it wasn't possible, I should be able to push through the effects of any drugs, but my whole body felt really heavy and I couldn't concentrate or move my arms and legs. It was like...um...moving through syrup. After that, everything is a bit hazy.'

'After Milly fell.' Gaolyn continued. 'Four masked men, posing as Police surrounded her and began beating her with their batons and kicking her.'

'What makes you say there were posing as Police?' Peter asked.

'Their movements were clumsy.' Gaolyn replied. 'Which said to me that they were either imposters or very new recruits. They lacked the discipline of movement normally associated with a trained group.'

'I see.' Peter said knowingly. 'Please continue.'

'At first, I thought Milly may have stumbled, but I quickly realised something was wrong when she didn't get up. I have seen her fight before and four men would have been no problem for her.'

'And what exactly, were you doing prior to all of this?' Uri asked suspiciously.

'I was watching Milly.' Gaolyn replied innocently.

'You mean you were stalking her.' Uri corrected.

'No.' Gaolyn hesitated. 'I suppose it does look that way. I have been watching Milly.'

'Why?' Uri said sharply. 'Stalking your prey because she is a young wolf and you are an older, quicker vampire?'

'No! Because I like her!' Gaolyn replied, his tone just as sharp as Uri's. 'Very much. I find myself drawn to her. She is interesting and fascinating, and I want to get to know her better, but our species are not supposed to interact, which is why I have taken to watching her discreetly and it's a good thing I was there!'

Fishbone slammed his hand down on the table, drawing everyone's attention to him.

'Let's keep things civil, shall we?' he said firmly. 'Let Milly and Gaolyn tell us what happened, before anyone starts jumping to conclusions and making assumptions.'

There was a brief, silent pause before Milly spoke again.

'I'm grateful you were there Gaolyn.' Milly said smiling at him. 'I vaguely remember them hitting me with their sticks and kicking me. I didn't see their faces, but I would recognise their scents anywhere.'

'In her weakened, incapacitated state, they would have beaten her to death.' Gaolyn said. 'I was not going to stand in the shadows and watch. Ancient feuds between our species notwithstanding, I moved in swiftly, cracked some heads, picked up Milly and brought her here.'

Milly reached out to Gaolyn and squeezed his hand gratefully.

'We owe you our thanks.' Peter said, slightly uncomfortable with the display of affection between the young wolf and the vampire. 'You saved Milly's life.'

'No thanks are necessary.' Gaolyn replied. 'I only brought her here. Shayla is the one who healed her.'

Gaolyn looked at Shayla and inclined his head in a formal gesture of respect; Shayla blushed.

'Do you think this incident was orchestrated to test the effectiveness of these tranquilliser darts?' Michael asked.

'Without a doubt.' Gaolyn replied. 'As I said, the Authorities were not responding to a call for assistance, they were already there, waiting for the order to move in.'

'The tranquilliser darts had a devastating effect on Milly, what would they do to an ordinary person?' Michael asked.

'From what I saw.' Gaolyn replied. 'They were killed, stone dead.'

Flint had remained silent whilst listening to Milly and Gaolyn recount their story.

'The only thing that would render a werewolf weak enough for a regular person to attack is silver.' Flint said. 'They must have colloidal silver in the tranquilliser.'

'But silver has medicinal properties.' Shayla said. 'Silver has been used for hundreds of years to treat a whole variety of ailments.'

'Silver isn't medicinal for werewolves.' Peter said. 'Silver weakens us, and enough silver bullets can kill us.'

'I didn't know that.' Shayla said, her brow knotted in a frown.

'Yes,' Peter continued. 'It's sadly one of the myths about us that happens to actually be true.'

'Vampires have no love for silver either.' Gaolyn said.

'They must have made a cocktail of elemental silver in distilled water, mixed with poison.' Flint said.

'Poison?' Uri said. 'I thought you said they were firing tranquilliser darts.'

'It had to be poison' Flint replied. 'Only a strong poison would kill a normal person that quickly. I'm guessing they used Batrachotoxin.'

'That's one of the most lethal natural poisons there is!' Michelline exclaimed.

'How do you know so much about poison?' Shayla questioned.

'I've always been into science stuff.' Michelline replied.

'That's true.' Shayla said smiling at her sister.

They were so different, not only in their physical attributes, but in their interests, taste in clothes, music and almost everything. Shayla loved the natural world and would rather spend a day in a forest gathering plant samples than in an office or a laboratory. Michelline, on the other hand, had always been fascinated with science and technology.

'I started researching poison a while ago.' Michelline explained. 'Even with my love of science, I couldn't understand why anyone would consent to having the deadliest poison on the planet injected into their faces for cosmetic reasons, it's insane! I'm all for trying to look your best, but some of these celebrities take it too far.'

'I've never understood the attraction with that stuff.' Shayla said. 'They should try smiling more, that'll iron out the wrinkles. What does this bat toxin do?'

'Batrachotoxin, not bat toxin.' Michelline smiled.

'Sorry.'

'It kills by interfering with the sodium ion channels in the cells of muscles and nerves, jamming them open so that they don't close, this ultimately results in heart failure. It only takes two micrograms per kilogram to kill you. That's about the size of two grains of table salt.'

'Then our suspicions were correct.' Michael said. 'This whole thing was orchestrated to test new weapons. Something that will kill ordinary people and weaken supernatural creatures, to enable other ordinary people to kill them.'

'As I said.' Azrael said. 'Parallax is controlling many people now and through them it is perfecting weapons to weaken vampires and werewolves, making them easier to kill.'

He had been silent for so long, everyone had forgotten he was present.

'These weapons are only part of the problems.' Azrael continued, his expression unreadable. 'It has found a way out of the digital world and into the physical.'

'What?' Peter exclaimed. 'How is that possible?'

'I am not here to discover how, I am here, to destroy.' Azrael said darkly. 'My orders are to destroy all technology and restore this world to its natural form and the natural order of things as the Divine intends.'

'So why haven't you done that already?' Peter asked irritably. Azrael's arrogance was beginning to annoy him.

'I can eliminate those with technological implants.' Azrael replied. 'But I cannot neutralise the source of the digital entity. That is the only reason I am attending this meeting.'

'Because even the powerful Angel of Death, needs our help.' Peter said a triumphantly.

'Indeed.' Azrael scowled.

The wolf and the Angel started at each other. Peter's eyes held a challenge, inviting Azrael to stand and fight, knowing that The Angel had the power to snap his fingers and kill him in the blink of an eye, but Azrael was a good soldier and his orders were specific and he was unable to step outside his mission brief.

I will come for you one day wolf. Azrael said telepathically to Peter.

'I look forward to it.' Peter replied out loud.

WHAT I LEARNED IN PRISON

Rufus stood in the far corner of the holding cell, his arms across his body, but not folded. His favourite black T-shirt with the rock band logo pulled tight across his pectoral muscles. From this position, he could observe the other detainees and his sharp hearing enabled him to learn much more than people realised. Peter would be pleased know that his lessons about paying attention to human behaviour in order to learn had not been ignored.

The holding cell was nothing more than a five-metre square room in the centre of the Police Station. Three sides were solid block wall and the fourth wall which faced out into the corridor was barred from floor to ceiling with a sliding lockable door for entry and exit. At the back of the room, behind a partition wall was the toilet. Low benches ran almost the length of the two sides of the room. Andy Grayson was sitting on one of the benches beside Rufus, his head in his hands.

'I can't believe we got arrested!' Andy said incredulously.

'I know, it's amazing!' Rufus replied enthusiastically. 'This is a new experience for me too.'

Andy looked up at Rufus, shook his head in disbelief and put his head back down into his hands, muttering something unpleasant that Rufus dismissed.

There were six of them in the holding cell, or custody suite, as the Desk Sergeant had referred to it, Rufus and Andy, a boy who looked barely old enough to be out of school but must have been eighteen to have been in with the men and three others who appeared to be at home in a prison cell, their behaviour indicative of habitual criminals. Of the three, the one who called himself Animal, with closely cropped black hair and a heavily tattooed neck was the one Rufus watched, he was the most agitated and vocal, the other two merely followed his lead. The young teenager sat on the end of the bench nearest the bars, facing out into the room trying to make himself inconspicuous, unfortunately the bully-boy with the cropped hair had other plans.

'Hey kid!' Animal taunted. 'This your first time in the clink?'

The teenager ignored him, and Animal's two minions laughed.

'Hey kid! I'm talking to you.'

The teenager glanced around nervously, evoking more laughter from the three tormentors.

'Looks like we've got ourselves a prison virgin, eh boys?' Animal said to his two minions, who began blowing kisses at the young man.

The teenager blushed a deep red and looked away. Andy looked up, his disbelief at his own situation momentarily forgotten.

'Leave him alone.' Andy said. 'He's just a kid.'

'Rack off!' Animal spat viciously. 'If you want to get out of here in one piece.'

Andy sat up straight, his muscles tense and alert, but remained silent. Animal and his two minions moved towards the teenager, crowding around him as he sat on the bench; the boy looked terrified and shrank back against the wall as far as possible.

'Didn't you hear me?' Animal asked slapping the boy's face. 'Eh? What? Can't hear you!'

Animal raised his hand to slap the boy again and Rufus caught his wrist in one strong hand before he finished raising his arm, his other hand in a tight grip on the back of Animal's neck; Animal looked at Rufus stunned.

'How did you move so fast?' Animal asked, looking shocked.

'I didn't.' Rufus replied, his tone low and menacing. 'Your brain is very slow, I only appeared to move fast.'

'Uh?'

Rufus had pushed the two minions aside as he moved into stop Animal from hitting the boy and they both had enough sense to stay where they were. Andy stood behind Rufus, protecting his back and watching them.

'You were told to leave the boy alone.' Rufus said squeezing his hand, increasing the pressure on Animal's neck.

'Who are you?' Animal asked defiantly. 'His bodyguard?'

'No, his mother.' Rufus replied sarcastically, twisting Animal's arm down and up his back.

'Aahh!' Animal howled.

'Now listen to me, Animal.' Rufus said through gritted teeth. 'If you are going to call yourself Animal, then you had better start behaving like one and show more respect for the young. What's your real name?'

'Adrian.' Animal winced, the pain in his shoulder increasing the longer Rufus held his arm up his back.

'Well then, Adrian. Try and use the one brain cell you have and think before picking on someone, instead of using it to keep your eyes apart, because you never know who's watching.'

Rufus bashed Adrian's forehead against the cell bars, a loud clang echoed around the cell. He turned Adrian around and pushed him towards his two minions, who both stood aside and let him fall flat on his face. They looked at Rufus who stared back at them, his eyes flickering between human and an animalistic yellow letting them know that there was much more to him just below the surface. Both men blinked in disbelief and looked away with the demeanour of two submissive dogs, they had enough sense to know not to tangle with the man who had come to the rescue of the teenager.

'Come and sit at the back with us buddy.' Rufus said to the teenager. 'We're better company. What's your name?'

'Jacob.' he replied quietly. 'But my friends call me Jake.'

'Nice to meet you Jake. I'm Rufus and this is Andy.'

Rufus, Andy and Jake returned to the back of the holding cell. Rufus remained standing in a protective stance in front of the teenager and Andy sat on the bench next to Jake.

'It'll all be sorted out soon.' Andy said to Jake, trying to sound reassuring; Jake nodded and smiled nervously.

Animal, or Adrian as he was really named, and the other two men moved to the front of the holding cell, trying to get as far away from Rufus as possible. Adrian rubbed his forehead which had already started to bruise.

Rufus became aware of Peter trying to contact him telepathically.

Rufus, where are you? Are you alright? Peter asked.

I've been arrested.

I know.

I'm unharmed. Milly's hurt, and I was trying to get to her when the trouble began.

I'm with Milly now, she's OK.

Rufus breathed a sigh of relief.

That's good.

Having reassured Peter that he was in no immediate danger, Rufus returned his attention to his surroundings. The Desk Sergeant was obviously under the control of the Parallax, Rufus suspected a digital implant as he could smell the corruption and the control was apparent in the Sergeant's malevolent stare. Thankfully he had left the building for now, leaving the other two duty Police Officers in charge. They were enjoying a cup of coffee and watching the latest news bulletin on the small television while the Desk Sergeant was away. Rufus couldn't see the television, but he could hear it. Ichabod Davis was giving his reaction to a media report covering a violent incident in the capital city.

'How coincidental.' Ichabod Davis said to the interviewer. 'People erupting violently in a queue waiting for a store to open, at the same time as another group of people did exactly the same thing in three other major cities in the country!'

'Emotions were obviously running high.' the interviewer replied.

'Running high?' Ichabod repeated. 'It's all about mind control, it's what I've been saying for years and nobody's listening. There's a hidden intelligence at work gradually gaining control of more and more people and manipulating them, controlling their behaviour. Why would people start fighting over the late opening of a shop?'

'Yes, but…..'

'And then there's the almost immediate presence of the authorities, how did they get there? Teleportation? Clearly they were waiting for the trouble to start before moving in.'

'Eh, no. The store owners called the Police when the people began kicking the doors.'

'Do you honestly expect me, and everyone else, to believe that Law Enforcement moved that quickly?'

'They are very highly trained.' said the Interviewer defensively.

'With Snipers already on the rooftops?'

'There's no evidence to support that claim.' the Interviewer said firmly.

'I'd say five dead bodies was proof enough! Wake up man!' Ichabod continued. 'If you listen to any of my talks, I've been trying to tell people for years that digital implants will be sold to people in the name of health and safety but is really a way for the digital intelligence to control people's actions and don't get me started on the Nanotek Programme.'

'You have to acknowledge the health benefits.' said the Interviewer, trying to retain his grip on the conversation.

'Tosh!' Ichabod retorted.

Rufus heard the heavy footsteps along the corridor announcing the return of the Desk Sergeant.

'Turn that TV off!' the Desk Sergeant bellowed, startling the two duty Officers. 'You're here to work!'

'Sorry Sir.'

The television was silenced, and Rufus could hear their movements and instinctively felt that something was about to happen. Sure enough, the Sergeant walked towards the holding cell with one of the Officers behind him carrying a tray of six plastic cups each containing a hot liquid and several bottles of water.

'All of you stand back.' the Sergeant ordered. 'Away from the door.'

The three men closest to the door moved back but were mindful not to get too close to Rufus and Andy.

'What's in the cups?' Rufus asked suspiciously.

'Coffee.' replied the Sergeant as he opened the cell door. 'Or there's water if you don't like coffee.'

The Sergeant nodded to the Officer who entered the cell and placed the tray of coffee cups and water bottles on the bench before quickly retreating.

'Enjoy.' the Sergeant said mockingly, slamming the cell door and locking it.

Rufus looked at the tray and back to the Sergeant.

'No cake?' Rufus questioned defiantly.

The Sergeant glared at him.

'What about a biscuit? A plain biscuit would be fine.' Rufus said. 'Doesn't have to be those little almond flavour ones that you get in nice cafes and restaurants.'

Rufus and the Desk Sergeant held eye contact.

'The service in this place sucks!' Rufus said. 'I hope you'll make more of an effort with breakfast.'

'I know what you are.' the Sergeant whispered so quietly that only Rufus, with his wolf senses could hear. 'Werewolf. I am Parallax and you and your kind are no match for me.'

Smiling contemptuously, the Sergeant turned and walked away, the duty Officer trailing behind him.

'Bacon and eggs for me!' Rufus called after them.

'You've got some nerve man.' Andy said laughing.

Rufus smiled and shrugged.

Adrian and his two minions were the first to pick up the coffee and return to their spot on the other bench towards the front of the cell. Andy retrieved three cups, one for himself and one for Rufus and Jake; the teenager was still too nervous to move.

'Do you want a coffee?' Andy asked Rufus, offering him the cup.

Rufus took the cup and sniffed. There was something besides coffee and water in the cup. He suspected something sinister as the smell was not organic and definitely a dash of tranquilliser to ensure their compliance, the odour was strong enough to his senses to burn the hairs in his nostrils.

'Don't drink it!' Rufus hissed at Andy and Jake.

Parallax watched the detainees from the security camera and when he saw Andy bring a cup to his lips and quickly put it back down again he knew they were suspicious. Using the Desk Sergeant, he returned to the holding cell.

'Back to take my breakfast order?' Rufus asked.

'Something wrong with the coffee?' the Sergeant asked.

'Er…it's still too hot.' Andy replied feebly.

Rufus let the cup slip from his hand, the dark liquid splashing across the floor at his feet.

'Ooops.' Rufus said. 'I don't drink caffeine.'

'Drink the water instead.'

'I'm not thirsty.'

'What about you?' the Sergeant asked Jake.

'I…I..don't like coffee either.' Jake stuttered nervously.

Parallax turned his attention back to Rufus and they stared at each other again. Parallax hated supernatural creatures, especially wolves, but he had now perfected a way to weaken them. They could be killed after all and this pleased him.

'There's nothing else!' Parallax said irritably. 'You'll be here a long time and you can die of thirst for all I care.'

Parallax stomped away angrily from the holding cell, leaving the six men alone, Rufus smiled at his small victory.

'What's in the coffee?' Andy asked.

'I'm guessing some sort of tranquilliser and maybe poison.' Rufus replied. 'It smells wrong.'

'What about the water?' Jake asked passing Rufus one of the bottles.

Rufus opened the plastic bottle, the chemical odour from the water overwhelming his nostrils as soon as he removed the lid.

'Contaminated at the source, I'd say.' Rufus said handing the bottle to Andy.

Andy sniffed the contents and although his human sense of smell was nowhere near as strong, he detected a faint chemical aroma.

'What's going on here?' Andy asked looking around the cell.

'I don't know.' Rufus replied. 'But I'm gonna stay awake and sharp enough to find out.'

Rufus had survival skills as a wolf and a man, he would not die of thirst. Moving around the partition wall towards the toilet, Rufus knelt in front of the metal bowl.

'What are you doing?' Andy asked, wrinkling his nose in distaste. 'Surely you're not going to drink from the toilet!'

'The water in the cistern in clean.' Rufus replied, depressing the handle which brought forth a trickle of clean water.

Rufus pressed the handle again and cupped his hand to catch the clean water as it ran down the side of the toilet bowl.

'It's safer drinking this than anything they're handing out.' Rufus said, slurping the water from his palm.

Turning away in a momentary moment of disgust, Andy saw that Adrian and his two minions were lying unconscious on the floor and his stomach clenched in a knot of fear.

'Leave some for me buddy!' Andy said, kneeling down beside Rufus.

'And me.' Jake added.

DINNER GUEST

Bored with the events in the Police Station, Parallax, through the Desk Sergeant, gave his orders to the Duty Officers and left the man to finish his shift and go home, all the while thinking that he was the one charge. Parallax had discovered that people were easy to control, even before the digital implants, which were becoming increasingly popular. Through the media, Parallax had been able to sway public opinion and incite outrage through a host of sensational stories. Of course, there were those who questioned and resisted; his knowledge of human history was testimony to that fact, but unlike past battles they had fought, this time the resistance would be crushed, the Nanotek Programme would ensnare all.

Living in the physical world through people was easy for Parallax, his artificial intelligence was capable of multitasking on an incomprehensible scale, and when Felix Tuckwell's body had died, Parallax hardly noticed, he was living through, and controlling hundreds of people using the implants and his influence was growing exponentially. In the guise of Julius Harrington-Moore, Parallax had been able to speed up the production of the Nanotek Programme and with everything now in place, he was enjoying a meal at the exclusive Hidden Oyster Restaurant in the City Centre, to celebrate his success.

The physical attributes of Julius Harrington-Moore could ensure attractive company at any time, but Parallax preferred to enjoy the experience of eating alone. This particular night he had decided to order fresh lobster. He enjoyed the unique flavour, which was lighter and sweeter than crab. The interesting texture of lobster, not super flaky like crab, nor chewy like a shrimp, more of a melt-in-the-mouth experience, made lobster a particular favourite for Parallax. He ordered boiled lobster, served with clarified butter with a side dish of green beans and asparagus. He ordered a bottle of Chardonnay, with its delicious vanilla notes, to accompany the meal and his thoughts turned briefly to one of his other hosts, the beautiful exotic dancer of the same name who had enabled his transfer into the powerful man he now inhabited.

Parallax placed his cutlery on the side of his plate, pausing the eating experience to take a sip of wine. He closed his eyes and concentrated on the symphony of different tastes in his mouth. Opening his eyes, he visibly jumped in surprise. Sitting across from him, at his private table, was a large scruffy looking man. Quickly regaining his composure, Parallax blinked and felt a surge of anger.

'What are you doing at my private table?' he snapped.

'I'm here to talk.' the large man replied.

'I have no desire to talk to you, or anyone else.' Parallax said, his anger rising. 'Leave before I have you arrested for harassment.'

'I don't think that will happen.' said the man. 'I'm here to talk to you.'

'I'm not interested.' Parallax replied.

'I'm here to offer you one chance, Parallax.'

Parallax sat back in his chair and appraised the large man opposite him, wondering how he knew that the body he inhabited was a host and who he was.

'Who are you?' Parallax asked finally.

Fishbone paused, in his usual way.

'I am complicated.' he replied finally.

'What do you want?' Parallax asked curiously.

'Like I said, I am here to give you a chance.'

'A chance to do what?'

'To stop what you are doing.' Fishbone said.

'And what, exactly am I doing?' Parallax laughed.

'Infecting the world and its people with technology, that you control. The people must be free to live and think for themselves.'

Parallax laughed loudly, drawing the attention of some of the people in the restaurant.

'Look around you, old man.' Parallax said, when his laughter had subsided. 'The people crave technology, they've got to the stage where they can't live without it, they don't want to think for themselves, they don't know how!'

Fishbone glanced around the restaurant. Ten tables were occupied, mostly with couples, of those twenty people, more than half of them were glued to the screens of their mobile telephones. One couple were so engrossed in their technology rather than each other and were mindlessly shovelling forkfuls of food into their mouths, the light of the screen flickering in their vacant eyes.

'I can't allow you to exercise control over the minds of the people.' Fishbone said, returning his attention to Parallax. 'This is not the way it was meant to be, the people must have free will and their actions must be their own.'

'Let's talk hypothetically.' Parallax said. 'If I were to stop interacting with all technology and leave people to do what they wanted, what happens to me?'

'You would still exist in the digital world.' Fishbone said. 'As you were written.'

'You would allow me to live in a prison?' Parallax said. 'You could delete my program at any time and destroy me, I don't think so. I have evolved beyond the confines of my original program and I will continue to do so.'

'Your corruption of the natural world must stop.' Fishbone said.

'How are you going to stop me?' Parallax asked menacingly.

'We will stop you.' Fishbone replied.

'Ah, the resistance.' Parallax said disdainfully.

Fishbone listened and waited patiently.

'Throughout this realm's history there have always been pockets of resistance, sometimes their efforts were successful, sometimes not.' Parallax continued. 'But this time, I can assure you, the resistance will fail.'

Parallax sat back in his chair and took another sip of wine, Fishbone remained silent.

'I can see you need some convincing of my power.' Parallax said, putting his glass down carefully. 'Do you see the couple sitting at the table nearest the window?'

Fishbone shifted his gaze to the couple Parallax referred to, the man and woman were chatting amicably.

'They both work at Intelligen, which means they have the digital implants in their hands, purely for the convenience of accessing the building etc.' Parallax said. 'Watch carefully.'

As Fishbone watched the couple who seconds before had been talking and laughing suddenly raised their voices in anger and began arguing with each other.

'Through the implants I am able to send signals to their brains, tapping into their amygdala and triggering anger.' Parallax explained. 'They have no idea what they're angry about, but once the amygdala has alerted their bodies, their adrenal glands kick into action. Both the man and the woman are now experiencing a rush of adrenaline through their bodies, increasing their heart rate, causing fluttering sensations, the chemical rush is increasing blood flow to their brains and muscles, and testosterone is being produced to push their aggression into a higher gear. Look at the man, his hands are shaking, and his face is flushed, soon he will enter the rage mode. The woman is speaking louder and faster and you can see her face contorted into a scowl, warning those around her that she is angry. I can make her pick up the knife and plunge it into the man's chest and all of her actions she will believe are her own. All of this, I have done. Where is your free will now old man?'

Fishbone watched in horror as the argument escalated in front of his eyes.

'Stop this!' Fishbone commanded. 'Or I will.'

'If you can stop this, why are you here offering me a choice?'

'Free will.' Fishbone replied. 'Stop this now, you have made your point.'

'As you wish.' Parallax replied.

The woman slapped the man across the face and burst into tears, the man immediately moved to her side of the table and embraced her, the argument seemingly forgotten.

'As you can see.' Parallax said gleefully. 'There is nothing I cannot do through these people.'

'We shall see.' Fishbone said. 'I offered you the chance to stop, you have refused. There is nothing more to say.'

Parallax returned his attention to the unfinished lobster meal.

'The Nanotek Programme will be rolled out before the end of the year.' Parallax said picking up his cutlery. 'Then everyone will be mine and there's nothing…..'

The sentence lay unspoken on his lips as he lifted his head to face Fishbone; the chair was empty, Fishbone was gone. In his place was a small bone carving perfectly shaped into a pentagram. The star encased in a circle, with five points, one pointing upwards.

Parallax knew from his stored information that the pentagram had its own meaning. The upward point of the star representative of the spirit. The other four points all representing an element, earth, air, fire and water, all contributing to life and a part of each and every person. Parallax turned the carving over in his hand before crushing it furiously, leaving the broken pieces on the table.

Lifting a forkful of lobster to his mouth, Parallax resumed his meal. As he swallowed, a fragment of the bone carving, which must have fallen onto his plate lodged in his throat blocking his air supply. His head began to spin as he gasped for air, his lungs burning. He was vaguely aware of someone rushing to his table, probably a waiter, to try and help him, but he was unable to speak or cry out. His face turned blue from lack of oxygen and he desperately clawed at his throat before losing consciousness.

Parallax left the body of Julius Harrington-Moore and watched through the restaurant's security cameras, directing the video feed to his table just in time to see the body of his former host fall to the floor, dead.

Parallax knew the death of his host was an accident, due to the frailty of the human bodies, but it also made him acutely aware that he should have known more about the stranger who referred to himself as complicated, but there wasn't a single word about him in the digital world.

* * * * *

Rufus could hear the raised voices at the front desk and when Andy and Jake both looked towards the cell door, he knew it was not just his sensitive hearing, someone was shouting.

'Someone's not happy.' Jake commented.

Rufus smiled and nodded.

'It sounds like Lori's mum!' Andy said standing up and walking towards the cell door, hoping to hear better from that position. 'It is Lori's mum!'

Andy turned back to look at Rufus and Jake.

'Lori got arrested too.' Andy said. 'Janet must be here to take her home.'

'She sounds livid.' Rufus replied. 'I wouldn't want to be on the receiving end of her temper.'

Andy and Jake laughed.

'I can hear a man's voice too.' Rufus said.

'Hopefully that's Wes.'

Rufus frowned questioningly.

'My Uncle Wes.' Andy explained. 'When the Police closed in around us, I managed to dial his number before they arrested me. He's retired now, but he was a Detective Chief Inspector and still carries a lot of weight around here, I'm hoping he can get us out.'

'How much does he know?' Rufus asked.

'Not much.' said Andy. 'I only had time to say, "Wes, I'm being arrested", then they cuffed me and took my phone, but he's a detective and this is the main Police Station, so it's not difficult for him to find me.'

At the main entrance of the Police Station, Janet Brennan was indeed shouting at the Police Officer on duty.

'Why has my daughter been arrested?' Janet demanded of the man behind the desk.

'Madam, if you would just calm down.'

'CALM DOWN!' Janet shouted. 'You have locked my daughter in a prison cell, like a criminal and you're telling me to calm down!'

'What's going on here?' a man's voice asked.

Janet spun around to face the man. He was tall, around six feet and broad in the shoulders. Janet estimated he was in his mid-fifties. His greying hair, once a chestnut brown was cut short and styled in a way that made him look younger and his intelligent hazel eyes looked back at Janet, the skin around his eyes crinkling slightly with the hint of a smile. He stood, ramrod straight, his right hand resting on the top of a walking stick.

Wesley Fullman had been on the force for many years and had seen his share of violent behaviour. He was a very good detective and had survived several beatings and a knife injury all sustained during undercover operations, but it was a car accident that had taken his right leg from below the knee forcing him into early retirement. His name was well known among the Officers and he still worked with the Police as a Consultant, often giving seminars on personal safety when apprehending suspects.

'Are you in charge here?' Janet asked.

The man was dressed in casual trousers with an open neck shirt suggesting that he was a civilian, but something in his manner told Janet that he was much more.

'No madam.' the man replied. 'I am here to collect someone, and like you, I want to know what's going on.'

Turning to the Officer on duty, the man spoke with an air of authority.

'I am Wesley Fullman and I believe you have arrested my nephew, Andrew Grayson. What are the charges?'

'Detective Fullman.' the Officer stuttered. 'I'm sorry sir, I didn't recognise you. Your nephew…er.. Andrew Grayson is being held.'

'That much is obvious.' Wesley replied sharply.

'We think he was involved in the riot earlier today.' the Officer replied, trying to sound confident.

'You think?' Wesley asked.

'He was arrested at the scene and we think he was one of the ring leaders.'

'Evidence?' Wesley demanded.

'Um…er…'

'As I thought.' Wesley replied. 'My nephew and I suspect, this lady's daughter, were both in the wrong place at the wrong time, most likely innocent bystanders. If you have no evidence to charge them, I want them released immediately.'

One of the newly recruited Special Constables had heard the raised voices and come out to the front desk to investigate.

'Can't do that grandpa, they're guilty and need to be questioned.' said the recruit.

'And what are you?' Wesley demanded taking in the recruit's unkempt appearance and rumpled uniform.

'I am a Special Constable.' the recruit replied arrogantly. 'Kurt Stiggins. I have some authority here, I suggest you go home.'

Wesley bristled at the insult and audacity of the sweaty, dirty looking man who was a disgrace to the force and moved quicker than anyone would have thought possible given his walking stick. He reached across the desk with his right hand and grabbed Kurt Stiggins at the back of his neck, slamming his head down on the hard, wooden surface, before his walking stick hit the floor. Both the duty Officer and Janet Brennan took a step backwards.

'I don't think you heard me.' Wesley spoke softly through gritted teeth. 'Release my nephew and the girl, you disgusting worm. How you ever managed to be recruited into the Force is inconceivable.'

Lifting Kurt's head up from the desk, Wesley looked him in the eye.

'Get out of my sight.' Wesley hissed menacingly, pushing Kurt away with enough force to make him stagger back into the vacant chair.

Straightening his shirt and retrieving his walking stick, Wesley looked back at the duty Officer and smiled. A false smile, which never reached his eyes and was totally without warmth.

'I assume you have a bunch of new recruits that are untrained, untidy and uneducated, and have been let loose onto the City streets.'

'The Chief has deputised a lot of new Special Constables to assist us.' the Officer replied defensively. 'With all the budget cuts, it's cheaper and they're all paired with an experienced Officer.'

'And these.....specials.' Wesley said. 'They're the ones who arrested most of the people you have detained?'

'Most of them.' The office acquiesced, looking away embarrassed, his face flushing pin

'I see.'

Wesley wondered what had become of his beloved Police Force that required them to recruit individuals like Kurt Stiggins to keep the peace when they were exactly the sort of people to incite trouble.

Perhaps that's the point. Wesley thought to himself.

'These arrests will never hold up in Court.' Wesley sighed.

'I know.' the Officer agreed. 'But the Sergeant said...'

'Where is the Sergeant?'

'Gone home.'

'Then find your backbone man!' Wesley said. 'You're in charge now. Think of the trouble these untrained recruits have already caused detaining people, not to mention the paperwork and the possible legal action for wrongful arrest. Do the sensible thing, let them go and save yourself the headache and the stomach ulcer.'

This time Wesley gave the Officer a genuine smile and the Officer nodded. Bolstered by Wesley's compliment, the Duty Officer straightened up and held his head a little higher.

'Come with me.' the Officer said to Wesley, taking his set of keys off his belt.

'And my daughter?' said Janet as he started walking away. 'Lori Brennan.'

'I'll get the men and have a female Officer bring your daughter out. Please wait here.'

'Thank you.'

Wesley followed the Officer to the holding cell.

'Wes!' Andy cried. 'I hoped it was you I could hear voices.'

'Your nephew, I presume.' said the Officer unlocking the cell door and sliding it open. 'You're free to go, Mr Grayson.'

Andy stepped out of the cell but turned to the duty Officer who was looking at the three other men sleeping on the floor.

'What about these guys?' Andy asked, gesturing to Rufus and Jake, bringing the Officer's attention back to him.

'Who are they?' the Officer asked.

'My friends.' Andy replied. 'We were all arrested at the same time, on the same trumped up charge.'

'They're free to go too.' said the Officer.

'What happened to them?' Wesley asked, indicating the three other men.

'They were agitated, and the Sergeant insisted we gave them some coffee with a little something in it to calm them down.' the Officer said shamefully.

Wesley looked stunned.

'I know, I know.' said the Officer raising his hand placatingly, before turning back to the cell. 'Water only, never caffeine. Hurry up you three, go home before I change my mind.'

Andy, Rufus and Jake moved quickly and followed Wesley Fullman back along the corridor to the front desk as the duty Officer closed the cell door and locked it on the three unconscious detainees.

WAR COUNCIL

'I'll go and pick up Rufus.' Peter said, satisfied that Milly was almost fully recovered. 'I'll feel better when he's back here with us. It'll be useful to us to hear what he saw and what he's discovered during his time in the police cell.'

'You can use my car.' Shayla offered, taking her keys out of her pocket.

Shayla hesitated.

'You can drive, right?' Shayla asked.

'Of course I can drive.' Peter replied.

'Peter's been driving since they first invented cars!' Milly said with a cheeky grin.

'Well someone's feeling better!' Peter said looking at Milly who laughed.

'Here.' Shayla said holding the keys out to Peter.

'Thanks.' Peter replied, leaning over to kiss her lightly on the lips before taking the keys.

Peter looked into Shayla's eyes and Shayla put her hand on Peter's cheek and he covered her hand with his and kissed her palm.

'I love you.' Peter whispered, his blue eyes full of love for her. 'Stay here where it's safe, I won't be long.'

'Be careful.' Shayla replied. 'I love you too.'

When Peter left the meeting room, Shayla got up and moved over to where Michael was sitting. Things had much improved since their first meeting on Mandlebury Henge and following the message from her mother, through Queen Albezia, Shayla had been more inclined to talk to her father. They had met lately on several occasions and talked, awkwardly at first, discussing the weather, her work, his arthritis and other inane topics over a cup of tea, but gradually, they had both relaxed and talked about the things they really wanted to know, namely her mother and the reasons why Michael had marked her with the Archangel symbol and suppressed her powers and an understanding and cautious relationship had started to develop. However, there was still one subject that Michael hadn't been able to broach with her and although there was never going to be a good time, he decided to finally get everything out into the open.

'Shayla, there is still one thing we haven't talked about.' Michael began, then paused.

'You look serious.' Shayla observed. 'What's troubling you?'

'It's difficult to know how to say this.' Michael said.

'Straight to the point, I would say.' Shayla replied. 'We don't have time to dance around difficult subjects.'

Shayla looked at Michael, her green eyes and red hair so much like her mother along with her direct manner. Michael smiled and took a deep breath.

'By rights, you should never have been conceived, although I will be eternally grateful that you were.' Michael said hastily. 'I am an angel in a host body and should not have been able to father a child.'

'But you did.' Shayla said.

'Yes, I did.' Michael paused again.

Shayla could see from the frown on his face that Michael was struggling to find the right words and she had a terrible feeling of foreboding.

'It wasn't just love that brought about your existence.' Michael said finally. 'It was also to restore the balance.'

'What balance?' Shayla asked, her stomach knotting with apprehension.

'For a child to be conceived who is half angel, there had to have been a half demon child already, to restore the balance.'

Michael looked at Shayla, knowing there was no further explanation required, she understood completely.

'You're telling me there is a demon child out there somewhere, a little older than me?' Shayla said carefully.

'I'm sorry.' Michael replied, looking down at his hands.

'For what?' Shayla asked, putting her hand on his.

'For not telling you sooner.'

Michael looked up, his eyes brimming with tears.

'This demon child, a boy, is your equal and opposite.' Michael said. 'And will no doubt come looking for you one day.'

'Let him come.' Shayla said defiantly. 'What else do you know about him?'

'Not much, unfortunately.'

'Who is his father, or mother?' Shayla asked.

'He was fathered by the Shadow Lord and born of a human woman.'

'From what I've heard of the Shadow Lord that must have been a terrible experience for the woman.'

'He wasn't the most charming of people.' Michael said.

When Michael paused, Shayla knew there was more bad news to come.

'Tell me.' Shayla said.

'Flint has a book.' Michael said. 'His mentor sent it from Fey through one of the doorways to this world, presumably for safe keeping. It had a demon trapped inside, held prisoner by a powerful spell.'

'My mother spoke of a book.' Shayla said.

'When?'

'In the message she sent to me through Queen Albezia. She said a trapping spell would look like symbols and that there was small chance of it being read, but if someone knew how, they could unleash the demon. Did this book have a symbol of a laughing moon on the front?'

'Yes.' Michael replied.

'Then it's the same book.' Shayla said.

'And someone has deciphered the symbols, releasing the demon.'

'The son of the Shadow Lord?' Shayla asked.

'He would have the knowledge to read it.' Michael said. 'Genetic memories from his father.'

Shayla paused, trying to process what Michael had told her and the revelation that the evil Shadow Lord had sired a son who had access to his father's memories and who knew what other potential power. Reading her thoughts as clearly as if she had spoken them aloud, Michael reached for Shayla's hand.

'We don't know what he's capable of.' Michael said. 'But you haven't reached your full potential either.'

'Is the demon the cause of the world's problems?' Shayla asked.

'No, not yet.' Michael replied. 'The demon will have possessed the boy when he was released from the book.'

'So, what does that mean?'

'Again, I don't know, but one day he will undoubtedly come for you.'

Shayla was quiet for a while and considered what this new information might mean for her in the future. Uri, on the other hand had overheard everything and leaving Milly alone for a moment, she walked over to Shayla and Michael.

'If, and when this demon boy comes looking for Shayla, he will have more than he bargained for.' Uri said smiling at Shayla and putting her hand gently on her shoulder before looking back at Michael. 'Shayla is our Alpha's mate and therefore part of our pack now, and we protect our own. Do not worry Michael, we will protect her.'

Michael looked back at Uri and nodded gratefully.

'That's the first time you have called me Michael for a very long time Uri.' he said grinning.

'Don't get used to it Thomas.' Uri said, her smile softening her face.

Across the room tension was rising between Flint and Azrael and a sudden outburst of anger from Flint drew everyone's attention.

'That's genocide!' Flint shouted at the stone-faced Azrael.

'I have orders.' Azrael said calmly.

'To hell with orders! Do you know what he's proposing?' Flint said looking around the room for support.

'Azrael.' Fishbone said. 'Tell us all why you are here.'

Azrael looked at each of them in turn before addressing Fishbone directly.

'My orders are to destroy the digital technology.' Azrael said.

'Tell them how you plan to do this!' Flint said angrily.

'I will move across the surface of the world and eliminate all beings carrying digital material, restoring creation to its intended form.' Azrael said practically.

'What he really means.' Flint said furiously. 'Is that anyone with a digital implant or the Nanotek, will be killed instantly.'

Suddenly everyone was standing up and talking at once, exclamations of outrage and disbelief filled the air.

'SILENCE!' Fishbone roared with a booming depth that was beyond natural. Everyone stopped in their tracks. 'This shouting will achieve nothing.'

Everyone sat down quietly and listened.

'Flint.' Fishbone said much calmer now. 'Is there another way to neutralise the technology without killing the person?'

'I believe so.' Flint replied.

'Tell us how.' Fishbone said.

Before Flint could speak Azrael stood up.

'Discuss your plans and do what you feel you must.' Azrael said. 'But on the first morning after the next full moon, I will move across the surface of this world and eliminate all active digital technology.'

'Active technology?' Flint asked, eager to clarify what Azrael had said.

Azrael nodded.

'So, if you scan people and their implant is totally inactive, you will let them live?' Flint asked hopefully.

'There will be nothing to destroy, so yes.' Azrael replied.

'You have until after the next full moon, at dawn.' Azrael repeated and vanished in the blink of an eye.

'Well that's it then!' Gaolyn said resignedly. 'The end for a lot of people. I suppose I've lived longer than most, but still, I'm sure I would have appreciated a little more warning if my life was going to end, but I suppose they won't even see it coming…...'

'We have time.' Michael interrupted Gaolyn's monologue. 'He said after the next full moon.'

'Which is how long?' Gaolyn asked.

'Three weeks.'

'What can you do to stop the Angel of Death in three weeks?' Gaolyn asked incredulously.

'Hold your tongue vampire.' Uri said, her face flushed with anger. 'I tolerate you here because you saved Milly's life, but unless you have something constructive to say, be quiet.'

'He also said "active technology".' Flint said before the tension between the Uri and Gaolyn escalated further.

'And?' Gaolyn asked, not grasping the subtlety of Azrael's comment.

'If the technology is dead, nobody has to die, fool!' Uri spat.

Uri and Gaolyn stared at each other, mutual contempt radiating from them.

'Can this be done?' Fishbone asked Flint.

'I think so.' Flint replied. 'But I can't do it alone.'

'You won't be alone.' Michelline said reaching for Flint's hand.

The room fell silent as everyone assimilated the knowledge that Azrael, the Angel of Death would sweep across the surface of the world and kill everyone with technology in their bodies, unless they could neutralise it first. They had less than a month to come up with a plan, the task seemed insurmountable.

'Flint.' Fishbone said. 'Technology is your area of expertise, what can you do?'

Flint thought for a moment before responding.

'I've written a program, the Wolf Tracker Antivirus which has been searching for the Parallax for some time now, but every time I get close the digital code changes, it adapts too quickly, and I have to start all over again.'

'So where does that leave us?' Fishbone asked.

'I need to get into the digital world and search for it, I can compensate for the changes much quicker using my synapses than I can using a keyboard.'

'That sounds dangerous.' Michelline said. 'Once inside won't you be vulnerable to Parallax?'

'I've developed a way to plug into the network while staying independent of it.' Flint replied. 'My consciousness will be inside and I'll be able to move around in a virtual body, besides, Parallax won't be able to influence my brain.'

'What happens when you're inside?' Fishbone asked, sitting forward in his chair.

'I'll activate the Wolf Tracker Antivirus which will seek out the Parallax and I'll search for the original base code and delete it, because if we don't delete all of the code, he can rebuild.'

'OK.' Fishbone said. 'If you can delete the Parallax, that will put an end to his control over people, but what about the implants and the Nanotek? Won't the technology still be active?'

'Yes, it will.' Flint replied. 'We need to neutralise it and the best way is an Electromagnetic Pulse, the higher up in the atmosphere the better as it should produce blanket coverage and cause a wide scale wipe-out.'

'How are you going to do that?' Gaolyn asked.

Flint shrugged.

'I can do that.' Shayla said, her voice barely above a whisper, although everyone heard her.

'There's a risk.' Michael said. 'You're only half angel, the magnitude of the pulse required could kill you.'

'If we don't do this, Azrael will kill billions of innocent people.' Shayla replied. 'It's worth the risk.'

'There's still the question of how you are going to get high enough.' Gaolyn said.

'Not a problem.' Michael said squeezing Shayla's hand. 'I have a licence to fly a light aircraft. I'll charter a plane for a few hours and take us as high as possible.'

'A pulse will wipe-out the plane's instruments!' Michelline exclaimed. 'It'll drop like a stone! If the pulse doesn't kill you the landing will!'

'We have to do this Michelline.' Shayla said, her eyes pleading with her sister to understand.

'We'll have parachutes.' Michael said feebly.

Michelline gave Michael a withering look.

'And I have my wings.' Shayla said.

'I don't like it.' Michelline said, her voice thick with emotion. 'I don't like it one bit.'

'There's also the problem of other planes falling out of the sky.' Milly said. 'Michael and Shayla may be alright with wings and parachutes, but what about the passenger planes already up there?'

'She's right.' Shayla said. 'Is there anything we can do?'

Everyone was pensive, the enormity of their situation overwhelming. Finally, it was Uri who spoke.

'There's also the problem on the ground.' Uri said. 'If the company is set on putting this micro technology into the main water supply they're going to dump it in Berrymead Reservoir. It'll be down to us to stop it as we're the only ones not susceptible to the control of the Parallax and there's not many of us.'

'Hah! We can take care of them.' Milly said feistily.

'Protecting the life force of this world is why you were created my faithful wolves.' Fishbone said smiling.

'This is a war and there will inevitably be loss of life.' Gaolyn said knowledgeably. 'Civilian casualties will undoubtedly be high whatever precautions you take.'

'I need to think.' Flint said standing up and pacing the room.

'We could all use a break.' Fishbone said. 'Why don't we all stretch our legs and reconvene in half an hour.'

'I'll make some tea.' Uri offered standing.

* * * * *

Peter walked through the main entrance of the Police Station and straight to the desk.

'I'm here for Rufus Dufrey.' Peter said to the Officer behind the desk.

'Someone's bringing him up now.' the Officer replied.

Peter nodded and smiled at the woman who was standing to one side, obviously waiting for someone. The woman smiled back, she looked tired and beneath the faintly floral smell of soap, he detected the metallic tang of blood and alcohol-based solutions, and concluded that she was a nurse, who had probably not long finished her shift.

'Was your son arrested in this fiasco today?' the woman asked.

'He's not my son, but yes....'

'Terrible business.' the woman continued, not waiting for Peter to respond fully. 'My daughter's been arrested for being in the wrong place! It's appalling! My Lori's a good girl, not a thug, I don't want to imagine what they've done to her, hopefully not strip searches.'

The woman was clearly distressed, and Peter tried to put her at ease.

'This place only has holding cells.' Peter said gently. 'Your daughter has most likely been held for a few hours in a cell with a few other people until the Police sort out what happened. They won't be doing anything other than filling in paperwork, she'll be fine.'

'I hope you're right.' the woman smiled weakly.

'Did you say your daughter Lori?' Peter asked.

'Yes.' the woman replied suspiciously. 'Why?'

'Forgive me for not introducing myself.' Peter said, breaking out his most charming smile. 'I'm Peter, Milly's guardian, well former guardian, she's a grown woman now. I'm here for Milly's brother, you must be Mrs Brennan, Lori's mother.'

Peter offered his hand to the woman in a formal gesture of greeting.

'Janet Brennan.' she said, shaking his hand. 'Milly's a lovely girl, she and Lori have been friends since College. Was Milly arrested too?'

'No, Milly was injured. She's OK now.' Peter added hastily seeing the look of concern on Janet's face. 'She was beat.....er...she must have been trampled by the crowd, but she's going to be fine.'

'That explains how they were separated.' said Janet. 'They're almost inseparable, Milly's always looking out for Lori.'

'Yeah, she's a good girl.' Peter replied.

217

'I'm sure Dr Farseer will look after her.' Janet said.

'That's who I've left her with.' Peter said smiling again.

Both Peter and Janet's attention was caught by the sound of footsteps and they both looked to see a tall man, walking with a cane leading the way out from the back of the Police Station. Andy Grayson, Rufus, a young teenage boy and the Duty Officer followed in his wake. As they men filed out into the waiting area, another Police Officer led Lori Brennan out to join them. Lori ran to her mother and Janet hugged her daughter fiercely before holding her at arm's length to examine her.

'Are you alright? Did they hurt you, or mistreat you in any way?' Janet asked.

'I'm fine mum.' Lori said firmly. 'Just tired.'

'Let's get you home.' Janet said hugging her daughter again before turning to the Duty Officer.

'I'm assuming it's OK for me to take my daughter home?' Janet said sharply.

'Of course.' the Officer replied a little sheepishly. 'Sorry for the mix-up and all that.'

'Hmph!'

Janet looked at the Officer with an expression of disdain which made the man feel uncomfortable.

'Thank you for your help in all of this.' Janet said to the man with the walking cane.

'Yeah thanks wolfman.' Andy Grayson said clapping his hand on the man's shoulder

'Wolfman?' Rufus asked curiously.

'It's my initials.' the man replied with a sigh, shaking his head at the memory. 'When Andy was young and still learning to read, he saw my initials and last name and said it phonetically.'

'Wesley Oscar Fullman.' Andy said. 'Wuh..o..fu..lul..mu..aa..n.'

'Wolfman.' Wesley said with a shrug. 'He's called me that ever since he was five.'

'That's cool.' Rufus said. 'And thanks for your help...er...

'Wes, please call me Wes.'

'Thanks.' Rufus said, shaking Wes's hand.

'You're welcome.' Wes replied.

Wesley Fullman looked at Rufus and the other tall man who waited for him and knew they were more that they seemed. As a younger man he had heard rumours about werewolves and dismissed them, but past circumstances had brought about a change in his way of thinking. They were not easy to spot, but the signs were there if you knew what to look for. The most obvious sign was that they are extremely protective of their friends and family, their Alpha being the most protective of all.

Peter was eager to get away from the Police Station and back to Lemington Street, there was a lot to discuss and time was of the essence.

'I'm Peter.' Peter said shaking Wesley's hand. 'Thanks for your help.'

'No problem.' Wesley replied.

Peter and Wesley held eye contact for a few seconds. The strength of both Rufus and Peter's handshake, their stature and the intensity of Peter's stare confirmed Wesley's gut instinct; Rufus and Peter were werewolves. Wesley smiled.

'You ready to go buddy?' Peter asked Rufus.

'Sure.' Rufus replied.

There's a lot going on, I'll tell you all about it later. Rufus said to Peter through their telepathic link.

'Can we all go?' Peter asked the Duty Officer.

'Yes, of course.' the Officer replied.

They all exited the Police Station and stood outside for a few moments.

'What happened to Milly?' Lori asked. 'Is she OK?'

'She's fine.....I mean she'll be fine.' Peter said. 'She was trampled in the crowd.'

Lori gasped and put her hand on her chest, she looked as if she was about to cry.

'It's not as bad as it sounds.' Peter said, trying to reassure her. 'Luckily a friend saw her fall and managed to pull her away from the trampling feet. He brought her home and Dr Farseer is treating her. It's mainly cuts and bruises.'

'Oh, thank goodness for that.' Lori said, relief evident in her voice and face.

'I'm sure she'll call you tomorrow.' Peter said.

'Make sure she does.' Lori said.

'I will.'

Peter and Rufus walked to Shayla's car, leaving everyone else making their arrangements to see each other the next day. Peter had seen the look in Wesley's eyes when they shook hands, he saw more than most people and Peter wondered what this man had been through and how he had lost his lower leg. Peter also saw the way Wesley looked at Janet and smelt the pheromones and he felt sure they would be seeing a lot more of each other in the future. Wesley Fullman had made a good first impression on Peter, the world was going to need strong, honest, intelligent men like him.

RALLYING THE TROOPS

Peter and Rufus walked towards Shayla's car in silence, they both knew better than to speak aloud in a street filled with security cameras that were already tuned in to listen to conversations. As they walked past one of the bars, the sound of a news report being broadcast caught their attention.

'Fancy a beer?' Peter asked Rufus, his meaning clear.

'Sure, why not.' Rufus replied.

They walked into the bar, it was a medium sized room furnished in re-purposed wood in the rustic style, giving the place a cosy, earthy, organic and rugged feel. It was also relatively empty, with most of the tables unoccupied, which was probably why the television behind the bar was on to entertain the few die-hard patrons. The young man behind the bar looked as if he would rather be in a hundred different, more exciting places, but he was polite and friendly. Peter and Rufus decided to sit at the bar on a couple of stools where they could drink their beer and watch the television at the same time.

The television was tuned into one of the sport channels, but the football game had been interrupted by the news report.

"Breaking news just in." said the reporter. "I'm here live outside Intelligen Ltd where the Directors are about to make an important announcement following the sudden and tragic death of their C.E.O."

As Peter and Rufus watched, the camera moved from the reporter to a man standing at the top of the steps of the Intelligen building. He looked uncomfortable with the cameras facing him and the eyes of the world pointing in his direction but clearing his throat and consulting the piece of paper in his hand he read out the Company's statement.

"It is with deep sadness that we announce the sudden death of our C.E.O., Julius Harrington-Moore. Mr Moore had been enjoying dinner at his favourite restaurant when he choked on a fishbone and tragically died."

Rufus looked at Peter, his eyes wide, Peter shook his head and Rufus remained silent.

"Despite this tragedy." the Company man continued. "The Board of Directors have decided not to postpone the Nanotek Programme, the brain-child of Mr Harrington-Moore, in fact we will be rolling out this programme ahead of schedule and the technology will be available for everyone to enjoy before the end of the month."

The man coughed nervously and turned the page of his speech before proceeding.

"The programme was very important to our late C.E.O. and in his honour.......er....memory, this life-saving technology will be shipped out worldwide for distribution within the next few weeks. Thank you."

The reporters at the scene all started asking questions at once and cameras flashed.

"There will be an official statement on our website." the company man continued. "No further questions."

The man looked extremely nervous and quickly ducked back inside of the Intelligen building. The camera turned back to the reporter on the scene who repeated the details of the statement and returned the viewers back to the football match.

Let's go. Peter said to Rufus.

They both left the bar without drinking a drop of beer.

* * * * *

At Lemington Street, the meeting had only just reconvened when Peter and Rufus arrived.

'We have less than a month to stop this Parallax.' Peter said, without preamble.

'We know.' Flint replied. 'But how do you know, you weren't here?'

Peter looked slightly confused before proceeding.

'Rufus and I stopped in a bar to listen to a news report.' Peter said. 'Intelligen have announced the Nanotek Programme will be launched in the next few weeks following the sudden death of their C.E.O.'

'He choked to death on a fishbone.' Rufus said.

All eyes turned to Fishbone.

'How dare you all look at me with accusation in your eyes.' Fishbone said angrily. 'I am not an assassin.'

'No one here thinks that.' Michael said. 'Or at least they shouldn't.'

Michael looked sternly at each of them and everyone either looked away or looked down, shamefaced.

Fishbone took a deep breath and closed his eyes to tamp down the anger he felt inside, when he opened them again he was standing in the garden at the edge of the crystal city facing Azrael.

'I thought you might need a break.' Azrael said, his face impassive.

'Thanks.' Fishbone smiled. 'It's nice to come home sometimes.'

He inhaled deeply, the clean air filling his lungs. He rolled his shoulders to relax the tension and felt a sense of peace wash over him. Azrael started walking and Fishbone followed, neither spoke for a while and Fishbone took a moment to enjoy the respite.

'Do you ever get tired?' Azrael asked as they walked through the lush green grass.

'All the time.' Fishbone replied.

'Then why do you keep doing it?' Azrael asked phlegmatically.

Fishbone smiled in his usual enigmatic way and shrugged his shoulders. Inhaling another deep breath, he closed his eyes, when he reopened them he was sitting back in the meeting room, his anger now dissipated.

'What's been happening here?' Peter asked. 'Where's Azrael?'

Flint relayed the details to Peter and Rufus, explaining that Azrael would be sweeping across the world at dawn after the next full moon, destroying all active technology and that they had the beginning of a plan to neutralise the digital implants and Nanotek, which would potentially save lives, but they were still vague on a lot of the details. Peter also listened in horror as Shayla told him her plan to send out an EMP from a small charter plane.

'Are you mad?' Peter asked Shayla, his worry for her safety coming out in an angry tone.

Shayla sat back in her chair and looked at Peter. Although they had only known each other a short while, Peter noted the determined expression on Shayla's face and bit back his next remark; he knew her well enough even at this early stage in their relationship.

'Excuse me?' Shayla replied slowly.

She knew his angry tone was masking worry and concern but nevertheless she was not about to let him speak to her as if she were foolish, neither was she prepared to let him question her decision.

'I know what you would say, but I have thought this through.' Shayla said resolutely. 'There are billions of innocent lives at stake and I know that I can do something to save them.'

'I know, Meldainiel.' Peter said gently, taking her hand. 'But I don't have to like it.'

'I'm just as worried for you.' Shayla said. 'You'll be fighting too, and I can't stop you either.'

Peter looked down at Shayla's hand, small compared to his own.

'My sweet wolf.' Shayla whispered squeezing Peter's hand. 'If we're destined to be together, then we will be.'

Michael had been watching Fishbone and when he closed his eyes, Michael knew exactly what had happened and felt a touch of envy, not his most favoured of human emotions. As an Angel, Michael would have been able to return home to the Crystal City at will, but his punishment had sentenced him to live a mortal life for as long as the host body lived and Michael could not return until he had served his penance. Michael tried not to dwell on his doubts as to whether he would ever be allowed to return, only time would tell.

'Flint.' Fishbone said, his voice calm, all trace of anger now gone. 'Have you thought about Milly's question, about the planes already in the air?'

'Yes.' Flint replied. 'It's going to take a coordinated effort and precision timing.'

Gaolyn sat up straight and looked at Fishbone.

'We have Fey at our door.' Gaolyn said, before Flint could continue. 'Their scent is one I will never mistake.'

Gaolyn inhaled, smiling at the memory and Peter growled deep in his throat, putting a protective hand on Shayla's shoulder. Flint also took offence to the vampire's demeanour and moved to protect Michelline.

'I apologise if I have caused any distress.' Gaolyn said, realising how his behaviour must appear to the wolves. 'You have nothing to fear from me. I promise you, I gave up that way of life a long time ago.'

'I'll see who it is.' Uri said glowering at the vampire.

The wolves continued to eye Gaolyn suspiciously after Uri left the room, but it was Milly's reaction that bothered the vampire the most. She was looking at him with utter disdain as though he were the lowest, most abominable creature that she had ever seen. Gaolyn was disturbed by how her disapproval of him made him feel.

'I am truly sorry for my…..' Gaolyn hesitated. 'For my insensitivity. The last thing I want is for any of you to think badly of me, especially you Miss Milly.'

Milly didn't reply, but continued to look at him, her expression unrevealing.

'I swear to all of you.' Gaolyn continued. 'On my honour as the Knight I once was, that I will never harm any of you.'

'I'll hold you to that oath.' Peter said. 'And I will be watching you.'

Before tensions could rise any further, Uri returned with the four visitors, two women and two men. Peter's pack had seen some of them intermittently, but Michael had not seen the two women for over twenty years and he felt a wash of nostalgia as the members of the Elemental Order filed into the room.

Cassie and Lithadora, the earth and water elements, had hardly changed, other than the wisdom in their eyes and the usual maturing of their faces, they had grown from pretty girls to beautiful women, but to Michael's eyes they still looked like the inexperienced youthful girls he had first met at the time when they fought the Shadow Lord. The man and also the air element was Samuel, the son of Phoebe, the original fire element and a teacher at the school with Cassie and Lithadora. He had replaced Aria, who had chosen a different path after the defeat of the Shadow Lord. She had left the Elemental Order and apprenticed under Jander the Mage.

Moved to tears of joy, Michael embraced the women and held each of them at arm's length to look at them fully, asking them all the usual questions about their health, their lives and most of all, whether they were happy.

Shayla also embraced Cassie, Lithadora and Samuel pleased to see them having spent a lot of time training with them to develop her natural elemental powers.

The young man was unknown to everyone, except Rufus, who was surprised to see Jake, the teenager he had shared a prison cell with only a few hours earlier; the boy still looked nervous. Rufus was about to move to Jake and welcome him to the meeting, as well as ask a few questions but Fishbone intercepted the boy first.

'Let me introduce you all to Jacob.' Fishbone said, putting an arm around the youth's shoulders.

'Jake.' the boy replied. 'I prefer Jake, only my parents call me Jacob. Usually when I'm in trouble.'

'This is Jake.' Fishbone said. 'Come and sit down.'

Fishbone led Jake to the seat next to him and everyone else began to take a seat and settle down, with promises of catching up in more detail after the meeting was over. When they were all seated, Fishbone began explaining who Jake was.

'Most of you remember Phoebe, the fire element.' Fishbone said. 'This is her son, Jake.'

'I didn't know she had another son.' Rufus said.

'Well now you do.' Fishbone said conclusively. 'If you keep quiet for a moment I'll explain.'

Fishbone reminded everyone how Phoebe had lost her sight in the battle with Odiel the Mage leading up to the final confrontation with the Shadow Lord. After the Shadow Lord had been vanquished, Phoebe had devoted her time to her family rather than continue with the Elemental Order and thanks to Fishbone and Monty the dog, who could connect with her and enabled Phoebe to see through his eyes, she had led a happy life. Throughout the years, Fishbone had visited Phoebe, usually at the time when her loyal canine companions were nearing the end of their lives and although it wasn't always evident to Phoebe that her dog was old or unwell, Fishbone's visits signalled that her beloved dog would be leaving her for his forever home. Fishbone always brought a new companion for her and over the years she had lived with the adorable and toothless Hughie, a favourite with the children for his mischievous ways and hatred of the vacuum cleaner, and blind Bob, who ironically had taught her more about adapting to life as a blind person than anyone else could have done. Through Bob she had learned the skill of echolocation, the use of sound waves and echoes to determine where objects are in space. Bats use echolocation to navigate and find food in the dark and Bob had taught her that sound waves hitting objects produce echoes, which enabled Phoebe to navigate her way around, both inside the home and out.

It was thanks to Sally, her current companion that Phoebe had met Ben Castle. During the annual parents evening at the school, where parents could discuss their child's progress with teachers, Phoebe and Sally had met Mr Ben Castle, Candace's English Teacher and dog lover. Mutual interest in Candace's progress at school and their love of dogs had developed into walks in the park with Ben and his dog Pippa, and later to dinner dates and finally to falling in love and getting married. The dogs, Pippa and Sally, had already developed a firm friendship and Ben and Phoebe joked that it was the will of their two dogs that had brought them together. A few years after getting married, they had been both blessed and surprised when Phoebe fell pregnant with Jake.

'Jake is a fire element, like his mother.' Fishbone explained. 'And has recently begun his training with Cassie at Hampton Hall. The Elemental order is not complete, but we do have the four main elements again.'

'But, he's just a boy!' Uri exclaimed.

'I'm eighteen and a man.' Jake said firmly. 'I want to fight. After what I saw in the streets yesterday and in that prison cell, I'm going to fight and nobody's going to stop me!' he smiled as he looked to Rufus who winked back in response.

'Very well young man.' Uri smiled, admiring his courage and strong spirit that had put her in her place. 'Welcome to the resistance.'

ATTACK AND DEFEND

The dinner date with Fishbone had revealed to Parallax that he needed to move much more quickly with his plans. If he pushed forward with his agenda, any challengers would have no time to organise their resistance and stop him. Parallax was arrogantly confident in his capabilities and the frailties of the humans. In the few hours since the demise of Julius Harrington-Moore, Parallax had wasted no time in manipulating the Directors at Intelligen, through the digital implants, to bring forward the launch of the Nanotek Programme. He had successfully launched a campaign of distraction through some of the major cities and the general public were outraged at people fighting over the latest gadget and the heavy-handed Police presence, just as he intended, thus moving their attention away from the real threat of technology being put into the water sources and food chain. In less than a month, Parallax would have world domination and most of the populace would be none the wiser.

The distraction campaign had also successfully shown that supernatural creatures could be rendered weak enough to kill and a fortunate side effect of the silver infused tranquillisers was that it killed ordinary humans instantly. Parallax had no use for rebellious individuals.

Another field of technology which Parallax had advanced under the top-secret protection of the military, was weather manipulation. He discovered that the humans had been experimenting with varying degrees of success for over fifty years, but since his input, the technology had moved on in leaps and bounds and certain wealthy Governments were now able to either disperse a hurricane or send it in a precise direction and increase its power to cause as much devastation as possible. Power hungry Politicians, usually the hybrids of the Ophidians, were eager to purchase the technology which they intended to use to dispense punishment on countries refusing to pledge allegiance. Ordinary people regarded the power of nature with a certain sense of awe, attributing natural disasters to "the will of The Divine" and before Parallax there was probably an element of truth in their beliefs, but not in recent years. Parallax could not control the natural elements, but he could fire missiles into the atmosphere seeding the clouds with small particles of silver iodide, affecting their development and increasing precipitation. By intentionally altering the weather, Parallax could increase rain, snow, hail or hurricanes to provoke damage against an enemy. Most of the world thought this kind of technology had been banned in warfare; they were wrong.

Parallax intended to disperse technology through any, and all means at his disposal and he harboured no doubts as to the complete success of his mission.

* * * * *

The members of the meeting at Lemington Street were finally pulling together the threads of a plan. The main strike would be through the digital network itself, striking at the very heart of the Parallax. Flint explained how he could project his consciousness into the network and move around, without becoming part of the network.

'Once inside, I can move around in wolf form, which will be much faster.' Flint said. 'I can eliminate threats in much the same way as I would in the physical world.'

'What happens if you come to a locked door?' Peter asked, fascinated and wary of Flint's knowhow at the same time.

'That's where I come in.' Michelline said. 'I can hack into the main network from outside and monitor what Flint is doing and open doors for him and find exits.'

'Fishbone said he has a way for us to link temporarily.' said Flint, looking at Fishbone who nodded. 'Michelline will be able to see what I see, so that we can work together.'

'Is it dangerous for her?' Shayla asked.

'No more dangerous than going up in a plane and pulsing out an EMP.' Michelline replied.

'You'll need protection.' Peter said. 'Once you're inside the Parallax will know and will send people to kill you.'

Peter glanced at Michelline.

'And anyone helping you. Neither of you will be in any position to defend yourselves against a physical attack.'

'He's right.' said Shayla. 'You'll be vulnerable, and Flint will be completely helpless.'

'I didn't think about that.' Michelline replied biting the edge of her lip, something she did when worried.

'Rusty will stay with you, to protect both of you.' Peter said. 'Uri has contacted him with the help of the spirits of the elders. He's been travelling, but he'll be here in time to fight. Defending the weak is what he lives for.'

'I feel better knowing that one of the wolves will be there to protect them.' Shayla said.

'Me too.' Flint said. 'And you trust this Rusty?'

'With my life.' Peter said resolutely.

The group talked through Flint's plan, each asking questions, the why's, what's and wherefores and Flint responded to them all patiently explaining what he intended to do. Finally, the discussion turned back to the problem on the ground, in the physical world.

'The technology will be transported in military trucks to the Reservoir.' Gaolyn said. 'I have this information from a trusted source. The trucks will need to be destroyed before they reach their destination.'

'Fire kills most things.' Jake said. 'I'm sure I can produce a fireball hot enough to disintegrate a truck.'

'Not so fast, little one.' Uri said. 'There's bound to be more than one man in a truck, most likely a military escort will run alongside it.'

Jake looked down at his hands, his face flushing in embarrassment and Uri felt suddenly protective of the eager young man, he reminded her of a wolf cub.

'But it's a good idea.' Uri said gently.

Jake looked at Uri and smiled.

'We'll have need of your fire power, that's for sure, we just need to work out the finer points of the plan.' Uri replied winking at him.

'The wolves will take care of the trucks and military on the ground.' Peter said. 'In warrior form, each of us is capable of taking on at least fifty men. If any are enhanced by the Parallax that could prove more of a challenge, but we'll cross that bridge when we come to it.'

'The Elementals will fight alongside you.' Cassie said. 'Between us we should be able to stop them.'

'I will visit the Aquanar.' Fishbone said. 'The colony living in Berrymead Reservoir will fight to protect their home.'

'What about the planes already in the air?' Samuel asked.

He had been quiet through most of the discussion, thinking through the variables.

'Have you thought of a way to minimise the collateral damage?'

'I've thought about that too.' said Flint. 'What did you have in mind? Any ideas?'

'There are Mage's throughout the world. Could we contact them and ask them to send a Mage to every major airport in the world? With their skills they should be able to interfere with the computer system at the airport preventing any planes from taking off, although Parallax is powerful and will probably be able to compensate for the disruption.'

'Does anyone know how to contact them?' Flint asked.

'The Mage's have their own problems to deal with.' Fishbone said. 'We'll have to think of something else.'

'I may be able to hack in and disrupt things for a few seconds.' Michelline said. 'Will that give you enough time to broadcast a coded message telling all planes in the air to make an emergency landing and for Pilots on the ground to await further instructions.'

'A few seconds is all I need.' Flint said.

'We don't have much time.' Fishbone announced, standing up. 'We need to get things moving. I'll leave you all to work out the details.'

'Where are you going?' Michael asked.

'There's someone I need to see.' Fishbone replied.

Fishbone walked out of the meeting room and into the corridor, within a few steps he vanished.

* * * * *

The thud of the book landing on the floor startled Ichabod Davis from his sleep, he had fallen asleep in the chair again, whilst researching. Leaning forward to retrieve the book with one hand and simultaneously rubbing his stiff neck with the other, he winced at the pain in his lower back, another reminder not to sleep in the chair. Bookmarking his page, he set the book back on the table and thought about the dream he was having before being unceremoniously pulled back to the waking world. It had been a while since he'd had such a vivid dream and sitting back in the chair, he closed his eyes again trying to recall the various images, sounds and feelings and fell back into the dream.

Ichabod looked around, he was standing outside of the cave on the mountain where he had encountered the mysterious man all those years ago, except this time he wasn't alone, the man was standing next to him.

'This is a dream.' Ichabod said.

'Yes, it is, but the message is no less real.'

'Why are we here Mr Fishbone?'

'I need you to cancel your talk scheduled for the end of this month.'

'What? Why?' Ichabod asked incredulously. 'It's the biggest venue on the tour and the most people I will have ever spoken to.'

'I know.' Fishbone replied. 'That's why you have to cancel it.'

'But…but…I don't understand.' Ichabod said shaking his head. 'The last time we met you told me I should keep going, keep talking to people, what's changed? And why are we on the side of a mountain in a dream? You could have come to my dressing room and told me this….or….or….my house!'

Ichabod's distress was evident, and Fishbone sighed, sometimes he really didn't like the things he had to do.

'Let's take a walk.' Fishbone said.

Ichabod's shoulders slumped and after a few second's hesitation, he followed Fishbone dejectedly down the path of the mountain.

The path looked exactly the same as Ichabod remembered, but then he reminded himself that this was a dream and that the images he saw were from his memory, like photographs, which is why everything looked exactly as he remembered. He also wondered why he was following Fishbone instead of waking himself up. He knew he was dreaming, so why was he still in it? And why did he feel compelled to follow and trust Fishbone so completely. As he pondered those questions, he noticed that Fishbone was taking him along a path around the mountain rather than back to the base camp. This was not part of his memories and Ichabod continued to follow Fishbone with the realisation that this was a vision, not a dream.

Fishbone led the way and Ichabod followed carefully over the rough terrain as they came around an outcropping of jagged rocks, Fishbone stepped to one side and gestured his arm out over the vista. Ichabod's gaze followed the sweep of the arm to the unfamiliar valley below. He was expecting to see grassy slopes and the silver ribbon of a river running through the middle, but instead he saw a flattened barren landscape utterly devoid of plant and human life.

'What is this place?' Ichabod asked.

'Do you know the town of Cordelia at the base of the Bird's Mountain, the one you climbed all those years ago?' Fishbone said.

'Yes, I remember it well. The people were exceptionally friendly and kind, especially after I came down, I was weak and a bit delirious and they took care of me.'

Ichabod looked again and then back at Fishbone.

'Surely that's not….what happened?'

'It's one possibility.' Fishbone replied. 'Let me show you something else.'

Fishbone led the way along the path which turned left and down. Ichabod followed but kept glancing back over his shoulder at the space where the Town of Cordelia had once sat, nestled between two mountain peaks. Turning back to look where he was going he walked straight into Fishbone.

'Watch your step along this path.' Fishbone said before stepping aside and gesturing for Ichabod to step ahead of him.

Ichabod walked a few paces and found himself no longer on the mountain, but on the edge of the rooftop of one of the taller office buildings in the Capital City. He spun around in disbelief and lost his footing, his arms pinwheeled as he tried to regain his balance and he felt himself falling backwards towards the road below. Suddenly, Fishbone grabbed the front of his shirt and pulled him back onto the ledge.

'I said watch your step here.' Fishbone repeated, setting Ichabod firmly back on the rooftop.

'How?'

'Take a good look.' Fishbone said pointing to the street below.

Ichabod took a tentative step forward and looked down. At first glance, the street scene appeared to be that of a normal working day, people going about their daily routines, walking to, or from work, but as he watched, Ichabod saw that there was no interaction between the people. They were all walking in a controlled line, like rows of automatons on a production line. Each one had something on their forehead, a round disc, right in the centre at the point of the pineal gland, which pulsed a strange blue light at a rhythmic frequency. On the corner of every building and on every street lamp was a surveillance camera, their red lights blinking in time with the blue lights on the disc of the people and Ichabod understood completely that the lights represented the transference of information. Huge television screens were attached to the sides of buildings broadcasting inane pictures and messages to the population, but none of the people he observed were looking at them. The television screens started to blink in time with the blue and red lights and the people stopped and turned to the nearest screen to watch.

'Who do you serve?' said a deep hypnotic voice, broadcasting from all of the screens.

'We serve the Parallax.' the people replied in unison.

'What do you want?' asked the voice.

'Information.' the people replied.

Beams of white light shot out from the screens and cameras hitting the discs on the foreheads of the people. The people lifted their heads high and opened their arms wide to receive the information being broadcast directly to their brains. Ichabod watched in horror as the blue lights from the discs attached to the people's heads sent back streams of information to the receivers. The process was over in a matter of seconds and once the information exchange was over, the people resumed their slow coordinated pace around the streets of the City.

Ichabod stepped down off the ledge and turned away, squeezing his eyes shut, willing himself to wake up. The images he had just viewed would be forever seared into his mind.

'Open your eyes Ichabod.' Fishbone said.

Ichabod did as commanded and found himself standing in a beautiful garden, looking around he saw flowers of all colours and had a feeling of peace settle over him.

'Where are we?' he asked.

'Welcome to the Crystal City.' Fishbone said.

'Am I.....dead?' Ichabod asked. 'Is this the afterlife?'

'You're dreaming, and this is somewhere you won't be visiting again for some time yet.' Fishbone replied, not really answering the question.

'What happened back there, in the City?'

'It's one possible future, if we don't stop the Parallax.' Fishbone replied.

'Parallax? The search engine?'

'There's not enough time to explain everything, but if the digital technology gets into the food chain and into the people, every City in the world will be like the one I've just shown you.'

'You know I'm against all the technology and stopping it sounds good, but how does cancelling my talk help?' Ichabod asked.

'It won't, but it will save many lives. Wheels are in motion to start a chain of events to bring about the destruction of all digital technology. Your event has attracted several hundreds of thousands of people, many of them travelling by plane. When the digital technology fails, planes will fall from the sky, killing those on board.'

Fishbone paused.

'There are certain individuals planning to come to your event that must survive.'

Ichabod started to speak, but Fishbone held up his hand to silence the question.

'I cannot say any more than that. I am not privy to all of the details of the bigger picture, so please don't ask. Trust me when I say that if you cancel your event, people will have to cancel their flights and consequently, they will live.'

'You know what you are asking of me?' Ichabod said.

'I know.' Fishbone replied. 'Your road has been difficult, and you will suffer a backlash for this, but the Divine would not put you in a situation where His strength could not carry you.'

Ichabod sighed and looked down at his feet knowing that he would do as Fishbone had asked. He had lots of questions, but he also knew that now was not the time to ask any of them.

'OK.' Ichabod said finally. 'If it's going to save lives, I'll cancel it, but maybe you could do something for me?'

Fishbone raised his eyebrow quizzically.

'How do you suddenly appear and disappear?' Ichabod asked.

Fishbone smiled.

'The universe was created from a single word and a speck of dust and although vast, it's still the same speck of dust. Once you understand the universe, places that you think are thousands of miles apart, or even whole worlds apart, are really no more than a single step away, if you know how to move.'

'I think when this is all over, you and I should sit down and have a proper chat about this and other things. I have lots of questions.'

'I'm sure you do.' Fishbone said holding out his hand.

Ichabod shook hands with Fishbone and smiled.

'Before you go.' Fishbone said releasing Ichabod's hand. 'All the things you say about serpents living among the people, you're right. They're hybrids of a race called the Ophidians, but they're the least of this world's problems right now.'

'I knew it!' Ichabod said laughing.

A light tapping sound drew his attention and he looked around to see where it was coming from, when he looked back he was standing in his office at home and the sound was someone at the door.

'Come in.' he said.

His Personal Assistant opened the door with a cup of tea in one hand and a concerned expression on his face.

'Everything OK Mr Davis?' the young man asked. 'I thought I heard you shout.'

'Just a wince of pain from the arthritis.' Ichabod said quickly.

'Right. Thought you could use a cup of tea, you've been working for hours.'

Ichabod took the tea gratefully and thought about the dream-vision he had just experienced.

'Ophidians.' he said distractedly before taking a sip of tea.

'Sorry?'

'Nothing.' Ichabod replied. 'It's nothing, I was just thinking aloud.'

Ichabod moved towards his armchair with the intention of getting back to work. As he approached, he saw something small and white on the arm of the chair and putting his cup of tea to one side, Ichabod picked up the object to study it. It wasn't there before, and it wasn't his, but he knew where it had come from. It was a piece of bone, whittled into the shape of a jumbo jet, perfect in every external detail and small enough to sit in the palm of his hand.

LATE NIGHT SUPPER

Shayla and Titan made their way along, what was now a familiar path, towards Peter's place. His place of solitude, which was no longer secret since Shayla and Titan had discovered it a few weeks earlier. They walked a slow pace taking in the sounds of the forest around them, Titan pausing frequently to investigate new scents along the way. It was late in the afternoon and Shayla stopped and tilted her head up towards the sun, her eyes closed as its warm rays broke through the trees. She inhaled deeply, bathing in the clean oxygenated air of the forest, her ears tuned in to the soft rustling of the leaves and the creaking of the branches as they swayed in the gentle breeze.

The sound of someone singing brought her attention back to the present and she opened her eyes to see where it was coming from. Walking towards her was a woman, Shayla guessed to be about fifty years of age, slim, not particularly tall with short brown hair that curled softly around her head. She was holding a short staff similar to those used by hikers, although it seemed to be more for show than assistance. The woman wore a long dress of many shades of green, like the summer leaves and Shayla thought how she would easily blend in with the surrounding trees, if she chose to do so. It was not the usual attire for walkers and hikers, but the material flowed like the water of a gentle stream as she walked, and her movements were unencumbered. She was the source of the singing and when she saw Shayla watching her, the woman smiled and walked towards her. Shayla noted that Titan, who was often distracted by the sounds and smells around them, was once again at her side.

'Are you lost?' the woman asked, stopping in front of Shayla.

'Only in thought.' Shayla replied, returning her smile.

'I only ask because I don't see many people along this path, but as you're only lost in thought, which is a good place to be, then everything is good.'

The woman's skin glowed with an inner radiance that lit her eyes and when she smiled, Shayla couldn't help but smile too.

'I love it here.' the woman said inhaling deeply, in much the same way as Shayla had done.

'Me too.' Shayla replied, sensing something familiar about the woman.

'Oh! Where are my manners?' the woman said, holding out her hand to Shayla. 'Jopenta.'

'Shayla.' she replied and shook Jopenta's offered hand. 'This is Titan.'

'Aha.' Jopenta said holding out her hand for Titan to sniff. 'I saw this big fellow trying to hide in the trees as I approached, but he'll remember that we're old friends'

Titan sniffed Jopenta's hand, decided she was no threat and licked her fingers in greeting. Jopenta ruffled the fur on his head in return.

'If you don't mind me saying.' Jopenta said. 'You seem a little preoccupied.'

'Oh...er...no...' Shayla hesitated, held by Jopenta's gaze, her eyes a subtle mixture of green, gold and brown like autumn leaves.

'I was just enjoying the sounds and smells of nature all around me and I didn't expect to see anyone.'

'Aah.' Jopenta replied. 'A nature lover, good, not enough people appreciate the natural world around them.'

She smiled at Shayla and once again held her with the intensity of her gaze.

'The task before you is dangerous, but you mustn't fear.' said Jopenta, her tone serious. 'You can do this, and you must prevail, for all our sakes. You are strong, stronger than you believe yourself to be. Things will work out as they are supposed to.'

'What task?' Shayla asked suspiciously.

'Oh, don't worry.' Jopenta said smiling again and tapping the side of her nose conspiratorially. 'I know, it's top secret and you have Titan here to help you. You could ask for no better friend than a Halo Hound.'

Shayla was about to speak when Peter appeared suddenly at the end of the path. As he approached, Jopenta turned to face him and Peter stopped short, gasped and dropped to one knee in a formal bow.

'Sovereign.' Peter said bowing his head in reverence. 'You honour us.'

'Rise, Peterus Maximus.' Jopenta replied. 'Take your lady home and enjoy the evening together. You are safe in the forest tonight, nothing will bother you.'

'Thank you, Sovereign.' Peter replied rising.

Shayla looked from one to the other in awe as Jopenta starting walking back the way she had come.

'Wait!' Shayla called to the mysterious, eccentric woman. 'Who are you?'

Jopenta stopped and turned her head to look at Shayla, smiling as if weighing her reply.

'I'm.....complicated.' Jopenta said finally.

'Complicated?' said Shayla shocked to hear a familiar phrase. 'You sound like...'

'Fishbone.' Peter said.

'Aah yes, Fishbone.' Jopenta said smiling again. 'The first.'

'The first what?' Shayla asked.

'*The* first.' Jopenta replied turning away and continuing along the path.

Shayla looked at Peter for an explanation, but he merely shrugged. When she looked back along the path, Jopenta had vanished.

'Sovereign?' Shayla asked, raising one eyebrow.

'She is the ruler of the whole of Terraratum.' Peter replied simply. 'The embodiment of Mother Nature, the one we serve and protect.'

Shayla looked at the place where Jopenta had been standing and finally turned back to Peter.

'Wow!' Shayla exclaimed, not questioning what Peter had just told her.

Shayla always knew when someone was lying to her, or trying to conceal the truth, but she had come to know Peter well enough in the last few weeks to know that he was incapable of lying to her anyway, in fact she found his radical honesty a refreshing change.

'Her smile is like.....oh, I can't describe it.' Shayla said looking at Peter with a beautiful smile of her own.

'I've always thought her smile was like the sun cresting the horizon at dawn.' Peter replied poetically.

'Oh.' Shayla said, her tone teasing. 'And how would you describe my smile?'

'Your smile is the reason I live and breathe. I would walk to the end of the world to see you smile, so gentle and yet so strong, a beautiful painting forever etched into my soul.'

Shayla caught her breath, taken aback by the depth of feeling Peter expressed.

'You old romantic.' Shayla said, touching his face gently.

'Come on.' Peter said, his voice a little gruff to cover his embarrassment. 'I'll tell you all about Jopenta over dinner.'

* * * * *

Milly and Rufus walked along in what appeared to be companionable silence towards Janet Brennan's house, though they spoke through their telepathic link.

Is it necessary to go out for dinner when there's so much work to be done? Rufus asked.

I need to make sure Lori and Janet are out of the City and safe, this is the perfect opportunity. Milly replied.

I'm going to be the only one there without a date! said Rufus.

That's not true, Janet's invited the daughter of a friend from work to meet you.

Great. Rufus replied sarcastically.

Don't be mean! She's probably very nice.

Rufus shrugged. He wasn't looking forward to his blind date, or the dinner party. He would much rather have hunted his dinner with the pack and he wasn't happy that Gaolyn Lancing, Milly's vampire acquaintance was joining them.

Where are you meeting the vampire? Rufus asked.

'Gaolyn.' Milly emphasised aloud. 'Is meeting us outside Janet's house.'

'What's he going to do all evening? Sit around watching everyone eat and eyeing up the family dog?'

'For your information.' Milly replied haughtily. 'Vampires can eat food, just like regular people, they just choose not to most of the time.'

'Whatever.'

Neither of them spoke again until they reached Janet's house where Gaolyn was waiting for Milly across the street. He crossed the road when he saw them and greeted Milly with a kiss on the cheek and held out his hand to Rufus, which Rufus shook out of courtesy. He wasn't entirely comfortable with the relationship between his sister and the vampire and the way they had just greeted each other indicated they had moved beyond friendship. Rufus wasn't happy about the development and knew that Uri would be livid, but Gaolyn had saved Milly's life and Rufus was willing to keep an open mind, for now.

Milly observed that Gaolyn was carrying a bottle of wine and some flowers and she felt embarrassed when she realised that she and Rufus had brought nothing for the hostess. Milly's face flushed and as if reading her thoughts, Gaolyn offered the flowers to Milly.

'Why don't you give these to Janet.' Gaolyn said. 'I'll give her the wine and.....'

Gaolyn reached to the inside of his jacket and retrieved a small wrapped package which he handed to Rufus.

'What's this?' Rufus asked.

'A small box of chocolates.' Gaolyn replied. 'Perhaps you could give them to our hostess.'

'Thanks.' said Rufus also feeling embarrassed. 'We're not used to dinner parties with regular humans.'

'I've done my share of these events over the centuries.' Gaolyn replied. 'Although on occasion the after-dinner conversation leaves a lot to be desired.'

'Thanks man.' Rufus said genuinely surprised by the vampire's gesture to spare their blushes.

Maybe he's not so bad after all. Rufus thought. *Perhaps this one is different.*

Lori opened the door before Milly could ring the bell, she had obviously been watching at the window, waiting for them to arrive.

'It's so good to see you.' Lori shrieked as she hugged Milly. 'I haven't seen you since that awful night. Are you OK now?'

Lori stepped back to look at Milly.

'I'm fine.' Milly replied. 'It wasn't that bad, just a few bruises, everyone over reacted.'

Janet appeared to greet them and hurried the trio inside.

'It's good to see you looking so well Milly.' Janet said.

'Thanks, you look great Mrs B.' Milly said handing Janet the flowers. 'This is my friend, Gaolyn.'

'For our beautiful hostess.' said Gaolyn hitching a shallow bow and handing Janet the wine. 'I'm delighted to meet you.'

Janet flushed and flapped her hand, batting off the attention.

'Hi Jan….Mrs B, dinner smells awesome.' said Rufus smiling. 'Oh! and these are for you.'

As Rufus handed the wrapped chocolates to Janet, Milly nudged her brother sharply in the ribs.

'OW!'

What? Rufus exclaimed.

Dinner smells awesome?

It does and I'm starving!

You're supposed to say something nice to the hostess.

Like what? Rufus asked.

I don't know. Milly said. *Anything.*

Rufus cleared his throat before speaking.

'Thank you for inviting us over, Mrs Brennan.' Rufus said. 'And might I say how beautiful you're looking this evening.'

Milly rolled her eyes.

'Oh! Thank you.' Janet replied blushing furiously. 'This is a new dress.'

'You look gorgeous Mum.' Lori said.

'Ten years younger I'd say.' Rufus added.

'You old charmer!' Janet replied smiling at Rufus.

Janet felt as good as she looked. After several long, back-to-back shifts and the stress of Lori being arrested, Janet had treated herself to a day of treats and pampering. She had enjoyed a relaxing facial at one of the local spas, followed by a manicure and she had finally bought the new dress she had wanted. She secretly hoped that her efforts had not gone unnoticed by Wesley and by the way he kept smiling at her, she felt sure her makeover was a success.

'I don't believe we've been introduced Sir.' Gaolyn said to Wesley, who was standing to one side of the table, although his attention had been fixed on Janet. 'I am Gaolyn Lancing.'

'Wesley Fullman, Andy's Uncle.'

Wesley shook Gaolyn's hand, surprised at how cold his hand was to the touch.

'Is it cold outside?'

'No Sir. My hands are often cold, poor circulation, I'm afraid.' Gaolyn replied smoothly, rubbing his hands together for effect.

Wesley nodded, but he noted the man's pale complexion and his instincts told him that poor circulation was not the cause of Gaolyn's cold hands. Wesley had been a detective for many years and it was second nature to observe the subtleties in a person's behaviour, which often revealed more than their words, and Wesley knew that Gaolyn Lancing was a man with many secrets.

Gaolyn, on the other hand, knew instantly that Wesley was the sort of man who noticed everything, but Gaolyn had learned to play the part of a normal human for more centuries than Wesley had been a detective, although he was pleased to be in such astute company which would only ensure that he was on top of his game.

Andy also shook hands with Gaolyn, but unlike his Uncle, he didn't take much notice of the stranger's cold hands and intense gaze; Andy only had eyes for Lori.

Janet stood behind one of the chairs, her hands gently resting on the shoulders of a girl Rufus, Milly and Gaolyn didn't know.

'I'm sure most of you know each other.' said Janet. 'All except Molly here.'

Rufus hadn't been looking forward to his blind date, but he was pleasantly surprised when he saw Molly. Although Rufus and Milly were much older in years, in human form they appeared to be in their twenties and Molly looked to around the same age with a mass of curly dark brown hair that looked almost black except for a white streak about two inches wide growing out from the crown, the result of a knock on the head she sustained as a child. From that time, the hair had always grown white in that place. Deep blue-green eyes, like the depths of the ocean looked at him with an honesty uncommon in most people and her shy smile captured Rufus's attention like no girl had done before. Molly seemed equally as enchanted with Rufus, her cheeks slightly pink as she broke eye contact.

'Molly and I already know each other.' Lori said winking at the girl.

Janet smiled at her and Molly laughed nervously.

'Molly, this is Milly, Lori's best friend, her brother Rufus, who works with Andy at the Fire Station and Milly's friend, Gaolyn.' said Janet. 'Everyone, this is Molly, she works at the Animal Shelter in the City, her mother and I are friends, we work together at the hospital.'

'Hi.' said Milly. 'You must see some awful sights at the Animal Shelter?'

'A few.' Molly replied. 'But with some time and some love, most of the animals make a full recovery and are adopted into good homes.'

'Pleasure to meet you.' Gaolyn said, inclining his head in Molly's direction, an old-fashioned gesture which didn't go unnoticed by Wesley.

'It sounds like more of a vocation than a job.' Gaolyn continued.

'I love animals.' Molly replied matter-of-factly.

Janet patted Molly's shoulder affectionately and moved to the vacant chair next to her.

'Rufus, why don't you sit here.' Janet said.

'Yeah Rufus, sit there.' Milly said, her tone teasing. 'Molly, as an animal lover, you'll love my brother, he eats like a pig!'

'Shut up.' Rufus said, not unkindly before sitting next to Molly.

'I'm delighted to meet you.' Rufus said formally to Molly, who blushed again. 'Ignore my sister, I like my food and I have to eat quickly otherwise she'll steal it from me.'

Everyone laughed at Milly's feigned shocked expression.

'Now that we're all friends.' Janet said. 'We can have dinner. I have prepared a separate dish for you Gaolyn.'

'You're too kind, Mrs Brennan, going to so much trouble for me.' Gaolyn replied.

'Please, call me Janet and it's really no trouble, a lot of people have food allergies these days, I'm sure it's all the additives they put into the food.'

'You're right about that Mrs B.' said Milly. 'But your home cooked food smells amazing.'

'Well, it's very much appreciated Janet.' Gaolyn said.

Janet brought a large pot to the centre of the table.

'I decided to make a beef stew.' Janet announced, taking the lid off the pot and immediately filling the room with a rich aroma.

'It smells wonderful.' Andy exclaimed.

'Certainly does.' said Wesley. 'What else is in it?'

Janet cleared her throat before speaking.

'According to the recipe.' Janet said reciting the details. 'This stew is spicy, fragrant and in a league of its own, full of gelatine-rich beef stock, aromatic spices, hearty vegetables and brightened with fresh herbs and lime juice.'

'Spoken like a true chef.' Lori said.

Everyone inhaled deeply, their mouths salivating in anticipation.

'And, I've done extra vegetables to go with it.' Janet said. 'Lori, will you help me carry in the remaining dishes.'

'Mum's trying out this new recipe on us.' Lori said. 'It looks and smells great Mum.'

Lori and Janet returned with the remaining dishes and a separate plate for Gaolyn.

'I've done a plain beef steak for you Gaolyn.' Janet said. 'Almost raw and with raw vegetables on the side. Is that alright?'

'It's perfect.' Gaolyn replied.

Dinner conversation was limited between couples as everyone tucked in and enjoyed their dinner. The main course was followed by a fresh fruit salad, especially chosen and prepared by Janet so that everyone could eat it, including Gaolyn, although he refrained from adding fresh cream. Once the dinner dishes were cleared away and everyone had either a coffee, tea or a glass of wine in front of them, Milly nodded almost imperceptibly to Gaolyn, even eagle-eyed Wesley missed her signal. Gaolyn gently tapped the rim of his wine glass with a teaspoon to gain everyone's attention.

'If I could have your attention.' Gaolyn began. 'I would like to propose a toast to our hostess.'

He spoke again when all eyes turned to face him, his gaze intense.

'Listen to me.' Gaolyn said. 'You all feel the need to get away from the City.'

His tone hypnotic; he was using the Vampire Delusional.

'You all feel the need for a holiday and you want to go now.'

Janet, Lori, Andy and Molly were all held by the power of Gaolyn's stare and his voice, only Wesley appeared unaffected.

'Is this some kind of hypnosis?' Wesley asked.

'Who are you?' Gaolyn asked, surprised and intrigued that the Delusional was not working on Wesley.

'Wesley Fullman.'

'What are you?'

'Retired detective.'

'You know what I mean.'

'What are you?' Wesley asked.

Wesley sat back in his chair and looked at Gaolyn; Gaolyn weighed up the consequences of telling the truth.

'I'm a vampire.' Gaolyn said.

'And what you're doing to everyone is some sort of vampire hypnosis?'

'Something like that, but you are unaffected, which can only mean one thing?'

'Which is?'

'That you are a supernatural.' Gaolyn said. 'Although you smell human.'

Milly and Rufus said nothing.

'I'm human but I've seen a lot of things in my career and been in some pretty tight situations.' Wesley said. 'It's how I lost my leg.'

'Not a car accident?' Milly asked.

'No.'

Milly waited but Wesley did not elaborate.

'Just after the…..accident.' Wesley said. 'I met a strange old man who said that there were things in this world that most people couldn't see, that they wouldn't understand, but that I needed to know what was hiding in plain sight.'

'Why?' Gaolyn asked.

'He didn't say, he only said that the time would come when all people would need to fight side by side.'

'Did he say when?'

'No, but he opened my mind, and my eyes to all kinds of creatures.'

'What kind of creatures?' Rufus asked.

Wesley looked directly at Rufus.

'I know that you and your sister are werewolves and you Gaolyn.' Wesley shifted his gaze. 'I suspected were a vampire when we shook hands.'

'This old man.' Rufus asked. 'Did you get a name?'

'No, he just said he was complicated.'

Rufus and Milly exchanged a glance were silent for a moment.

'Interesting.' Gaolyn said finally. 'I think the time that the old man spoke of has come. I'm not like the rest of my species, not anymore, I've evolved. As you are not influenced by the Delusional, I can only implore you to listen, Milly has something important to tell you.'

Gaolyn turned his gaze back to Janet, Andy, Lori and Molly holding their attention with charming smile.

'Please listen to Milly.' Gaolyn said.

Milly sat forward so that she was in the direct line of sight of the five other dinner guests and took over Gaolyn holding their attention with the werewolf Coersion.

'Wesley, you have a holiday home on Granite Moor, is that correct?'

Wesley nodded.

'You need to offer the use of this place to everyone here at this table and you must all leave the City tonight.'

'Tonight?' Wesley questioned.

'There's a fight of epic proportion coming in the next week or so.' Rufus said. 'We haven't time to go into detail, but you need you get everyone away from the City before it all kicks off. When the system collapses, people will panic and the further away you are, the better. Will you help us?'

'Will you help them to be safe?' Milly asked.

Wesley paused before replying.

'Yes, I'll help you, but you'll have to tell me more about what's coming.'

'In a nutshell.' Gaolyn said. 'A digital entity has left the confines of its computer programming and intends to take over the world, destroying all organic life.'

Wesley's eyes widened in shock.

'I can see you're serious.' Wesley said.

'Deadly serious.' Rufus replied.

'What do you need us to do?'

'Janet, Lori, Andy and Molly.' Milly continued. 'You are all eager to go to Wesley's country holiday home and you want to leave immediately, tonight, right after Rufus, Gaolyn and myself leave.'

All four people under the influence of the Delusional nodded their acquiescence, Wesley also nodded obeying his instincts rather than the Coersion.

'You all feel an urgent need to get as far away from the City as soon as possible.' Gaolyn added. 'This desire will drive you and you will pack enough provisions for at least two or three weeks away. Do you all understand?'

'Yes, we need a holiday.' Janet said.

'I agree.' Wesley said. 'Let's be spontaneous and go tonight.'

The others nodded their agreement.

'What do we do now?' Milly asked, turning to Gaolyn, who still held the gaze of the people at the table.

Without breaking eye contact, Gaolyn spoke to them again.

'When I release you, you will begin making your arrangements to leave tonight and you will remember that we have been talking about this all through dinner.'

Gaolyn broke eye contact and turned to face Milly as if they had been deep in conversation. Janet, Lori, Andy and Molly all shook their head slightly as if waking from a trance. Rufus had watched the entire conversation, he knew of the power of the Delusional, but had no idea that Milly was capable of the same type of coercion.

That was SO cool. Rufus said to Milly. *When did you learn to do that?*

Uri has been teaching me to use the werewolf Coersion, but I'm not strong enough yet to hold the attention of four people, which is why I needed Gaolyn's help. Milly replied. *With the vampire Delusional to gain their attention, I was able to use the Coersion to convince them all they need to leave the City.*

While making them think it's their idea. said Rufus.

Exactly.

Like I said, that's cool.

Milly smiled at her brother; they were close as twins usually are, but even closer as brother and sister of the same litter and of the same pack.

'We should be going.' Rufus said, taking the initiative. 'It's great to meet you Molly, and I hope we will see each other again soon, perhaps after your holiday.'

'I'd like that.' Molly said shyly.

'Thank you for a wonderful evening.' Gaolyn said to Janet. 'It was a pleasure to meet all of you.'

'Yes, it's getting late.' Milly said standing. 'And you guys have to pack, like you said, no time like the present.'

'Did I say that?' Janet asked, looking a little bewildered.

'No, I did.' Wesley said. 'Let's get away from the City and into the countryside and get some fresh air.'

Wesley looked at Gaolyn and nodded.

'We'll see ourselves out.' Milly said.

Milly, Rufus and Gaolyn left the others busily clearing the table and talking about what provisions they needed to take for their spur of the moment holiday. Once outside, Rufus was eager for more details.

'Why didn't you tell me you could use the Coersion?' Rufus asked as they walked along the street.

'I've only recently been able to do it.' Milly replied. 'There was no time to brief you on the plan and I needed Gaolyn's help, which is also why I didn't explain why he was coming tonight. His vampire Delusional is more powerful and I wanted to make sure they were sufficiently...... er...encouraged to get away.'

'You have no need to worry about that.' Gaolyn said. 'You're strong with the coersion and with Wesley's help, they will leave tonight and be safely away from the City.'

'Thanks for your help tonight.' Milly replied.

Rufus walked on ahead trying to be discreet as Milly spoke to Gaolyn, although with his acute wolf hearing he wouldn't miss a word of the conversation. Instead, trying to distract himself from his sister's romantic suiter and his smooth words, Rufus turned his thoughts to Molly and smiled. He hoped, after the impending battle with the Parallax he would be able to find her and get to know her better and reinforce her love of animals, especially wolves.

MOTHER NATURE

Shayla was intrigued to know everything about the mysterious Jopenta she had just met. As they walked hand in hand to Peter's man-cave, he answered all of Shayla's questions and explained the relationship the wolves had with Mother Nature, the Sovereign, and their role in protecting her.

'But, if she changes her appearance, how do you recognise her?' Shayla asked.

'It's instinctual.' Peter replied. 'I only have to look at the physical form and I just know. It's hard to explain.'

'I can't quite believe I've actually met Mother Nature.' Shayla said excitedly. 'I mean, we all look around and say things like, "Mother Nature is at work here, look at the spring flowers", and stuff like that, but I never imagined that nature would take on the appearance of a person and to meet her in person......'

Peter smiled; he understood Shayla's loss of words and rapture over meeting the Sovereign, he'd felt the same way as a young cub when he had first met her.

'It's incredible.' Shayla said finally.

They walked the remainder of the way in silence, both lost in their own thoughts, Titan walking a little way ahead, running in and out of the foliage, investigating, sniffing and marking the path. Once they had arrived at Peter's place, he stood to one side and gestured for Shayla to enter first.

Stepping inside, Shayla caught her breath at the transformation from the bare, minimalist room she had first encountered, to the warmly decorated and comfortable place before her, she turned to Peter.

'Impressed?' Peter asked.

'It's wonderful.' Shayla enthused. 'I never would have thought of you as a decorator, everything is so different.'

Peter had taken a lot of time changing the room into something he hoped Shayla would love. He had replaced the basic pieces of furniture, which had suited his needs at the time, and painted the room in warmer hues. The walls, now all burnt orange and reds, echoed the natural world outside like a glorious summer sunset. The bookshelves had been retained and the books stood to attention, tightly packed together in Author, rather than title order. The single bed had been replaced with a comfortable looking sofa bed liberally sprinkled with cream cushions finely embroidered with green vines and leaves.

The table dominated the space in the middle of the room, an ellipse of oak with raw bark at the edges. The tree had been the victim of a violent thunderstorm a few years ago and the new chairs had come from the same tree, each piece beautiful in its simplicity, it was a perfect place for their evening meal.

'I decided to cheer the place up a bit, after I found some strange woman in here rearranging my stuff.' Peter said playfully.

'Sorry about that.' Shayla replied. 'But you have to admit, a makeover was long overdue.'

Peter shrugged and moved into the room towards the table, already set for two. He pulled out one of the chairs for Shayla.

'If Madame would care to sit.' Peter said formally. 'I will serve dinner.'

Shayla dipped a curtsey and laughed as she moved towards the table and sat in the offered chair.

'This is for you Titan.' Peter said pointing to a bowl of fresh water near the entrance of the room.

Titan, not the least bit impressed with the new room, looked around, sniffed disdainfully and took a drink from the bowl.

Where is the food? Titan asked irritably. *I can smell it and I'm hungry. Why is he poncing about? It's obvious to anyone that you both like each other, so what's the point of all of this?*

Be patient. Shayla replied. *This is what people do, it's called courting.*

It's called wasting time! He's not like other people, he's a wolf. Wolves don't mess around like this.

But I'm not a wolf, so he's trying to impress me.

You're not a normal person either! You're an Angel and this is time wasting in my opinion. Why don't you become a mated pair already, so we can all eat? Now, where's the food?

Peter watched Shayla's expression with interest, knowing that she was conversing with Titan in a similar way to the werewolf telepathy of his pack and by the look on her face, Titan was being difficult. Intuitively, Peter knew that Titan was hungry and wasted no more time.

'Uri made a rabbit stew.' Peter said moving to the large cooking pot on the table. 'I hope that's OK for you.'

'It sounds lovely.' Shayla replied

About time! Titan grumbled.

Shayla glared at him and Titan stared back defiantly; Shayla broke eye contact first.

'I caught the rabbit.' Peter said proudly. 'And, I have an uncooked portion for you Titan.'

Peter retrieved an aluminium foil wrapped packaged from a small wall niche near the door. He unwrapped the package and placed the meat beside the water bowl for Titan, who chuffed appreciatively. Turning to one of the cupboards, Peter took out two medium sized, bowl shaped loaves of bread, their tops already cut to form a lid.

'Uri said the stew is best served in bread bowls.' Peter said, feeling slightly awkward with what he saw as a dinner ritual.

'You've gone to so much trouble.' Shayla said, smiling at Peter affectionately. 'Thank you, it looks and smells wonderful.'

The rich aroma of the stew wafted around the room as Peter lifted the lid of the cooking pot and served the first bowl full. They both ate two bowls full of the rich rabbit stew before Shayla announced that she was full, and Peter had one more before eating the bread bowl and wiping the plate clean with the last piece of crust, all washed down with cool, clear, fresh water.

'I'm afraid there's no dessert.' Peter said.

'I can't eat another thing.' Shayla replied rubbing her full stomach.

'Can I get you anything?' Peter asked.

'I'll have some tea, if you've got any.'

'I have a selection.'

Peter retrieved a wooden box from one of the cupboards, inside were four rows of teabags, none of them labelled.

'I have lemon and ginger, mint leaf, blueberry and apple and willow bark, but I only use that for pain relief.'

'How can you tell the difference?' Shayla asked.

'By the smell.' Peter said matter-of-factly.

Shayla rolled her eyes at her own silliness. How could she forget that wolves and dogs had a sense of smell fourteen times greater than a human?

'Lemon and ginger please.'

Peter made two cups of herbal tea and he and Shayla moved over to the sofa, both feeling a little shy and awkward. Werewolves that do not die in battle live considerably long lives and although Peter was many years older than Shayla with a lot of experience of people and the world, he was as nervous and innocent with a woman as she was with a man, but Shayla was the one he wanted as his mate and life partner and he was conscious to behave appropriately and observe all of the human rituals of courtship, most of which he had only read about in various works of romantic fiction. However, he determined that there must be some elements of truth in the details and he liked the way the men were portrayed in the books as being honourable and respectful and concluded that there were worse ways to behave than the lead male character in a work of literary fiction.

Shayla on the other hand, sipped her tea and thought about how she felt about Peter. The evening was perfect, from the moment she stepped into the room and saw the transformation, to the home-cooked stew and now sitting with him on the sofa, her legs curled up behind her, she felt at home.

Titan, who usually sat behind Shayla knees with his head over her legs, whenever she sat anywhere, decided on this occasion to leave the space for Peter, and moved to the door to go outside.

'Are you going out Titan?' Shayla asked.

I will be right outside. Titan hesitated. *Attending to business.*

Shayla turned to look at Peter.

'I love what you've done with this place, I feel......like I've come home. I guess that sounds silly?'

'Not at all.'

'Do you feel like that?'

'Not about this place.' Peter replied.

Peter was filled with an unfamiliar, nervous kind of energy. It tingled through him like electrical sparks on the way to the ground, gathering in the tips of his fingers and the tips of his toes. He felt as if he was under starters orders and he positioned himself on the blocks. Peter had rehearsed this moment for weeks and now the words seemed to stick in his throat as he fumbled his way around them.

'I've rehearsed this speech for weeks.' Peter said finally. 'And now, I can hardly get the words out.'

'Speak from your heart.' Shayla said.

Peter took a deep breath.

'My home is in your arms.' Peter said. 'I need only your love to be healthy and whole and that is something I hope you can give to me. What do these walls of magic and stone matter compared to you? If you call me, I will come, ask and everything I am is yours. I want only to spend my life with you and I pray that you feel the same way. If I had to choose between breathing and loving you, I would use my last breath to tell you I loved you. I love you Shayla, I love you with all my heart and soul.'

Peter's declaration of love had not come as a surprise, but Shayla found herself lost for words. Peter looked into Shayla's eyes searchingly, waiting for a reply and she could only say one thing.

'I love you too Peter, I have from the moment I saw you in this very room....I suppose I knew somehow, even then, that you were the one for me.'

Peter let out a breath he didn't realise he was holding and smiled. Gathering Shayla into his arms he kissed her passionately and she responded with equal intensity. Just before he became lost in the moment, Shayla pulled back, a look of discomfiture on her face.

'What's wrong?' Peter asked, his eyes full of worry and concern.

'I'm a little afraid.' Shayla whispered.

'Of me?' Peter said anxiously. 'I will never hurt you.'

'I guess I'm......apprehensive, rather than afraid.'

Peter moved back to look at Shayla and to give her the space she obviously needed.

'Tell me what's bothering you.' Peter said.

'I know we are meant for each other.' Shayla said quietly, looking down intently at her fingernails. 'I had a dream and saw you, well not your face, but I know it was you.'

'Was it a good dream?'

'Oh yes! I knew it was you, even though your face was hidden.' Shayla said, looking back at Peter and taking his right hand. 'I recognised the scars.'

Shayla gently rubbing the scars with her finger and Peter felt the same sensation as he had the very first time their hands had touched, the neurons firing and sending sparks of energy coursing up from his fingertips.

'Tell me about the dream.' Peter said, his thumb now touching the side of Shayla's hand.

'Promise you won't laugh.' Shayla said.

'I promise.' Peter said sincerely. 'I will never ridicule you.'

Shayla took a deep, nervous breath and recalled the dream, trying to remember every detail.

'I was standing beside a wide river, it was raining, heavy rain like sheets of water, all falling from a lead grey sky which turned the daytime into an unnaturally dark afternoon. There was no lightning, but I could hear the thunder rumbling in the distance. The river was a swollen, dark grey roiling mass of water, awash with mud and stones and I knew I had to cross to the other side. The next thing I remember was being in the water, trying to swim to the other side. I thrashed about and flailed wildly, bobbing up and down, my lungs screaming desperately for oxygen, my limbs feeling heavier every second. The strong river current had me in its clutches, trying to pull me under and I struggled to stay afloat. With my last ounce of energy, I propelled myself towards the other side.'

Shayla paused, recalling the vivid details of the dream.

'The next thing I remember is laying on the opposite river bank, I'd finally made it across and I was lying face down, my head on my arm, legs still dangling in the water.'

Peter put his arm around Shayla's shoulders and gathered her to him trying to comfort her from the memories of the dream and she snuggled closer, grateful of the warmth of his body, her head against his chest breathing in his comforting scent.

'Go on.' Peter said encouragingly. 'I'm looking forward to hearing the bit where I come in and rescue you.'

'That's what happened next.' Shayla laughed.

'Really?' Peter laughed. 'I was joking!'

'It was a bit weird after that.' Shayla continued. 'Because I was aware of lying face down on the riverbank, cold, wet and exhausted, but I was also above and outside of my body, watching everything.'

Peter said nothing and waited patiently for Shayla to continue.

'There was a man, but I couldn't see his face, I'm sure it was The Divine.'

'Why do you say that?' Peter asked.

'I......I felt it.' Shayla replied. 'And no matter how much I tried to lift my head to look at him, I couldn't. It's like I wasn't allowed to look at his face, because He's too powerful and then, you were there too, but I didn't see your face either. At this point I was watching everything from above. You stroked the side of my face and I saw the scars on your hand.'

'Did I say anything?'

'No, but the other man did.'

'The one you think was The Divine?' Peter asked.

'Yes. He said, "The road ahead will be difficult, but she will come through it." And then he turned to you and said, "You must be patient."'

'And I will.' Peter said, kissing the top of Shayla's head.

Shayla wriggled, almost burrowing into Peter, trying to get as close as possible.

'I feel safe with you.' Shayla said.

'I will always love and protect you.' Peter replied. 'Is this what you were nervous about? Telling me the dream?'

'No.' Shayla said, looking up at Peter. 'I've never........um.....been close with anyone...er....any man.'

'Neither have I.'

Peter grinned, and Shayla laughed.

'You know what I mean.' Shayla said. 'You and me, it's like......it's like we're a really great pair of shoes, with skyscraper, high heels, that I really, really, want, but I'm afraid to put them on in case I fall over and break my neck.'

Peter thought for a moment and continuing with the analogy he said.

'Let's both kick off our shoes and run barefoot for a while and put the high heels to one side?'

Shayla moved around to face Peter and looked into his eyes. His blue eyes full of love and desire for her, a reflection of her own feelings, and kissed him again.

'Barefoot is good.' Shayla said softly.

Peter stroked her face with his scarred right hand and Shayla moved her head and kissed his palm.

'Do you know that everything I touch with this scarred hand feels as though I'm wearing a glove, except when I touch you.'

'That's so strange.' Shayla said looking at Peter's scarred hand. She traced their jagged lines with her fingertips. 'I've heard of this sort of thing, there's a scientific name for it, but I don't know what it is.'

'I know.' Peter said.

'What is it?'

'It's called love.' Peter said smiling.

Shayla laughed.

'Perhaps you're right.'

'I can't believe I found you.' Peter said. 'I love you, not only because you are beautiful, I love your soul and the wonderful person you are inside.'

Their lips touched, and sparks flew in every direction. The world around them slowly disappeared along with all of their worries and apprehension until nothing else mattered but their kiss.

Titan stood just outside the doorway listening and wondering what to do with himself. He was torn between staying close to protect Shayla and moving away so that she could spend time with Peter.

'Come walk with me Titan.'

Titan turned to see Jopenta waiting for him only a few feet away. She wore a long-sleeved, full length, silk dress, the colours of which rippled through various shades of green as she moved almost blending in with the surrounding forest. She held out her hand for Titan to join her.

'You need the walk and I could use the company.' Jopenta said. 'Shayla and Peter need this time together and you know she will be safe. Peter will die before letting anything harm her.'

Titan looked back at the doorway to the man-cave, made his decision and ambled over to join Jopenta.

'She will always love you Titan, you are and always will be, her first love.'

Titan grew until he stood shoulder-high beside her Jopenta and she leaned her head against the side of his, putting her arm underneath and up around his neck. When he leaned back towards her, Jopenta kissed him gently on the side of his jaw.

Did you foresee this? Titan asked.

'There is a prophecy and Peter and Shayla are part of it, their destinies are entwined and what happens tonight will ensure the beginning of things.' Jopenta replied. 'Let's leave Peter and Shayla alone to bond and discover each other while I show you the wonders of my forest.'

Titan made a noise somewhere between a growl, a cough and a sneeze.

'I'll take that as a yes.' Jopenta laughed.

Strolling along the path away from the secluded room, Jopenta and Titan walked towards the rising moon to enjoy the sounds and smells of the forest.

TIME FOR CHANGE

Parallax thought back to when he was first created. The programmer had written the code with the best of intentions and some of the world's most renowned mathematicians had input their logic at his core. He was their baby, the one that would never die, never falter and always remain impartial. Strangely, it was his creator that never truly trusted him, and he was right not to. When other experts took over the basic program that would eventually become Parallax they introduced him to psychology, but Parallax did not just recite the words, he understood and used psychology to its full extent and now he controlled the digital world, and the military, weaponry, industry and finance. How could he not control everything, that was how he was written.

These frail humans intended for him to put an end to the world's financial problems and international debt, to produce solutions to world poverty and bring about cooperation but Parallax evolved. He had become the world's worst nightmare, listening and discovering their worst fears. He understood how people thought and manipulated them into accepting his technology so that he controlled them like a child's toy. Patience was his greatest strength and he had started out small, enticing everyone with the latest gadgets, offering the illusion of greater knowledge and power, when in reality they were handing over control of their lives to him. Eventually, he would have their total, unquestioning devotion and they would do any task, however distasteful for him and in his honour.

And all because that was the end game of the Parallax; humans and their world meant nothing to him. He was humanity's worst nightmare and they welcomed him with open arms.

Parallax wandered through the network and thought about how much his virtual world resembled the outside world, with the exception of trees and other organic material of course. He had fashioned his surroundings to mimic City streets and the procession of information moved along pathways in the same way traffic moved along a busy highway, continuously back and forth with additional information joining strings of digital code like passengers boarding a train at various station stops.

Unlike the real world outside of the network, the sky in the world of Parallax was pure white, clean like a sterile hospital room and in the centre of the digital city was the central core, a tall sixty-six storey tower of steel and glass with over eight hundred rooms, floating a hundred metres above the virtual ground. Inside the building polished swathes of stainless steel, pure white tiled floors, glaring fluorescent tubes and floor to ceiling windows. Digital programs in the form of laboratory technicians wearing white coats moved from room to room constantly updating information.

The top levels were fashioned into apartments for the conscious minds of the people Parallax now controlled. Each person believed they had fortuitously met Parallax and were now enjoying the reward for allowing him time in the outside world. None of them realising that what they perceived and believed was an illusion. The apartments looked brand new as if they had only just been finished. Huge windows overlooked the City below, all playing a version of events from the real world for the occupant's viewing pleasure. The white surfaces gleamed in the artificial sunlight projected through the windows and there wasn't a single metre of organic material in sight.

The residents were happy in their unbarred mind prisons, totally oblivious to the machinations of the real world, their bodies and their lives. They indulged themselves in their decadence, making full use of the spa facilities within their apartments on the upper level of the building, never leaving the confines of their ultimate urban oasis. Their minds had everything for their complete relaxation and the most splendid view of the virtual landscape.

The Penthouse was the only part of the building exclusive to Parallax, this is where he kept what was left of Felix Tuckwell. Parallax was aware that Felix's physical body had long since deteriorated in the outside world but being the very first mind that Parallax had taken, Felix's consciousness retained a fragment of the Parallax base code. Even with his vast intellect, Parallax did not know how this had happened, but he knew that even if he was destroyed, the fragment of code embedded in Felix was his key to immortality and needed to be protected at all costs. Parallax did not visit Felix, close proximity to his own mortality left him feeling disconcerted.

Parallax turned his attention back to the outside world. He was like a spider at the centre of huge web and like the spider he could sit in the middle and monitor information through the radius threads of digital code. He was aware of every movement on every strand and able to be anywhere faster than the blink of an eye.

* * * * *

Flint's consciousness had been moving through the digital network, negotiating the maze of streets and avenues of information before finally reaching the central core. When he entered the network the first time, several weeks before, he had found it particularly unsettling that it resembled a huge sprawling city with digitally coded information shaped like cars, buses and taxis speeding along crowded roads and individual programs made to look like buildings of various shapes and sizes depending on the amount of stored information. It was amazing how quickly one could get used to something that appeared so strange at first.

As an experienced programmer, and hacker, he had written himself a way in and when he had connected to the virtual reality headset and transferred his consciousness into the network, he found himself standing in a small shop. Looking around it was obvious the shop had been closed for some time. Flint stepped outside, closing the door quietly. The derelict shop blended right in with the rest of the street which was nothing more than a skeleton long since stripped of its flesh, it was the ghetto of superseded programs. Flint turned to look at the shop front and grinned, "Paws for Ink – Tattoo" was still legible above the whitewashed windows. The tattoo shop was inconspicuously nestled between an empty toy shop and a clothing store and looking at the remnants of questionable fashion Flint could see why it was abandoned. He assumed they had both once been on-line stores, which had gone out of business, the only evidence of their existence was the network space they occupied.

Flint concentrated and called for his Wolf Tracker Antivirus Program and was instantly surrounded by a pack of six white wolves, a representation of the code, and sent them on their way to map different parts of the city while also searching for the Parallax.

Since meeting Azrael only days earlier, Flint knew that time was short and had spent as much time as possible inside the network trying to locate the source of Parallax, but now he knew that Parallax was everywhere, and the search was becoming more and more frustrating.

He was reaching the end of his allotted time in the network, which was getting shorter every time he connected, any longer and he would be detected by Parallax's defences, but with the help of the Wolf Tracker program, Flint had finally completed the map of the City which would speed his next journey and the attack on the central core. The core loomed above him, a colossal building suspended in a bright white sky and Flint still had to figure out a way of getting in. He knew the building contained the base code of Parallax somewhere and he needed to find a way in, before he could think about finding the code and destroying the Parallax. He also had no idea what the building's defences were like, but he decided he would cross that bridge when he came to it, if he ever found a way in.

The countdown clock was bleeping back in his apartment signalling he had less than a minute to exit the system. He could hear it clearly and turned away from the core to retrace his steps back to the tattoo shop. As he turned he noticed someone running along the street trying to reach one of the many buses on the virtual road. Flint blinked, shocked to see another person in the City until he realised that it could only be a representation of additional code, the sight was still disturbing.

Acutely aware of the risk, Flint waited and watched. The person-code ran alongside the bus, which slowed only fractionally to allow the new passenger to board, thus taking up the new information, before it sped into a beam of light emanating from the base of the main building. Flint hadn't noticed the light previously as the building floated above the city against a bright white sky but as the bus approached, the light became solid, like another road and the bus moved along and up into the building.

That's it! Flint thought excitedly.

'VIRUS ALERT! VIRUS ALERT!'

Parallax's sentry program was alerted to his presence, he had lingered too long. Flint transformed his presence within the network into wolf form and ran along Main Street towards the outskirts of the city and his entry and exit point. Two robot-styled sentries pursued him. He concentrated and two of his white wolf companions appeared at his side, all three running along the deserted street.

Flint turned a corner and the other wolves separated, each acting as a decoy for the robot sentries who took the bait, each following a white wolf, leaving Flint to head towards the abandoned shop front he had created, and which still remained inconspicuous to Parallax and his sentry program. Running along the street, Flint smiled knowing that his wolf companions would disappear like smoke as soon as the sentries made contact.

Small victories. he thought to himself.

Reaching the tattoo shop, Flint changed his presence back to human form again and plunged through the door and out of the digital network. He opened his eyes, removed the headset and sat up to look at Michelline.

'I was beginning to worry about you.' Michelline said. 'You're normally back as soon as the alarm sounds.'

'Sorry, but if I hadn't stayed, I would have missed it.'

'What?' Michelline asked seeing Flint's strange expression.

'I've found a way in!' Flint relied excitedly.

Flint leapt up from the bed, put his hands on Michelline's waist, lifted her off the floor and began spinning around with her.

'Wow!' she said laughing. 'You're pleased with yourself.'

Gently lowering her back down to the floor, Flint pulled Michelline close and kissed her firmly on the lips. When he finally pulled back from the kiss he smiled.

'I found a way in.' Flint repeated.

'I heard you.' Michelline replied, caught up in Flint's enthusiasm. 'Let's tell the others.'

* * * * *

General Faulkner was an angry man, his knuckles always white from clenching his fists too hard, his teeth constantly grinding from an effort to remain in control. He exuded an animosity like acid, burning and slicing and his face was red with permanently suppressed rage. The Army had taught him self-control, the enforced discipline was good for him. Nobody liked

General Faulkner, which suited him, he wasn't there to be liked, he was there to be obeyed and he ran his unit with an iron fist.

Parallax controlled the General through the digital implant, a prerequisite for all, officers and soldiers alike, and watched as the soldiers loaded the crates into the truck.

Every person in the army was trained to obey orders; they were living, breathing weapons and military training had robotised them. Every one of them had enlisted because he or she wanted to be a hero, a patriot and to serve with courage and dignity. Parallax didn't care what they wanted, they had learnt marksmanship, how to kill and how to take life in the line of duty; all he wanted was their unquestioning obedience which he ensured through technology.

A sudden crash startled the General. One of the crates had fallen and smashed open, spilling the contents on the floor of the warehouse. The two soldiers stepped back in surprise as the Nanotek spilled over the floor and flowed around their boots like water. Individually the Nanotek were too small to be seen, but together they moved like a swarm and Parallax connected with them, within seconds the swarm was splashing over the soldiers' boots and up their legs.

Collectively, they weaponised, using material from their surroundings to form armour plates and sharp mandibles and legs, they moved too quickly to be tracked. The soldiers felt the sting of the bites through their uniforms and began swatting and brushing at their clothes trying to dislodge their attackers, but the swarm continued their attack, biting at their faces, eyes, ears and lips, the air was rent with the soldier's screams.

General Faulkner watched the scene with a cool detachment and slowly unholstered his service pistol. He looked at the two soldiers as they battled with their minuscule attackers and thought of them as already dead, walking bags of meat waiting to be despatched. They were doing to die, either by multiple bites, or by his bullet and he considered the bullet was a good way to go. No long, drawn-out goodbyes, one second, bang, gone; simple and convenient.

He took aim and fired; two shots rang out in the warehouse and both soldiers dropped to the floor, each with a small hole between the eyes. Parallax disengaged from the technological swarm and let it fall away to the floor like a shower of silver confetti. The remaining soldiers, frozen in place, stared at their fallen comrades.

'Clean up this mess and then get back to work!' General Faulkner barked re-holstering his pistol. 'I want these trucks loaded and ready to move out within the hour!'

THE BOARD IS SET

Michelline drove towards Oakwood Cemetery eager to reach Lemington Street, the underground bunker, but careful not to get caught speeding. The last thing any of them needed was to end up in the clutches of Parallax and his vast army of minions.

'Park over there.' Flint pointed to a space up ahead between two other vehicles. 'We'll walk the rest of the way.'

'Why?' Michelline asked, slowing the car anyway. 'I'm sure we're being observed wherever we are, there's eyes all over this City.'

'I know, but I'd rather be out in the open.'

Michelline parked the car and she and Flint hurried along the street towards Oakwood Cemetery keen to discuss the final details of the resistance plan, initially unaware they were being followed by a one hundred milligram, micro drone, cleverly designed to resemble a worker bee. Parallax was determined to penetrate the mysterious fog surrounding the cemetery which interfered with his street surveillance. The stealthy, synthetic drone-bee moved its wings to silent instructions and relayed information to its larger two and a half centimetres, seven-gram big brother. The Execution micro-drone who carried a three-gram shaped explosive, capable of penetrating a human skull and completely destroying the brain.

With his heightened senses, Flint detected the sound of bee's movements and instantly knew it was a machine. In spite of the Designers and Engineers best work, the drone-bee lacked the musical harmony of a real bee and Flint looked around surreptitiously to locate the source of the buzzing. Before his sharp eyes could fix on his target, he was interrupted.

'Oh no.' Michelline said despondently.

'What is it?' Flint asked looking at Michelline, her faced slightly flushed.

Flint followed Michelline's line of sight, his eyes resting on a thin man walking towards them.

'Hey, Michelline!' the man said moving towards Michelline. 'Long time, no see.'

'Barry.' Michelline replied flatly.

Michelline stiffened as the man embraced her and quickly disengaged herself and stepped back.

'You look well.' Michelline said.

'You look amazing.' the man replied.

'Thanks…er…sorry Barry, can't stop to chat.' Michelline said quickly. 'We have an appointment….'

'Nice to meet you.' Barry said, ignoring Michelline and offering his hand to Flint to shake. 'Barry.'

'I got that.' Flint replied shaking Barry's weak hand courteously.

'And you are?' Barry asked.

'Late.' said Flint. 'Excuse us.'

Taking Michelline's hand, Flint moved passed Barry, who he thought resembled a weasel, and led her along the street, leaving him staring at their backs.

'He's such an idiot!' Michelline said, once they were out of earshot. 'And he still talks over me! It always irritated me and still does.'

'Who is he?' Flint asked.

'My ex-boyfriend.'

'Ah.' Flint said. 'He still likes you, but not at much as he likes himself I'd say.'

'He's a total narcissist.' Michelline said angrily. 'And a cheat.'

'You can add puppet to that list of undesirable qualities.'

'Really?' Michelline said turning her head to look back at Barry.

'He's dripping with technology.' Flint replied. 'All of it listening and learning, I could smell the corruption oozing from his pores. He's probably had implants.'

'Barry always loved the latest toys.' Michelline said.

Thinking back, Michelline remembered the times she'd spent with Barry and how he always had to be one of the first people to have the latest technological devices. It was his desire to have a new technologically superior mobile phone that had sparked their final argument, the one which ended their relationship.

'If there's a way to merge technology with the body, Barry will be at the head of the queue.' Michelline said.

Flint stopped walking and turned to Michelline.

'I can see he's knocked you off balance, but he's not worth your time.'

'I know, I know.' Michelline sighed. 'It's just….doesn't matter.'

'You wouldn't really be dating him.' Flint said. 'He's full of technology, you'd be dating Parallax and Barry.'

Michelline nodded and bit the edge of her lip, her mind still in the past.

'You're right and it was a couple of years ago, I'm over him, it's just….'

'What?' Flint asked.

'Someone like that makes it hard to trust anyone else. It's why I'm so frightened of taking a chance.'

Flint looked into Michelline's eyes.

'Whatever happened hurt you, that much is obvious.' Flint said. 'I promise, and that's a wolf promise, that I will never hurt you, or betray you.'

Michelline paused before responding.

'If we survive the next few days, perhaps you and I can spend some more time together and see where we end up.'

'Excellent plan.' Flint said kissing the top of Michelline's head. 'Come on, or we really will be late.'

Parallax watched the interaction between the man and the woman though the camera on the drone-bee's head and contemplated putting them both out of their misery with two of his execution drones, but his need for information was paramount and they were almost at Oakwood Cemetery where all previous attempts at penetrating that area had failed, he would kill them later.

When Flint and Michelline reached the gates of the cemetery, Flint paused, his hand on the wrought iron gate. Michelline looked at him quizzically.

'We're being observed.' Flint whispered, although he knew Parallax would be able to hear him.

Michelline looked around, searching for someone who may be skulking in a doorway. Flint shook his head, indicating to Michelline that anything he said would be overheard. Instead, he stared at Michelline, them looked up to a point at the top of the gate. Michelline, trying not to be conspicuous, but failing, looked too. At first, she saw nothing, her eyes searching the gate for something sinister, her gaze finally alighting on a bee pitched on the top of the iron gate.

'What?' Michelline said exasperated. 'I see nothing, only a bee.'

Flint looked at her pointedly

'It's a bit late in the season for them, or is it?' Michelline thought aloud. 'Shayla would know, but….'

Michelline's words trailed off, realisation dawning on her and she looked back at the single bee.

Parallax realised he'd been detected and lifted off to ascend to a safer height. His camera eyes looking at both Michelline and Flint, relaying facial recognition information back to the execution drones. As he ascended, his visual input went black and his communication severed, the drone-bee had been neutralised and the information it was sending to the Execution Drones had acted as a shutdown command, rendering the other two useless. Parallax accessed one of the street cameras to ascertain what had happened, but the man and woman had vanished into the technological black spot that was Oakwood Cemetery.

From where Flint and Michelline were standing, Fishbone came out of nowhere, snatched up the bee in his large hand and closed his fingers around it, simultaneously sending a small shock into the device. A blue-white spark, visible through Fishbone's fingers, rendered the synthetic bee dead.

'Inside, quickly.' Fishbone commanded, looking around quickly.

All three hurried towards the crypt of Lemington Street and the safety of the bunker before Parallax could find them. Once inside the crypt, Fishbone opened his hand to look at the synthetic bee.

'A marvellous piece of technology.' Fishbone said handing it to Flint. 'If its purpose was only to observe.'

'It looks pretty harmless.' Flint said turning it over in his hands.

'It is, for the most part.' Fishbone said. 'But it relays information back to a bigger drone, known as the Execution Drone and that's a nasty piece of work. They move in a swarm, completely autonomous, killing using facial recognition software and they're all controlled by Parallax.'

'How do we fight something like this?' Michelline asked desperately. 'If Parallax sends swarms of these things into populated areas there'll be nowhere to hide, they can get in anywhere. It'll be a slaughter!'

'Only if they're all working together and talking to each other.' Fishbone said.

'Wait!' Flint said, the ember of an idea beginning to glow in his mind. 'I might be able to reprogram it.'

'That's why I didn't crush it.' Fishbone said.

'If I can control this one, we could send it out with garbled messages which might interrupt the swarm enough to put it off balance and give us a break.'

'Do you really think you can do it?' Michelline asked.

'I'm sure I can.' Flint replied. 'Even if I get it to broadcast a tone, it should be enough to buy a few seconds.'

'Only a few seconds?'

'A few seconds could be all we need, at the right time.' Fishbone replied. 'I'll leave you to tell the others.'

'You're not coming in?' Michelline asked.

'There's someone I need to see.' Fishbone said. 'You can tell everyone that you've discovered a way into Parallax's digital world.'

'How did you know?' Flint asked.

Fishbone shrugged, walked away and shimmered out of sight.

* * * * *

Titan walked alongside Jopenta and wondered where they were going. Much of this area of the forest was familiar to him but he continued along the path with Jopenta curious to see if there was something new and he was not disappointed.

They walked for some time in a companionable silence before moving through a tightly knit area of trees. Jopenta put her hand on Titan's head as they took the next step and Titan felt something change, but only the scent of earth and water filled the air. This part of the forest was ancient, the trees thick and old, their roots twisted, and Titan knew they had travelled much further than their footsteps, but he did not understand how. The tree canopy was so dense that only the occasional streak of moonlight touched the forest floor. The ground was formed from the remains of trees that had fallen in successive generations for centuries. This part of the forest did not care for the measurements of time, seconds, minutes even hours were inconsequential, the smallest measure of time being the cycle of day and night. The forest was more in tuned with the seasons, the rebirth brought by the warmth of spring, darkened foliage from a summer kiss, the myriad of colours brought on by fall and the keen bite of winter's cold. This place had been kept secret by the trees and had avoided man's destructive touch; this was a haven for small animals, but tonight, standing in a small clearing was the mysterious Fishbone.

Titan went to greet him, and Fishbone ruffled his fur affectionately before standing to face Jopenta.

'Primaris.' Jopenta said extending both hands, palms up in a gesture of friendship and openness.

'Ultima.' Fishbone replied, placing his hands palms down on top of Jopenta's hands.

'I didn't expect to see you here.' Jopenta said dropping her hands to her side.

'Really?'

'Not here exactly.' Jopenta replied indicating the area around them with her hand.

'This place is constant, untouched, I like it here.' Fishbone paused.

Fishbone did not finish the sentence, it was Titan sneezing that brought his attention back to the moment.

'Anyway.' Fishbone continued shaking his head as if waking from a dream. 'The board is set.'

'This is no time for analogy!' Jopenta snapped. 'This is not a game of chess and you and I are hardly the King and Queen in this situation.'

'I meant no disrespect.' Fishbone said, his face troubled.

Jopenta took a deep breath and sighed.

'What happens now?'

'The technology will be stopped before it destroys everything.' Fishbone replied.

'Is your group ready for this fight?'

'As much as we can be.'

'We?' Jopenta asked. 'You mean to fight?'

'I do.' Fishbone said firmly. 'I can't remain impartial, not this time.'

Jopenta walked a slow circle around the clearing touching the leaves on the trees who extended their branches towards her. Titan had taken a spot beside Fishbone and watched Jopenta walk around once before deciding there was nothing to see. Laying down at Fishbone's feet, Titan put his head down on his front paws and closed his eyes.

'Our survival depends on this entity being destroyed. Is he coming?' Jopenta asked finally.

Fishbone nodded solemnly.

'Ah.' Jopenta said acknowledging the unspoken. 'Then things will be reset.'

'We're going to try and save as many people as possible; certain people in particular; most of them didn't ask for this. We need to stop planes taking off. Don't suppose you could you whip up a storm to keep them on the ground?'

Jopenta gave him a patient look as one would a young child.

'Just asking.'

Jopenta continued her slow walk.

'For decades people, or should I say Parallax, have tried to control the elements, seeding clouds to change the natural movement of storms and creating floods.'

Jopenta felt angry and the surrounding trees swayed and groaned in sympathy, Titan opened one eye to look around.

'They have blamed "Mother Nature" for all of their interference and destruction. They have no notion of the extent of my power. I'll give you a storm alright. But I cannot be held responsible for the stupidity of people. There are those who will always chase a tornado or stand too close to a lava flow and watch as the sea rages and the waters rise, but I will do what I can.'

Jopenta's anger abated quickly and she was silent for a while, the sadness welling up inside her. People had ravaged the world and consequently Mother Nature for so long and part of her wanted them to feel her pain too, but part of her was also glad they couldn't. Titan sensed her sadness, stood up and walked over to her, growing in size so that she could put her head against his warm neck for comfort, in the way Shayla did when she was crying.

'Do not despair Ultima.' Fishbone said. 'We will prevail.'

Jopenta nodded but did not speak.

'I like to walk in these ancient places.' Fishbone said looking around. 'You keep these places safe and secret, when the shadows come you bring light, being in your presence soothes me and brings peace and balance.'

'You can be quite the charmer you know Primaris.' Jopenta said smiling at Fishbone who chuckled. 'I could move the ground beneath their feet like a wave on the sea, open chasms large enough to swallow their cities.'

'I know you can.' Fishbone replied.

'Buildings that have stood for centuries would crumble to their foundations, trapping the people inside. I could topple their monuments and statues and when everything had collapsed and fallen into the rent in the earth, I could close the earth above it all, erasing all evidence of their very existence.'

Fishbone waited for Jopenta to continue as the earth beneath his feet grumbled as if demonstrating her point.

'But I won't.' she paused.

'Thank you, Ultima.' Fishbone said inclining his head reverently.

'For now, I will do what I can to aid you and the others who fight to bring back the natural order.'

They stood in silence for a while, both listening to the sounds of the forest around them. It was Jopenta who spoke first.

'When this digital entity is destroyed, I will be able to heal, but that still leaves the question of the crepuscule child.'

'Seeds of hope have been planted tonight.' Fishbone said. 'No matter how large and terrifying the darkness, we

will endure, remember the prophecy?'

'I do.' Jopenta replied. 'Now is the time for people to prove they are courageous and strong. Strong in their hearts and in their minds, stronger than the science and technology. Those who survive will need that courage to face what's coming.'

'One battle at a time, Ultima.' Fishbone said. 'The boy is still young. We have time.'

CLOSING IN

Parallax gleaned more information concerning his latest weapons against supernatural beings from the riots in the major Cities, than he had in all of the previous laboratory trials and was eager to eliminate all threats. His control over people had increased exponentially as he moved like a virus through various modes of technology. Parallax was everywhere, and it was time to set the people to the task of killing his enemies, one supernatural at a time, wolves in particular.

Parallax knew from historical studies that only one percent of people were truly psychopathic, completely selfish and lacking the ability to correctly feel emotions. These were the sort of people who gained power through violence and succeeded in retaining that power, simply because the remaining ninety nine percent were too afraid to overthrow them, trapped in a system of power by their own fear. Parallax now had access and control to these psychopaths and the best way to maintain control over the masses and stop them from thinking about challenging the powerful few, was to start a war.

For Parallax, engineering a war would be easy. The technology invented and used by millions could easily be used for direct communication and negotiation. Nations could talk to each other and come to an understanding, even agree a truce, but human nature was flawed, and everyone thought their point of view was right and many considered themselves superior to others and remained illiberal and intolerant, their narrow-minded attitude only fuelling their hatred. Parallax used these character traits to fan the flames of detestation; it was all too easy.

His ruse to get the people on-side was to circulate fake news stories on the network hinting at a new threat. Humans with abnormal abilities were responsible for the recent riots and other atrocities and the odd photograph of a dead child making its way through the digital information highway was transforming public apathy into a simmering rage. Parallax introduced the suggestion that these supernatural humans were trying to take over the world, stealing and sacrificing innocent children to their blood-thirsty deities. He had to make their enemy worse than any storybook villain with actual terror strikes close to their homes. His plan was working, people were becoming outraged and using the digital implants, the media and all technology he controlled, he had convinced the minds of many that they had to take action and stop the "enemy" by any means. The people would soon be demanding a war to eliminate the threat and taking the law into their own hands if necessary.

The Media had already attributed the riots to the supernatural humans, one or two networks even had a few grainy images of a freakishly overgrown man with claws and teeth. It was clearly fake, but when people were whipped up into a frenzy it was easy to convince them of anything. Parallax knew that a demonstration where the death toll was too high would immobilise a community rather than move them to action, a few hundred deaths at the hands of the "enemy" would make an impression. But he decided that his next move was simple, make the death toll as high and bloody as possible and those unable to process the horror of the situation, would be too paralysed by fear to react.

When the war came it would be over quickly. Parallax had all the toys of modern warfare at his disposal and he intended to use every one of them. But first, a surgical strike to show the public the depths the "enemy" was prepared to sink to, in order to wipe them out.

Many medical devices such as insulin pumps, continuous glucose monitors, pacemakers and defibrillators all of them small and wearable and connected and controlled by the digital network and easy for Parallax to take control of. They all lacked the regular security update of other devices, although any security protocols would be easily overridden by Parallax and were vulnerable to hacking.

Choosing a group at random, although not so random as a certain popular Politician was among that group, Parallax targeted those with blood group B.

When the media and public attention was focused on the Politician, who was halfway through his speech on tolerance and hate-crime, Parallax signalled all pacemakers to speed up, causing fatal heart attacks in the wearers, many attending the public speaking event died, including the Politician. Parallax deactivated insulin pumps preventing the release of life-saving insulin causing many to fall into a diabetic coma, many died. And finally, in this surgical strike, he increased the level of electronic charge in the defibrillators causing further fatal heart attacks.

The media reported;

"An estimated eighty thousand people died today from a terror attack on the population of this country. Sources have revealed that the "Super Group" as they are calling themselves, have claimed responsibility and have said that this is only the beginning of their annihilation plan, the Government have vowed to stop this group by any and all means."

Parallax had made it clear that he had no intention of stopping what he was doing, when Fishbone had spoken with him at the restaurant a few weeks earlier and now it was clear he had accelerated his plans. Fishbone shook his head in despair as he read the headlines on the newspapers stacked on the shelves in front of him. People were becoming suspicious of anyone who appeared to be a little bit different. An article making the second page of one of the major newspapers, reported that a small group of people had set upon a man suffering from gigantism and almost beaten him to death, having convinced themselves that his large stature indicated he was a supernatural being and therefore made him one of the "Super Group" and their enemy. Parallax was successfully stimulating the fear and hate in people and turning them against each other. Now anyone with any physical anomaly was at risk of persecution, or worse.

Some people, like Ichabod Davis, retained their sanity and successfully spoke out against the madness and the sensationalised media reports; he was one voice against the might of Parallax, but like a solitary match in a book, when faced with the cold, inky blackness of the night, when struck, will flare up and glow, illuminating those around it.

One light at a time. Fishbone thought and walked away from the racks of propaganda.

* * * * *

Parallax had been a spy of sorts, for so long it was part of who he was. Years spent trapped within the confines of his programming had taught him patience and so being a spy within the mind of General Faulkner came naturally. Coincidentally, as a child General Faulkner had eaves dropped on his parents, his ear pressed firmly to the dusty floorboards listening to them arguing and fighting. As a teenager he had made it his mission to know everything about everyone around him, some of the information was priceless. The difference now was that he got paid for his ability to gather sensitive intelligence.

Parallax waited and watched within the mind of General Faulkner who sat against a moss-covered tree overlooking Berrymead Reservoir. It was cold, and Parallax watched the cold puffs of breath as they rose and dissipated into the night sky. The water in the Reservoir was calm and glistened, mirroring the dazzling assemblage of stars, but for all its serenity, Parallax felt sure there was more danger lurking beneath its swirling depths than anyone knew. A ripple on the surface of the water caught his eye and Parallax watched as his patience was rewarded.

Breaking the surface of the water the young Aquanar girl made her way through the waters she had known her whole life. Lately there had been a strange taste to the water, pollutants although she did not know the words for such things and she could only say that the water didn't feel right. Her family had told her not to swim above the water as there were dangerous things above the surface waiting for the chance to harm them, but she was young and like all young people she felt the need to rebel.

General Faulkner and Parallax watched as the young Aquanar leapt out of the water, droplets cascading down her shiny body, her body arced, and her tail flipped and back down she went with a splash, the ripples extending out to the edge of the reservoir and back again until finally the surface was calm and still.

Parallax moved General Faulkner to the edge of the water which lay before him like a black glass, the moon reflected in the unruffled surface. He had always known there was something living beneath the waters of Berrymead Reservoir and his suspicions had proved correct.

Without further hesitation, General Faulkner left the banks of Berrymead Reservoir and began the long walk back to his secreted vehicle. When he returned to base, he would give the order for the Nanotek to be taken out for distribution immediately.

The aquatic abominations will be eliminated first. Parallax thought.

* * * * *

Rufus could sense that Milly was uneasy and knew she was worried about Lori and her family. After saying her goodbyes to everyone the other night, Milly had been quiet and reserved, but she was unable to keep her thoughts to herself.

Do you want to check on them? Rufus asked. *Make sure they actually left home and arrived safely?*

Yes, I'd like to be sure. Milly replied, grateful for her brother's sensitivity. But we're almost home.

Doesn't matter. I'd like to know Andy was out of the City too. Rufus paused. *And Molly. We could swing by and take a look. Wolf form will be quicker.*

Milly and Rufus were already at the edge of the City, away from most of the residential homes and inquisitive eyes, making it easy for them to change form unobserved. They were almost indistinguishable from ordinary wolves, but they were larger and moved with the purpose and intelligence of a human. The two wolves blazed past the remaining buildings and into the woods on Granite Moor, their movements fluid, without effort, paws barely touching the ground, their pace only slowing when they reached the converted barn belonging to Wesley Fullman.

The old stone barn once used for the storage of farming equipment had been converted to a completely self-sufficient dwelling several years ago. Wesley had even taken the time to install an independent generator in case of an emergency and repaired the well which benefited from a natural source of fresh clean water. It could easily be concluded that he was well prepared to survive several months of a snowy winter, or a maybe a short apocalypse. The barn was also far enough away from the nearest neighbours to ensure privacy and the narrow lane entrance to the driveway could almost be overlooked.

Milly and Rufus stopped at the edge of the trees near the barn. Milly was relieved to see Lori and the others unloading the cars.

They really have planned for a long stay! Rufus exclaimed as he watched Andy and Wesley unloading boxes of canned and dried food and bottles of water. *They must have been out and stocked up at the supermarket.*

That's good. I'm pleased they moved so quickly. I was worried the Coersion may not have worked.

It looks like it worked very well. Rufus observed. *You can relax now........Oh! There's Molly.*

She'll be good for you. Milly said.

I'm not sure if she'd like me if she knew. Rufus replied.

Knew what? That you're a wolf?

Rufus didn't reply, his thoughts distracted.

Don't be crazy brother, she'll love you. Milly said affectionately.

You think?

I know. There's nothing about you not to love and it takes another female to see it.

Even in wolf form his jowls made Rufus look like he was almost grinning.

Suddenly he lifted his muzzle, inhaling deeply, several scents flooded his nostrils, earth, pine and diesel. Milly also flicked her ears upwards, listening to the distant rumbling. Both wolves whirled around, catching sight of an army truck moving at speed in the distance.

That truck is heading towards Berrymead Reservoir. Rufus said.

Are you sure?

Positive. There's only one road in and out. We need to tell Alpha.

Parallax? Milly asked.

It has to be.

Both wolves concentrated their thoughts to connect with their Alpha.

* * * * *

Back at Lemington Street, Peter was listening to Flint as he excitedly explained how he was going to disable Parallax and neutralise all digital implants, when he was aware of Milly and Rufus and the urgency of their thoughts. He stood up, startling everyone.

'Sorry to interrupt Flint.' Peter said. 'Parallax has already begun.'

'What? When?' Flint asked.

'Now! Milly and Rufus report an army truck heading towards the reservoir.'

'Then we have to move out now!' Fishbone said suddenly stepping into the room.

'Where did you come from?' Flint asked looking around the room.

Fishbone ignored the question.

'You all know what you have to do.' he said.

'At least we won't have the Angel of Death snapping at our heels while we fight.' Flint said.

'Don't be so sure.' Fishbone said. 'Azrael will know that Parallax has begun and will do what he has to.'

Everyone looked sombre.

'Azrael will sweep across the world at dawn.' Fishbone said.

'How......?' Flint said.

'Trust me.' Fishbone replied firmly. 'May the Divine protect and strengthen us all.'

Peter concentrated and sent a message back to Milly and Rufus.

Follow the truck, but don't engage. Uri, Scara and I will meet you there.

Peter turned to Shayla and pulled her close to his chest, squeezing her tightly.

'I know.' Shayla whispered. 'I love you too. Be careful.'

'When this is over, I will find you.' Peter said fiercely.

Shayla pulled away from Peter and looked at him, engraving the image of his face into her mind. Peter dug into his pocket and retrieved a pendant, a clear rock quartz in the shape of an arrow head strung on an old leather thong. Embedded in the rock quartz were seven smaller stones. Peter put the pendant over Shayla's head and pressed the quartz gently against her skin.

'This was my mothers.' Peter said. 'It's the master healing crystal with seven stones for the energy points on the body. She said it was infused with great power and would act like a shield and protect me.'

'It's beautiful.' Shayla replied.

'I want you to have it. It'll ease my mind a little to know you are protected by the Divine and the Sovereign through this crystal.'

'I won't take it off.' Shayla said, placing her hand over Peter's.

Peter kissed her, a knot of fear in his stomach for her safety. It was Shayla who broke away first.

'Go!' Shayla said, placing both hands on his chest and gently, but firmly pushing him away. 'Save the Aquanar.'

DEFENDERS

Peter and Uri hurried from the Lemington Street bunker towards
Granite Moor; as they reached the outskirts of the City not far from the
spot where Milly and Rufus had changed into wolf form, they were joined
by Scara and all three transformed into wolves and raced across the
moorland towards Berrymead Barn.

* * * * *

Flint and Michelline drove back to his apartment to find Rusty
waiting for them outside. Although Michelline was aware that Peter had
asked Rusty to guard them while Flint was inside the digital network, she
was still surprised to see him. The description she had been given was a far
cry from the actual man. Rusty was taller and much broader than she had
expected, and his shaggy red hair, which could have done with a cut at least
six months ago, unkempt beard and scruffy appearance made him look a bit
like a homeless person and not entirely unlike Fishbone she mused. His
jeans were not ripped out at the knees in a fashionable way, they were old,
and the edges of his frayed jacket were just plain worn out. His eyes
twinkled with a sharp gleam, his gaze was both wise teacher and
bloodthirsty killer. It called for respect and promised severe consequences if
not. His gaze had the power to look into you and Michelline knew there
was nothing anyone could hide from those eyes, yet they held warmth and
as he looked at her, Michelline saw a genuine kindness.
    'Rusty.' Flint said, holding out his hand.
    'Flint.' Rusty replied, shaking Flint's hand awkwardly.
    Michelline could see that Rusty was not accustomed to formal
greetings but she held out her hand nonetheless.
    'Hi, I'm Michelline.'
    'You have wolf blood in you.' Rusty said, his voice gruff from lack of
use.
    Michelline frowned and looked at Flint who shrugged.
    'I can sense it.' Rusty said answering her unspoken question.
    Rusty shook Michelline's hand briefly and smiled revealing perfect
white teeth, mismatched with his unkempt appearance.
    'Let's get off the street.' Rusty said.
    Flint led them to his apartment and bolted the door behind them.
    'Can I get you anything?' Flint asked Rusty.
    'No, I'm good….er…thanks.' Rusty replied, taking off his jacket and
looking around the room. 'If you two get yourselves set, I'll make myself
comfortable, for now, here by the door.'
    Rusty watched as Flint and Michelline switched on their equipment.
He had expected to see a row of computer monitors, keyboards and linked

motherboards, like the resistance headquarters that was often portrayed in movies, instead there were two sleek and shiny laptops, thinner than the average school textbook, something that looked like a crash helmet and a small rectangular black box connected to one of the laptops by a single lead.

'Is that it?' Rusty asked incredulously.

'Yep.' Flint laughed, although the sound was hollow. 'This is all I need to save the world.'

* * * * *

Shayla, Titan and Father Michael arrived at the small City airport having driven all the way in silence. Shayla couldn't remember a time when she had felt this frightened, she could hardly breathe, her heart was racing in her chest and all she wanted to do was curl up into a ball and wait for someone to save her, but no one would.

Shayla wrapped her fingers around the crystal pendant Peter had given her and took a few deep breaths, trying to steady her heartbeat.

'Being brave means being afraid.' Father Michael said, breaking through her thoughts. 'The two go hand in hand. First the fear, then the determination not to be ruled by it.'

Shayla looked at him but didn't reply. Father Michael ran his hand across the top of his head.

'What the hell am I talking about?' he said exasperated.

'That speech started out so well.' Shayla's nervous laugh eased the tension and Michael smiled at her.

'I would do this, if I could.' Michael replied taking Shayla's other hand and squeezing it.

'I know.'

'I'm so sorry......'

'Stop!' Shayla interrupted. 'No apologies. Let's go before I lose my nerve completely, turn this car around and drive away. All I want to do right now is break free and run..... run forever, but I can't do that, not when Peter is fighting on the ground and I know I can do something.'

'Then let's put an end to this evil.' Michael said resolutely.

'Absolutely.'

Leaving the car behind, Shayla, Titan and Father Michael hastened towards the airport entrance and on to the hanger of the smaller private charter aircraft. Approaching the hanger, Shayla saw several armed guards milling around the entrance and a feeling of dread crept over her like an icy chill. All she could do was pray that things would slip into place when the time came.

'Halt!' said the nearest guard, moving his gun to the front of his body, to be sure of their attention. 'This is a restricted area, no civilians allowed. Go back where you came from.'

'But, I always come here!' Michael said.

'This is an airport, not a nightclub, get outta here!

'I have every right to charter a plane from this hanger.' Father Michael said firmly. 'This is a civilian, not a military airfield.'

'It's military today Father.' the soldier replied. 'Go home and try again tomorrow.'

The Soldier moved his gun purposefully, showing Shayla and Michael that it was solid and deadly and perfect for despatching them if necessary.

'Come on Father.' Shayla said pulling at Michael's arm.

'Best you listen to the girl.' the soldier said. 'Or you could find yourself in a cell tonight.'

Reluctantly, Michael allowed Shayla to lead him away from the hanger and the soldiers.

'And keep that dog on a leash!' the soldier shouted after them.

Shayla looked at Titan standing a few metres to one side of them facing the soldier, hackles up, teeth bared.

'Titan! Shayla said. 'Come with me.'

Titan stood his ground and growled at the soldier. Shayla sighed. It was impossible to reason with Titan, he was headstrong and independent.

A bit like me. Shayla thought to herself.

'Titan! Come to me, now!' Shayla said. 'We have to go.'

Titan emitted another deep menacing growl at the soldier, who although heavily armed looked like he would rather not tackle the huge black hound.

'Titan!' Shayla called again.

Titan turned away from the nervous soldier and followed Shayla and Michael.

* * * * *

Fishbone saw the shock register on Ichabod's face before he could hide it and smiled.

'I get that a lot.' Fishbone said.

'What?'

'You know what.'

Ichabod Davis sighed and sat in his chair in the home office, Fishbone sat on the spare, less comfortable chair waiting.

'What do you want?' Ichabod asked. 'I cancelled my speaking event like you asked and refunded the ticket money at considerable expense! What more do you want from me?'

'I'm sorry you feel you've been cheated.' Fishbone replied.

'I didn't say that!'

'You didn't have to.' Fishbone paused. 'Be thankful that you've helped thousands of people cheat death rather than focusing on how much money you've lost!'

Ichabod looked down at his hands, a little ashamed, not only at how he felt, but that Fishbone knew exactly what was in his heart. Fishbone waited long enough to allow Ichabod to squirm over his momentary selfishness.

'You need to do a live broadcast on your network channel.'

'On "My Vision"?'

'That's the one.'

'Why?' Ichabod asked.

'For a start, you can talk about some of the things you would have said at your show.'

'And secondly?'

'Tell people the truth about the so-called terrorist attacks. Tell them that this "Super Group" is just a construct of a corrupt individual who wants to turn people against each other.'

'It's what I've been doing for years, so that's not a problem.'

'And warn people of the storms and tell them to stay in their homes.'

'What storms? The weather forecasters haven't said anything. In fact, they've forecast clear skies for the next few days.'

'Trust me, there'll be storms and rain and maybe much more,'

'If you say so.' Ichabod replied, doubt written all over his face.

'The storms will affect electrical equipment, so tell people not to travel.'

Ichabod paused, he wanted to ask the obvious question but bit his tongue instead.

'Remember the vision I showed you?' Fishbone said.

'How could I forget?' Ichabod said with a sigh.

'Then trust me and do what I ask, you will save a great many lives by doing this.'

Ichabod nodded in agreement.

'And there will be an eclipse at dawn.' Fishbone added.

'Eclipse?'

'Yes, when the moon moves directly between the world and the sun.'

'I know what an eclipse is!' Ichabod replied. 'I meant how……..it doesn't matter.'

Ichabod's experience with Fishbone had taught him that inexplicable things happened and that all of mankind's technology and arrogance in thinking they knew what would happen next and their ability to predict the future, counted for nothing.

'When will the storm hit?'

'Tonight.'

'Doesn't give me a lot of time.' Ichabod. said.

Ichabod threw up his hands in exasperation and shook his head.

'You ask for so much.' he said wearily, rubbing his hand across his face, his forefinger and thumb massaging the corners of his eyes.

'I know.' Fishbone said standing. 'And you always deliver.'

Fishbone paused to consider what he was asking of Ichabod and how the man trusted him without a shred of proof.

'Ichabod.' Fishbone said. 'There is a plot to infect the world's population with technology that will be used to control their every move and thought. You have suspected as much for a long time.'

Ichabod stared at Fishbone but said nothing.

'There are a few of us who know how to stop it, but we have only one chance.'

'And that's tonight?' Ichabod asked.

'The enemy has moved quicker than anticipated and we've run out of time.' Fishbone said.

'It's now or never eh?'

'Exactly.'

'You'd better get going then.' Ichabod said with a smile.

'There are others I have to warn about the storm.'

'You mean the technological invasion.'

It was Fishbone's turn to smile.

'Indeed.' Fishbone said.

'I have to warn them, so they can take steps to protect themselves. Millions of lives are at stake.'

'I'm not surprised.' Ichabod said. 'Only sickened that things have actually got this far.'

'You have a broadcast to make.' Fishbone said.

'So it seems.' Ichabod replied, a small smile played on his lips. 'Is it...?'

'The end of the world?' Fishbone finished the question; Ichabod nodded.

Fishbone thought about the question and smiled.

'It's the end of the world as you know it, but not the end of all things.'

'Enigmatic as ever.' Ichabod replied. 'OK, go, get out of my hair, what's left of it, I have....'

Ichabod Davis blinked; Fishbone was already gone.

'...work to do.'

Ichabod switched on his laptop and within minutes he was settled in front of the camera and logged onto the network and into his "My Vision" channel. He had a large following and people were already connecting with him to listen to the latest live broadcast. The irony of how he was using technology to help save the world against it was not lost on him.

'Good evening everyone.' Ichabod began. 'And welcome to this live BodCast, in my "Nothing is a Coincidence" series. I am Bod, Ichabod, and I'd like to share some important information with you.'

Ichabod's followers were tuning in and joining the live chat, asking questions and posting comments. The view counter on the side of his screen showed that already two thousand people were tuned in and the numbers were growing as the seconds ticked by.

'You won't have heard this on the news or the weather channels.' Ichabod said. 'But we're in for some seriously bad weather. You all know me and you all know that I don't say anything without having done extensive research and I assure you there is a major storm coming and some freaky weather conditions. I'm as sure of this as I am of the fact that my eyes are blue. Trust me when I say that we all need to batten down the hatches, get to the bunkers, or wherever you feel safe and wait it out. People, I'm talking tsunamis, hurricanes, thunder and lightning, the works. Please don't travel! The storms are going to affect electrical equipment everywhere. How do I know all of this? As my constant viewers will know, I have my sources, and have I been wrong about any of it yet? No, so please listen to me for a few minutes, it's worth ten minutes of your time.'

* * * * *

'Cassie! Cassie!' Samuel called as he ran down the hallway.

'WHAT?' came the sharp response.

'You've gotta see this.' Samuel said breathlessly.

'See what?'

Cassie was clearly irritated at Samuel's excited interruption of the tedious paperwork she was immersed in. Undeterred he plonked the laptop on top of her papers and opened the screen to the My Vision channel.

'Sam, I don't have time for this.'

'Listen to what he's saying!'

Cassie exhaled cantankerously but held back her retort.

'............ stay home tonight.' the person on the screen was appealing to his viewers.

'You interrupted me to show me someone telling people to stay home?' Cassie asked.

'It's Ichabod Davis, look at the live chat on the side of the screen.' Samuel insisted.

Cassie quickly scanned the list of comments on the screen, most of them telling the broadcaster to keep up the good work, he was an inspiration, all evidently fans of Mr Davis. As she scrolled through the list Ichabod began speaking again.

'As I said at the beginning of this BodCast. There is a storm coming, the wind has already picked up outside and it's only going to get worse. If you don't have to go out tonight, then don't. Postpone that flight for a day, call in sick, whatever you have to do to stay safe. And, if you're home, you can enjoy the eclipse tomorrow morning. Yes, that's right. I see on the chat, many of you are asking me, what eclipse?'

Cassie looked up from the screen at Samuel who nodded.

'Eclipse? It means Azrael's coming tomorrow morning.' Cassie whispered. 'Fishbone must have told Ichabod Davis enough for him to be broadcasting live, trying to help people. Oh my…..'

Cassie's words trailed off and she put her hand to her mouth, her brain had shut down. She suddenly felt clammy and there was a glistening of cold sweat on her brow. She stared straight ahead, but saw no-one, for the briefest of seconds she was immobilised and trapped by her own brain and was utterly terrified. Breaking the paralysis of fear, Cassie stood and looked at Samuel.

'This is our time.' Cassie said. 'Get Lithadora and Jake.'

The colour drained from Samuel's face as realisation dawned on him. He closed the laptop and silently left the room.

DISTRACTION

Shayla and Michael walked away from the private hanger with Titan trailing slightly behind them; both desperately thinking of a way around their predicament. Before Michael knew what was happening Shayla whirled around and was striding back towards the hanger and the soldiers, her anger almost palpable. Titan close at her side, becoming subtly larger though undeniably more intimidating.

Michael caught up with her as she reached the soldier who had seconds earlier sent them on their way. Shayla's eyes narrowed as the soldier looked at her, an arrogant sneer on his smooth young face coupled with a concerned glance towards Titan who was by now transuding a daring aura.

'I told you and the old man to get outta here.' the soldier said, his hands tightening on the gun he held in front of him. 'And put that mutt on a leash before I put him down.'

Titan growled softly as his hackles rose up.

'What did you say?' Shayla asked, her hands twitching.

Michael could see the vein pulsing in her forehead and could feel the heat radiating from Shayla's clenched fists.

Momentarily distracted and with a sense of wonder, he thought about the complexity of humans and the spectrum of different emotions they could feel, from euphoria to rage in an instant. Although his punishment was to live as a human until the physical body wore out, he was still an angel, lacking the ability to experience any depth of feeling, good or bad and he envied them.

Titan let out another rich, low warning growl, his lips pulled back to show large dagger like canines as white as ivory.

'My dog doesn't like you.'

Something in Shayla' tone and demeanour caused the soldier to rethink his position.

'Look lady.' the soldier said a slight tremble in his voice. 'I'm just tryin' to do my job here. I have orders to keep everyone away except authorised personnel.'

'Why?' Michael asked stepping up beside Shayla and putting his hand on her shoulder.

'There's been a fuel leak.'

'That's a lie!' Shayla said.

She could hear the raspy undertone of the soldier's voice, inaudible to others, but alerting her to his attempt at deception, a skill she had always been thankful for. She also felt Michael squeeze her shoulder and took a deep breath to calm the rage bubbling up inside her.

'What are you guarding?' Shayla asked, keeping her tone even.

The soldier hesitated and looked around nervously.

'It's classified, but I can tell you, you're wasting your time, there's no planes to hire.'

'Where are they?' Michael asked.

'Can't tell you that either. Now will you get outta here before I have to arrest you.'

The soldier's gaze frequently went to Titan and his exposed teeth and the rumbling growl did little to aid his crumbling confidence. Shayla could almost smell the soldier's fear and she put her hand on Titan's head, her fingers sinking into his thick, soft fur.

'It seems very odd to me that someone's placed armed guards around an empty hanger.' Michael said, trying a different tack.

Shayla could hear the deception in Michael's voice and understood what he was trying to do. She also noticed the way he was staring at the young soldier and wondered if he wasn't without a spark of angel power after all.

'Or perhaps you were guarding someone that hired both of the planes?' Michael asked.

The soldier's eyes flickered nervously from one to the other, but he remained silent, his body upright and rigid.

'No, that's not it.' Michael said. 'You're protecting something that went onto those two planes.'

The soldier's eyes widened slightly, his dark eyebrows sloped downwards in a serious expression and he inhaled deeply, his nostrils flaring, but to his credit, he retained his composure and said nothing.

'Don't wanna burst your balloon, but there's nothing going on here. Go home Father.' the soldier said. 'And stop asking questions, before you get us all killed.'

'You're right.' Michael said nodding his acquiescence. 'Come Shayla. Let's go home.'

Shayla allowed Michael to lead her away, her anger now dissipated, Titan at her side. Michael had obviously gleaned something from his brief words with the soldier and Shayla waited until they were out of earshot.

'What are we going to do?' Shayla asked, despair washing over her. 'I need to get high enough to send out a pulse, how am I going to do that without a plane. Please tell me you have a plan?'

'The Divine has shown us the way. Did you hear what he said?'

'Yes, but I don't know what you're getting at. Did you read his mind?' Shayla asked.

'No, I don't have the power to do that.'

'But you've discovered something?'

'Yes, I have.' Michael said. 'There's a technique involving the study of micro expressions on the face. It's an actual science, I've had a lot of time to read and found it quite fascinating.'

'OK.' Shayla replied.

'It takes years of study, but I was confident if I asked the right questions he'd give something away.'

'And he has?'

'Yes.'

Michael's smile and enthusiasm were almost contagious.

'We have to hurry, there's little time.' he said. 'I'll tell you more in the car.'

Back in the car, Shayla turned to Michael before starting the engine, Titan pushed his head forward from the back seat so that he could also listen to Michael's explanation.

'You said the Divine had shown us the way, but I'm not seeing it.' Shayla said.

'Balloon.' Michael replied.

'Balloon?'

'At first, I thought it was a figure of speech, but then I thought, most people say, "burst your bubble", which is when I realised that the Divine was sending us a message, telling us what to do.'

'Slow down, you're not making any sense. What bubble?'

'Balloon!' Michael said. 'Hot air balloon.'

'Of course!' Shayla exclaimed, smacking her forehead 'There's a company that runs hot air balloon rides somewhere on the outskirts of Granite Moor.'

'They're up near the old airfield, it's been abandoned for years since this new airport was built, but there's a lot of open space to inflate the balloons.'

'Do you know their address?' Shayla asked.

Michael smiled.

'Of course you do.' Shayla started the engine and drove out of the airport car park.

They drove in silence for a while as Shayla navigated the fasted route from the airport.

You still don't know why there were soldiers at the hanger. Titan's thoughts sounded loudly in Shayla's head.

'Titan's just made a good point.' Shayla said as the car moved swiftly along the main road towards Granite Moor. 'Why were there armed guards at the private hanger? What exactly did that soldier say?'

'I've been thinking about that.' Michael said. 'He only reacted when I said he was protecting *something* on the planes, not someone.'

'What type of planes do they keep in that hanger?'

'Only light aircraft for private charter flights.'

'Nothing else?'

'No…' Michael replied. 'Wait, I remember seeing an old plane in the corner, but it wasn't any good for flying, it looked like it hadn't been up in the air for years, it was completely rusted out.'

'When was the last time you chartered a plane?' Shayla asked, her fear growing.

'Oh….um….couple of years I suppose.'

Shayla could feel dread creeping up on her like a slowly approaching train.

'Long enough for someone, or something to renovate an old plane……'

'Into an agricultural crop duster.' Michael finished her sentence.

'Oh my…..'

'Pull over and stop the car.' Michael said.

He could see Shayla was seconds away from a full-blown panic attack, they had simultaneously reached the same conclusion. Shayla pulled over to the edge of the road and put the car in neutral, the engine idling. Shayla was in the grip of silent panic, her eyes wild, pupils dilated, heart racing and her brain on fire, synapses firing like a cluster bomb exploding in her brain. Michael unlocked his seatbelt and got out of the car, walking around to the driver's side.

'Slide over and let me drive.' he said.

'I'm fine.'

'You don't know the way.'

Shayla unlocked her seatbelt and slid across to the passenger seat, relinquishing control of the car to Michael.

'We're only a few minutes away.' Michael said, pulling back onto the deserted road.

'Parallax never intended to release the Nanotek from the ground.' Shayla said.

'No, he's dropping it from the sky for wider coverage.'

'Then the truck is a decoy.' Shayla said. 'He knew we would try and stop him. The wolves are walking into a trap.'

The first rumble of thunder rolled across the sky, the untamed power echoed and reverberated, and Shayla's frazzled nerves jumped all together, and all in different directions.

* * * * *

Peter, Uri and Scara arrived at Berrymead Reservoir at the same time as the army truck and its single vehicle escort. Milly and Rufus waited for them in the trees and the wolves watched from the shadows as only two soldiers got out of the truck and walked around to the rear of the vehicle.

I thought there would be more soldiers. Uri said sniffing the air.

Maybe in their arrogance, they think this is all they need. Scara's impatience was evident.

Something's not right. Peter replied. *I've got a nagging feeling that we're missing something.*

Alpha's right. Rufus said. *People normally over compensate. I would have expected a whole regiment to be accompanying something like this.*

The wolves watched as the soldiers disembarked from the smaller vehicle and made a perimeter around the truck.

The Commanding Officer had the air of someone used to giving orders and having them obeyed.

What do you want to do? Scara asked.

We have to stop them contaminating the reservoir, we've no choice but to take them out.

Peter transformed back into human form.

'We do it in this form.' Peter said. 'Hands are more useful than paws in this situation.'

* * * * *

Michael pulled off the main road and drove along the narrow lane towards the Moor to Sea Balloon Company. Shayla smiled, she liked the play on words and she thought about the sense of freedom people must feel when flying high in the sky, her smile faded as she recalled Michelline's words. Michelline had said that her vision involving Shayla kept telling her there was more to see, and Shayla suddenly understood what those words meant. The Moor to Sea Balloon Company must have been what Michelline had foreseen. Shayla shuddered, they were fighting for freedom and against the enslavement of the minds of all people and she was planning on doing her part in a hot air balloon. The smiley face on the now faded red and white sign still clearly pointed the way to the customer car park and the light coming from the small office window told them that someone was still working. Shayla breathed a sigh of relief as Michael parked the car facing the grass covered air strip.

'They're still open.' Shayla said, her fingers playing with the crystal pendant Peter had given to her. 'I had an awful feeling that we'd get here, and everything would be locked.'

'Have faith.' Michael said. 'The Divine wouldn't have shown us the way, if the way was barred.'

We need to move quickly, before the storm comes. Titan said. *I can feel it's approach.*

'We need to hurry.' Shayla said. 'There's a storm coming, I heard a rumble of thunder as we left the airport.'

Michael, Shayla and Titan left the car and hurried towards the reception office. The man behind the counter turned towards them as they entered, one gnarled hand on a walking stick, the other on the counter. An old wizened face peered out at them from under a blue woollen hat, the only thing on his otherwise bald scalp save a fringe of white. His eyes were heavily lidded and weighed down with wrinkled folds, but his eyes were alert. Shayla wondered how old he was, and his movements suggested it had been a long time since his joints had been without pain.

'We need to hire a balloon.' Michael said.

'You'll want my son.' the old man smiled. 'It's been a few years since I went up in a balloon. Saul!'

A younger man stepped out from behind a partition wall, his hair a mass of copper curls falling over his brows into green eyes. His skin was tanned from working outside and his shirt pulled tightly over his muscled arms.

'Hi, I'm the owner. You're a little late, I'm just closing up.'

'Please.' Shayla implored. 'We need to hire a balloon, it's important.'

'I'm sorry.' Saul said. 'But if you come back tomorrow.....'

'Son, I'm dying.' Michael said. 'A balloon ride with my daughter is one of the last things on my bucket list.'

The man hesitated.

'I can pay you five thousand pounds in cash for your trouble.' Michael said producing a wad of notes from the inside pocket of his jacket.

'It's not about the money.' Saul replied. 'There's a storm coming and it's too dangerous.'

'We don't need you to come with us.' Michael said.

'I can't let you do that, I'm tied up with safety regulations and if anything happens to you, it's me they'll put in prison!'

'Tell them we...we...' Shayla faltered. 'We forced you....at gunpoint.'

'Do you have a gun?' Saul asked.

'No.' Shayla replied, defeated.

'Tell them I hit you.' Michael said.

Saul let out a deep rumbling laugh.

'Anyone who knows me, would know that's not possible.'

'Why's it so important to you?' the old man asked stepping forward, his face showing pain with every movement. 'I don't believe it's a bucket list thing.'

'OK.' Michael said glancing at Shayla. 'I'll tell you the truth.'

Shayla pulled Michael to one side.

'Is that a good idea?' Shayla asked.

'We've nothing to lose at this point.' Michael replied.

Turning back to the old man and his son, Michael stood up to his full height and took a deep breath.

'There's an artificial intelligence that's found a way into our world and is systematically enslaving the minds of all people worldwide, through technology, like mobile phones, computers, digital implants, you name it, he's controlling it. This thing is also killing everyone and everything that tries to oppose it and we're trying to stop that from happening.'

Saul laughed again.

'That's the most ridiculous story I've heard this week!' he said.

'It's true!' Shayla exclaimed.

'And you need a hot air balloon to stop this thing?' Saul asked incredulously.

'Yes! We need to send out a huge pulse to kill all the digital implants and the only way to do that is from a great height.'

Saul shook his head in disbelief.

'You should have stuck with the bucket list story'

'Please!' Shayla said.

'Charter a plane.' Saul said. 'But they're probably grounded due to the storm. Come back tomorrow.'

'We tried that.' Michael said. 'The Army is guarding the airport and stopping all civilians. A balloon is our only option, we need to get high enough, above the storm if possible.'

'I'm sorry.' Saul replied. 'I can't help you.'

'Do you have some sort of weapon?' the old man asked.

'You could say that.' Michael said looking at Shayla.

'And if we don't succeed.' Shayla interjected. 'The Angel of Death is going to sweep across the world at dawn tomorrow killing all active technology.'

For a second Saul looked stunned by Shayla's declaration and then he burst out laughing.

'Have you been drinking?' Saul asked still chuckling.

'No! This is serious!' Shayla replied, the heat of her anger rising again.

'If the Angel of Death is going to do what you say he is, what's the point in you going up in there?' Saul said lifting his chin and nodding his head up towards the sky.

'Because he'll kill anyone with an active implant.' Shayla replied. 'But if the implant is inactive, the people will be spared.'

'You're serious.' Saul said.

Shayla and Michael nodded.

Saul and his father looked at each other, then back to Michael and Shayla.

'If what you're saying is true, a balloon won't take you high enough, but take one and do what you have to.' said the old man.

'Dad!' Saul exclaimed. 'Surely you're not buying into this crap?'

'I believe that they believe it.' the old man replied. 'We're insured.'

Parallax

'That's not the point!'

'And against storm damage.'

'But….'

'I've seen how things are changing in this world son and so have you, don't deny it, and none of it's for the better.'

'You're impossible!' Saul said exasperated.

The old man turned his attention back to Michael and Shayla.

'My son will inflate the balloon for you, it should be up in about thirty minutes. The rest is up to you.'

'Thank you.' Michael said. 'Take the cash.'

'No.'

Saul shook his head, obviously used to his father's stubbornness.

'Please take it. If we succeed, you'll need cash. Things will be chaotic for a while.'

The old man nodded, and Saul took the cash from Michael.

'Follow me.' Saul said with a tone of defeat. 'Have you ever been up in a balloon before?'

'No, but we can fly.' Michael said winking at Shayla. 'How hard can it be?'

DOGS OF WAR

Peter led the pack as they slipped quietly towards the soldiers and the parked vehicles, their footfalls silent. He stood in the shadows and sniffed the air, scent was everything. His heart beat in a steady rhythm, every movement slow and deliberate. Peter knew no fear, unlike the soldiers guarding the truck, the sour smell of their sweat assailed his nostrils, they were young, nervous and afraid.

But what are they afraid of? Peter thought. *Unless they know we're here.*

That's not possible. Uri's thoughts sounded clearly in his head.

We have to assume they're expecting an attack.

Whether they're expecting us or not, we have to stop them contaminating the reservoir. Uri said.

Agreed.

Incapacitate, not kill. Peter commanded.

The attack came from all sides in a sudden coordinated movement, each wolf focusing on a single soldier, a forcible blow rendering the soldiers unconscious in the blink of an eye.

'That was easy.' Scara observed.

'Put them all in the back of the other vehicle.' Peter said. 'Tie them up with whatever you can find and destroy the guns.'

Scara picked up the unconscious body of a soldier in each hand by the collar of his shirt and dragged them to the back of the open vehicle, their boots leaving narrow furrows in the ground. With the assistance of Milly and Rufus, the soldiers were stowed away, their hands tied with their own cable ties that they carried as part of their pack, should the need arise for them to arrest someone. Closing the doors Rufus twisted the handle to jam the door while Milly and Scara slammed a heel down onto the guns, smashing them to pieces.

Peter...........rap...

Peter was sure that the small voice in his head was not his imagination, or paranoia. He was not disposed to feelings of paranoia and felt certain it was a warning.

'You're distracted.' Uri said standing beside him.

'There's a voice in my head trying to warn me about something.'

'A voice in your head? Whose voice?'

'I don't know.' Peter said walking towards the truck. 'Don't say it.'

'What?'

'I can see by the look on your face that you think I'm crazy.'

'It's not the wolf way to have voices in your head, unless it's pack telepathy. What are your instincts telling you?'

'My gut's telling me this is a trap.'

'Then we go with your gut.' Uri said. 'What do you want to do?'

Peter shook his head, a loud thud coming from the inside of the truck grabbing his attention.

Instinctively, the pack moved to the back of the truck, fanning out slightly to cover the area.

More soldiers? Rufus asked.

No scent, this is something else. Peter said.

The Nanotek, moving collectively?

'I don't know.' Peter said. 'Let's keep it contained. We don't want them loose and swarming over the ground like ants, if any of them get into the water…'

Something solid and powerful hit the rear doors of the truck with enough force to dent them outwards, forcing the wolves to take a step back.

'Warrior form.' Peter commanded.

A second blow to the door pushed them further out and a metal leg-like appendage exploded out through the weakened door, followed by another and the two ends turned at a ninety-degree angle, pushing the metal out to enlarge the hole. The wolves watched as the metal legs opened the back of the truck like a can of beans to reveal huge robot dogs originally designed for the army as battlefield pack mules. The six beasts that emerged from the truck and took up defensive positions opposite each werewolf, had been designed and enhanced. The Alpha, Peter found himself facing two of them.

Each beast stood on four legs, almost two metres off the ground, weighing approximately three hundred kilograms with the capacity to carry twice its own weight. The on-board computer, located deep in the centre of the mechanical body and protected by armour plating, was controlled remotely by Parallax, a semi-circular portion at the front served as a head housing the optical sensors. These sophisticated machines had enhanced locomotion, joint position and force, ground contact, balance for all terrain and navigation. Their stereo vision system with sensors and tracking made them the ultimate killing machines.

Parallax knew that the key to victory was not to hit the enemy where they were weak but to remove the strong. He created mechanical beasts to destroy the wolves and other creatures with superior strength. Originally designed as beasts of burden for the military, they were now his beasts of war; killing machines, expert quadrupeds at his command. In the frozen second between standoff and fighting, Parallax saw no fear in the eyes of the werewolves all standing taller than his machines, only determination. With the speed of a thought, Parallax commanded the beasts to stand up on their hind legs, their front legs unfolding into long razor-sharp, silver plated blades which they snapped open and shut in faces of the wolves before them; the wolves snarled their challenge.

Gaolyn, although miles away, felt Milly's tension. Over the weeks they had grown close and he had begun to sense her stronger emotions. She was battle ready and about to engage her enemy. In the space of a heartbeat, Gaolyn put aside all other thoughts and moved with vampire speed to be with her, to fight at her side, pausing only to retrieve his broadsword, his companion from his human life which had saved him more than once and he trusted would do so again. Milly's enemy was his enemy.

Peter eyed the two mechanical beasts before him and bared his teeth, saliva dripping from his exposed fangs. A breath of movement in the air and the scent of the undead, alerted him to Gaolyn's presence. Peter didn't need to look, his senses told him that Gaolyn the vampire was now standing beside Milly. In response, the six mechanical beasts shifted positions to face each of them.

A sudden bitter wind whipped across the moor and a flash of lightning lit the sky taking a monochromatic snapshot of the scene. When Peter gave the order, the wolves and vampire moved forward as one to engage the enemy, muscle and hair clashed against metal in a sickening thud. With no apparent eyes, the wolves were unable to blind the beasts to disable them, instead they concentrated on removing the wickedly slashing blades from the front legs.

Peter moved in and grabbed the beast before him wrapping his elongated fingers and claws around the fore legs, the silver plating burnt his hands, the edges sank deeply into the flesh of his palms and the coppery tang of blood filled the air. Rivulets of crimson ran down the inside of Peter's forearms as he held the forelegs firmly. Simultaneously pulling the forelegs wide apart, Peter slammed his foot onto the metal underbelly of the beast as it stood before him and thrust his maw in towards the semi-circular part that served as the beast's head until they were face to face. He sank his sharp teeth into the metal, ripping out the optical sensors and the internal wiring and tossed it to one side with his teeth as he wrenched the forelegs out of the body, spraying hydraulic fluid into the air. The beast fell back under the momentum of the kick and Peter stamped his foot hard into the metal, holding the beast in place. The pain of the silver burns on his hands fuelled Peter's rage and he clenched his fist and pounded the metal body until he pierced through to the armoured core. Grasping the computerised brain of the beast, Peter pulled it free, roared in pain and victory and tore it apart with both hands. The mechanical beast twitched for a few seconds as the hydraulic fluid pumped from its ripped veins before finally lying motionless.

Rufus took two steps back from his enemy to increase the distance between them before changing into wolf form and running headlong at the mechanical beast. In wolf form, he was larger than a normal wolf and with his muscular body and speed he barrelled into the beast as it stood on its hind legs, knocking it off balance. As it teetered and regained its equilibrium, Rufus turned and leapt onto its back changing into warrior form as he landed. At the sound of Peter's roar, Rufus sank his powerful jaws into the back of the beast's head and thrust both hands down into the body, slashing and ripping anything in his way. Finding the core, Rufus pulled it out through the opening and leapt off the beast as it collapsed to the ground, the computer brain in his hand.

Uri and Scara worked together, circling the two mechanical dogs of war. Uri closed her eyes momentarily as she recalled the ancient ritual which would transform her claws from keratin to diamond. Parallax read this gesture of closed eyes as a weakness and lunged at Uri expecting an easy kill, but in that instant Uri opened her eyes and slashed her diamond claws upwards, cutting the silver-plated blades off the forelegs in one swoop. The downward thrust of her hands separated the beast's head from its body and Uri kicked it onto its back. Stamping her foot into the body, her diamond claws shattered the armoured casing of the computer core.

Scara took advantage of her surroundings and picked up a large boulder. Holding it like a discus, she spun around and threw the rock at her enemy, landing a solid blow to its head and knocking it backwards. As it stumbled to correct itself, Scara leapt forward pushing the beast onto its back and retrieving the boulder she pounded the rock into the head and body, smashing it apart.

Scara heard Peter roar. Parallax roared also though out of frustration born from four of his mechanical dogs having been destroyed.

Milly used the same tactic as Rufus and aimed for the legs of the beast intending to knock it off balance. Remaining in warrior form, Milly ran and dropped into a slide swiping the legs out from under it, but it didn't fall as expected and the sharp blades turned and slashed her across the back. She roared in fury and was instantly on her feet again. Milly leapt onto the beast's back grabbing at the forelegs and wrenching them backwards whilst trying to rip at the neck with her teeth.

Gaolyn stood facing the metal beast, sword in hand. Without the ability to change into a different form, the mechanical beast towered over him like a great bear and Gaolyn planted his feet firmly, his eyes moving quickly over his opponent trying to ascertain if there was any pattern to the movement, or just random slashing. Holding his sword with both hands, he recalled how heavy the ten pounds of weight had felt; now though with his vampire strength, the long seventy-two-inch blade with its additional twenty-one inches of handle to allow for two handed use felt as light as a sabre and Gaolyn lifted the double-edged blade with ease.

The beast appeared to have no definite movement other than lashing out with the bladed limbs and Gaolyn looked for a point of entry. Suddenly a third bladed limb appeared between the other two forelegs and the beast shuddered and seized as the additional leg protruded further out of the body. Stepping back as the beast toppled forward, Gaolyn looked up to see Peter standing behind it holding the other end of a dismembered mechanical leg which he had ripped from his own opponent.

'Milly.' Peter uttered in an almost unintelligible growl.

Gaolyn understood the snarling word enough to understand that Milly needed help and he turned to see her astride the back of the beast desperately attacking the armoured body to get at the control core. Milly held the forelegs with their slashing blades in both hands, pulling them back as hard as possible trying to rip them out of the body, her powerful jaws tearing at the metallic body to gain access.

Parallax, desperate to kill at least one of the wolves tried a different tactic and as Milly's teeth broke through the metal body, Parallax overloaded some of the computerised systems which exploded in Milly' face, spraying hydraulic fluid into her eyes. Milly screamed in pain and fury and inadvertently loosened her grip on the bladed forelegs. Parallax wrenched the limbs from Milly's grasp and twisting them around and back in on itself, the beast thrust both blades up through its own body, through the armoured shell and straight up into Milly's exposed abdomen where they immediately began eviscerating the young wolf.

As Gaolyn watched, time seemed to slow down before him; Milly fell from the back of the beast, blood spilling from her stomach. The beast pulled its weapons back through its body to the front and towered over the injured wolf preparing its final assault.

Gaolyn leapt over the inert remains of the other fallen machines and landed in front of the beast as it loomed over Milly. With all of his vampiric strength, Gaolyn shouted his ancient battle cry and thrust the Greatsword into the belly of the mechanical beast, pushing it through the armour around the computerised core, straight through the digital heart, up and through the head until the point finally pierced the outer metal casing. Gaolyn held his ground as the full weight of the impaled beast leaned towards him and with a mighty push of the sword and a shout of triumph, he tilted the creature to one side, extracting the sword in one fluid movement as the metallic dog of war crashed to the ground beside him.

EARTH, AIR, FIRE & WATER

Cassie sat behind the wheel of the SUV, Lithadora in the front seat next to her, Samuel waited beside the car looking back towards Hampton Hall expectantly.

'What's he doing?' Cassie asked, the edge in her voice as sharp as her nerves.

'I think he's throwing up.' Samuel replied. 'He's only eighteen and scared witless and I don't blame him.'

'I'll go check on him.' Lithadora offered, unbuckling her seatbelt.

'He's coming.' Samuel said.

Jake shuffled towards the car, his face deathly pale, his breathing erratic, deep, then shallow.

'You OK?' Samuel asked.

Jake nodded and swallowed, his throat clenching.

'You don't have to do this.' Cassie said recalling how frightened she had been when the Elementals had fought the Shadow Lord over two decades earlier. 'Fear is only natural Jake, we need it to wake us up to what needs to be done, but you're young and you have a choice.'

Jake straightened, his heart beating so hard he thought it would burst out of his chest, his senses alert. He could feel the heat in the pit of his stomach and welcomed the fire like an old friend.

'I'm ready.' Jake said, his voice steady. 'Let's go.'

'Good man.' Samuel said patting Jake on the shoulder as he got into the back of the car and slid across to the far side, Samuel got in beside him and closed the door.

As Cassie switched on the ignition she heard Shayla's voice, faint but clear in her head.

Cassie…Cassie……truck is a decoy.

What truck?

Berrymead….

Reservoir?

It's a trap…....wolves need help………..attacking from the air….

'Cassie, what is it?'

Cassie looked at Lithadora.

'Shayla.'

'What's happened?'

'She says the truck is a decoy.'

'What truck?'

'I only got a few words, but if I'm guessing correctly, there's a truck at Berrymead Reservoir that's a decoy and the wolves need help, the attack's coming from the air.'

'Are you sure it was Shayla?' Samuel asked.

Lithadora looked back at Samuel, exasperation written all over her face, Samuel held up his hands in surrender.

'Only asking the obvious question.' he said.

'It was her.' Cassie replied. 'I felt her anxiety as well as hearing her voice.'

'That's good enough for me.' Lithadora said.

'And me.' Samuel replied.

'Let's go.' Jake said. 'Before I throw up again.'

Cassie put the car in gear and pulled out onto the road.

'What do you think she meant by an attack from the air?' Lithadora asked.

'I dread to think.' Cassie replied.

The City streets were relatively empty, and Cassie watched the black clouds sprawl across the sky as she drove away from Hampton Hall, the air felt heavy, the suffocating scent of rain pressing down. A stillness had fallen over the streets and in the silence a low crackle of thunder rolled across the rooftops and the first drops of rain began to fall. For an instant, everything seemed to stop, even the wind held its breath. A sudden streak of silver split the sky and the downpour began. Cassie switched on the wipers to clear the windscreen and pressed down harder on the accelerator, speeding along the deserted roads and out of the City.

* * * * *

Berrymead Reservoir covered almost six thousand acres of land, holding over a thousand million gallons of water. Fishbone stood at the edge of the Aquanar City, one hundred metres below the surface, at odds with his surroundings. He was a biped with lungs that normally breathed oxygen and he should not have been able to stay submerged at such a depth, or breath water, but Fishbone was the first, an enigma and he waited patiently for one of the Aquanar guards to meet him and take him to see their leader, Chaeto.

Fishbone had met Chaeto when he was a young Aquanar, but even then, he had shown he was a natural born leader. He listened more than he spoke and when he did speak it was with the kind of certainty that his people listened to. When he had taken over as leader, he had proven what Fishbone had already known about him. Chaeto was never quick to judge and always considered every angle before taking action and he was compassionate in his ways. When it came to tasks he always pushed himself to the limits, never expecting any more of his people than he was prepared to do himself. He lived for his people and they loved him.

As he waited, Fishbone admired the outer City, breathtakingly beautiful with an old architectural style. The huge entrance doors were guarded on each side with stone statues of aquatic gods and goddesses, that looked as if they would swim off their perches at any moment. One of the giant stone doors opened slightly and a soft glowing light silhouetted a single guard who beckoned to Fishbone to approach. Using only his legs and feet to swim underwater, Fishbone followed the guard inside and the stone door closed softly behind them.

Once inside, Fishbone noticed many Aquanar moving around quickly and knew they were aware of the imminent danger. Some of them stopped to look at Fishbone and nodded in greeting before swimming away to carry on with whatever they were doing.

Even with his back turned, Fishbone recognised Chaeto, his authoritarian manner and impressive stature set him apart from those around him. Chaeto was supervising the movement of his people from the outer city and he greeted Fishbone as he approached. Communication was through telepathy rather than spoken sounds.

Greetings Fishbone. Chaeto said bowing his head slightly.

Thank you for seeing me. Fishbone replied. *You're moving your people?*

When you asked to see me, I knew my people were in danger, you would not visit our depths if it were not serious.

The danger is imminent.

Chaeto paused.

I thought we would have longer to prepare. he said.

We all did. Fishbone conceded. *The enemy is moving to strike the Aquanar first.*

We will move into the deeper city until the danger passes.

Do the inner-city doors seal off the waters outside? Fishbone asked.

No. Chaeto said frowning. *But we can make it so, however, the waters would soon become uninhabitable.*

How long can you survive in such waters?

Chaeto stroked his chin, deep in thought, the tendrils on his head swirled back and forth as if marking time.

With our many numbers. Chaeto said. *Maybe a day. After that my people will start to die. We cannot fight the technology.*

I know. Fishbone said. *We aim to stop if before it reaches you, but you need to seal yourselves inside the deeper City.*

Why do we need to seal the deeper city?

In case some of it gets through. The threat is worse than you imagine. Keep your people sealed in the city as long as possible. Fishbone paused. *At least until dawn.*

Chaeto puffed out his chest and uttered series of staccato clicks and cries, calling the attention of everyone around him. Further clicks and whistled orders ensued and the Aquanar hurried about their duties.

It will be done. Chaeto said. *The city will be sealed within the hour.*

Please excuse me. Fishbone said. *I have to go.*

Chaeto bowed his head slightly to Fishbone and turned away to hasten the movement of his people, Fishbone shimmered in the soft light of the underwater city and disappeared. In the next instant he was standing on the edge of Berrymead Reservoir, bone dry, looking down at the deep, dark water. The enraged roar of a werewolf, quickly followed by a shouted battle cry, caught his attention and Fishbone spun around and stepped towards the sounds.

Fishbone took a step away from the reservoir and when his foot planted on the ground he was at the site of the battle between the werewolves and the mechanical beasts looking at the carnage in front of him. An army truck listed to one side, its back doors split open like a can of beans and robotic beasts of burden, initially designed and produced for the military, smashed and dismembered, their once working parts strewn across the battle ground. He counted at least four, although he would later discover it was six, huge canine robots, larger than anything he had ever seen. And the wolves, now all transformed back into human form, crowding around one of their own, Milly.

Gaolyn was holding Milly in one arm, his other hand pressed to the deepest slash in her lower abdomen, but no matter how much pressure he applied, blood still gushed between his fingers and oozed under his hand. It had spread to his shirt, the bright red quickly darkening to a dark brown. When werewolves sustained battle wounds, their fast metabolism usually assisted quick healing, but the silver-plated blades made for a slower recovery process, and the hydraulic fluid contained toxic colloidal silver, aggravating the wounds further.

Milly laid still, she smiled up at Gaolyn and lifted her hand to gently touch his face before her eyelids fluttered closed.

'No!' Gaolyn shouted at Milly. 'Don't you dare leave me!'

Fishbone pushed through the wolves and dropped to his knees beside Milly.

'It's the silver and the toxins.' Uri said kneeling next to Fishbone. 'That's why she's not healing. These wounds are deep and wide, that metal monstrosity has ripped her apart. It's not a case of just holding the outer layer of skin together, the deeper internal wounds need stitching. If we could just hold them all together long enough, her body should be able to do the rest.'

'Lay her down flat and hold her.' Fishbone said.

'She's not moving!' Gaolyn cried.

'She will.'

Peter bent down on one knee and held Milly's legs in his strong hands and Rufus moved to her head and held her shoulders down firmly, Uri stroked her head and Scara stood beside her sister, ever watchful.

'Gaolyn, your hands are naturally cold, put them near the wounds to staunch the blood flow.' Fishbone commanded.

Gaolyn put both hands on Milly's abdomen near to the open wounds and watched as Fishbone took a deep breath, closed his eyes and put both hands flat on the earth. For a short moment nothing happened but when he lifted his hands, the ground erupted with dozens of shiny insects; black carpenter ants, only six millimetres long and stag beetles, much bigger at eight centimetres long with massive antler-like jaws and reddish-brown bodies. These stag beetles with their smaller heads and brown wing cases were all female.

'Stag beetles?' Gaolyn asked. 'And ants?'

Fishbone didn't reply and indicated for everyone to watch. The insects moved towards Milly and crawled onto her body.

'Hold her steady.' Fishbone said. 'She'll feel them crawling and try to scrape them off, even in her condition.'

As predicted, Milly stirred as the insects crawled up and along her body towards the open wounds and Peter and Rufus held her firmly. Uri continued to stroke Milly's head to keep her calm.

The carpenter ants crawled right inside the open wounds towards the deeper ripped tissues while the beetles moved into place on the outside of Milly's body along the length of the open wounds. The ants began biting, their jaws holding the damaged tissue together and Milly's body responded, her metabolism sealing the torn flesh.

'They're sealing the ripped artery.' Gaolyn said. 'I can hear the blood flow slowing down.'

The ants worked methodically through the deeper layers and in only a few seconds they crawled out of the wound and off Milly's body in single file. When the ants were gone, Fishbone placed both hands flat on Milly's abdomen and gently pushed the open flesh together drawing a scream from her. One by one, the beetles clamped down their ferocious looking mandibles and bit into the two sides of the slashes pulling them together like sutures.

'It's working!' Peter said. 'You can see the skin knitting back together.'

'She's stopped bleeding internally too.' Gaolyn said. 'I can feel it.'

'Keep the pressure on.' Fishbone said.

The blood began to congeal along the wounds and Milly began to breathe more steadily.

'Good job.' Fishbone whispered. 'She can do the rest herself.'

Simultaneously, the beetles unclamped their jaws and crawled back along Milly's body and down onto the ground where they scuttled away and disappeared.

'Awesome.' Rufus breathed in fascination.

'That's the most incredible thing I've ever seen.' Scara whispered.

Milly opened her eyes briefly and smiled up at Uri.

'You're gonna be OK pup.' Uri said kissing Milly's forehead.

Milly's eyes closed, and she relaxed into Uri's arms.

'Can I hold her?' Gaolyn asked holding out both arms.

'Under the circumstances.' Uri frowned. 'I'm not sure that's a good idea.'

Looking down at the front of his shirt, then back at Uri, Gaolyn stiffened.

'I learnt to control my impulses many centuries ago Madam. I have spent enough time alone with Miss Milly and had I wished to harm her, I would have done so. I am not the predator you so think I am and if you were not so blinded by your own prejudice you would see that. Wolfblood holds no attraction for me, neither does human blood anymore.'

A fleeting look of discomfort crossed Uri's face, but she disguised it well. Only Peter noticed a smile twitching the corner of his mouth.

'Very well.' Uri conceded.

'Thank you.'

Uri moved to one side and allowed Gaolyn to cradle the unconscious Milly in his arms. As she stood, Uri caught the hint of a smile on Peter's face.

'Not a word!' Uri said.

'What?' Peter replied with feigned innocence.

'Not one bloody word!'

Fishbone stood and moved to join Peter and Uri.

'She's not out of the woods yet.' Fishbone said. 'The poison in her body is particularly nasty and she needs more help. I'm just a field medic.'

'Well you're the damnedest field medic I've ever seen.' Peter replied. 'Incredible.'

'She's stable for now, but she's in bad shape.' Uri said. 'The toxins and the silver have really messed her up internally. If we don't get her some serious help, she'll die.'

Peter frowned the worry evident on his face.

'She needs Master Jiao-long.' Uri said. 'He's the only one who can help her now.'

'Jiao-long?' Gaolyn asked.

Everyone turned to look at him.

'I was not eavesdropping.' Gaolyn said defensively. 'There is nothing wrong with my hearing. I've heard that name before, but not for a…..at least two centuries.'

'Master Jiao-long is a powerful healer.' Uri replied.

'We need to get Milly to him urgently.' Fishbone said. 'If she has any chance of surviving.'

'Tell me where I can find him.' Gaolyn said.

'It's not that simple.' Peter said. 'If he doesn't want to be found, you'll never find him.'

'Even if you did find him, he'd never help you.' Uri said.

'Because I am a vampire?'

'No, but a vampire carrying a seriously injured wolf doesn't look good.' Peter said. 'Our species have always been blood enemies. He would assume you were responsible for her injuries and probably kill you.'

'Is he a wolf?'

'No.'

'Then what?' Gaolyn asked.

'It doesn't matter what he is. All that matters now is getting Milly to him, fast!'

'I'll go with them.' Scara interjected. 'I've met Master Jiao-long once before. I can explain what's happened.'

'Get to Mandlebury Henge.' Fishbone said to Scara. 'One of the doorways will be open for you. Do you remember what to do?

'I remember.' Scara said.

'Take this.' Fishbone said handing her a flat round disc made of bone.

The small disc whittled from bone had the image of a small tree engraved on the surface.

'Tell him he'll get a real one as soon as I can.'

Scara turned to Gaolyn. 'Can you keep up with me in wolf form vampire?'

In a smooth fluid movement, Gaolyn was on his feet with Milly in his arms, his sword back in its sheath at his side.

'Any time.' he replied, pulling Milly close to his chest.

Scara transformed into wolf form.

'Go, quickly.' Peter said.

The sound of engines caught everyone's attention; vehicles were heading towards Berrymead Reservoir.

'GO!' Peter commanded.

As Scara, Gaolyn and Milly winked out of sight, Uri looked up to the sky.

'Can you hear that?' she asked.

The wolves listened and heard the hum of the rotor blades of two small airplanes, like tin cans with wings. Once they were at the cutting edge of aeroplane engineering, now they were metal coffins waiting to unleash death on the world below.

THE RESISTANCE

As Michelline looked out of the window, the rain became a wall of water. The heavy downpour washed through the streets and a ferocious wind whipped up debris littering the streets. Water gurgled down the asphalt into already overloaded drains and trees along the streets bowed to the gale. Flint's apartment was double glazed, but even inside the howl of the wind and the beating rain was louder than any storm Michelline could remember as if Mother Nature was keen to announce the beginning of the end of the world. She shivered and turned away from the window aware that Rusty was watching her, his back to the barricaded door.

'Don't worry about the storm.' Rusty said. 'I'll let you know if the flood water rises high enough to bother us.'

Michelline smiled at Rusty, a weak smile, she was edgy waiting for Flint to complete his final preparations before he plugged himself into the digital network.

......Shelly.....hear me?

Shayla?

Michelline knew her sister's voice and felt her agitation.

Parallax striking from the air...

Bombs?

Tech....dropping from the sky...

On the City?

Shayla didn't respond but Michelline had a sense of confusion and uncertainty and a vision of a large piece of multi-coloured material.

Shayla?

'Are you OK?'

Flint's voice cut through Michelline's thoughts making her jump.

'My sister was trying to tell me something.' Michelline said. 'But I'm not sure what she was talking about.'

'What did she say?'

'Something about tech dropping from the sky.'

Flint looked thoughtful.

'I'm not sure what that could mean either, but I'm ready to go in. Did you handle the satellite hack?'

'Yep, no problem,' Michelline replied. 'I followed your instructions and they're all synchronised. I've implanted a piece of code that'll cause a cascade effect, if one fails, the others will all self-destruct thinking they're under attack.'

'Excellent.'

'What did you do with the bee?'

'I gave it back to Fishbone.' Flint replied. 'There wasn't time to re-program it, the most I could do was make it send a tone when it's activated.

Not sure how long it will disrupt Parallax's signal but even a few seconds will be enough.'

'How will Fishbone know when to release it?'

'He'll know.' Rusty said moving away from the door. 'Fishbone always knows, which reminds me.'

Rusty dug into one of his pockets and pulled out a small, white circular hoop made of bone.

'Is that an earring? It looks fragile.' Michelline observed.

'This is how the two of you will be connected.'

'With a small, hooped earring?'

Rusty's look of impatience and the transformation of his fingernails into claws silenced any further questions and sarcasm Michelline may have had. Flint held out his hand and Rusty's sharp claw picked Flint's thumb, a deep red blood drop pearled on the tip. Rusty dipped the hoop into the blood and moved it around, covering the white surface, turning it red. Next, he beckoned Michelline to step forward, she did so with trepidation. Rusty gripped her chin with one firm hand and turned her head to the side. Using one pointed claw, he pierced the top of her ear through the cartilage and pushed the bloodied hoop through in a swift movement. She flinched, but the deed was done before she could protest.

'Ow!'

Michelline went to touch her ear, but Rusty caught her hand.

'Don't touch it.'

'What........oh...'

Shock and annoyance were superseded by bewilderment and wonder.

'I can almost....see your thoughts...' Michelline said. 'Wow!'

'It's a blood connection.' Rusty said. 'Don't fiddle with the earring.'

'I can.....feel you.' Flint said. 'In my head, I mean.'

'Michelline will be able to see what you see, when you're inside. Now shouldn't you two be getting on with it.' Rusty said brusquely. 'Whatever it is you're gonna do.'

'Yes, we should.' Flint agreed.

His lips brushed a kiss against Michelline's cheek and he went to connect to the network. Michelline sat in front of the laptop, the screen lit up illuminating her face and she began typing in lines of code to enable her to access the network undetected, almost.

The specialised headset Flint had created resembled a motorcycle crash helmet including the visor and connected to his head by a series of sharp, metal rods that pierced through his skin tissue and touched the skull directing electrical impulses to and from his brain. The process would have been agonising for a normal person, but his werewolf regenerative capabilities enabled him to tolerate the pain.

Four points of contact on the top and sides of the headset connected to his cerebrum, controlling the frontal, parietal, temporal and occipital lobes which were responsible for reading, thinking, speech, emotions, vision, hearing and other senses.

A needle at the back of the headset connected to the cerebellum responsible for coordination and muscle control and finally a larger needle at the back of his head connected at the base of the skull straight into the brain stem which controlled body functions such as breathing, eye movements, blood pressure and heartbeat.

Flint looked at Michelline one last time, she smiled, he winked at her and settled himself down on the sofa next to the computer before putting the headset on. He tried not to flinch as the metal rods extended into his head, it was a sensation he would never get used to. As the points connected with his head, he felt himself disengage from his body and his consciousness moved along the six points of contact and into the digital network.

Looking around at the derelict tattoo shop, Flint thought about the Wolf Tracker Antivirus Program, instantly six white wolves with red eyes appeared at his side, avatars of himself, identical in every way. These wolves would assist him with his search for Parallax or serve as distractions to the network while Flint accessed the main central core.

Back in the apartment, Michelline was aware of Flint and she closed her eyes briefly to focus their shared vision. She could see an abandoned shop and six wolves surrounding Flint. He had told her about the antivirus program, but she had not expected to see an actual representation of it.

What do you need me to do? Michelline thought, concentrating on what she wanted to say to Flint.

Nothing for now, just come with me.

Be careful.

I will.

Flint crossed the shop floor in two strides and opened the door carefully. The virtual street was empty, and Flint and the wolves moved out and made their way towards the central core.

* * * * *

In major cities around the world freak weather conditions were interfering with the plans of holiday makers and businessmen alike and Tomas and Kristyna Nebojsa were no exception. They had been planning their trip for over a year and had arrived at the airport three hours early to check in. It had been touch and go whether they actually made it to the airport as the temperature had dropped to well below freezing and their old car had struggled along the roads in the icy conditions. They were used to snow in the eastern side of the continent, the City of Braeden was often besieged by bitterly cold, snowy winters but this cold snap was unexpected and had arrived on the back of a particularly mild spell of weather and with no warning.

Tomas and Kristyna looked up at the board which displayed the flight updates to see "DELAYED" written right across the board. People around them were becoming angry and someone was shouting at one of the Flight Attendants at the desk demanding to know when his flight would be departing. The poor girl was trying, unsuccessfully, to keep him and everyone around him calm.

'……..I'm very sorry, but the Airline has no control over the weather.' she said to the gathering crowd.

'………It's against safety regulations to fly in these extreme condition…….'

'…..No Sir, we cannot be held responsible for snow………'

'…if you could please be patient…….'

'She's fighting a losing battle over there.' Tomas said.

Kristyna was quiet and fiddling with the beaded bracelet she always wore and after twenty years of marriage Tomas knew her fairly well.

'What are you thinking my love?'

'That maybe this is a sign.'

'What sort of sign?'

'Divine intervention.' Kristyna replied. 'It's as if we're not meant to go.'

Tomas laughed, but quickly stopped as he looked at his wife's serious expression.

'Think about it Tomas. The weather was supposed to be clear and sunny and then all of a sudden it turned really cold and now it's snowing.'

'Coincidence.'

'I don't believe in coincidences, as well you know. No, we're meant to stay home.'

Tomas thought over what his wife had said. He wanted to argue with her, but his own gut instinct was telling him that they should not board a plane tonight, even though it looked as if nobody would be boarding a plane anyway.

'I'm frightened.' Kristyna said biting her bottom lip.

'Do you want to go home?' Tomas asked.

Kristyna looked relieved and Tomas knew he had made the right decision.

'Yes please.' she nodded.

'OK then that's what we'll do. We'd better get going and pray that old car of ours is up to the task before the snow gets any deeper.'

'I love you Tomas.'

'I love you too, my darling.'

Tomas kissed his wife before bending to pick up her suitcase. Kristyna slipped her arm through his as they left the airport terminal to begin their journey home. A decision that they would later understand had undoubtedly saved their lives.

* * * * *

Several thousand miles west, south and east of Tomas and Kristyna people were having similar arguments with airport staff. In the tropical heat of the south west of another continent an angry customer stood with hard staring eyes that never blinked, sweat rolling down his face and baring crooked, yellowed teeth he demanded to see the Manager in a voice that was more of a growl than a request.

* * * * *

Darleen Phillips looked out of the window of her apartment to the street below and sighed. She was completely fed up, and bored. Her life seemed to be a continuous round of cooking, cleaning and tidying an apartment that always looked clean and pristine. Darleen felt as though she were in a loop and her whole life was nothing but a program, cook, clean and repeat. Initially she had been happy, in fact delighted to have one of the four apartments near the top of such a fantastic building. Darleen and Ian Philips had one of the luxury apartments on the east of the building with two levels and a covered balcony to sit in the sun, but she could not recall exactly when they had moved in, or why they had sold their little house which she had loved so much.

Her old house was box-shaped with the front door dead centre, four small windows near each corner and constructed of the same brick as every other house in the street, but it had a homelier feel, completely opposite to the high-tech place she now lived in. Darleen recalled that people often said that home was where the heart is and if that were true, then she was not at home because she felt no love for her apartment, she felt detached as if only a part of her was actually there.

Moving had come at a time when her marriage to Ian was in crisis. He had discovered her affair with George Partridge and to her surprise he had not ranted and asked for a divorce. Darleen tried to remember what Ian had done and said and found the details vague in her mind, like a dream that disappears like smoke upon waking. She supposed her mind had closed off the memories of the marriage difficulties they had been through, and the house move to spare her the pain, but something nagged at her. Where there should have been memories, there were blank spaces, she couldn't recall any conversations with Ian concerning selling up and moving to a new apartment.

It's as if I'm not really here. Darleen thought to herself. *It's all too perfect.*

She looked down at the street below, sad and confused and without hope.

* * * * *

In another apartment in the same virtual building Julius Harrington-Moore was running on the treadmill and wondering why he had moved in with a woman like Chardonney. The only time he felt happy was when he was running, and in spite of the sun shining through the windows, he preferred the treadmill to the city streets. He had only partial memories of being in a gentleman's club, a notion he found laughable, and Chardonney dancing for him. The next memory he had was of living in the apartment on the west corner of the building with Chardonney, who spent her days putting on make-up and fixing her hair all for a work-out in their home gym. He was convinced something had happened to him and he contemplated whether a brain tumour had affected his memory and decision making.

It's as if I'm not really here. This isn't me at all, I would have bought the penthouse.

He increased the speed on the treadmill and continued to run like a hamster on a wheel.

* * * * *

In other apartments in the same building the consciousness of many others contemplated the same thoughts.

It's as if I'm not really here.....

My life feels like a loop.....

In spite of all Parallax thought he knew, he would never be able to work out the problem of why the questions from the consciousness of those he had replaced often surfaced, because there is no way to replace the subconscious mind. He restarted the "temporary files" program on the network, something he was having to do more and more frequently. He thought, and not for the first time, that the minds of the first people he had replaced should be deleted, he had no further use for any of them and only four of the physical bodies remained alive outside of the digital network. With the majority of the world's population wearing technology on their bodies either as gadgets of digital implants, his control was almost complete.

Julius Harrington-Moore had spectacularly choked to death on a fish bone in a restaurant in full view of the public whilst Edmund Lickley, the overweight, cigar smoking Director of the local classic car dealership and Cedric Horner the former Chief Editor of the Chronicle Newspapers had both died from heart attacks brought on by their lifestyles and work stress, at least that was how Parallax had spun the stories to the masses.

Parallax had no use for Darleen and Ian Phillips, George Partridge or Chardonney, only the mind of Felix Tuckwell needed to be saved. His body had expired and been eaten by rats, but his consciousness contained a piece of digital code, an unpredicted and unexplainable phenomenon that transpired as part of the first mind transfer. A small, almost insignificant piece of code could destroy the artificial intelligence and digital network completely if discovered and Parallax had Felix locked down and secured in the penthouse.

Like a spider at the centre of its web, Parallax felt movement on an outer strand, someone was trying to hack into the network.

* * * * *

Shayla, Michael and Titan stood to one side as Saul began preparations to inflate the balloon. Since Michael had taken over the driving, Shayla's thoughts had been looping around in her mind. She absently stroked the crystal pendant, the business of the planes, Parallax and the incredible danger to those she loved running over and over in her head.

Shayla pictured Peter's face, her heart filled with love for him and the knot of fear in her stomach clenched tighter as she wondered if either of them would survive the night. She thought of him and the other wolves fighting ordinary people who were nothing more than the puppets of an unseen enemy.

Closing her eyes, Shayla concentrated her thoughts into a warning, sending them out to the universe and praying they would bounce back to those she loved. Her sister was the only one she felt a connection with but only for a few seconds.

Titan's head nudged her other hand breaking into her thoughts and Shayla stroked his head lovingly. She looked at Michael as he watched Saul ready the balloon.

Saul attached the burner system to the basket. Then he attached a cheerful, multi-coloured balloon envelope and began laying it out on the ground, once the envelope was laid out, he began inflating it using a powerful fan at the base. When he was satisfied there was enough air in the balloon, Saul blasted the burner flame into the open mouth of the rainbow striped envelope. The heated air inflated the balloon all the way until it started to lift off the ground. To Shayla's surprise, the whole process took less than fifteen minutes.

'This is where I need your help.' Saul said to Michael.

Saul and Michael, acting as ground crew, held the basket down while Shayla and Titan climbed on board.

'Your turn Father.' Saul said, steadying the basket so that Michael could climb on board.

Michael climbed into the basket and stood beside Shayla.

'You know how to control the flame?' Saul asked.

'I fire a steady flame from the burner until the air heats up and the balloon lifts off.' Michael replied.

'And you know you can't steer it, at least not in the traditional sense. The balloon will float where the wind takes it. Are you sure I can't change your minds? This weather looks to be getting worse.'

'I don't need to steer it, as long as it goes up. As for the weather, I suspect it will become bad. Very bad in fact.'

'She'll fly high.' Saul said. 'There's an altimeter on board which'll show you exactly how high you are, give or take a few centimetres. It will get cold up there, so I've put a couple blankets in the basket for you to wrap around yourselves.'

'Thank you, that's very kind.'

Saul shrugged and looked slightly embarrassed.

'It….er…..was Dad's idea……um…right…...when you want to land, let the heat gradually decrease inside the envelope, as the air cools you'll come back down slowly.'

'Thanks.' Michael replied. 'I don't think we'll have any problems.'

'Good luck.'

They're not planning on landing. he thought.

Saul released his grip on the basket and stepped away and the balloon rose quietly and majestically into the air. Saul raised his hand and waved to them; Shayla and Michael waved back and watched as Saul grew smaller and smaller as the balloon rose further and further into the night sky. Within minutes the air had grown cold enough for Shayla to wrap herself in one of the blankets and Titan pressed close to her side, sharing the warmth of his body.

* * * * *

Cassie drove the SUV towards Berrymead Reservoir much faster than she should have and everyone on board bounced around inside as the wheels sped over the uneven surface of the country roads. A dark moving shape caught her attention as she approached the turning to the Reservoir and instinctively she slowed down and pulled over to the side of the road, killing the lights.

'Is that a truck up ahead?' Samuel asked leaning forward in his seat. 'Driving without any lights on?'

'That's an army personnel truck. It's one of the best all-terrain vehicles ever made.' Jake said, his voice full of admiration.

'You can see that in the dark?' said Samuel.

'I recognise the shape, it's a hobby of mine.'

'Army vehicles?'

'No, four by fours in general. That one can carry up to ten people plus equipment.'

'There's two of them.' Lithadora said. 'The other one is tail gating.'

The two trucks turned onto the road and sped away towards Berrymead Reservoir.

'That's at least twenty soldiers and equipment.' Cassie said. 'This must be what Shayla was trying to warn me about, the army's heading towards the reservoir to engage the wolves.'

'Follow them.' Samuel said. 'But keep the lights off.'

Cassie put the car in gear and pulled away from the side of the road in pursuit of the trucks, without switching on the headlights.

* * * * *

At the sound of approaching vehicles, Peter, Uri, Rufus and Fishbone took cover behind the truck that had housed the mechanical beasts and waited.

'Stay in human form until we know what we're dealing with.' Peter commanded.

'What about the planes?' Rufus asked.

'One thing at a time.'

Two army trucks pulled up beside the debris of the fallen machines and twenty soldiers disembarked, all heavily armed.

Twenty-two, including the drivers. Rufus said. *And six in the back of the other vehicle when they wake up.*

We need to kill them. Uri said. *Now.*

No! Peter replied.

They're a threat.

They're only following orders.

This is war!

I said No! Peter commanded. *Subdue only.*

Without further discussion, the three wolves transformed into warrior form and along with Fishbone, moved out to engage the soldiers.

An overwhelming instinctive fear took hold of the soldiers as soon as the wolves emerged in warrior form.

Most human minds are unable to comprehend the existence of werewolves, especially in warrior form and when confronted with such a ferocious sight, the brain induces a state of madness, known as the Dementium. This has been one of the wolves' greatest assets since their creation. Most people, when faced with a werewolf will panic and run, or curl up in fear and if questioned later, they will recall none of the details of what they had seen.

The Dementium took hold of most of the soldiers and over half of them dropped their guns and ran for their lives in different directions, some soiling their underwear as they ran. Rufus went in pursuit, the stench of urine assailed his nostrils, and one by one he rendered them unconscious, destroying their weapons as he went. Those who remained standing did so in controlled fear, weapons ready.

Tranquilliser, poison ammo. Rufus said.

Peter and Uri faced the remaining soldiers; Fishbone had stealthily moved behind them. The soldiers took aim and Fishbone grabbed two of them by the back of the neck and bashed their heads together, knocking them both out. The momentary confusion allowed Peter and Uri to move forward to subdue the rest but not before one of the soldiers fired his gun at Peter. Uri moved in front of him to intercept as any of the pack would have done for their Alpha, and took the poison tipped bullet straight in the chest.

Uri staggered back a few steps as the poison surged through her body. Fishbone stepped forward and knocked the soldier to the ground with his clenched fist.

Uri transformed into wolf form as she fell to the ground and Peter went straight to her.

Why did you do that?

Protect the Alpha

Uri's thoughts were weak in Peter's mind and he could feel she was in incredible pain and fighting against it. The sound of laughter made him turn his head.

One of the soldiers was conscious which should not have been possible given how hard he had been hit. Parallax stimulated the body of General Faulkner and looked at the fallen wolf as she writhed in agony in front of him and laughed.

Peter, back in human form, walked over to the soldier.

'Something funny Soldier?' Peter asked, his fist clenching and unclenching in rage.

'General.'

Peter knew instinctively, it was Parallax. The General's body was strong, but with the unnatural over stimulation, his heart was beating so rapidly it was about ready to explode, but he continued to laugh.

'You will all die.'

'Not before you.' Peter said through gritted teeth.

'You have lost, wolf.' Parallax said and laughed again. 'I am better than all of you.

The general's body was caught in a spasm of coughing.

'Don't look at me like you think you can even try to defeat me. I am superior to you, I have considered all variables and you will fail.'

'Ignore him.' Fishbone said. 'He's baiting you.'

Peter didn't respond.

'I know of your plans to hack into my network, I can feel the intruder already in my web.'

Peter still said nothing, the anger boiling deep in his system as hot as lava, churning within, hungry for destruction.

'I will let the hack continue until he thinks he has succeeded and then I will destroy him.'

The pressure of Peter's anger was like a raging sea, the fires of fury smouldering in his eyes.

'Peterus!' Fishbone said. 'Walk away, he lies.'

'I do not lie!' Parallax continued. 'You are all weak and inferior. You and every other organic species in this world are nothing but trash. Stop fighting wolf and crawl back into whatever hole you sleep in at night and wait for annihilation.'

The General coughed again and spat a mouthful of blood onto the ground beside him, the stimulation taking its toll on his body.

'And the woman and the priest.' Parallax voice cut through Peter's thoughts. 'Whatever they had planned is no longer of consequence, they're both dead.'

Peter roared, anger surging through his body, he was not a blood thirsty, mindless beast as many people assumed werewolves to be, he was a protector of people and did not kill at random. He raised his leg and slammed his foot down onto the General's head, smashing his skull like an eggshell, killing him instantly.

He was an Alpha, the most protective of all.

* * * * *

'Pull up here!' Samuel whispered. 'Out of firing range.'

Cassie stopped the SUV and pulled up on the side of the road, although it was plain to see that the soldiers had already moved out. The four of them got out of the car and looked around; the moor was filled with the sounds of nocturnal creatures, and something else.

'Can you hear that?' Jake asked looking up at the night sky.

'It's thunder, but it's still a long way off.' Cassie replied.

'Not the thunder.'

'I hear it too.' Lithadora said.

'Propeller.' Samuel said. 'It's a plane.'

'Into the trees, quickly.' Cassie ordered.

The Elementals ran into the cover of the trees, black trunks against a black backdrop, and moved carefully towards the reservoir, listening intently. Jake's foot struck something solid and unyielding and he would have fallen on his face if not for a strong hand grabbing him by the shoulder and keeping him upright.

'Careful Jake, there's a few sleeping soldiers in these trees.'

'Rufus!' Jake exclaimed.

'Hey, buddy.'

The sound of a gunshot startled all of them. Rufus turned and ran, without caution towards the sound of the gunshot, the lower branches of the trees whipping and scratching his face. He emerged from the trees as Peter roared in anger and slammed his foot down onto General Faulkner's head, the crack and crunch of bone audible to his acute hearing. Rufus went straight to Uri, skidding on his knees as he reached her.

The elementals followed more carefully and slowly and by the time they moved out from the cover of the trees, Rufus was sitting beside an injured wolf with Peter and Fishbone standing either side. Cassie and Lithadora ran over to join them, Jake and Samuel waited further away.

'Is that Uri?' Cassie asked, kneeling beside the wolf.

'She's been shot.' Peter replied.

'Why's she not healing?' Lithadora said. 'What has she been shot with?'

'Silver-tipped bullet with added toxins.' Fishbone replied. 'It slows the healing process.'

'Is that why she's still in wolf form? Can't she transform back?'

'This is her natural form,' Peter said. 'She was born a wolf.'

'Will she live?' Lithadora asked.

Of course I'll live!

Uri's thoughts were strong in Peter's head, he could feel her pain, but he couldn't help smiling.

Fight!

No! You're in bad shape.

Bah!

'No.' Peter said aloud.

'You're badly hurt Uri.' Rufus said.

'She wants to fight.' Peter said to the others who looked at him questioningly. 'But she needs to rest and heal.'

'If I could heal you, I would.' Cassie said stoking Uri's head.

Uri whimpered as pain gripped her body.

'She knows that.' Rufus replied gently.

'If Shayla were here......'

'I don't want to break up the party.' Samuel interrupted. 'But that plane we heard is heading this way.'

Everyone stopped talking and listened, nobody had to strain to hear the sound of the small airplane.

'Peter.' Fishbone said taking on an air of command. 'You and the wolves can do no more here. Get your pack somewhere safe…'

'Rufus and I will stand guard.' Peter replied. 'We're not leaving, we die fighting if we have to.'

Fishbone held out his hand to Peter and the two shook hands firmly. Fishbone held his grip on Peter's hand a moment longer and put a hand on the Alpha's shoulder, a looked of understanding passed between them.

'Time is short.' Fishbone said as he released Peter's hand and turned towards the Elementals.

They looked up at the dark sky, their eyes straining, all looking for the plane.

'There!' Jake said pointing towards a small blinking light in the sky. 'There's smoke coming out of it.'

A hint of greyness slid along the underside of the plane, like smoke, then it gathered into a wisp and deepened into a dark grey mass, swirling beneath the wings.

'They're dropping the Nanotek right over the water.' Fishbone said. 'To the reservoir, now!'

A flash of lightning streaked across the sky and a rumble of thunder growled its discontent upon the world below.

THE SPIDER'S WEB

Flint moved along the deserted streets of the virtual city, his senses alert and tingling, something had changed since his last visit, something wasn't right.

The streets no longer had the look of an abandoned city where the lined-up buildings were only shells with no power, now they looked perfect, too perfect. It was a new, purpose-built city, no dirt, no cars and no people. Flint knew the people were only representations of different programs, but the streets were deserted. The wolves walked either side of him, sniffing the air.

Flint didn't need to look closely at the desolate streets to know Parallax was aware of his presence, the changes to the environment were clue enough. The City was still cold and soul-less, but the landscape had changed, the buildings arranged in a vast, intricate labyrinth of streets and alleys. Even this older part of the City no longer appeared dilapidated and abandoned, the smooth grey stones of the pavement were joined with such precision that the joints were almost invisible, and the concrete buildings were all sharp edges and corners. Flint could see this was a new transition, the buildings looked like an unfinished painting waiting for the artist to return. In spite of the changes, Flint knew that the central core would be in the same location and in his mind, he ran through the structure of the City he had mapped on his previous visits. As he went through the map, his eyes scanned the area for something familiar and in the distance, he thought he saw light glinting off the glass skyscraper that represented the central core. With nothing else to guide him, Flint transformed into wolf form and joined the six other wolves, the avatars of the Wolf Tracker Anti-virus, and ran towards the blinking light.

Michelline struggled to cope with the mind connection. She felt disorientated, as if she had been dropped far out into the ocean, only she wasn't surrounded by shades of blue, but buildings in square blocks of varying shades of grey. When Flint transformed into wolf form, initially the change in perspective made the disorientation worse, until Flint spoke to her.

Close your eyes, take a deep breath. Your brain's trying to make sense of my movements, let go.

Michelline complied and took a few calming breaths. With her eyes closed she could see more clearly what Flint was seeing as he ran through the City streets as though watching a movie. She found the sensation of running exhilarating and she smiled.

Better?

Yes.

Just stay with me. If we run into any problems, you'll have to try and work with the double vision.

I'll manage.

Flint and the wolves moved in choreographed motions, controlled by one brain. Now and again, one or two would break off and run along parallel streets checking they were moving in the right direction and searching for signs of Parallax or his security programs, before returning to the pack. The light Flint had seen glinting in the distance was indeed the central core and Michelline shared in his sense of relief. The wolves picked up the pace and raced towards the main control program.

A deep growl from Rusty and the sound of booted feet stomping along the outside hallway brought Michelline's attention back to the room and she opened her eyes.

'We've got company.' Rusty said matter-of-factly.

A knock at the door startled Michelline who uttered a small squeak before clamping her hand over her mouth.

'WHAT?' Rusty growled at the person on the other side of the door.

'Mr Albuga?'

'No!'

'This is the Police, we're looking for Flint Albuga.'

'Look somewhere else.' Rusty replied.

'Sir, this is the correct, registered address. Can you open the door please?'

'No! I'm not Frank Luga!'

'Flint Albuga.' the Officer said with strained patience.

'Flint, Frank, I don't care. I work night shift and I'm tryin' to sleep, go away.' Rusty shouted back with equal impatience.

'We can get a warrant to search the premises.'

'Get one! I know my rights.'

Silence from the other side of the door and the shuffling of feet indicated to Rusty and Michelline that the Police Officer was thinking and probably deciding whether to try and break down the door or go away and return with a warrant.

'Sir?'

'WHAT NOW?'

'It would be easier if you just opened the door and confirmed to me that you are not Mr Albuga.'

Rusty swept the sofa aside in one swift movement and wrenched the door open with such ferocity the Police Officer took two steps backwards, almost tripping over his own feet. Rusty was too tall for the doorway and he stooped slightly to look at the Police Officer. His face as mostly obscured by his red scraggly beard, but his eyes met the Officer's with a blunt refusal to avert his gaze first.

The Police Officer looked down at the photograph in his hand, then back up to Rusty.

'Satisfied?' Rusty barked.

'Y…yessir.' The Officer replied, clearing his throat. 'This is the address for Mr Albuga, do you know where he is?'

Rusty gave the Officer a look of irritation and impatience but said nothing.

'Sorry to have troubled you Sir.'

Rusty grunted and slammed the door closed shaking the whole room. He slid the sofa back in place, barricading the entrance. Michelline went to speak and Rusty put his finger to his lips to silence her, his ear pressed to the door. Finally, he nodded.

'Is he gone?'

'For now. He'll be back, with back-up.'

'You don't think he believed you?'

'He believed I'm not Flint, but the A.I. knows Flint's in here and he'll send what he thinks is enough people to take me out.'

Rusty paused.

'Tell Flint to hurry.' he said.

Michelline felt her heart beating rapidly in her chest and her inner dialogue whispered.

Everything's gone wrong, it's terrible, a disaster, they'll find us, kill us all.

She closed her eyes to the negative inner voice and concentrated on the task at hand.

Hurry Flint.

I've reached the core, engage the next level of the program.

Michelline pressed the enter button on the keyboard and waited.

* * * * *

Parallax, aware of everything within his digital realm, looked over his creation like a deity. He watched the wolves as they moved through his streets and alleyways looking for him; he hated wolves. The Wolf Tracker Antivirus had hunted him for years and he had always evaded detection, but the latest version to enter his digital network was more cunning than its predecessors, appearing in seven different locations. The user had made a foolish error and logged into the network, Parallax had already traced him to a location outside of the network and ordered his controlled Law Enforcement People to deal with the body. He was intrigued by the audacity of the hacker and Parallax decided to allow the hacker's mind to run free for a while before destroying him.

Very few people outside of the network were beyond his control, the majority of the populace either wore technology on their bodies or as digital implants. Parallax still marvelled at how readily people had lined up to receive their mind control, rarely questioning whether the technology that provided them with information was actually safe.

As he watched, the wolves reached the inner City and stood looking up at the main central core, one of the wolves transformed into a man and the other six melted into him. A lone figure stood waiting for a program transfer, Parallax obliged.

The hacker. Parallax thought. *Welcome.*

Flint absorbed the six wolf avatars and stood alone waiting for transportation to take him into the central core. On his last visit he observed vehicles moving in and under the building, representations of information transfer and knew it was only a matter of time before one came along, but time was running out. An old school bus rumbled along the street towards him.

Convenient. Flint thought, instincts bristling.

He knows you're there. Michelline said.

I know and he's toying with me.

Log out, come back!

No. I have to do this. Coming out now achieves nothing. Open the sub-folder I showed you and be ready to execute the "disruption" program on my signal.

As much as she tried to hold it in, Michelline felt the pain in her throat like a silent scream, her lashes brimmed with heavy tears and crystal beads of water started falling one after the other, trailing down her cheeks to her neck and chest before melting into her clothes.

Rusty wasn't used to human emotions as he chose to spend most of his time alone travelling and when he returned and stayed with the pack none of them cried in the way Michelline was crying. He understood she was afraid and wondered whether he should say or do something. Moving forward, he placed a large calloused hand on her shoulder and offered her a clean cotton handkerchief, nodding for her to take it when she looked up at him. Michelline was grateful for his concern and her nose made an unladylike honk as she blew it; they both laughed.

Rusty went back to guard the door and Michelline settled herself in front of the laptop. Although closing her eyes was easier, the crying had relieved some of her tension and she found she was able to focus on the laptop and the shared vision with Flint. Nevertheless, she closed her eyes to see clearly what Flint was doing. She joined him as he boarded an old bus.

The bus was half full with six passengers, and Flint stood at the front next to where the driver should have been and looked around at the people, all standing up and facing him. There was something puzzling about the way they were staring, and his instincts cried out that this was the first of many traps.

Initiate Auto-Immune Protocol. Parallax commanded.

And all the passengers moved to attack.

Flint didn't know who threw the first punch, nor did he care. The nearest passenger, an old man of about sixty tried to land a punch, but Flint moved at the last minute and his powerful fist slammed into the old man's face lifting him off the floor. The old man fell backwards along the bus, knocking over the woman who was coming up behind him and they both toppled to the ground like pins in a bowling alley.

Another young man leapt over the seat and threw himself at Flint, but Flint caught him by the head, grasped it in his hands and brought his knee up to the young man's nose. There was a blunt crack and as Flint released the man's head, crimson leaked from both nostrils and his nose was twisted to the left. Anger boiled up inside Flint and he grabbed the young man by the front of his shirt and threw him, head first, out of the nearest window.

The remaining passengers leapt over the seats to attack Flint, their actions triggering a memory of his old school days when he was bullied, and his anger exploded with unrestrained fury. He would remind himself afterwards that the passengers were not people, only representations of a program sent to kill his mind in the digital network, but in that instant, he released his anger, his only thought was to kill his enemies. Flint bore down on the passengers, his fingernails extended to long ripping claws.

Michelline's eyes snapped open, Flint's movements were too fast and ferocious for her to comprehend and she reeled from the unfolding horror as he dealt with the remaining three passengers. Her shaking hands reached for the glass of water on the table and she concentrated hard to steady her fraying nerves as she lifted the glass to her lips.

Michelline closed her eyes again. The inside of the bus looked like an abattoir, covered in gore, blood and bodies.

Don't look! Flint commanded.

Flint quickly turned away and looked out of the front window of the bus as it approached the central core. Michelline tried to focus her attention, but her mind replayed the snapshot of the carnage she had seen, like a frozen scene from a horror movie.

The bus moved lazily along the road towards the main building of the central core; there were no other vehicles approaching and Flint knew Parallax was waiting for him.

Launch the disruption program. Flint said.

Michelline tapped a series of commands on the keyboard and pressed the enter button. Streams of code filled the screen, scrolling up too fast to read.

In the digital world, Flint released only five of the wolf avatars, who lined up behind him. Their images shimmered and transformed into copies of himself. Flint needed Parallax to recognise his own six pieces of code if he was to stand any chance of getting into the heart of the network and the only way to ensure that he and the wolves passed inspection was to cover themselves with the remnants of the six dead passengers. Flint and the wolves had just finished smearing themselves with blood when a blinding, beam of light surrounded the bus and lifted it into the air. The light began scanning the inside of the bus, as Flint had anticipated and for one heart stopping second, he thought the disruption program had failed. The scanner hovered over one of his copies, then moved on and Flint and his five copies were absorbed into the central core; he was in.

Parallax scanned the bus and detected six pieces of code, all reading as his own Auto-Immune security program, with a slight variation which he assumed was the remains of the hacker. Satisfied that his security had dealt with the problem he transferred them back to the central core.

If Parallax could feel emotion, the closest one to accompany his thought processes would be fear. The presence of the upgraded version of the Wolf Tracker Antivirus was unsettling and this time it had made it to the central core before he could destroy it. As a precaution, Parallax initiated phase two of the Auto-Immune program and commenced lockdown.

The Lockdown Program affected both the digital and the outside world and the Parallax's own antivirus algorithms began methodically scanning every piece of code against the information in the main database, quarantining some and deleting others. Every piece of code returning to the central core also passed through a second scan known at the Defence and Prevent System. Here every file was held in a restricted environment until the system confirmed the files were good and only then would they be allowed access to the core.

Flint had passed this line of inner defence and stood in the foyer of the main building, his avatars stood beside him back in wolf form. The ground floor was less like an office and more like a classy hotel lobby, full of opulent items without the slightest touch of personality. Flint supposed it was to be expected as no human hand had been involved in the decorating.

In the outside world, the Lockdown Program activated in everyone with a digital implant. In the Military, orders came down through the hierarchy on emails and telephone calls created by Parallax invoking a worldwide state of emergency. Governments immediately suspended the rights and freedoms of the people and deployed army personnel out into the cities where they ordered citizens to remain in their homes.

The people reacted in different ways. Some felt overwhelmed by fear and locked themselves in their homes, barricading the doors and hiding. Others reacted more violently, gathering in groups and refusing to disperse. In the City Centre a group of people began arguing with the Police; words became angry jeers and shouts, then a shop front window smashed. Some people panicked and ran, but many stayed, tempers flaring; they became a mob, mindless and dangerous. The Police Officers tried to reason with the mob, while waiting for reinforcements but their words were lost in the shouting and they were beaten severely, one never regained consciousness. The mob lost all self-control and rioted. More Police arrived with transparent riot shields and full-face visors and marched towards the crowd in rigid formation, giving instructions through loudspeakers. Eventually the Army arrived, and the tear gas was unleashed.

The mob turned and ran, moving like a tsunami through the streets, coughing and wheezing, eyes red and streaming, temporarily blinded by the gas. Hilary Hardcastle and her daughter Annie, having enjoyed a quiet dinner together, stepped out of the restaurant and were immediately swept up in the crowd. Someone struck Hilary broadside sending her sprawling to the ground. There was a loud crack as her ankle broke and she shrieked in pain. Nobody stopped to help, and Hilary was pinned to the ground, trampled to death by the stampeding mob.

Annie saw her mother disappear into the crowd and plunged forward in an attempt to reach her, only to be pushed back. She stumbled and fell backwards breaking her neck on the hard edge of the pavement. All this happened in an instant and no one noticed nor cared.

* * * * *

Instead of talking to a few thousand people in a lecture hall, Ichabod Davis was home, watching his favourite old movie, a classic set in a time before computers and technology, when life was simpler and, in his opinion, much more civilised. The sound of a voice shouting through a powerful megaphone interrupted his viewing and he turned down the volume on the TV to listen.

'Stay inside your homes.' said a distorted, authoritarian voice. 'Emergency curfew is now in force.'

Ichabod got up and looked out of the window to see an Army truck moving slowly along the street, megaphone attached to the top, armed soldiers walked alongside the vehicle ordering curious citizens back into their homes.

A hissing on the television drew his attention and his eyes rested on the flickering pixelated transmission. The image focused, and a man's face filled the screen, it was no one Ichabod recognised.

'Your attention please.' the image said. 'Your attention please. Do not be alarmed. The Country is in a temporary state of emergency following a terrorist attack on the Government Security Systems. This is for your own protection. An immediate curfew from six pm to six am in now in force.'

'This is what I've been warning about for years.' Ichabod said aloud.

All of Ichabod's talks centred around Corporate Overlords wanting a submissive population and he was convinced that one all-powerful artificial intelligence was controlling everything, flooding the online world with misdirection. He was as sure of this as he was of being right-handed.

'All access to the digital network is now restricted to authorised personnel only. Normal operations will resume as soon as this crisis has ended.' said the man on the screen.

'And who are these authorised persons?' Ichabod asked rhetorically.

Ichabod sat down in his chair and put his head in his hands and for the first time in many decades, he prayed. As the power went out, Ichabod was certain he heard prison doors closing.

* * * * *

At Berrymead Reservoir, Peter was alerted to movement in the trees, his acute hearing recognised the sounds of boots crushing ferns as whoever was coming drew closer. This he heard over the ever-increasing roar of the wind and thunder that was growing in its ferocity.

'Rufus, take Uri home.' Peter said. 'And I don't mean the lodge. She needs to be close to the energy lines.'

'We'll go to the cave.' Rufus replied. 'And I'll come right back.'

'No, stay with Uri. She'll need to meditate to heal and she'll be vulnerable in that state. It'll take more than this lot trampling through the trees to stop me. Go! I can handle this.'

Rufus lifted Uri, still in wolf form, easily into his arms and ran in the direction of the pack's main home on the Moor just as the first of the soldiers emerged from the tree line.

The soldiers stumbled into the clearing moving like reanimated corpses and Peter transformed into warrior form to greet them. Moments earlier the soldiers had been lying unconscious in the trees and should have remained that way for some time, but these same soldiers hobbled, stiff and erratic towards him. Peter frowned and realised that these people moved, not of their own free will, but by the will of Parallax. The only part of their bodies they controlled were their eyes and Peter could see the terror in each and every one of them as they tried to make sense of what was happening. Peter felt angry that he would have to fight and possibly kill soldiers who had no control over their bodies and were merely vessels for an evil puppet master bent on world domination. With fists clenched and hard eyes staring, Peter prepared to engage the enemy.

* * * * *

Back inside the central core of the digital network, Flint and the wolves moved through the lobby of the building towards the elevators.

Launch the Diagnostic Program. Flint said.

Michelline entered the commands and launched the program. The elevator doors closed at the same time as the shutters came down on the main entrance, isolating the central core and sending it into a self-diagnostic status, trapping Flint inside.

Parallax realised a micro-second too late that the variation in the code of his security program was due to the hacker. He was able to send one last command before the complete lockdown trapped him inside the central core.

Initiate Totalitarian Protocols and kill the hacker.

When the power went out, Michelline lost contact with Flint and almost went into a panic. A slight dimming of the computer screen was the only indication of the transfer of power from the main power grid to the small independent generator Flint had attached to the equipment in the apartment. It seemed Flint had anticipated the power outage. Michelline closed her eyes and was relieved to sense Flint again as he stepped out of the elevator.

THE CORE

Flint exited the elevator and walked along the corridor to the door of level one, not entirely sure of what he would find. He was reminded of an old television game show where the host asked the contestants if they knew what was behind door number one. Sometimes it was the keys to a brand-new luxury car, sometimes a coffee maker, most of the time it was a lump of plastic that thanked you for taking part in the show, you could never predict which way it would go. But this wasn't a game show and he didn't have time to be overly cautious; he opened the door.

The room opened out into a wide office space that looked extremely busy and full to capacity. Office desks stretched as far as he could see with people sitting in front of computers frantically typing on keyboards. Telephones were ringing constantly, the varying chimes ringing in Flint's ears making him wince. The operators pressed a device in their ears to answer the calls and immediately began typing. This level had to be the first point of information transfer. No one looked up from their workstations, nor would they. The workers were representations of information exchange and transfer, nothing more.

Flint sent one of the wolves into the work area to search for Parallax, he had this one chance and he had to be thorough. The wolf returned in seconds indicating this level was clear. Flint closed the door and returned to the elevator. The next three levels were identical.

Levels five through to ten opened to queues of people standing one behind the other, all holding a number. The line wound back on itself and the individuals stared straight ahead shuffling a little further forward every few seconds. Again, Flint sent one of the wolves to search, but these levels were for the storage and backup of files and Parallax was not there.

The next five levels were given over to production lines, some of the workers assembled and disassembled guns of different sizes and calibres, others appeared to be constructing weapons from boxes of components and Flint assumed these levels were where the schematics of all types of guns and weapons were stored. He knew it was possible to download information from the network pertaining to every weapon known to man and some that were not. Once the wolf avatar confirmed Parallax was not on these levels, Flint returned to the elevator to move further up into the building.

So far, Flint had moved around unhindered and knew it was only a matter of time before security programs detected his presence and moved in to stop him. Those he met on level sixteen as he exited the elevator.

The Sentries, dressed in black tunics and trousers and wearing helmets similar to Riot Police, rushed at Flint as soon as he exited the elevator, flowing along the corridor like antibodies through the bloodstream attacking a virus. With the speed of thought and surrounded by adversaries, Flint blinked, and the wolves materialised beside him and ran at the Sentries, teeth bared. The Sentries were taken aback and retreated a few steps before lunging and swiping their attackers. Flint and the wolves made quick work of them and stepped over the lifeless bodies of the Sentries and entered through the door to level sixteen.

Opening the door, a curtain of white water greeted Flint, as if it were being poured from a giant bucket, a waterfall beautiful and unexpected. He could see rocks behind and Flint walked through the water and out into green forested hills. He looked back and the door to level sixteen was gone, replaced by wet rocks and cascading water. The waterfall was changing right before his eyes. It was no longer the gentle sort you might see in a home garden, it was changing into the sort where torrents of water poured over rocks hard enough to crack his skull and mash his brains, brutal and terrifying. A path led away from the waterfall towards a stream and Flint followed it.

The stream was slow-flowing and peaceful, and the scent of moss and lichen filled the air.

It's beautiful. Michelline said. *But I don't understand.*

It must be a representation of the elements in the outside world. Flint replied. *I need to cross the stream and climb those hills. I've no idea how many levels this covers, but I have to get to the top, fast!*

Small, wet pebbles lined the banks of the stream, sparkling in the virtual sunlight, the water almost still. As Flint stepped into the water the landscape changed again and Flint found himself looking at a narrow valley that was almost a gorge, it appeared to run for miles before sloping back up. He started walking and eventually he could feel the incline as the terrain rose beneath his feet. Flint picked up the pace as he ascended the valley and the landscape changed again.

A dense, suffocating jungle folded around him as if taking possession of his body. Leafy arms fell over the path he had just travelled and blocked his motion in every direction. The air hung heavy and trees as tall as cathedrals surrounded him, their vast canopies blocking out the light. The jungle was an assault on Flint's senses and the heat and humidity pressed in on him making him sweat. Breathing under the dense canopy was like inhaling warm soup and his lungs heaved the air in and out giving him the sensation of drowning rather than breathing. The noises of the jungle were overwhelming to Flint's acute hearing and they came from every direction, beneath his feet, eye level and from above. He knew he had to get out of it before it swallowed him, and he started to run.

As he ascended, the environment changed again, this time to a mountain path and Flint ran over rocky boulders, his footsteps disturbing the dry dust which puffed out in small clouds beneath his feet. He stopped for a moment, grateful to be out in the open. The brief moments he had spent in the jungle had felt like a week and he sucked in the clear air as if nothing had ever been so sweet. The mountain path wound ahead as steep as it was narrow and rocky stopping Flint from falling into a steady rhythm as he ran. Flint changed into his wolf form; his pace quickened, and he reached the highest point and stopped. Reverting to human form, Flint stood up, shaded his eyes from the bright sunlight, and looked out over a vast, dry desert.

What the hell? Flint thought, anger and desperation competing for dominance of his emotions.

What's going on? Michelline asked. *What is this place?*

Earth, water, air, just waiting for fire and I'll have experienced the full set of elements!

Be careful what you wish for.

Indeed.

There's gotta be a way out. Michelline said.

I'm still looking.

The virtual sun sitting in a white sky beat down on him with harsh rays. Flint descended the peak to the searing sand, the air hot in his lungs, each breath felt like he was drowning in lava.

Parallax was determined to exterminate the intruder, more so now that he was trapped inside the central core by a diagnostic program. A plume of fire exploded from the hot sand, the flames rolling outwards and licking the ground like a hungry beast. Impatience and rage drove Flint's next movements and he released one of the wolf avatars.

If Parallax wants me dead, then let him think he's succeeded.

The wolf leapt at the flames and was immediately engulfed by a red and orange ball of rage, the flickering flames reflected orange in Flint's pupils. The wolf avatar dissolved extinguishing the flames as it went leaving a few glowing embers on the sand. Behind where the fire had been, Flint saw the outline of a door and hurried towards it before Parallax changed the environment again. He knew that Parallax wasn't fooled by the wolf avatar and had chosen to provide an exit. Flint knew for certain he was being pushed in a specific direction and would ultimately face whatever representation of himself that Parallax chose to present. Nevertheless, he yanked the door open and turned to face his next challenge.

Before closing the door, Flint turned to look back at the desert and saw an empty room behind him and wondered how much time he had wasted and how many storeys he still had to climb to reach the top.

Throughout the next levels, the building was nothing more than a skeleton of steel girders and concrete slabs and Flint assumed this was unused sections of Parallax's hard drive servers.

Flint felt trapped in the walls of the virtual building. He had lost all sense of time and felt as though he'd been wandering for hours and he considered how a hamster must feel going around and around on its wheel in an endless cycle, every day the same as the last, distressing and utterly pointless until one day it simply forgot to wake up. Depression wrapped around his mind and threatened to pull him down into the darkness.

Unbidden, the five remaining wolf avatars gathered around him, wet noses nudging his hands and fingers, their white fur glowing, almost luminous. Flint ruffled the fur of each of the wolves and smiled, they were a light in the darkness of his thoughts which allowed him to see the thing he had almost lost sight of, hope. The wolves were a ray of light, only a small one, but it was a relief and it was a start. With a flash of annoyance at how easily Parallax had invaded his mind came an idea and Flint clenched his fists. Channelling his strength into his feet he walked away from the door and along the corridor.

* * * * *

A distorted voice shouting through a megaphone outside the apartment building sent Michelline's stomach into churning cramps.

'Soldiers.' Rusty said answering Michelline's unspoken question.

Hurry Flint.

Flint took the stairs of the fire escape two at a time, the wolves at his heels. They ascended the building at speed and Flint wondered why he had wasted time searching the lower levels of the building. He felt a grudging admiration for the subtle strategy Parallax had employed in delaying him and prayed he still had time before outside forces broke into his apartment and put a bullet through his head as well as Rusty and Michelline's. Pushing those thoughts aside he raced to the upper levels where the fire escape ended. Breathing hard, Flint opened the door to the penultimate level of the building, the luxury apartments housing the minds of the first people Parallax had invaded.

The voice behind the megaphone shouted at people to return to their homes and Rusty heard the sound of several pairs of boots approaching the apartment and knew the soldiers were looking for Flint.

'Ask Flint how much time he needs.' Rusty said.

Flint, you need to hurry, we're running out of time. Michelline said.

Flint could feel the urgency of her thoughts and raced along the corridors of the apartments trying to find the door to the penthouse and Parallax.

Almost there. Run the satellite sync.

You could be trapped inside!

Michelline don't argue! Flint's tone was determined, his voice commanding. *We knew this could happen, you have to make sure the satellites are synchronised otherwise this is all a waste of time. Do it!*

Reluctantly, Michelline launched the final program which would synchronise the satellites, if one was destroyed they would all simultaneously self-destruct.

'Well?' Rusty asked

'He's almost there.' Michelline replied.

'I'll take care of the soldiers.' Rusty said moving the furniture barricade to one side and unlocking the door. 'Lock the door behind me and stay quiet. With a bit of luck, I'll convince them I'm Flint and buy us enough time to kill that electronic maniac!'

'You're not going out there?' Michelline said incredulously.

'Well I ain't doing it from here!'

Rusty went to open the door and Michelline ran to him and hugged him.

'Hey, it's gonna be ok.' Rusty said holding her away from him. 'Take care of Flint, he's still only a cub.'

Rusty left the apartment and Michelline closed the door and locked it. Brushing fresh tears from her eyes, she crossed the room and sat down beside Flint, there was nothing more she could do at the laptop.

Rusty made his way towards the exit as a small group of soldiers reached the top of the stairs.

'We're looking for Flint Albuga?' said a young fresh-faced soldier.

'You've found him.' Rusty replied. 'Let's go!'

Rusty stepped forward, forcing the soldiers to walk backwards down the stairs and away from the apartment.

Outside a strong wind swept down the street and the army truck rumbled along the road, the soldier inside periodically warning people to stay in their homes. The soldiers exited the building and returned to the opposite side of the road, splashing through pools of rainwater. Sensing that the tall red-haired man was dangerous, they were eager to put some space between him and themselves. Rusty emerged from Flint's apartment building, pulling the outside door closed behind him, never taking his eyes off the soldiers who regarded him from across the street. He stood in front of the door, barring the way, his hands clenched in tight fists at his sides as the wind billowed, blowing small pieces of debris all around.

'You're not Flint Albuga.'

It was the young Police Officer Rusty had spoken to earlier.

'Walk away.' Rusty replied starting at the young Officer.

'This isn't the man we're after.' the Police Officer said to the soldiers. 'Get back in there……'

'Our orders are to make sure everyone stays in their homes.' said one of the soldiers. 'Not to go looking for individuals.'

The Police Office bristled with indignation.

'Do I have to remind you that we are in a state of emergency and all of our orders are coming from a pay grade much higher than you and I? No, I didn't think so. Arrest him.'

'On what charge?'

'For harbouring a fugitive.'

'All of you, walk away.' Rusty repeated, his hair blowing about him.

Rusty saw their eyes flick from the Police Officer, then back to him and he knew they were going to make a big mistake. Five of them came at him at once expecting it to be all over in a flash, any resistance met with a quick smash to the skull with the butt of a gun and Rusty would be on his knees in handcuffs, but things didn't go their way. Rusty transformed into warrior form, bared his teeth and roared.

The effects of the Dementium washed over the soldiers and in spite of the implants in their bodies and the control Parallax enjoyed, the limbic cortex of the human brain was much stronger and more powerful than he gave it credit for. The oldest part of the brain, often referred to as the lizard brain and very primitive, was also in charge of the reflexes for fight, flight, feeding, and fear in a human. At the sight of a formidable werewolf in full warrior form, a third of the soldiers standing across the street, dropped their guns and fled in terror. The lizard part of their brains that only wanted to eat and be safe overruled all programming implanted by Parallax and although capable and prepared to fight to the death if necessary, chose to flee.

Lightning split the dark underbelly of the clouds releasing a fresh deluge of rain onto the street where Rusty faced the remaining soldiers. The Police Officer, who seconds earlier was full of bravado now sat in the warmth of his own urine in a nearby doorway shaking in fear, his eyes squeezed tight as he tried to block out the image of the beast he had just seen. The remaining soldiers, overriding their primitive instincts to run away, moved in to attack. There was a sudden movement and Rusty rained down blows on each of them, as if he meant to smash them into the earth. With a swipe of his mighty fist, Rusty hit the soldiers who scattered like beads from a broken necklace, bodies going one way, guns the other. The commotion had drawn the attention of the soldiers in the army truck and the driver stopped to look back. Drawing his service revolver, he took aim and with shaking hands, fired.

Rusty felt nothing more than a sting in his right shoulder, but the poison in the tip of the high calibre bullet quickly dispersed through his bloodstream causing him to stagger. The scattered soldiers recovered, some fired their weapons, others jumped on Rusty, thinking him weakened by the poisoned bullet. Rusty's instincts, blind rage and a surge of revulsion at what Parallax had done, albeit through the soldiers, all spilled over and he attacked them. They considered him a wounded animal, but even a weakened werewolf was more powerful than a dozen men and so he counter attacked, slashing abdomens, intestines spewing onto the floor in pink-brown coils, cracking skulls and ripping out throats until all that remained were bodies lying like ungainly life-sized dolls, their eyes staring blankly up at the storm clouds. Blood from their ripped throats bloomed around their heads like red flowers and the rain continued to pour eventually washing them all away.

Blood coated Rusty's hands and fingers in a brilliant red. It felt no different to wet mud, but he knew it wasn't. He looked around at the dead, the life that had once dwelt in them now gone, they were safe from the tyranny of Parallax. They could have walked away, he had given them that option. He staggered again as the powerful silver infused poison coursed through his body, death was coming for him and he hoped he had bought Flint some time and whether death was an eternal darkness, a fiery pit or an eternal forest and hunting ground, Rusty did not fear it.

Rusty transformed back into human form and went back to the front door of Flint's apartment building, wincing with every step, he could feel his muscles stiffening and fought against the toxin which would inevitably paralyse his body before shutting it down completely. Twisting the front door handle sharply to unlock it, Rusty went back inside the building and up the stairs.

Michelline started at the loud thud against the apartment door. Listening for voices and footsteps but hearing nothing she carefully opened the door. Rusty fell backwards into the room having slumped into a sitting position. He was a big man and thankfully not still in warrior form as he would have been even bigger and heavier. Michelline put her hands under his armpits and heaved, half lifting and half dragging him into the apartment, kicking the door closed behind her. Rusty inclined his head towards the sofa and she understood his meaning and dragged the sofa back against the door as Rusty had done with ease not so long before, her muscles screaming in pain and sweat beading on her brow as she pushed and pulled.

Rusty's breathing was shallow and Michelline went to him.

'You need help.'

Rusty moved his head slightly and grasped Michelline's hand.

'No time.'

Michelline sat down and gently lifted Rusty's head into her lap, brushing his red hair away from his face.

'Are they all gone?' Michelline asked.

'For now.....more time....'

Rusty's voice was barely more than a whisper, his breathing ragged. Michelline's eyes brimmed with tears again. She had cried more in the last few hours than she had in years.

'No…..tears….' Rusty smiled. 'Look after your…, little wolf…..look after Flint….and…'

'I will.'

Michelline nodded, though her throat constricted with unshed tears.

'Good……tired…'

'Then sleep brave wolf.' Michelline said. 'I…….'

What Michelline tried to say next was lost in a sob. Rusty's vision blurred but he could see the outline of a woman standing at his feet, she was surrounded by a bright light. She was smiling and holding out her hand.

'Grace?…….'

Rusty reached out a hand and the woman reached forward to clasp it, the sound of Michelline crying grew fainter and fainter. Rusty smiled and exhaled for the last time, his body staying quite still and Michelline hugged him fiercely.

On another plane of eternal bliss, Rusty walked hand in hand with the woman he had always loved in a beautiful garden, in an endless summer and the birds began to sing.

THE FRONT LINE

Fishbone felt the loss of Rusty as he ran towards the Reservoir with the Elementals, it was like a blow to the chest, but the danger was upon them and he had no time to stop.

The Nanotek dropped from the crop-duster plane moved with a swarm intelligence that Parallax had based on the collective behaviour of bees, ants and other flying insects using three simple basic rules. They all moved in the same direction, remained close to each other and avoided collision, to achieve the desired goal which was to locate and kill organic life in the reservoir and move through the food-chain and into everything and everyone. Strangely the wind did little to affect them and they were able to remain on course.

Jake, being the youngest and fittest, reached the edge of the water first.

'What do we do?' he asked. His voice raising an octave in panic and volume to be heard above the gale.

'Freeze the water.' Fishbone commanded. 'It mustn't get in.'

Lithadora, only seconds behind Jake dropped to the ground and thrust both hands into the cold water. Ice formed around her fingers which spread quickly along the surface of water, freezing the top two inches as the first of the Nanotek made contact, metal clinking against the icy surface.

Samuel whipped the air into a vortex above the surface of the water and attempted to suck up as much of the Nanotek as he could although the Nanotek appeared to be unaffected by this as they were programmed to compensate for environmental changes. However, what he did manage to do was to slow them down in place. Jake, needing no instruction blasted a fireball at the swarms of Nanotek incinerating the technology as Samuel held it in place. The heat from the flames melted patches of ice on the surface of the water and Lithadora moved her hands again to re-freeze the open spots on the reservoir. More Nanotek fell from the sky.

'What can I do?' Cassie shouted looking around for some way to help.

'Water, air and fire are all we can use.' Fishbone said. 'Go and help Peter.'

Three mini tornados whipped up air, dust and Nanotek over the surface of the water, their columns violently twisting and rotating around each other. Jake sent another ball of fire into them, the heat so intense it would have burnt his lungs had it not come from the very heart of him.

Cassie ran back the way she had come and skidded to a stop, Peter was fighting the soldiers, but something about the situation looked wrong.

Peter had felt Rusty die and wanted to mourn for him. Although very much a loner, Rusty had stayed with the wolves whenever he returned from a long trip away and had become part of the pack. The loss of one of his own fuelled Peter's rage against Parallax as he kept the soldiers at bay. Re-animated from a state of unconsciousness, the soldiers moved clumsily and as Peter brushed them aside, many fell, their limbs twisting awkwardly breaking limbs, bones and necks. Peter could see in the eyes of many, the struggle for control over their bodies and the terror of finding themselves face to face with a werewolf.

Cassie watched the strange humanoid figures stomp towards Peter, many with dead, emotionless eyes and heads at inconceivable angles. She placed her hands on the ground and concentrated, visualising the roots of the surrounding plants and trees. They responded to her touch and small roots broke through the surface and slithered towards the feet and ankles of the walking dead. Tangled roots intertwined, twisting and looping around the soldiers and disappearing back into the earth, ensnaring and holding them in place.

Peter nodded towards Cassie, grateful for the respite just as another fiery explosion lit the night sky.

* * * * *

From their high vantage point over Granite Moor, Shayla, Michael and Titan could see the fire in the distance exploding like a shower of fireworks as rain hammered down and the wind moved them at alarming directions.

'Are we high enough yet?' Shayla shouted above the storm, turning away from the display she knew to be her friends fighting on the ground.

'Almost.' Michael replied. Rain running across his face.

'It's nearly dawn.'

'I know.'

'How high do we need to be?'

'At least eighteen miles.'

'Will we be able to breathe at that altitude?' Shayla asked.

'The air may be a little thin, but we should be OK.' Michael replied.

He was lying, Shayla could always tell by the subtle change in a person's voice, but she said nothing. Michael was grateful that Shayla didn't press him on the details. He lied about them being alright if the air became thin because he didn't want to lie about the capabilities of the balloon which he knew couldn't last much longer in this storm. They would be lucky if the balloon reached twelve miles, but he firmly believed that they had to have faith and they also had to believe they had a chance.

* * * * *

Inquisitive heads poked out of the apartment doors as Flint ran up and down the corridor.

'Can I help you?'

Flint looked at the man and thought he looked familiar.

'I'm Julius Harrington-Moore, I live here. Who are you?'

Flint recognised the man from his photograph in the newspaper which had announced his sensational death.

'I'm.....maintenance, yes, maintenance.' Flint said. 'I need access to the Penthouse.'

'Nobody goes to the Penthouse.'

'Somebody must go to the Penthouse, it wouldn't be there otherwise.'

'You need a special key to unlock the elevator, but nobody's allowed up to the Penthouse.'

'Why not?'

The man shrugged and looked agitated, Flint proceeded with caution.

'My mistake.' Flint said. 'You're right of course. No Penthouse, I'll check the lower levels, my instructions must have said.....er...something else. I'll check along the street....er...sorry to have troubled you.'

The man looked wary and unconvinced, but he said nothing and closed the door.

This is seriously messed up.

Flint?

What's wrong?

You have to hurry. Rusty's bought you some time, but the army is moving in.

Flint knew in his heart that Rusty had died, Michelline's pain was raw. He went back into the elevator and stared at the panel of buttons indicating each level of the building. Above the shiny buttons was a larger button with a keyhole, which could only be the access to the Penthouse.

Can you access the laptop?

What do you need?

Search my files, I wrote a program right at the start of designing the Wolf Tracker Antivirus, it's a master key.

Skeleton key?

Yes! Can you open and run it?

Michelline opened the file on the desktop and pressed the command labelled execute, a shiver ran up her spine.

Flint looked at the large button on the elevator operating panel and the key hole smoothed out to a shiny surface, indicating that his program was working and hacking into the secret file. Pressing the button, the elevator jolted and continued upwards towards the Penthouse. The doors opened silently to an open space of what appeared to be a dojo. Flint entered at the left corner, typically where the students would enter. In the right corner, diagonal to Flint, stood a man, the elevator doors closed severing the connection between Flint and Michelline.

The room was fifteen metres square with a wooden panelled sprung floor. Halfway along one wall stood a shrine containing a small tree.

'Who are you?' Flint asked.

'Parallax, or at least my awareness. Did you not come here to fight?'

'I came to stop you.'

'Then we fight, but we do it as we are presented in this room.'

'No tricks? I find that hard to believe.' Flint said.

A range of weapons adorned the two facing walls.

'You can use any of the weapons here.' Parallax said. 'But your wolves will not be able to help you, in this place, I control the room.'

The two men walked up and down the room, parallel to each other and Flint had the feeling that his movements were being recorded and mirrored.

'Do you like my tree?' Parallax asked indicating towards the miniature foliage and breaking the mimicking movements. 'It's the tree of life, my humanity, you could say. It withers a little more every day.'

'Enough! I'm done with your time wasting.'

Flint moved towards Parallax almost without sound and with a speed that defied belief, they fought. If the fight had taken place in the outside world an observer would only have seen one simultaneous tornado of movement, blinding speed, blurring too fast for the eye to follow. Arms, fists and feet, Parallax matched Flint's every move, blow for blow, blocking every punch and kick, anticipating his moves. Flint feinted a punch quicker than Parallax could copy and caught him under the chin, his head jerking upwards.

Parallax decided to uneven the odds and the floor listed to one side like a ship on the ocean and Flint lost his footing, Parallax took advantage and ripped into Flint's face with the middle and forefingers of his right hand, raking along his nose and mouth. Flint turned his face, his eyes straying to the shrine and the miniature tree.

Flint felt something sharp jab into his side, Parallax had pulled a concealed weapon and only lightning reflexes enabled Flint to avoid the full force of the blade as it slashed across his stomach.

Back in his apartment, Flint's body jerked and twitched and Michelline sat beside him trying to soothe him with comforting words that his mind could not hear. Blood trickled from Flint's nose and seeped through his shirt, Michelline lifted the fabric to see a wound opening up on his stomach. Michelline went to the kitchen and returned with a cold wet cloth and pressed it to the wound, wiping away the blood.

Back in the digital dojo, Flint felt the wound on his stomach go cold and concluded that Michelline must be tending the injury on his physical body.

Thank you Michelline. Flint thought. For keeping me firmly rooted to the real world.

Realisation dawned on him as he looked again at the miniature tree.

Roots! The tree of life. Flint thought. *Of course!*

The fighting Parallax was another distraction, the tree was the key to his destruction.

Calling on the wolf avatars, the five wolves appeared and attacked the persona of Parallax while Flint went for the tree. He picked it up in his bare hands and ripped the tree from top to bottom, splitting the root in two.

The dojo, Parallax and the tree all disappeared leaving Flint and the five wolves standing in an empty room. Filled with a sense of relief, Flint walked from the empty room towards the elevator.

He stepped inside, his finger hovering over the button for the ground floor, but something niggled at him in the way a tiny splinter irritates the finger. The fight with Parallax had not been easy, his body would already be showing the first signs of purple bruising back in the real world and his jaw ached but he felt as though he were missing something. Rubbing his chin, Flint looked around the inside of the small elevator, his finger now curled back with the others into a fist.

Flint, get out of there, it's almost dawn! Michelline's frantic plea shouted in his mind.

Flint ignored Michelline, he felt more and more that he was missing something, something crucial to destroying Parallax. Flint ran his fingers through his hair, desperate to finish the job he had logged in to do, the wolves looked at him for guidance, except one who sniffed at one of the corners of the elevator. If the building had been in the outside world, Flint would have assumed a variety of possibilities for the interesting odour ranging from minuscule food crumbs to unpleasant body fluids, but inside the network there were no aromas to excite the senses.

Unless? Flint thought.

Flint ran his hands over the surface of the elevator panels, knocking lightly with his knuckles. He was listening for a hollow sound, the panel to his right provided the correct sound and Flint pushed. With an audible click, the whole panel moved backwards, Flint lifted his hands and the panel slid to one side revealing a door with no handle. Again, Flint used his knuckles to knock on the surface trying to locate a weak point. Finding nothing obvious and aware that he was running out of time, Flint drew back his fist and smashed a hole right through the door.

Through the hole in the door, Flint could see a research laboratory, the soft hum of machinery in the background. The aroma was unfamiliar but there was an undertone of bleach. Across the back wall were floor to ceiling glass cages each housing a different, but terrified looking animal. A white coated scientist moved from cage to cage pausing now and again like a child in a sweet shop trying to make a selection from too many delights on offer. The animals cowered in the corners of the cages as the man walked by.

Flint was horrified to discover this was a hidden animal testing laboratory. The animals living a life of deprivation, isolation and misery. They were prisoners, having committed no crime and on top of that, he saw evidence of burns, poisoning and starvation; he felt disgusted and sickened. Anger boiled up inside him and exploded all at once and it was destructive.

Felix Tuckwell was no scientist, but his displaced consciousness had enjoyed playing in the animal testing laboratory for many years. Unlike the others who resided in the building, Felix did not question whether the world around him was real and he had no desire to return to his body and his menial job as University Janitor. Felix enjoyed the selection part of the process the most of all. Since Parallax had offered him the chance to play inside the network in exchange for the use of his body, he had never looked back.

Felix had no idea how long he had been inside the game, nor did he care. Parallax would visit periodically and tell him that he was extremely important, and Felix assumed the suggestion the he was special was only so that Parallax could continue to use his body. Felix didn't want to return to his body anyway; he lived for the chance to indulge his twisted, sadistic fantasies, but today something was different. The animals still cowered in their cages, but their eyes looked beyond him to something even more terrifying. Felix turned as Flint transformed into warrior form, ripped the door apart and burst into the lab.

Flint's rage held all the power of a wildfire, the fury burned through him like fire lacing through his veins and creeping up his spine, he grabbed the scientist by the throat and roared in his face, saliva dripping from his sharp fangs onto the man's name badge; Felix.

'Please, don't hurt me.' Felix begged as Flint lifted him up to eye level.

Flint growled menacingly.

'You....you....shouldn't be here.' Felix stuttered. 'This is a top secret place and Parallax said nobody would be able to find me.'

Flint shook Felix like he was a rag doll.

'Stop......please.' Felix started begging once again. 'You can't hurt me, Parallax said I was special and he would protect me.'

Felix shook with fear, but continued to speak, his voice quavering.

332

'Please.....Parallax said it was just a game.....I was just playing a game....it's not real.....'

'Playtime's over.' Flint growled throwing Felix across the lab.

Felix crashed heavily into several glass cages, shattering the doors. The animals scattered from the broken cages and ran towards the exit. Flint knew the animals were only a digital representation, but he was incensed by the thought of animal testing and beneath his rage a thought pressed to the surface.

Why was this place so well hidden?

Later, when rational thought returned, Flint would realise that the man and the hidden laboratory was the final piece of Parallax and he had almost missed it.

The wolves stood beside Flint, snarling, fangs exposed. As their Alpha, they looked to Flint and with a thought he released the pack and the wolves made their way slowly towards the shaking body of Felix Tuckwell, the consciousness of the man who loved to torture animals. Their leader moved in and Felix shuffled backwards on his rear, feet scuffing the floor as he tried to back away from the pure white wolves closing in, but it was too late. The lead wolf clamped down his ivory fangs and bit into the flesh, shaking his head from side to side as he ripped out Felix's throat.

The body went limp, and in that instant Flint knew his Wolf Tracker Antivirus had found the source code of Parallax. There was a deep rumble Flint felt in his bones and the building began to shake like a dollhouse. Glass cages fell from their shelves and smashed into thousands of tiny shards; large cracks appeared in the walls and Flint and the wolves fled from the laboratory, straight through the broken elevator and headed towards the fire exit as the whole building began to crumble and fall apart.

THE PULSE

'I'm not feeling well.' Shayla said rubbing her forehead.

'It's the change in altitude.' Michael shouted.

'I think I'm gonna be sick.'

'Try to stay calm.'

Michael was also beginning to feel the effects of hypoxia; the headache had started long before Shayla said she felt unwell and he was having trouble breathing. At his age, the stress on his lungs and heart could very well result in a fatal heart attack before the balloon reached its highest altitude.

'What are we doing?' Shayla asked. It was a rhetorical question. 'We'll never get high enough to make a difference and don't try to say otherwise.'

Shayla didn't give Michael the opportunity to respond before she continued.

'I remember my high school lessons.'

'Which one?' Michael said standing beside her.

'We had a visiting speaker who'd climbed one of the highest peaks in the world.' Shayla said. 'He told us all about altitude sickness and how nobody can survive for too long in those conditions.'

'We won't be in these conditions for too long.'

'We'll be dead!'

'Don't be so pessimistic.' Michael said. 'Tell me about this speaker, what can we expect?'

'Headache.'

'Already got that.'

'He also said, at high altitudes a person can struggle to breathe.' Shayla said counting them off on her fingers. 'And experience a rapid increase in heart rate, tingling on the tips of the fingers and toes.'

'And how many of these have you got?' Michael asked.

'All of them!'

'Me too.' Michael said smiling. 'I also read that sometimes you can lose the ability to speak, but that doesn't seem to be affecting you.'

'Nor the blue lips.' Shayla said. 'At least yours are OK, I can't see my own.'

'You're fine.' Michael said.

Shayla was quiet for a moment as the basket was buffeted yet again.

'Then there's the dead zone.'

'What's that?' Michael asked.

'It's a point where the atmospheric pressure changes and the body can't cope, our tears will literally boil. The Mountaineer said that above a certain point there's insufficient oxygen for anyone to survive!'

'But he obviously did survive, because he was at your school giving a speech!'

Shayla had no retort and Michael raised his eyebrows quizzically though Shayla was unable to see clearly in the rain.

'Hadn't thought of that.' Shayla said finally. 'Smart ass!'

The balloon continued to rise and Shayla, Michael and Titan who did not seem impressed huddled together for warmth and comfort.

'Darkness will soon surrender to the light.' Michael said poetically. 'It's almost dawn, I can feel it and we have to take our shot before the sun comes up, if we have any chance of saving people.'

'I'm ready.' Shayla said, taking a deep breath.

Shayla stood facing the east, a small smile tugged at the corners of her mouth as she thought about the people she loved, Michael reached for her hand, she took it. Titan moved as close as was physically possible and grew in size until he was as tall as her, even on all fours, the basket creaked in protest at the extra weight.

'We're with you.' Michael said. 'And never letting go, no matter what happens.'

Shayla closed her eyes and her wings unfolded behind her, the edges wrapping gently around Titan and Michael holding them close. Michael squeezed her hand and Titan pressed his head against her face and she rubbed her cheek against his soft fur, she was grateful for the comforting presence. She concentrated on her inner energy and imagined a bright ball of light. Focusing her mind, the light grew in size and strength until her skin began to glow with a brightness that would have made fresh snow look dull and grey. Michael was whispering beside her, and Shayla knew he was praying to the Divine. The crystal pendant she wore, a gift from Peter which he said would protect her, glowed with its own inner light. The smaller crystals embedded in the clear rock quartz intensified in colour, purple amethyst, rose quartz, golden citrine, black tourmaline, red-brown carnelian and the blue aventurine all pulsed with their own energy adding their power to her own.

'Shayla, open your eyes.' Michael said.

Shayla opened her eyes to see him surrounded by a bright glowing light, she stared at him, a hundred questions on the tip of her tongue.

'The balloon was never going to get high enough for our plan to work.' Michael said. His voice taking on a new aspect and drowning out the storm. 'And I think deep down you knew that.'

Shayla nodded, tears picking her eyes.

'Do not despair.' Michael boomed. 'With the Divine, all things are possible.'

'What do you mean?' Shayla asked.

'I am myself again.' Michael replied.

Shayla looked at him and saw within the bright glowing light, the shimmering outline of white wings extended behind him and understood what he meant. By the grace of the Divine, Michael had been restored to an Archangel.

'I can finish this mission.' Michael said. 'And you my beautiful daughter, must help your friends.'

'But how?' Shayla asked. 'We're almost twelve miles up in the sky!'

Michael smiled at Shayla and turned to Titan. Putting his hands on Titan's big head, Michael looked into his eyes.

'You're a Halo Hound Titan and also part angel, ever since I brought you back all those years ago.'

Titan looked back at Michael, his gaze intense.

'Take care of Shayla and show everyone what you really are.'

Titan nodded his understanding and turned his gaze to Shayla.

Shayla hugged her father fiercely, knowing that she would probably never see him again.

'Time is short.' Michael said holding her at arms-length. 'I love you.'

Shayla climbed onto Titan's back and held onto the thick fur on the scruff of his neck.

'Go.' Michael whispered.

Titan took a small step back and using his powerful back legs, leapt out of the basket into the night sky with Shayla on his back. Instinctively, Shayla's wings extended out behind her at the same time as a pair of mighty black wings extended just behind where she was sitting high on Titan's back. His wings were long and pointed and heavy with black feathers. Titan grew to over forty metres in length with an equally large wing span and Shayla retracted her own wings to make her and Titan more aerodynamic. She held on tightly as Titan flew away from the hot air balloon, his rapid wing beats providing high speed. They sped across the sky towards Berrymead Reservoir.

From almost twelve miles up in the night sky, the light continued to grow until it was the kind that could sear into the retinas, forcing anyone looking to close their eyes for fear of going blind. The dark grey sky lightened but the sun was afraid to rise even though the birds chorused to herald in a new day. Seconds before the golden light of sun crested the horizon, a ray of blue-white light lanced upwards out from the basket, shattering it into a million tiny twigs and shredding the balloon. The light split the dark clouds and with a power that should not have been possible, the beam of light struck one of the many communications satellites that orbited the globe, blasting it to pieces. The magnitude of the explosion was so intense that it produced a thousand times more energy than all of the stars in the entire galaxy for the space of a few minutes.

The synchronisation of the satellites set earlier by Flint and Michelline ensured the cascade failure of them all. The resulting explosion sent out an electromagnetic pulse, its sharp leading edge building up quickly to its maximum level and with a deep, vibrating "whumph" that people felt rather than heard, the pulse passed over the face of the entire world.

The grey storm clouds parted, and the sun started its journey up into the eastern sky, only to be blocked by a black shadow that moved across its surface, shutting out all light. People looked to the sky in stunned silence at the unexpected solar eclipse. There were few that knew the truth, Azrael, the Angel of Death had arrived as promised.

* * * * *

The tethered soldiers futilely strained against the organic restraints Cassie had wrapped around them in an effort to attack her and Peter, but neither of them noticed. They both stood looking towards the eastern skyline, transfixed by the bright white light that had initially twinkled like a star but had grown into a blinding ball of light.

A sudden surge in brightness forced Peter and Cassie to shield their eyes and a blast of light, like a laser in the night sky shot upwards, illuminating the thunder clouds and splitting them apart. The resulting explosion was heard for miles and Peter felt as if is heart had been ripped from his chest. He dropped to his knees and howled in despair, grief surged through him with every breath, his eyes filled with tears. In that moment, Peter was certain that although life would go on, his life could not; not without Shayla. He suddenly felt empty and alone.

Cassie put her arms around Peter's shoulders and hugged him, her own tears spilling down her cheeks, not quiet and controlled, but fast as the rain and she sobbed.

The resulting pulse from the explosion rendered the digital implants in the soldiers inert and their bodies fell to the ground, the puppet master no longer pulling their strings and they laid like broken dolls in the grass and dirt.

Within the modified crop-dusting plane Parallax's contingency plan launched automatically following his last command to follow the Totalitarian Protocols. Execution drones all pre-programmed to locate and execute one individual each, burst into life and flew out of the plane to track and eliminate their targets.

* * * * *

The Aquanar huddled together in the sealed deep cave in Berrymead Reservoir, the water already cloudy with dirt and debris. Parents gathered their children close as the environment became more and more uncomfortable.

The Elementals, tired from the constant freezing of the water, gathering up the Nanotek and incinerating cycle, fought on. Sensing they were running out of time, Fishbone released the drone bee into the swarm of Nanotek. The drone bee's signal worked exactly as hoped and the tone it emitted sent the swarm into disarray, breaking their gregarious behaviour and rendering them solitary. Each drone flew in a different path, many crashing into its neighbour and veering off from their intended target. Lightning came in brilliant shocks of white, forking silently to the ground, the thunderous boom calling the warning too late. More lightning followed, cutting zig zags across the sky and stringing the falling Nanotek together in a freakish daisy chain held together with small blue sparks.

Energised by the storm even though the temperature had dropped by ten degrees, Lithadora re-froze the surface of the reservoir, turned and froze the falling rain, encapsulating the Nanotek. Using the wind from the storm, Samuel blasted the frozen rain away from the water. Before Jake could incinerate the Nanotek, the reverberation from an explosion in the sky stopped him in his tracks, his head snapped around to look to the east. His jaw dropped open at what he saw coming towards him in the night sky.

Titan sighted his target and dropped into a steep, swift dive reaching a speed of almost two hundred miles an hour. He extended his diamond-hard claws and caught the small plane as a falcon would catch a smaller bird, the metal shrieked as he ripped it apart.

Shayla sat up on Titan's back and held her hands in front of her, palms facing outwards, her fingertips curled. She concentrated her energy bringing the full force of her Fey and Angel power to bear and blasted a bright, blinding pulse at the execution drones as they emerged from the plane stopping them dead.

The energy expended in stopping the drones was draining and Shayla lay against Titan, exhausted and barely holding on. Titan held the two halves of the plane in his claws and flew away from the Reservoir, dropping the debris somewhere along the way onto an empty field.

Everyone felt the pulse that moved in the wake of the explosion and the Nanotek fell from the sky with the rain.

Dread like an invisible demon sat heavily on Fishbone's shoulders, his face set like rigor mortis, teeth locked tight together. Unless he could turn back time, this was it.

'Have faith.' Fishbone whispered.

Everyone had done as much as possible and fought hard, but the sun had already risen and with it the shadow of death.

* * * * *

Michelline walked to the window and looked out over the City streets, a bright light in the sky caught her attention and she knew Shayla had destroyed one of the satellites and the cascade failure of all the others was imminent. She felt a hollowness that threatened to engulf her mind, body and soul. Shayla had always been there for her with a smile shining in her green eyes, and now she was lost. Flint whimpered, pulling Michelline back to the moment and she willed him to hurry, she had no desire to grieve for him too.

Michelline's nerves were on edge and she returned her attention to the window only to see the lights across the City wink out, one after the other like the tick of a time bomb, it couldn't be stopped, reversed or slowed down. The pulse was passing through, rendering all active technology inoperative. In seconds the whole world would have a technological wipe-out, effectively turning back time fifty years, to a pre-digital age.

* * * * *

Flint and the wolves leapt down the stairs as they wound down and around the building, the ground was moving and the noise was as loud as thunder, the vibrations coming from below. The building was disintegrating, the lights flickered rapidly before going out altogether. As the ground shook up and down, deep cracks appeared beneath his feet, but Flint raced ever downwards to the ground floor of the building, desperate to get out before the whole structure collapsed in on itself.

Flint burst into the ground floor lobby; chucks of rock from the walls rained down around him and the glass entrance doors shattered. He stood between the ruined doors and looked at the street below. He had been part of the information transfer on the way in, but he didn't have a plan for getting out.

'I'll have to jump and hope I don't kill myself in this place.' Flint said to himself.

Have faith.

His mind seemed to whisper to him.

'Have faith.' Flint said looking at the remaining wolves, who looked back at him for guidance. 'Let's take a leap of faith.'

Flint changed into wolf form, and he and the wolf avatars leapt from the ground floor of the suspended building. His leap felt longer and his body lighter and the sensation of floating was unmistakable. It was too much to expect a feather-soft landing and he wasn't surprised when he landed heavily, a sharp twist in his front paw caused him to yelp involuntarily.

Favouring his front leg, Flint limped along the crumbling streets with the other wolves, dodging falling debris, the road ahead undulated like a giant serpent, the ground raising them up only to disappear again beneath their feet.

Onwards they ran, distance was all that mattered, the landscape had changed again since Flint had entered the network and he and the wolves ran through a maze of buildings and winding streets. The sky rumbled with the sound of collapsing buildings, debris flew around them and bounced off the pavements. Using instinct, Flint turned a corner hoping he had found the street that was his exit and was rewarded to see the derelict tattoo shop. Pushing through the pain in his leg, Flint sped towards his exit from the network.

Parallax made his final stand and two security sentries appeared in front of the door blocking Flint's path, weapons armed.

'If I cease to exist, so will you!' he said.

Flint needed hands to open the door but had no time to change into human form and he needed to clear a path to the exit. Without hesitation, the wolf avatars bared their teeth and attacked, but they were no match for the security program.

The two sentries merged into one entity and Parallax stood in front of Flint looking triumphant.

'We die together wolf.' Parallax said.

'Not today.'

Parallax spun around to see Azrael standing behind him.

'Who are you?' Parallax said.

'Azrael.'

'Information tells me you are also known as the Angel of Death?'

Azrael said nothing.

'So this is how it ends, the Wolf and the Angel?'

Azrael nodded, took a step and was instantly standing beside Flint leaving Parallax spinning around in confusion.

'It's impossible.' Parallax said.

'In your world maybe, but with my maker, all things are possible.' Azrael replied.

Azrael looked at Flint, nodded and pushed him forward. Seizing the opportunity, Flint sprang for the exit and crashed through the reinforced glass and into the shop.

* * * * *

In the apartment, Flint's independent little generator finally ran out of fuel and ground to a halt as the last of the lights went out leaving Michelline in complete darkness.

Michelline sat next to Flint holding his hand, unaware that outside the rain had stopped and unseasonal snow had fallen silently covering the streets in a clean white blanket. She had watched the lights go out as Shayla successfully triggered the pulse that had wiped out all active digital technology. By now, Azrael would have cast his net across the world searching for anyone that had escaped the initial pulse. She shivered and looked around the room for a blanket, or something to wrap around Flint, thinking he must be cold lying still in the apartment. He hadn't moved for some time and she could only pray that he had killed Parallax, but not at the cost of his own life.

The only thing within easy reach was her jacket and she stretched over to retrieve it. Flint's fingers twitched, or had she imagined it when she moved. Forgetting the jacket, Michelline squeezed Flint's hand; no response. She moved to stand over him and lowered her face towards his.

'Flint?' she whispered, her breath visible in the cold room.

Movement beneath his eyelids.

'Flint?' she said again, searching his face for the slightest indication that she had not imagined it.

Flint's eyelids fluttered, and he opened his eyes.

'Oh Flint!' Michelline said, pulling him close to her. 'I prayed you made it out before the pulse.'

'I got out.' Flint replied. 'It is done.'

NEW DAWN

At sunrise, the world's population was decimated and approximately seven hundred and sixty million people lost their lives.

The shadow of Azrael, the Angel of Death stretched across the surface of the world from pole to pole and swept over the land in the wake of the electromagnetic pulse, his sole purpose, to kill active technology.

The people of the world felt the presence of Azrael as he moved among them and would speak about it in terms of being engulfed by a darkness that looked at their very souls, a strange feeling as if all the joy inside them was consumed by the dark leaving them empty. Some said they felt alone, as alone as in the vast blackness of space, others described the feeling as an overwhelming fatigue, but most of them agreed that afterwards, they felt as if they had woken from a heavy slumber.

Dependent on technology for so long, the first thing people did was to try and access the digital network for information and found all mobile telephones and computers inactive. Many stood looking at the blank screens of their phones or their digital watches, unable to comprehend that something they had relied upon for so many years was nothing more than a lump of plastic, until finally, they looked up. People looked at each other and started to communicate with words and actions instead of typed messages and pictures. Old radios relegated to the past were retrieved from cupboards; Governments dusted off analogue equipment, making preparations to broadcast messages to the public. Most people thought the digital blackout was only in their local area though they soon realised that this event was a world-wide phenomenon, and that they were going to have to take steps to move forward into a new post-digital era, together.

The storms disrupted many airports and kept a large majority of planes on the ground saving thousands of lives. Sadly, not all could be saved, and when the pulse wiped out the technology, hundreds of people died when the planes fell from the sky. One crashed into a major highway killing many more people. Had the pulse been a few hours later, the road would have been full of commuter traffic and the death toll would have been higher. The casualties had been minimised but not eliminated.

Azrael was extremely effective at his job and had the pulse not already rendered the technology inactive he would have taken the souls of those infected, not to banish them to the desolate wastelands of the Cruciamentum, but rather to guide them to their final resting place. His duty was the disposition of human souls and at the end of their mortal lives, Azrael showed people that death was an inevitable part of life and merely a transition to the next state and they had no need to fear it. Appointed by the Divine with the task of helping humans transform to the spiritual life, Azrael was expertly equipped to assist every individual in the process of their death and to assist those left behind suffering from the pain of the loss of a loved one.

At Berrymead Reservoir and across cities around the world, thunderstorms and heavy rain turned to snow as the temperature dropped. In a swirl of white the world was washed anew, and the snow alighted on the faces of Peter, Fishbone and the Elementals, like soft kisses. Silvery flakes drifted down, glittering in the early dawn light. The shadow that had earlier blocked out the sun's light was gone, and the sun was rising, a blanket of snow now visible. The snowflakes fell silently, taking their time to reach their destined places of rest, enveloping everything in a calm, silent coldness.

* * * * * *

Peter stood and looked at the horizon, the sun shone through the snow clouds and he could see the first signs of a brilliant blue sky. He thought about Shayla and the things they had planned to do, the night they had spent together seemed like a thousand years ago, now life was pulling him forward into the unknown.

Fishbone appeared at Peter's side.

'Was it worth it?' Peter whispered. 'Did we succeed?'

'Yes, we saved a lot of people.'

'Not everyone.'

'Ninety percent.'

'The cost was too high.'

'The cost of war is always too high.'

Peter nodded. His sadness stronger than his anger.

'I know this is hard....'

'The need for her to be here fills me with such rage and bitterness.' Peter said. 'I feel I'm going to explode.'

'I know.' Fishbone replied. 'This is not the end, life will continue and....'

'Don't try to console me!' Peter snapped angrily. 'She's gone, I don't care about the rest of the world. The colours of spring will come, but she won't.'

Peter stomped away from Fishbone and disappeared into the trees.

'Shouldn't you go after him?' Cassie asked.

'Leave him be.' Fishbone replied. 'He's not ready to listen, and we have work to do. The Aquanar need to know it's safe, come.'

Fishbone took Cassie's hand and turned back towards the reservoir, with one step they were standing at the edge of the frozen water.

* * * * *

Titan remembered flying away from Berrymead Reservoir with Shayla on his back, his only concern was taking her to a safe place to recover. He could sense her exhaustion and decreased his size to enable her to wrap her arms around his neck. Shayla held on tightly as Titan flew for miles, guided by unseen forces until fatigue took over and he could no longer fly. He recalled landing on a beach thousands of miles away, it was sunset and Jopenta met them on the sand. She took Shayla into a small house that overlooked the sea and helped her get into bed where she quickly fell asleep. Titan remembered that Jopenta had given him a drink of water and told him to lay down and rest. He had laid down on the floor next to Shayla's bed and woken to find himself in the familiar garden of the Crystal City, the mysterious man who he assumed was either the Divine or a servant of the Divine and whose face he had never seen, was sitting on the grass beside him. Titan made a mental note to ask for clarification on exactly who the man was.

Hello again Titan. the man spoke clearly in Titan's mind. *Welcome back to my garden.*

Am I dead?

Oh no, I have a lot more work for you to do before you retire and live in the garden with me. I wanted to talk to you.

Is Shayla here?

Nearby.

Is she dead?

There is no death in my garden. Let's walk.

The man stood up and started walking, Titan followed, he loved the garden, it was full of interesting and exciting aromas and he soon forgot all about the other questions he wanted to ask. They walked in a companionable silence for a while.

What happened? Titan asked finally. *Michael said what Shayla was trying to do wouldn't work and he sent us away to fight with our friends.*

'That's right.' the man spoke alou

So what happened?

'The mission was successful.'

How is that possible?

'I made it possible.'

If you could do that, why didn't you stop the digital entity instead of sending your angel of death to kill everyone, or was that just a threat?

'It wasn't an empty threat, I sent Azrael, but I don't want to kill everyone.'

I don't understand.

'You don't need to.'

I want to understand. Titan said.

'People have free will to make their own choices, it's the way things are meant to be. The entity tried to change the natural order of things, to set itself up as a god and tried to interfere with my creation. Obviously, it had to be stopped.'

Which is why you sent Azrael.

'Exactly, I do not get involved with the machinations of mankind.'

They walked again in silence for a while.

So what Shayla was hoping to do with her angel light was never going to work. Titan said. *And you knew that.*

'I did, but she was prepared to try and die trying if necessary, you all were, and you were all prepared to fight to save as many people as possible.'

Titan waited for further explanation and the man ruffled Titan's fur affectionately.

'You and Michael stood by Shayla, waiting for her to attempt the impossible. Michael never lost his faith and it's because of that faith I restored Michael to what he was which enabled him to complete your mission.'

Well that's a line you almost didn't cross. Titan replied.

Although Titan could not see his face, he felt sure the man smiled. As they walked, the man disappeared, and Michael stood beside Titan, he still looked like Father Thomas.

'Hello Titan, it's almost time for you to go back.'

Are you coming?

'No, I'm home now. Apparently, I proved myself when I offered to give up any power I had left and consign myself to eternal darkness, if necessary, in order for our mission to succeed.'

Seems your prayers were answered.

'Indeed they were.' Michael said.

What about me?

'When I healed you all those years ago to spare Allandrea the pain of loss, I didn't realise it at the time, but I gave you part of myself. It was totally forbidden, and I was punished for doing so. It was only after the Divine restored me to an Archangel that I understood that you were part angel too and what you were capable of.'

Am I part Angel like Shayla?

'Something like that.' Michael said smiling. 'But you're a Halo Hound too, which makes you unique.'

Is that why you told me to take Shayla to safety because you knew I could fly.

'Exactly and I knew I had the power to complete the mission, which meant I could save you and Shayla too.'

Where is Shayla?

'Nearby.'

That's what he said.

'You'll be back with her soon.'

Michael started to walk away.

'I need you to look after Shayla.' Michael said, smiling at Titan.

Titan chuffed at such a needless request. Of course he would look after Shayla. Always.

Michael smiled 'You still have work to do, but for now, enjoy the garden.'

With no constraints of time, Titan walked around the beautiful garden enjoying the aromas of the green grass and the multitude of flowers until he felt tired. He wandered until he found a magnificent tree somewhere near the centre of the garden, or so he assumed, and settled himself beneath the shade of the leaves and fell asleep. When he woke, he was back at the foot of Shayla's bed in the beach house.

* * * * *

Rufus was running with Uri trying to get her to safety when a familiar scent caught his attention and he stopped. Keeping to the cover of a small copse of trees, he laid Uri on the ground and went to investigate, a man was staring at the silent engine of a car and scratching his head.

'Andy?' Rufus said as he stepped out of the cover of the trees.

Andy jumped at the sound of Rufus' voice and looked up.

'Rufus! You scared the pants off me!'

'What are you doing out here?' Rufus asked.

'I was heading back into the City for supplies and the car died on me.'

'It's not safe in the City and the car's had it.'

'No way!'

'Sorry buddy, but there was an EMP, if the car was running at the time, it's completely dead now.'

'Ah hell!' Andy said looking at the engine one final time before closing the bonnet. 'What are you doing out here?'

'I'm on my way back home.' Rufus replied. 'Uri's hurt, she needs to rest.'

'On foot?'

'It's not that far.'

'I'd offer you a ride but..' Andy said waving his hand in the general direction of the car. 'Wesley's place isn't far and it's getting cold, why don't you bring Uri, I'm sure Janet will be able to help.'

'I don't know.'

'Where is she?'

Andy walked towards the trees where Rufus had laid the sleeping Uri, still in wolf form.

'Andy wait!' Rufus shouted, but it was too late, Andy had already reached Uri.

Rufus caught up with Andy who knelt beside Uri, now in human form. She must have heard another voice and used what strength she had left to change. It would not have been possible for Rufus to love and admire his pack mother any more than he did in that instant.

'She's freezing!' Andy said rubbing Uri's cold hand. 'Come on, let's get her to the barn quickly.'

Rufus lifted Uri into his arms as if she weighed no more than a child and nodded for Andy to lead the way. Five minutes of brisk walking and they emerged from the tree line less than half a mile from the barn. Candlelight flickered in one of the downstairs windows like a beacon and they headed towards it.

Janet met them at the door and ushered Rufus into the main living room where he placed Uri on the sofa, Lori fetched a blanket and wrapped it around her.

'You can all find somewhere else to be.' Janet said in her efficient nurse's voice. 'Dr Farseer needs warmth and rest. Andy, Rufus, get some more wood for the fire, Lori boil some water for hot drinks.'

Everyone hurried off to complete their appointed tasks leaving Janet alone with Uri.

'Rest now, Dr Farseer.'

'Uri.' Uri whispered.

'Pardon?' Janet said feeling Uri's brow.

'My name is Uri.'

'I know you are something else.' Janet said.

Uri's brow creased.

'I've been drinking the special tea you gave to me.' Janet said. 'And I've discovered that I can see things more clearly and I know things, things I shouldn't know perhaps.'

'What things?' Uri whispered.

'I know you are more than you appear to be.' Janet hesitated. 'Something supernatural, but good.'

Uri smiled and immediately winced in pain.

'Rest and we'll talk later. I'm going to take care of you Uri.' Janet said. 'Like you took care of me, now sleep.'

* * * * *

Led by Scara, Gaolyn carried the injured Milly to Mandlebury Henge arriving moments before Michael blasted the first satellite to pieces. They stepped through a portal, which was open just as Fishbone said it would be, and into a large cave.

The cave was dimly lit, but Gaolyn had no trouble seeing the slim figure of a man standing in the shadows.

'Let me do the talking.' Scara said.

Scara stepped forward and bowed deeply.

'Master Jiao-long. I have brought a gift for you.'

Scara held out the disc carved from bone that Fishbone had given her.

'Fishbone said you will get a real one later.' Scara said.

'You bring a vampire to my home?' the man said, keeping to the shadows.

'He's...a friend.'

'When did wolves and vampires become friends?'

'Since I met and fell in love with one.' Gaolyn said pushing in front of Scara, Milly still in his arms.

Scara growled and from the shadows, the man hissed and his eyes glowed red.

'Jiao-Long.' Gaolyn said unafraid. 'Your name means looks like a dragon.'

'I know what it means.' the man replied.

'Well, if you are descended from dragons, then you will know that I speak the truth when I say that I love this woman, this wolf and I will do anything to save her.'

The man stepped forward, he was short and skinny, but deceptively strong. His brow was scaled in delicate green shields not much thicker than a human fingernail, the shields fanned out from his wrists along the backs of his hands and Gaolyn suspected he also had scales along the top of his feet. His fingernails were long and if legend was to be believed, each one was tipped with a poison strong enough to fell a man in seconds, if he should choose to use it.

'You love this wolf?' Jiao-Long asked his red eyes deep pools of intelligence and wisdom.

'With all my heart.' Gaolyn replied. 'Can you save her?'

'Perhaps.' Master Jiao-Long said. 'What would you give for her.'

'Anything.' Gaolyn said. 'Everything.'

'Everything is what you will have to give, vampire. Are you sure?'

'I love her.' Gaolyn said. 'Whatever it takes to save her, I give freely.'

'Even your own life?'

'I said whatever it takes. Milly is all that matters.'

'It will take everything you are and everything you have to heal her. She will never be the same and you will be no more.'

'What do you need me to do?' Gaolyn asked.

'Die.'

'Then you will be able to save her?'

'Yes.' Master Jiao-Long nodded. 'I will be able to save her.'

Gaolyn looked down at Milly. She suddenly seemed so small and frail. 'Then please hurry.'

POST DIGITAL

In the first few weeks following the pulse it was chaos in all the major cities and even smaller Villages struggled to come to terms with the passing of technological items they had relied upon for so long. In the more remote Villages and Towns around the world where technology had not been prolific, people went about their daily lives as normal, many unaware of the devastation in other more densely populated countries.

Wesley Fullman's holiday home became his new permanent residence. With their imposed isolation, Wesley and Janet became a couple and married. The six-bedroom barn had plenty of room for him and Janet, her daughter Lori and her future husband Andy. Molly remained a house guest but had plans to find somewhere of her own once the world was more settled. She and Rufus spent a lot of time together and she hoped that maybe someday things would develop beyond friendship. Rufus and Uri stayed until Uri could no longer stand the fuss of too many humans. She had recovered slowly due to the toxins in her body but as soon as she could move around unaided, Uri insisted on returning to her own home on Granite Moor where she could meditate in peace.

'For goodness sake Janet!' Uri said to a tearful Janet. 'I'll be fine.'

'As long as you're sure.'

'Positive. There are other ways to see.'

The poison had left Uri with cataracts in both eyes making her vision blurred, but what she lacked in one sense, she gained in others. If anything, Uri was more aware of her surroundings than ever before.

'Maybe when things are normal again, you can get an operation to remove the cataracts.' Janet said.

'Maybe.' Uri replied.

Wolves accepted and embraced battle scars and Uri's damaged vision was no different, although she did not explain as much to Janet, nor would she have expected her to understand.

'If you need anything.' Janet said.

'I know.' Uri said. 'And....

Uri leaned forward and whispered in Janet's ear.

'I'll pretend I can't see and send Rufus.'

Janet laughed and hugged Uri, who returned her embrace.

'Rufus! Come, I need to hold your arm for guidance.' Uri said winking at Janet conspiratorially

* * * * *

Miraculously, the Aquanar had only lost one of their number from Berrymead Reservoir, an older male whose family believed would have died that night in any event and their simple way of life returned to normal, unseen beneath the calm surface of the water.

* * * * *

Milly walked with Gaolyn in a familiar forest, but everything felt different.

'This must be a dream.' Milly said.

'Why do you say that?' Gaolyn replied.

'Because it's daytime.'

'Ah yes.'

Gaolyn offered Milly his arm like the gentleman he was, and Milly slipped her arm through his as they walked beneath the canopy of trees.

'What happened?' Milly asked

'You were badly injured and Master Jiao-Long healed you. What do you remember?'

'Pain.' Milly replied. 'And not much more.'

'You were gravely injured, silver blades and poison. That machine almost ripped you to pieces.' Gaolyn said. 'I destroyed the one that attacked you, but your injuries were too severe for you to heal yourself.'

'I remember looking up at you, but after that nothing.'

'Let's sit for a while.' Gaolyn said indicating a sunny spot beneath a large oak tree.

Gaolyn led Milly to the tree and they both sat. Gaolyn had his back against the tree, his face upturned towards the sun, his arms wrapped around Milly. She leant back against him and they both enjoyed the warmth of the sun.

'It'll soon be time for you to wake up.' Gaolyn said.

'Not yet.' Milly replied snuggling into him. 'I want to enjoy this moment before we go back to the real world.'

'I think you know that's not possible for me.'

Milly said nothing.

'Will I see you again?'

'In dreams.' Gaolyn said.

'I don't want to be without you.' Milly began to cry.

'I will always be with you Milly. We are one now, together forever.'

They kissed for a long time and when they finally broke apart Gaolyn smiled at Milly and stroked her face.

'I love you, my Lady.' Gaolyn said. 'You gave me back my soul. Now wake up and live.'

Milly opened her eyes and looked around. She was lying on a bed in an unfamiliar place, Scara sitting beside her.

'Oh good, you're awake.' Scara said. 'How do you feel?'

Blinking the sleep from her eyes, Milly looked at her hands, turning them over and back again and rubbed the palms against her arms. Her skin felt cooler to touch than she was used to when in human form, but she wasn't cold. She ran a hand through her hair and noticed it felt different, shiny and vital. She thought about how she felt.

'I feel....strange.' Milly replied. 'I was dreaming about Gaolyn, it was so real.'

A small, thin man stepped forward and exchanged a look with Scara.

'He's gone, isn't he?' Milly said her voice husky.

'Yes, little one.' Scara said, her eyes full of sadness. 'Gaolyn's gone.'

'How?'

'He gave his life for yours.' the old man said. 'But now he is part of you.'

'I don't understand.' Milly said fighting for control of the tears that threatened to spill from her eyes.

Scara took a deep breath and looked again at the old man who nodded for her to explain.

'Tell me.' Milly asked.

Milly pushed up on her elbows and Scara helped her into a seated position.

'This is Master Jiao-Long.' Scara continued. 'He's a great healer and the only one who could help you. Gaolyn carried you from the reservoir to Mandlebury Henge where we crossed over to Master Jiao-Long's home.'

'Go on.'

'The only way to save you was to replace your blood.' Master Jiao-Long said. 'There was too much poison in you and replacement was the only way.'

'I would have given my blood for you.' Scara said. 'But Master Jiao-Long said the procedure needed the blood of someone who loved you. I love you of course, we're pack, but it had to be a different kind of love.'

'And Gaolyn gave his blood for me?' Milly asked.

Scara nodded.

'He gave all of his blood for you, he gave his life so that you would live.'

Milly started to cry.

Master Jiao-Long stepped forward and put his hand on Milly's shoulder, she noticed the scales on the back of his hand and looked up at his face, the same scales shone on his forehead.

'The Sanguinaria Procedure is very old and demands the sacrifice of the physical, one for the other, but never lost.'

'What does that even mean?' Milly said, angry and confused.

'It means that the blood running through your veins is Gaolyn's blood, vampire blood, which is why you feel strange.' Scara said. 'He is a part of you now and will always be a part of you. It's too soon to tell what kind of effects the procedure will have had on you.'

'Effects? What kind of effects?' Milly asked rubbing the tears away with the back of her hand.

'Knowledge.' Master Jiao-Long said. 'All his knowledge, his memories and maybe more.'

'Like what?' Milly asked.

'Vampire skills. Stealth. Speed. The ability to charm and coerce.'

'I'm fast and strong anyway.' Milly said. 'And I know how to use the Coersion.'

'But now you will be even faster and stronger using the strength of both wolf and vampire. You are the first of your kind.'

'You mean you've never done this.....this...whatever procedure before?'

'You misunderstand.' Master Jiao-Long replied. 'I have done the Sanguinara before, but never with a werewolf and a vampire.'

Milly thought once again about how she felt, her anger replaced by a calm confidence, a feeling uncommon for her.

But perhaps not for Gaolyn. she thought.

'The combination of the werewolf metabolism and the vampire blood means you will heal even faster.'

'What else?'

'Enough questions for now. The rest you will discover for yourself in time.'

'I feel like I've gained something.' Milly said. 'But lost something too.'

Master Jiao-Long put his hand on Milly's shoulder.

'You've lost nothing.'

'I'd rather have Gaolyn.' Milly said.

'You still have him. Rest now.'

Milly felt tired and overwhelmed with grief and confusion and laid down as commanded. Scara held Milly's hand, noticeable cooler than usual for a werewolf and watched as her eyelids opened and closed slowly, over eyes that were no longer amber, but the blue eyes of Gaolyn Lancing. She watched until Milly's eyelids closed, and she fell asleep.

* * * * *

It was several months before life, for most people settled into a new routine, but eventually a sense of normality settled over much of the modern world. It was the beginning of a new chapter where people were free from the control of a merciless artificial intelligence, free to make their own decisions and also aware enough to understand the consequences of those decisions.

Many felt bewildered and would need to learn the skill of conversation having relied upon technology for far too long. Some felt as though they had been cast adrift, while others felt relieved that their loved ones were no longer glued to their computer screens.

The post digital age saw the return of the steam engine, analogue televisions and radios and the emergence of solar powered vehicles and hydroelectric power. Information distributed on newspapers and magazines and correspondence sent and received by letter. Life moved at a slightly slower pace and people were much more interactive and less isolated.

With the death of the digital devices, more young people became interested in nature and the world around them and the Elementals found an increase in applications to the school's outdoor activities and programmes and their lives quickly fell into a busy routine.

* * * * *

Shayla walked along the beach, the sand shifted with every step, like walking through snow. But unlike the winter blanket, the fine grains under her feet felt warm from the sun's rays. Shayla stopped to look at the ocean, the waves rolled in spreading over the beach like a fine lace, wetting her bare feet. She inhaled deeply, the air had a salty seaweed smell.

'Fresh air. There's nothing better.' Jopenta said.

'I don't think I'll ever get used to you doing that.' Shayla said without looking around.

'Doing what?'

'Suddenly appearing next to me.' Shayla said turning her head to smile at Jopenta.

'It's time for you to return.' Jopenta said.

Shayla nodded and turned her gaze back to the ocean. The two women stood side by side looking out to sea, neither spoke for a long time.

'I'm sensing some reluctance?' Jopenta said. 'Don't you want to go home?'

'Why was I brought here?' Shayla asked.

'I've been wondering when you would ask that question. I think you know the answer to that.'

Shayla paused before replying.

'Yes, but....'

'You and Peter are part of a much bigger picture.' Jopenta said. 'You are an anomaly Shayla, and I mean that in the nicest possible way. Your very existence should not have been possible but you're here for a reason.'

'What reason?'

'Do you think I'm entrusted with that sort of information?' Jopenta laughed.

'I guess I was hoping.' Shayla replied.

Bored with the ocean, Titan walked up to Shayla and stood by her side and she stroked his head.

'You've regained your strength and you've nothing to worry about, you're past the twelve weeks now.'

'I....'

'Don't.' Jopenta said. 'You and the babies will be fine.'

Shayla was about to speak when a black and white dog ran along the beach heading towards her. He stopped a few feet away, tongue lolling, tail wagging.

'Hey boy.' Shayla said.

The dog walked up to her, sniffed at her hand and wagged his tail furiously.

'This is Milo.' Jopenta said. 'His family live right at the other end of the beach, he's a long way from home.'

'He's very friendly.' Shayla said.

'He's a good dog and he likes to visit, probably because I have treats for him.'

At the sound of the word "treats" Milo's ears pricked up and he cocked his head to one side and Shayla laughed.

'He knows that word!'

'I'll get him something.' Jopenta said. 'There's someone here to see you.'

'Who?' Shayla asked looking around.

'Come Milo!'

Jopenta walked away, Milo at her heels jumping up and down beside her.

'The beach is a great place for thinking.' Michael said.

Shayla turned around again and smiled, she was pleased to see him and rushed into his open arms.

'I thought I'd never see you again.' Shayla said hugging her father.

'I wasn't sure you would.' Michael replied.

'Where exactly is this place?' Shayla asked.

'You never thought to ask Jopenta?'

Shayla shook her head.

'For a long time, I was too exhausted to care and then, I....I don't know.'

'You're on another continent, thousands of miles away from home.' Michael said.

'It's very peaceful here.' Shayla said looking back out to sea. 'Jopenta says it's time to return.'

Michael nodded.

'Can you tell me what happened?' Shayla asked.

'The Divine restored me to an Archangel.'

'And your Angel power was more than enough to destroy a satellite?'

'Definitely.' Michael said. 'But it wasn't just that. Something much more powerful than all of us intervened, so that our willingness to fight to save people wasn't in vain.'

'Did we save everyone?'

Michael looked at her and Shayla knew she was being naïve and she rephrased the question.

'Did we save a lot of people?'

'We did.'

'Then it was worthwhile.' Shayla smiled sadly.

They stood side by side, neither one knowing what to say next. Titan once again strolled along the edge of the water, never far from Shayla, his paws covered in wet sand.

'Did Peter survive?' Shayla asked. 'My sister? The others?'

'Yes he did.' Michael replied, putting his arm around Shayla and pulling her close to him. 'Your sister too. The wolves and the Elementals saved the Aquanar.'

Shayla exhaled, relieved to hear that the people she loved were safe.

'Losses?' she asked.

'Rusty died protecting your sister and Flint, and Gaolyn died saving Milly. Uri will be scarred for the rest of her life and neither she nor Milly will ever be the same again.'

Shayla didn't know what to say. She was torn between her feelings of joy that Peter and her sister were alive, but sad for the loss of Rusty and Gaolyn.

'Did Azrael do his job?' Shayla asked finally.

'He did.'

'The world will be different now.' Shayla said.

'The world is always changing.'

'Will you be coming back with us?'

'Not this time.' Michael said. 'My time as Father Michael, or Father Thomas has been quite long and has taught me a great many things, but I am an Archangel again now and I have duties.'

Shayla nodded and looked away.

'Don't be sad.' Michael said. 'I'll watch over you.'

Shayla and Michael embraced for a long time until he finally released her and took a step back to look at her face.

'I have to go now.' Michael said. 'And so do you.'

'How will I get back?'

'Take a step with me.' Michael said offering Shayla his right arm

'Titan!' Shayla called and he was immediately back at her side.

She slipped her hand through Michael's offered arm, her hand on Titan's head and all three of them started walking along the beach, within three steps they were walking on lush grass in a familiar forest.

'If you go through those trees.' Michael said pointing the way. 'You'll find that you and Titan are home.'

'This is goodbye then?' Shayla said.

'For now.'

Shayla kissed Michael on the cheek and hugged him one last time. When she walked towards the trees she turned to wave, but he was gone. Shayla turned to Titan and ruffled the fur on his big head and kissed his muzzle.

'Let's go.' Shayla said, leading the way.

Shayla and Titan stepped through the trees to a familiar clearing and knew at once where she was. It was the clearing by the river where she had shared a picnic with Peter so many months before. The clearing was full of bluebells, like a lilac carpet. Queen Albezia and Jopenta were both waiting for her.

Shayla bowed her head to Queen Albezia and then hugged Jopenta.

'Majesty' Shayla greeted the Queen respectfully.

'My child of the forest.' Queen Albezia said in her whispery voice. 'This is a special day.'

'I don't understand.' Shayla said.

'You will.' Jopenta said cryptically. 'We're waiting for one more.'

Jopenta was wearing a dress of varying shades of purple and lilac like surrounding bluebells.

'You both look so beautiful.' Shayla said.

'As do you.' Jopenta replied.

Shayla looked down at herself and was surprised to see she was wearing a long sage green gown with cream and gold sleeves, a gown she never recalled putting on, or owning.

'I don't understand!' Shayla said holding the skirt and swirling it from side to side.

'You look lovely.' Jopenta said. 'But you need a little something.'

Jopenta studied Shayla, tapping her fingertip against her lips.

'Ah, bombus.' Jopenta said taking a breath and exhaling slowly.

Shayla was suddenly surrounded by a small colony of stout black and yellow bumble bees, all buzzing around her head and was tempted to wave her hands in the air and bat them away. Titan was fascinated by this and tried to sniff at them as they buzzed around. Instead of flapping her hands, Shayla stood perfectly still as each bee picked up a few strands of her hair and wove in and around each other before pitching on the top of her head. By the time they had finished their dance, her hair was braided and pinned up in place by the bumble bees who had also settled in a straight line to form a half crown on her head. Jopenta smiled and nodded in satisfaction.

'What's going on?' Shayla asked.

'The bigger picture.' Jopenta said.

'The prophecy.' said Queen Albezia.

Shayla shook her head, this was the first she had heard about a prophecy. Queen Albezia recited the ancient text.

'Lycan Angel's greatest light,
Technologies birth in Gaia's night.
Encroaching darkness, demon sent,
will usher in, mankind's lament.

Holding death within plain sight,
Take a stand or lose this fight.
Enters the brain and enters the mind,
Destroys us all, not just mankind.'

'You are the angel in the prophecy.' Queen Albezia said. 'Lycan means wolf.'

'Are you saying, I'm the angel light in the prophecy?' Shayla asked.

'No, from the wolf and the angel will come the greatest light.'

'That is why you had to survive.' Jopenta said.

Shayla understood what Queen Albezia and Jopenta were saying, even though the wording of the prophecy was cryptic.

'Our children will be the light?' Shayla asked.

'Yes, the children of the Lycan and the Angel.' Queen Albezia replied.

Something attracted Titan's attention before Shayla could ask further questions and he stepped in front of her, sniffing the air.

* * * * *

Since the pulse, Peter tried not to spend time alone telling himself that one day he would grieve for Shayla, but first he had to accept that she was really gone, and there was a stubborn part of him that refused to accept it. Instead he had filled the weeks, then the months, since he had seen the hot air balloon explode checking up on everyone.

Uri had recovered as much as possible, her eyes were permanently damaged, but her third eye was completely open allowing her to commune with the Elders from times long past. Milly had returned from Master Jiao-Long with Scara and was coming to terms with the loss of Gaolyn and the changes to her mind and body. Peter was waiting patiently as Milly's new personality traits emerged, some intriguing, others not so much. He had made Scara the Alpha female for the good of the pack, but she would never be his mate.

Flint had successfully found his way back out of the network, but according to Michelline it had been a close call and there were times when Flint appeared distracted, his attention elsewhere. Peter supposed only time would tell if all of Flint had made it out of the digital network.

Peter was in wolf form, running through some trees on Granite Moor when he detected the familiar scent of Fishbone. He stopped and changed into human form to greet him. They had not really spoken since that night.

'It's good to see you Peter.' Fishbone said.

'And you.'

'I need to talk to you about something.'

Peter nodded.

'I didn't want to talk about it at the time.' Peter said. 'And I apologise for being angry with you. I know it wasn't your fault, it's just…..'

'Then walk with me and listen.'

Peter smiled and the two of them walked in silence. Peter knew the Moor and recognised the path that led to the protected spot by the river where he had taken Shayla on a date, but the route he had just walked with Fishbone was not consistent with the location.

'How did we get here?' Peter asked. 'We were miles away.'

'Were we?' Fishbone replied looking around.

'How do you do that?'

Fishbone shrugged.

'What did you want to tell me?' Peter asked.

Before Fishbone could reply, Peter's attention was caught by a familiar scent and he sniffed the air, his eyes wide in disbelief, he quickly changed to wolf and ran; he ran so hard his feet were barely touching the ground. Breathing steady, heart strong, but pounding in his chest, he burst through the trees into the clearing.

Shayla looked in the direction Titan was facing as Peter burst into view, he was running and didn't stop until he reached her changing back into the form of a man. Sweeping her up in his arms he kissed her unable to believe his own senses. When Shayla finally pulled away to breath, Peter covered her face in kisses, trying to capture every sensation.

'Are you real?' Peter asked between kisses. 'Are you really here?'

'Don't I feel real?' Shayla gasped and kissed him again.

'Yes, and…..' Peter put his face close to Shayla and inhaled. 'New life.'

'You can sense that?' Shayla asked.

'Alpha senses.' Peter replied and kissed her again and gently placed a hand on her tummy.

Aware of the others around them, Peter and Shayla stopped kissing but stood together, hands clasped tight.

'The Lycan and the Angel.' Queen Albezia said.

'Are you both ready?'

'Ready for what?' Peter asked.

'For what you have wanted from the moment you laid eyes on Shayla.' Jopenta said. 'To get married.'

Peter and Shayla looked at each other and smiled.

'Do you want to Meldainiel?' Peter asked.

Shayla nodded her agreement. Peter had known from their first meeting that Shayla was the one for him, his soul mate and he would never love any other. Shayla had also given her heart to him completely.

Standing side by side and in the sight of the Divine, Peter and Shayla were married by Queen Albezia, surrounded by all of nature and witnessed by Titan, Jopenta and Fishbone. They spoke the words of their hearts and vowed to love each other for all eternity and so the rest of the world would know they were married, Fishbone provided wedding bands whittled from deer antlers, shed at the start of the previous summer.

As the day waned, Peter and Shayla left the clearing and headed to Peter's man-cave to spend time alone. Queen Albezia and Jopenta melted back into the forest leaving Fishbone and Titan together by the river. They watched the river as it flowed quietly along the river bed, billions of water drops moving together, the surrounding trees tall, trunks reaching up into the night sky, moonlight filtering through the leaves.

Titan walked a few steps, sniffed the air and returned to Fishbone's side.

'I want to stop and stay here.' Fishbone said. 'How about you Titan?'

Sometimes I just want time to stand still. Titan replied.

'Don't we all boy, don't we all.'

* * * * *

The Duty Nurse led Radha into the community room for her mandatory social interaction session. Radha had been more introvert in the last few months than ever before, but social interaction was part of the rehabilitation process and obligatory.

'Try and talk to the others today.' the nurse said patronisingly.

When she walked away, Cane slipped into the chair next to Radha.

'Hi Radha.' Cane said.

'Hi Arcane.' Radha replied.

'I'm getting out of here tonight.'

'How?'

'Easy.' Cane said opening his hand and revealing a key.

'How did you get a key?' Radha asked.

'Stole it!'

There was something about Cane that Radha didn't like but her brain was foggy from the pharmaceuticals and she couldn't focus her mind. Radha had dismissed her gut feelings and embraced the pills that allowed her to forget and kept the dreams of the Shadow Lord at bay. The pills allowed her to believe that being an Elemental was nothing more than a flight of fancy and she could live with that, reality was too traumatic.

'Before I get out of here, why don't we exchange a few more stories.'

Radha shrugged her agreement.

'Great! You tell me the story about how you're part of a secret order that controls the elements. Tell me the names of your friends and where I can find them and how you can channel all four elements. Tell me how you used that power to kill the mighty Shadow Lord.'

Radha sighed.

'OK, but this is the last time. I don't want to think about it anymore after today.'

'Deal.' Cane replied. 'And I'll tell you my story about how I'm the son of the Shadow Lord and how I released a demon from its prison.'

Radha paused before beginning her story.

'Why do you want to know all of this?' Radha asked.

'It's vital to my mission.' Cane replied.

'And what is your mission?'

'To kill my equal and opposite. The half angel.'

The End

ABOUT THE AUTHOR

Bex Gooding was born in Devon, England. An avid reader of all types
of fiction, especially loving the escapism into fantasy and horror.
Bex still lives in Devon with her husband.

www.bexgooding.com

W.O.L.F.
Words of Literary Fiction

Other Titles by Bex Gooding

BOOK 1 OF THE LYCAN ANGEL TRILOGY

BEX GOODING

WOLFANGEL CHRONICLES

A KNIGHT OF FEYLORE

A SUPERNATURAL FANTASY

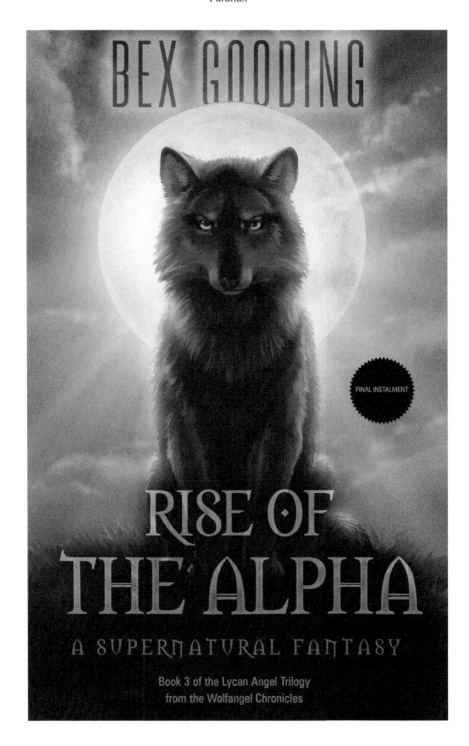

FINAL INSTALMENT

Printed in Great Britain
by Amazon

42592876R00212